Edward Hugessen Knatchbull-Hugessen

Other stories

Edward Hugessen Knatchbull-Hugessen

Other stories

ISBN/EAN: 9783744750356

Printed in Europe, USA, Canada, Australia, Japan

Cover: Foto ©Andreas Hilbeck / pixelio.de

More available books at **www.hansebooks.com**

OTHER STORIES

BY THE RIGHT HON.

E. H. KNATCHBULL-HUGESSEN, M.P.

AUTHOR OF "UNCLE JOE'S STORIES," "RIVER LEGENDS," &c.

WITH ILLUSTRATIONS BY ERNEST GRISET

LONDON

GEORGE ROUTLEDGE AND SONS

BROADWAY, LUDGATE HILL

NEW YORK: 416, BROOME STREET

1880

Dedication.

TO MY FAVOURITE ARM-CHAIR.

Respected and valued Friend,

To you I wish to dedicate this little volume, the contents of which are in no small degree the outcome of pleasant dreams and strange thoughts which have come to me whilst drowsily reclining in your arms. It is true that a jealous and censorious world may raise the objection that you cannot read my book; but, granting the correctness of the remark, I can see therein no reason why I should change my intention. If you cannot read you cannot find fault, and if you cannot find fault, that is the next best thing to praise. And although you may, from special circumstances, be unable to praise my book, you have at least done much in assisting the inspiration from which it has sprung. You are so soothing, so soft, so remarkably comfortable, that it is impossible not to think of amusing things when one is with you, and you never annoy or worry him who seeks you in his hour of leisure. From you proceeds no unkind word or hasty rebuke : no fault of temper on your part disturbs his tranquillity ; but, preserving ever the calm and unruffled demeanour of your race, you receive a happy occupant only to lull him to repose, to give him rest alike in body and in spirit, and to make him, for the time at least, forget the troubles and anxieties of this restless world.

To you, therefore, I respectfully and lovingly dedicate this off-spring of the idle moments which you have so often made happy, and though, as a member of Parliament, I enjoy "freedom from arrest," I hope still frequently to obtain a rest from you, and again to be honoured with the soothing inspiration which you are so well able to bestow.

With the most profound esteem, I subscribe myself your constant and contented occupant,

E. H. KNATCHBULL-HUGESSEN.

CONTENTS.

LIST OF ILLUSTRATIONS.

OTHER STORIES.

PRINCE MARAFLETE;

OR, THE TWO-NOSED PRINCE.

PART I.

THERE was once a Prince who differed in one respect
from all other Princes of his time, and, for that matter,
from all other Princes that I ever heard of, at whatever
time they happen to have existed. He had a most
peculiar defect, for which no one could account, and which
no one who had not actually seen him would ever have
believed him to possess. The generality of men, having
two eyes, a nose and a mouth, are satisfied with the
arrangement which nature has made for them. This
Prince, however, had not only two eyes but two noses,
each placed above his mouth, at an equal distance from
that organ, and each perfectly competent to have discharged the functions of an ordinary nose without the
assistance of a partner or the example of a rival. To be
sure, one of the two noses was a trifle better-shaped than
the other, at least in the judgment of those who prefer an
aquiline nose to one which is vulgarly called "snub." But
both were gifted with a keen sense of smell, both were
equally susceptible of the unpleasant consequences of the

catching by their owner of a cold in the head, and both were alike sensible of the startling effects of being roughly pulled by alien fingers, although the rank and dignity of their master naturally protected them from the probability of any such disaster.

It is not, however, to be disputed, that no man, whether prince or peasant, could be expected to consider such a condition of face to be entirely satisfactory. A prince, indeed, might be safe from insult: every alleviation of his misfortune might be afforded by medical skill; nay, the courtiers and nobles in attendance upon his person might endeavour to persuade him that the singularity of his appearance was by no means unbecoming, and that, to the unprejudiced eye, it was positively beautiful. But the fact would still remain, whatever might be said to the contrary, that he had one more nose than he required, and that the inconvenience of this arrangement greatly outweighed any possible advantage which might be derived from it. The Prince in question, being emphatically practical in all his views, could not regard the matter in any other light, and was excessively annoyed at his condition, the more especially as he was utterly unable to devise or imagine any expedient by which it could be improved. The removal of one nose would entirely spoil the symmetry of his face; the removal of both would leave him in a position positively worse than before; while the suggestion made by one eminent physician, that an artificial nose should be manufactured and placed between the two existing appendages in order to render the whole appearance of the face more symmetrical, was not only indignantly rejected, but went near to obtain condign and fearful punishment for the author of an idea so revolting to common sense and ordinary good feeling. There seemed nothing for it but to endure the misfortune with patience and resignation, and to submit to be known through life (and that, perhaps, a long life, for the Royal Family in that country were proverbial for their longevity) as the Two-nosed Prince. Fancy the jokes which would be made upon him, and, worse than these, the jokes which his sensitive imagination would always suspect to be in the hearts and upon the lips of those around him. To be accused of being double-faced would be bad enough, but even such an imputation of moral obliquity would be less painful to bear than the taunt of being double-nosed, which would carry with it the sting of truth to the inmost recesses of his soul. If told to "follow his nose," the question "which nose?" would be so obvious as to make the first remark clearly offensive; and if he ever should be inclined to "turn up his nose" at anybody or anything, he could scarcely venture to express his intention in those terms, lest a similar inquiry should at once be made to his discomfiture.

One man indeed there was who suggested a cure, and went so far as to invent a machine which he called the "Royal nose-compressor," which, duly fixed upon both the nasal organs of the Prince's face at the same moment, would, so the inventor declared, gradually bring both together until they should blend in one harmonious whole. As, however, he was obliged to confess that the process could not be otherwise than painful, and as the Prince had a great dislike to that kind of thing, the project came to nothing, and the inventor was sent away in disgrace; after which no one tried to invent anything, and the Prince's two noses went on flourishing after the usual fashion of noses, and causing him an uneasiness which time seemed unable to remove.

As the Prince's father and mother (who, as is not unfrequently the case with the parents of princes, were a King and Queen) had died very shortly after his birth, it will be seen that although I have called him a Prince, he was in reality a King to all intents and purposes, and I have only used the term prince on account of his youth at the time our story begins. He was just seventeen, the happy age at which, whilst the pleasures of childhood have scarce begun to be distasteful, those of manhood begin to dawn upon the youth, and, under ordinary circumstances, our Prince would have had before him a prospect of as much uninterrupted happiness as can well fall to the lot of mortal man. But, like a cloud which darkens the glorious sun, so the fell shadow of his nasal construction brooded over his young life, and turned to gall the honey of existence. As the months passed by, and his mind became more and more developed, Prince Marafleto (for such was his name among mortals) began to wonder whether there had been any special cause for the deformity which so greatly troubled him. Had his parents been particularly wicked, that they should have been thus punished in their off-spring? Had any of his relatives, either on the father's or the mother's side, been similarly afflicted? Was there any special occurrence to which the misfortune might be attributed? What steps had his parents taken when they first became aware of it?

These and similar questions constantly arose in Prince Marafleto's mind, and to none of them could he obtain a satisfactory reply from any of his courtiers or attendants. His father had been a very powerful monarch, and his mother's beauty had been proverbial in the country, and had been only equalled by her wit and virtue. Yet the two seemed to have departed without leaving any record behind them, or anything which could testify to the fact of their having lived and reigned, save a well-governed country and a two-nosed son.

"Surely," thought the Prince, "there must be some strange story connected with such a state of things;" and accordingly, as he approached the age of manhood, he determined to try and discover whether or no his conjecture was correct. He renewed his inquiries among the courtiers and attendants by whom he was surrounded, but with a result in no degree more satisfactory than before. The younger people knew nothing of matters which had occurred, if at all, before they were born, and the elder ones seemed to have very little more to say. The memory of the late king and queen appeared to have passed away from the minds of their subjects as completely as if they had never existed; and the Prince sighed to himself as he thought of the brevity and vanity of all earthly greatness, and even of royal glory.

One day, whilst his mind was occupied by thoughts of this description, he wandered forth into the palace gardens, and betook himself to a summer-house which had been the favourite haunt of his boyish days. It was a remarkably pretty summer-house outside, and a remarkably comfortable one inside, as indeed one might have expected in the case of a summer-house especially built for royal personages. It stood upon a green lawn, and at the distance of only a few feet from it, the ground in front sloped gently down to a babbling brook, which, when it had babbled up to a spot nearly opposite to the summer-house, had been made to supply with its cool fresh water a small pond at the foot of the slope, in which gold and silver fish displayed their glittering beauty in the rays of the sun, being protected at the same time by ample shade, when they might need it, from the leaves of the water-lilies, which grew there to great size and perfection. Immediately behind the summer-house was a wood, and a wood of no ordinary character. The trees at the side nearest the summer-house had been suffered to grow to a great height, but had been so carefully thinned when young, that they were not near enough to interfere with each other's growth and strength, but yet towered up sufficiently close to afford an uninterrupted covering of shade to anyone who sought their shelter. It was indeed most enjoyable to walk beneath them; and it was easy to do so, inasmuch as their height had stopped the growth of the underwood below, so that there were neither bushes nor brambles to hinder anyone who wished to stroll through the wood. This was the condition of the place for some distance behind the summer-house, right and left; but if you went into the wood and turned to the right, a few minutes' walk brought you out on to an open down, covered with heather, gorse, and grass, and studded with trees and thickets, which formed the most beautiful glades imaginable, and tempted you to wander along the paths by which they were penetrated in every direction, and which, every now and then, as you gradually ascended the slope of the downs, brought you into an open space from which the most magnificent view could be seen. The down was very large and beautiful, and was a favourite resort of the people of that country, and it was only separated from the wood adjoining the royal pleasure-grounds by a high park fence, through which one passed by a wicket gate, if one had the good luck to possess a key, although this was only the case with a few privileged persons, as the wood and gardens were of course sacred to royalty. The Prince was very fond both of the wood and the downs; and whenever he felt tired of the privacy of the former, he was wont to betake himself to the latter, and wander about just like the meanest of his subjects might have done, shaking off the dignity of his royal position and the restraints of his court. Upon the present occasion he had betaken himself to his favourite summer-house, as I have already mentioned, and, throwing himself upon the cushions of a sofa which stood therein, abandoned himself to his reflections, and thought over those matters which so constantly occupied his attention, and disturbed his mind. He felt very unhappy, not only on account of the actual affliction (if so it might be called) under which he laboured, but because of the mystery with which it, and all appertaining to it, was surrounded, and which greatly added to its intensity. Educated in the school of monarchy, he could not understand how it could be right that anything should be impossible to kings, or that any secret should be beyond their powers of discovery. According to his theories of right and wrong, a king's country and people should be entirely at the sovereign's disposal, all should yield to his sway, and his royal will should prevail in every matter, from the highest to the lowest. There was to him something incomprehensible in the circumstance that a king should not even have the absolute control over his own face; that such face, in spite of the royal will and pleasure, should be in the condition in which he found his own; and that not only should no one be found to obey the royal behest by setting matters right, but that the facts connected with his birth, and the probable cause of his nasal peculiarity, should be enveloped in an obscurity so contrary to his express desire. All this seemed to him very wrong, and he could not comprehend how such a state of things could be permitted by the Powers which regulate the universe.

So he lay upon his cushions and thought and pondered over these things, until a pleasant, drowsy feeling came creeping over him, such as not unfrequently comes, even to ordinary mortals as well as princes, if they recline in a comfortable position upon a warm summer's afternoon, and give themselves up to meditation. He listened for some time to the sounds that filled the air: the soft, homely, comfortable cooing of the wood-pigeons in the high trees behind the summer-house; the unwearying hum of the gnats which were rejoicing in the sun just outside the window near which his sofa stood, varied occasionally by the deep buzz of a humble-bee who was rushing hither and thither with apparently no other object in life but buzzing; the short, sharp, but pleasant twitter of the swallow as he darted by the summer-house door every other minute, to the great discomfort of the insects in search of whom he skimmed the brook; and, above all, the continual rippling, gurgling, friendly babble of the brook itself; all these were sounds soothing and composing enough to make anyone in the Prince's position forget all thoughts and cares of any kind whatever, and sink gradually into the sweetest of slumbers. This is precisely what Prince Maraflete proceeded to do, thereby proving beyond a doubt that assertion which has been so often disputed by historians and philosophers, that princes, however superior to other men in most respects, are yet subject to the influences of those causes which, in the case of the common herd of mankind, produce fatigue, drowsiness, and a desire to sleep. Yes: the Prince slept, or at least dozed in such a manner as to present every appearance of doing so. One of his royal arms was bent beneath his head, which rested upon it, the other lay listlessly by his side; his legs were outstretched upon the sofa; his soft and regular breathing became from time to time deeper drawn; his royal noses kept each other company in a low duet of musical respiration; and his whole frame appeared to be completely under the magic influence of the hour and the place.

The Prince undoubtedly slept, and his mind wandered away into the strange and unaccountable land of dreams. He thought he saw two shadowy forms enter the summer-house and approach the sofa; they were of stately and majestic appearance, such as betokened royal personages, and an expression of mingled dignity and sadness was displayed upon the countenance of each. The figures were those of a man and woman; the former presenting a model of manly strength and lofty bearing, the latter the perfection of female loveliness. They bent over the prostrate form of the sleeping Prince, who, by some inscrutable means, recognized beyond doubt that they were his parents, and felt, even in his slumbers, a thrill of affection, not unmixed with awe, which agitated his whole frame, and filled his soul with a strange excitement. This was increased and intensified by that which followed, and the Prince felt as if he was awake and yet not awake; as if he was trying to shake off some mysterious power which enchained and enthralled his senses, and kept on saying to himself, "It is only a dream!" when in his inner consciousness he seemed to know that it was no dream at all, but a marvellous reality which was passing before his eyes.

Presently he heard the figures speaking to each other in soft low tones that seemed very far off, like the echo of distant voices wafted by the gentle breeze to the listener's ear on some summer's evening, when the air is clear and every sound distinct.

"This is our dear son," said the father. "See how soundly he sleeps in spite of all the past sorrow."

"Yes," replied his mother, sighing deeply as she spoke; "he sleeps indeed, darling boy! But he cannot be happy while cursed with this horrible spell. Oh, why is it so? Are such things to be permitted for ever? Is there no hope and no help?"

"Hush!" returned her companion. "Do not repine, sweet one, nor complain of the decrees of Providence. Should Evil have power for the present, Good shall prevail in the end, and all will be well with our boy."

"But how is he to be saved from this sad affliction, and when shall the evil be overcome?" plaintively asked the lady.

"In the appointed way and at the appointed time," returned the other gravely.

"But how," she rejoined, "will he ever discover these?"

"Only on the downs," was the reply.

"And how there?" asked the mother anxiously.

"If he can only catch the Bilberry men off their guard he will know all fast enough," answered the other; "and he might easily do that if he went the right way about it."

"What *is* the right way?" inquired his questioner.

"Oh, the Nibblers are the people to tell him *that*," responded the kingly figure.

"But he cannot get them to do so," mournfully muttered the lady.

"Perhaps not if he tried by himself," replied her companion; "but then the haggister would help him without doubt."

"And pray how can he get speech of the haggister?" sighed the poor lady.

"For the matter of that," rejoined the other, "he has got only to go and ask Murlingford, the cabdriver."

At this instant the Prince suddenly awoke with a start and sat upright. There was no one near him. The wood-pigeons were still cooing at brief intervals; the shrill trumpet of the gnats was sounding its continual note, and the brook was brawling and babbling on as usual, talking to itself of all the curious things it had seen in its twistings and windings through the country. But no living thing was present, and no human voice was to be heard—the figures had departed; and yet it seemed to the Prince that they had certainly been there the minute before, and could not really be gone. Moreover, their last words were still ringing in his ears as if they had only just been spoken:

"Go and ask Murlingford, the cab-driver."

Ask him *what?* The Prince rubbed his eyes again and again, and endeavoured to collect his thoughts. What was he to ask Murlingford? After a few minutes he recollected that there were several things which he was to do by means of several different sets of beings, of none of whom he had ever yet heard. "Murlingford, the cab-driver," was to introduce him to the haggister, whoever or whatever that interesting creature might be; the haggister was to make him acquainted with the Nibblers, and through the agency of the latter he was to catch the Bilberry men off their guard, and by their help find out something which was most necessary for him to know, and would doubtless lead to some great benefit. Yes, he recollected the dream now, if dream it was; and it was all so vividly impressed upon his imagination that he was not at all likely to forget it. Everything seemed to hinge upon his speedy discovery of "Murlingford, the cab-driver," of whose existence he had not previously been aware. If, however, such a person dwelt within the Prince's dominions, there could be no doubt of his being found without difficulty. This must obviously be his first care, and accordingly he determined to lose no time in setting about it.

Returning to his palace, he desired the immediate attendance of his First Minister of Police, and informed him of his wish to discover the person whom he named. The high official to whom he spoke answered, with a low obeisance, that the name was not known to him at the moment, but that, supposing such an individual to exist in the kingdom, he would undertake to produce him in two days at furthest. With this reply the Prince was forced to be content, although he would have been very glad of an immediate interview with the individual upon whom so much depended. However, he waited with as much patience as he could muster, until the two days had passed, at the expiration of which time the Police Minister presented himself again, and was obliged to confess that his inquiries had been unsuccessful. Although his whole force had been employed in the search, no such person as "Murlingford" could be discovered among the cab-drivers, which body, he was bound to say, had received the inquiries of the Police with scant respect, and accused them in impolite language of "chaffing" them by asking after a man with such a name as a decent cabman would be ashamed to own.

At this news, or rather at the want of any news of him he sought, Prince Maraflete was vastly disappointed. He felt perfectly certain of the name, and equally so of the truth of the information given him in his dream in the summer-house. Nothing should persuade him but that " Murlingford, the cab-driver," was a real living personage, and one that could and should be found. Accordingly, he gave renewed instructions to the police, and ordered advertisements to be inserted in all the newspapers, and notices to be stuck up on all the church and chapel doors, offering a reward for the discovery of the individual whom he desired to meet.

But no Murlingford turned up: every effort to find him proved ineffectual ; and when ten days of fruitless search had gone by, the Prince began to despair of success. Several times he sought the summer-house again, hoping that he might be aided by another dream ; but somehow or other, nothing came of it. Either he could not sleep, or, if he did, it was a deep and dreamless slumber that fell upon him, and he awoke no wiser than before.

Another thing irritated him not a little, namely, the appearance of several people who claimed to be Murlingford, but turned out on investigation to be rank impostors. One came clothed in rags, with a long white beard, looking like a venerable hermit, which, in fact, he declared himself to be, having, he said, been a cab-driver in the city some fifty years before, and only recently heard of the Prince's advertisement from a traveller who had passed the cave to which he had retired, in order to carry on the hermit business in a proper manner. But when Prince Maraflete eagerly questioned him about the haggister, he stared in his face with blank astonishment, and was no better acquainted with either the Nibblers or the Bilberry men. As, moreover, the records of the police proved that he was a very different person from that which he represented himself to be, having been several times convicted as a rogue and a vagabond, and rejoicing in the name of Nibbs, and not Murlingford at all, he was promptly and severely whipped out of the city, for the warning and discouragement of other persons who might be similarly disposed to try and deceive the Prince.

Another person, tall, thin, bony, and angular in shape, loudly declared himself to be Murlingford, and as such claimed the reward offered for the discovery of that personage. Not being previously known to the police, he was presumed to be respectable, and accordingly conducted to the Prince. He stipulated for a considerable sum before he would disclose what he knew, and such was the anxiety of the Royal questioner, that he actually complied with the request. Then the person who called himself Murlingford explained that the haggister meant a person who ate "haggis," a kind of broth made with sheeps' heads, and that this particular food inspired people with a species of second sight, and enabled them to discover secrets and mysteries which were unknown to others.

As soon as this opinion had been given, everybody took directly to eating haggis, the demand for sheeps' heads was extraordinary, the price of the article went-up greatly in the market, and one would have thought that no secret or mystery would have been left undiscovered. But, strange to say, from the Prince downwards, no one was a bit the wiser for this change of diet, and the pretended Murlingford soon lost favour. He utterly failed, too, to give any reasonable solution to the " Nibbler" question ; and as no practical good had resulted from his first explanation, he was roughly treated by some of those who had at first believed him. Then, under the influence of terror, he confessed that his name also was not Murlingford, but Muggins the tinker, and that he had been tempted to play the part of the former personage by the offered reward. He received a severe punishment for his misdeeds, having his money taken from him, and being nailed by the ears to the pillory for two hours, during which time the mob pelted him with everything they could lay their hands upon, until he was half dead, and at the expiration of the appointed time, he also was whipped out of the city, his bleeding ears having previously been removed from his head, lest, in their wounded condition, they should prove inconvenient.

These two were the more prominent examples of persons who were foolish enough to attempt to deceive Royalty, a thing not only wicked in itself, but almost certain to lead to exposure and shame, wherever and whenever it may be practised. It will be easily understood that the course which things had taken was a great disappointment to Prince Maraflete, who, after his dream, had made sure that his path would be made easy for him, and that he should readily discover all that had previously been hidden from him. When princes are disappointed, there is only a choice of evils before them. Either they turn cruel, persecute their subjects, and make themselves generally disagreeable, or they pine away, become melancholy, and not unfrequently die. As the former alternative was impossible to a good and kind-hearted Prince like Maraflete, he not unnaturally took to the latter. He lost his appetite, grew pale and thin, ceased to be interested or amused by anything, gave up riding, scarcely looked at the morning papers, and was utterly careless in his apparel, frequently wearing a round hat and shooting-coat on Sundays, and at other times keeping his slippers on all the morning, and constantly forgetting to dress for dinner. All this was observed by the courtiers with regret, and everyone feared that the Prince was in a bad way altogether.

He was induced by his ministers to consult several doctors, each famous for his skill in curing people of some particular disease. As, however, it happened, fortunately or unfortunately, that the Prince had no disease at all save that which was mental, the doctors did him no good, and only damaged their own reputations by conspicuous failures. Nobody could do anything for the poor young man, and he grew daily thinner and more miserable. One day he had gone as usual to the summer-house, listened to the birds and the stream, vainly sought such a sleep as might take him once more to dreamland, and groaned in spirit at the continued disappointment of his hopes.

Suddenly he arose, impelled by an uncontrollable desire to go forth from the palace gardens on to the open downs behind the shrubbery. As it is part of the undoubted prerogative of royalty to gratify its desires, whenever they cannot be conveniently controlled, Prince Maraflete forthwith proceeded to follow his inclination, passed through the gate in the park fence which bounded the royal shrubberies, and stood at the bottom of the downs, up to which an old winding road led through an avenue of oak and yew trees intermixed. Slowly the Prince ascended, and presently the place grew still wilder. Thickets covered the ground, and amid the thickets were continually to be seen open spaces of green grass, in the middle of which either an oak or a yew reared its noble form. Then came large patches of gorse, which covered the upper side of the hill, and through which the path twisted and turned in several directions.

The Prince did not care to ascend as high as the gorse, but turned aside to the left, and presently sat down on the grass upon a spot whereon stood together half-a-dozen gigantic yew-trees, casting their shade for some distance around.

It was a lovely place—the rays of the sun flickered through the trees and bushes which fringed the hill-side, and lightened the sombre shadows made by the dense branches of the yew-trees without being able to pierce through them. There was scarcely a breath of air stirring; the little linnets sat on the top of the gorse and on the neighbouring boughs, uttering their sleepy, contented sounds, the sparrows lazily twittered about, and from the wood below came the soft, homely, comfortable cooing of the wood-pigeons. It was the very hour and the very place for dreams; and Prince Maraflete felt that if he was ever to dream again it must be now. Accordingly, he closed his eyes with a resolute determination to sleep, if he could, but had hardly done so when he opened them again in great surprise. Some one was speaking, and speaking very near him, too; so that when I said he opened his eyes, it was in order to assist his ears, which he had immediate occasion to use. Yes! there were certainly voices which appeared to come from within or close by the largest of the yew-trees; and what the voices said was so interesting and astonishing to the Prince that he listened with wrapt attention.

"Confound those fellows!—why don't they come?" said one voice.

"I can't imagine," replied another. "They never can have forgotten the day, can they?"

"No, surely not," said the first voice; "and old Murlingford is never late!"

At this word the Prince nearly jumped out of his skin, which would have been a pity, since he would never have got another to fit him so well. However, by a violent effort he restrained himself, kept both his skin and his seat, and continued to listen to the conversation which had arrested and rivetted his attention.

"No," said the other voice, musingly; "old Murlingford is sure to be true to time. Oh! here they are."

And even as he spoke the Prince heard the sound of wheels coming apparently down one of the grassy tracks which traversed the thickets by which the yew-trees were surrounded, and rapidly approaching the latter. At the same time he heard that which was still more important to him, seeing that all this time, whilst he plainly heard the voices, no living thing had been visible to his eyes. One of the voices exclaimed hastily to the other:

"Now, then, here is a branch of yew—let us rub our eyes quickly, that we may see well."

As soon as the Prince heard these words, it struck him that what made one person see might probably have the same effect upon another; and he accordingly looked round for a yew-branch, which he had no difficulty in finding, and immediately rubbed it carefully over both his eyes. The effect was instantaneous; the atmosphere appeared to be doubly clear, and he could see doubly well. The first thing he saw was, that the speakers to whom he

THE CAB OF MURLINGFORD. —p. 19

had been listening were seated upon the other side of the nearest yew tree, and that they were neither more nor less than a hare and a hedgehog. The hare had one fore-leg bandaged up, and was evidently hardly able to walk. She was, however, dressed in holiday costume; a vest of the finest white cambric surrounded her body, red ribands were tied round each of her legs save that which was bandaged, and a smart little cap with stripes of various colours was jauntily set upon her head. The hedgehog, for his part, was painted entirely of a vivid green, that being the custom of his race when making holiday.

The two friends were anxiously looking up the hill when the Prince saw them, evidently expecting the arrival of some one or another of their acquaintance, and at this moment an exclamation of "Here he comes!" burst simultaneously from the lips of both. Earnestly gazing in the same direction as the two creatures, Prince Maraflete now saw a small carriage rapidly descending one of the tracks on the other side of the yew-trees. It was a low, strong-built little open car, drawn by a couple of black rabbits, evidently well trained to obey whip and rein. In the carriage, however, was seated an individual upon whom the Prince's attention was at once earnestly fixed. It was a little stout man, with a wide-brimmed, low-crowned, glazed black hat upon his head, with a broad yellow riband round the hat. Beneath his hat, as is constantly the case with such people, was his face, which was a red and rosy-cheeked, though somewhat wrinkled, face, wherein two eyes, one on each side of a full-coloured nose, shone and sparkled with a cheerful expression, and underneath a mouth, which seemed always about to laugh, his chin came out into rather a peak, something like Punch, only not so long as the chin which distinguishes that remarkable personage. A blue-spotted handkerchief, wrapped in several folds round his neck, and ornamented by a gigantic gold pin with a fox's head on it, served to set off an ample waistcoat of undefinable colour, which reached very low down over the person of the wearer. A venerable pair of corduroys and top-boots, which had also seen their best days, completed his costume, whilst his name and condition were displayed in gold letters on the side of his cart — "Murlingford, cab-driver. Licensed to carry four inside." There *were* four inside, too, and they were comical passengers enough, for the matter of that. The front seats were occupied by a jay, with its wing in a sling, as if it had been recently broken, and an elderly rabbit, one of whose feet had been cut off by a trap, whilst opposite to these sat a venerable mole, fresh from his usual earth-grubbing occupation, and a small fieldmouse, who by his constant and joyous squeaks showed that he was out for a holiday. The cab drove rapidly up to the foot of the tree where the hare and hedgehog were sitting, and then the driver pulled up and touched his hat civilly as he assisted his passengers to alight. Having done this, they instantly began to salute the two creatures whom they had apparently come to see, whilst Murlingford stood patting his rabbits with calm satisfaction. Up to this time the Prince had been really struck dumb with astonishment, but the vehicle, the appearance of the man, and, above all, the sight of his name on the cab, all convinced him that he had at last found the individual for whom he had so anxiously sought, and he could keep silence no longer. Springing to his feet, and still clasping firmly the branch of the yew tree with which he had rubbed his eyes to such good purpose, he shouted aloud, "Murlingford!" As soon as he had done so a cry of alarm proceeded from all the animals. The hare hobbled off on three legs into the bushes without a moment's delay; the hedgehog also scuttled off as fast as he could, the jay hid behind a bramble, the rabbit crept into a hole hard by, the field-mouse went under the root of the tree, and the mole ran wildly to and fro, and presently concealed himself under a heap of leaves. But Murlingford showed no signs of the alarm which seemed to have possessed his friends and passengers. Turning round to see who had called him, he at once perceived Prince Maraflete, and, respectfully touching his hat, asked him what his pleasure might be? The Prince was still so surprised at the whole occurrence, that for a moment he could make no reply; then, taking a step forward, he eagerly exclaimed—

"Are you Murlingford, the cab-driver?"

"At your service, sir," replied the little man, with a roguish but not unfriendly twinkle of the eye.

"Then I have found you!" joyfully cried the Prince.

"Not a doubt of it, sir," rejoined the other, twinkling again with some vehemence.

"How is it that I have never found you before?" asked the young man.

"Never looked in the right place, I expect, sir."

"That must be it," said the Prince, thoughtfully; "but now that we have met, I have to ask your help. I am Prince Maraflete."

"There are no princes out on the Free Downs," interrupted the other—"we are all equals here. I am Murlingford, the cab-driver, and for two hundred years I have driven the old, lame, and feeble animals to and fro to visit their friends, and get fresh air. Perhaps I shall do so for two hundred years more, but not if anybody sets himself up as a prince or a ruler over me."

"I did not mean to do so," hastily rejoined the Prince; "for, although I am the sovereign of this kingdom, I have no doubt that you belong to a class of persons who are not required to own mortal sovereigns. I only meant to tell you who I am when I am at home."

"But I suppose you are the same person when you are out?" asked Murlingford, with a malicious twinkle.

"Certainly," responded Prince Maraflete; "but I do not claim the same authority, and from you I only ask a favour."

The little man took off his hat, disclosing as he did so a coloured pocket-handkerchief in the crown of it. With this he carefully mopped his brow, as if suffering from heat, and continued this interesting operation as he listened quietly to the Prince.

"I hope," continued the latter, "that you will be able and willing to do me this favour."

"That depends on what it is," calmly observed the other.

"I want you," continued the Prince, "to introduce me to the haggister."

"Introduce you to the haggister!" exclaimed Murlingford in a surprised tone of voice. "Why, what sort of a favour do you call *that*, I should like to know?—and what made you come to *me* for it?"

"I was told to do so in a dream," answered Prince Maraflete; "and I have been searching for you ever since, and at last almost began to believe that there was no such person as you in the world."

"I don't know what you mean by 'the world'—as if

there was only one," replied Murlingford. "There are a great many worlds, if you only knew the fact. There is the world of animals, the world of birds, the world of insects, the world of fishes, and a number more worlds of different degrees of importance. But you princes do not know more than other people, I find, and indeed very often not so much, because you look upon common things from an elevation which causes you to see them through a mist which prevents your clearly discerning and understanding them. Because you could not find me, forsooth, you thought I did not exist. Let me tell you that there are a great many things which exist, in the existence of which you and other foolish mortals do not believe, or only half believe. *I* have existed, thank God, for a great number of years, although you never might have known it or have seen me, if you had not happened to have sat under these yew-trees upon a Thursday, which enabled you to hear and understand the animals, and to have rubbed your eyes with the yew-branch which gave you the power of seeing me. But you will not do so long, since I have my business to attend to. My work is to help the weak and suffering among animals; and, as soon as I have got back to the top of the hill, I am bound by a promise to go and help a lame dog over a stile. Before I do so, however, I will certainly oblige you by bringing you to speak with the haggister, though why you should require it I cannot think. But, anyhow, I like to hear you call the creature by the good old-fashioned name, instead of Magpie, which, though more common, is not half so pretty."

The Prince stared in astonishment: he had never hitherto known that "haggister" and magpie meant the same thing, and being well aware of the habitual shyness of the bird, he foresaw some difficulty in obtaining a confidential interview with it, and at once expressed his fears upon the subject to Murlingford.

"Do not you be afraid, friend Prince," rejoined the latter; "there is a verse to be said, and a certain civility to be performed, after which you will find the haggister perfectly reasonable and full of talk, not to say chatter."

Then drawing from his car a couple of glasses, he poured into each some liquor from a flask which he next produced, and then, handing one of the glasses to the Prince, thus continued:

"Now take off your hat and repeat the words I say; at the word 'once' take a sip at your glass, another at 'twice,' and be sure to finish your glass at the last line, also taking care to bow civilly to the bird when she appears."

Then Murlingford sang to a sing-song tune, the following words, which the Prince carefully sang after him:

> " A pie sat on a pear-tree,
> A pie sat on a pear-tree,
> A pie sat on a pear-tree,
>   Sing hi, sing ho, sing he.
> Once so merrily hopp'd she,
> Twice so merrily hopp'd she,
> Thrice so merrily hopp'd she,
>   Sing hi, sing ho, sing he."

At the word " once," Murlingford took a large sip at his glass, the Prince dutifully following his example; they repeated the process at the word "twice," and finished off their glasses manfully by the last "hopp'd she"; although the Prince, as his glass was large, and Murlingford sang quickly, nearly choked himself in the attempt. Scarcely had they performed this feat, when a magpie suddenly appeared, sitting upon the bough of a thorn-tree hard by. The Prince instantly made her a low bow, according to the instructions of his companion. The bird, however, did not seem inclined to stand upon ceremony, and required no introduction, for she began to chatter away "nineteen to the dozen," as the saying is.

"Sheeps' heads and lambs' eyes!" she cried; "what a row you two fellows are making out here on the downs with your singing and what not! Why, 'tis old Murlingford, I do declare! Well, my old buck, and what are you up to? Glad to see you anyhow, my cheery one, twinkling your ancient eye as usual, and ready for a lark, I'll be bound. Now don't you look at me as if you thought I meant mischief. I don't—I really don't—I don't indeed. But I will if you tease me. I'll have your rabbits' eyes. Take care!" and the bird broke off into a merry chuckle at the idea of enjoying her favourite feast at the expense of Murlingford's team.

The worthy cab-driver took it, as it was meant, as a joke, and at once replied:

"I'll tell the keepers of ye, I will!" and then they both laughed together, after which Murlingford went on to say:

"Here is a gentleman who is by way of being a Prince in the man-world down here, and who wants the honour of an introduction to you. I am sure you will help him if you can, for he seems a decent kind of fellow enough."

With these words Murlingford turned short on his heel, gave a little nod to the Prince, as much as to say, "I'm glad to have done you a good turn," and then, without more ado, stepped into his car, touched his rabbits with the whip, and in another moment was out of sight.

Prince Maraflete had no time to speak to him again, or indeed to think of anybody or anything else but the magpie, who, as soon as Murlingford had taken his departure, turned upon him with a friendly look and began to talk directly.

"*He* doesn't give us much of his company, does he? A good old fellow, too, Murlingford, and no friend to those dratted keepers. Why, I've known that chap to take stoats and weasels out of number, let alone birds, out of those brutal traps. He is such an one for animals, he is! I suppose he is a friend of yours, master Prince, if that's your name or nature, for I didn't rightly understand which. Well, *you*'re dressed pretty fine for the downs, any how! One would think it was Epsom Downs, where you men have your swell racings, instead of our quiet, pleasant, rough, wooded downs—thank goodness it is *not*, though! I was up at Epsom one year when those races were going on. Pretty high up I flew, you may believe; but oh! the screeching and shouting and hullibaloo there was there, and the fresh air spoiled with bad tobacco, and the quiet turned into a racket and noise, and the green grass trodden bare—oh, it was no place for an honest haggister to be at, I can tell you. *These* are jolly downs, an't they? Fresh and green, and pleasant, and quiet! A first-rate place, this is! Now I wonder what brings *you* here, young man. I don't suppose you're after any mischief. Why are you all alone? It is bad for a fellow to be solitary. Why haven't you brought your sweetheart out for a walk? Perhaps you haven't got one. Ha, ha! Well, there's plenty of time, no doubt. But I wonder why you *are* here, and under the wise yew-trees, too ! I call them 'wise,' you know, because there is so much wisdom to be learned under them. How did *you* know that, though, I wonder? Oh, I suppose Murlingford told you, since you're a friend of his. *He* knows everything, *he* does."

The bird rattled on at such a pace, that the poor Prince began to despair of being ever able to get a word in, but at this point he determined to make a bold effort.

" Madam," he began, " I have come to see you——"

"To see me, have you," broke in the magpie hastily. " And very polite of you, too, I must say, young man. But you don't want *me* for your sweetheart, do you? Ha, ha ! I know I'm a good looking bird, and perhaps not altogether a dull companion, but it can't be *that !* But talking of companions, you've no notion what good society we have here on the downs. The very wisest of owls lives in one of those yew-trees, and then we have several hawks, and quite a number of pigeons and doves, and several pheasants and partridges, beside one or two others of my own family. These are the aristocracy, you understand ; and then there are a lot of those second-rate people, the jays; and as to blackbirds, and thrushes, and such-like, their name is legion. Oh, it is a very nice place *indeed* to live in, and I really do declare that if I had my choice of all the world, I would rather be here than anywhere ! "

At this point the Prince made another attempt to obtain a hearing.

" I wanted to see you, madam," he said, " in order to ask you if——"

" My dear sir," interrupted the bird, " you may ask me

anything you please—indeed, you may. I do assure you that if there is one thing on which we haggisters pride ourselves more than another, it is our readiness to answer questions, and to give every information in our power to those who seek it. Why, indeed, should it be otherwise? Why, for instance, should I, who am a friend (let me call myself so) of the worthy Murlingford, refuse to answer any question which you, *another* friend of the good fellow, might wish to ask? What object could I have in doing so? I fairly say, *none.* There is a pleasure, too, in telling other people things which *we* know, and *they* do not I don't mean the feeling of superiority to which such a position gives rise. *That,* I know, ought not to be encouraged, but there is a sense of satisfaction in being useful, which is most gratifying to those who are able to feel it, and——"

"Pray, dear madam," cried the Prince, interrupting her, "will you be so *very* kind as to allow me to ask you——"

"*Of course* I will," went on the bird, "that is just what I am saying, and you need not have interrupted me to say that. It is rude to interrupt people when they are talking, and depend upon it no one ever gains anything by being rude. I always make it *my* rule to be civil to every one. I am sure it is the best plan; long experience has taught me so. I would advise you always to do the same, young man. Now you have really made me almost forget what I was saying. Let me see—about asking questions, so it was——"

Here the Prince once more interposed.

"Yes, madam, and if you would only be so kind as to listen for one moment——"

"There is no one so good—or at least none better—at listening," chimed in the magpie before he had gone any further; "I was always famous for it, and I think it is most decidedly a mark of good breeding. I hate great talkative chattering fellows that will never let you get a word in. Now a jay is a dreadful creature for talking. *I* like the quiet creatures that talk but little themselves, and whose little is always to the point. Now the Nibblers are the sort of people *I* like. There is no chattering about them, but they eat up their supper quietly, and enjoy the fresh air, and will sit listening to you as long as you choose to talk to them."

As soon as Prince Maraflete heard the word "Nibblers," he pricked up his ears at once, and at the very first pause hurriedly exclaimed,—

"Who *are* the Nibblers, dear madam? I do so want to know them; that is the reason I asked to be introduced to you, as I was told you could help me if you would."

"Why didn't you say so before?" asked the bird quite hastily, "instead of jabbering on as you have been doing. What a lot of precious time you've wasted by not coming to the point at once. I *do* like people to come to the point at once, instead of standing for half an hour talking about nothing. The Nibblers! Of course I know them; know them well, too. Men and women call them rabbits, but that is a vulgar name, and means nothing; whereas 'Nibblers' conveys the idea of the animal, whose favourite amusement is to nibble young grass—unless it can get cabbage or parsley, either of which it likes better. But the Nibblers will never speak to you unless you understand how to approach them. They have a habit of scuttling away into their holes when they see a man, and there is only one way to get at them."

"Oh, do tell me what it is;" eagerly asked the Prince.

"Yes," replied the magpie somewhat peevishly, "if you will but let one speak I will; but you go on talking as if nobody else had a tongue but you. What you have to do is not very difficult. Keep your right hand over your left eye as you approach the Nibblers, and when I turn to you as a signal that you may speak, accost the largest of them you can see, who will probably be one of their chiefs, and say in a clear voice :

> ' Sons of Parsley, who by night
>   Tender plants and shrublings bite,
>   Since I mean your race no wrong,
>   Speak to me with friendly tongue.' "

The Prince listened attentively to these words, and at the magpie's desire, carefully learned them by heart. She then told him to follow her, which he accordingly did, and she flew slowly from tree to tree, stopping to have a chatter with him whenever he came up, until he thought they would never get to their journey's end. However, as he was afraid to offend the bird, lest she should fly off in a huff and refuse to help him, he bore the delay with as much patience as he was able, and after a little while they arrived at some scattered hawthorn trees, around which were many rabbits, seated outside a number of holes which betokened that this was a great rabbits' earth.

"There are the Nibblers!" cried the magpie; but the Prince did not think they gave her a very warm reception, which perhaps arose from the fact of birds of her race being more than suspected of a partiality for young rabbits as an article of food, and being confessedly prone to pick out the eyes of a dead or wounded rabbit when an opportunity for so doing happened to occur. At all events, whatever might have been the reason, the behaviour of the rabbits showed no particular delight on their part at seeing the magpie and her companion. Some of them drew in their heads which had been peering out above their holes, so that nothing but the tips of their ears were visible, and presently withdrew even these from sight. Others began to drum violently upon the ground with their fore-feet at short intervals, as if warning each other to look out, whilst some sat up on their hind quarters and stared at the new comers as if prepared to take flight at the shortest notice.

"Ferrets and weasels take them!" whispered the magpie to the Prince. "What fools these Nibblers are! If it wasn't for their eyes I should wish there were no such animals. But never mind, it will be all right presently, on the word of a haggister."

So saying, she flew forward, and perching on a stone near one of the hawthorn trees, began to chatter away at a fine rate, and so fast, that the Prince could hardly make out what she said, only that he saw she nodded towards him, and could plainly distinguish the word "Murlingford," by which he came to the conclusion that she was pointing him out as a friend of that worthy and respected individual. Anyhow, her conversation seemed to satisfy the rabbits, who remained outside their castles, and showed no more symptoms of disquietude. The magpie seemed to address herself particularly to one old buck rabbit, who seemed larger than the rest, and who wore a sprig of parsley cocked jauntily behind his left ear. So when she presently winked at the Prince as a signal that he might speak, it was to this animal that he looked, as he advanced with his right hand over his left eye, and carefully repeated the lines which he had been taught by the magpie. That excellent bird, meanwhile, having interrupted him by remarking that she had an appointment with a carrion crow relative to a sheep that had lately died, left him to mind his own affairs, and flew off in a zig-zag flight up the hill.

Having repeated his verse without a single mistake, Prince Maraflete stood opposite the old buck rabbit, eager to hear his reply. The rabbit appeared by no means anxious to make one; he gravely elevated one of his fore-paws and scratched himself behind the ear; then he performed the same ceremony with regard to his side by means of one of his hind legs; then he drummed pensively on the ground for full half a minute, and at last turned his head languidly round towards the Prince, and exclaimed, in a tone of voice which led one to believe that he was not particularly interested in the matter:

"Why not? My name is Bufflekins, and I am the oldest Nibbler on the downs."

At most times this announcement would have been received by the Prince with the most profound indifference, and even now it seemed somewhat superfluous. But as it was made in answer to the last line of his verse, which entreated the Nibblers to speak to him "with friendly tongue," it was of no little interest to our hero, and he at once inferred that not only was the speaker ready to comply with his request, but that his position, as the oldest of his race upon the downs, would probably enable him to speak with weight and authority, and as one who knew all about the matter on which he would be questioned. So as soon as the words were out of his lips, Prince Maraflete earnestly replied :

"Most excellent Bufflekins, I am indeed pleased to have made your acquaintance. My object is simple. I am told that the Bilberry men have possession of a secret which it is of the greatest importance for me to discover, and that you can help me to obtain what I want."

The rabbit gave a long, low whistle at these words.

" Oh, ho ! " he said, and then remained silent for a full minute, as if pondering deeply over the communication which he had just received ; then he spoke again in a tone little less indifferent than before. " The Bilberry men will tell you nothing," he said, " unless you catch them off their guard."

" I know it, I know it," said the Prince eagerly ; " but how am I to do it, when I don't even know what a Bilberry man *is* ? "

"A Bilberry man," gravely replied the rabbit, "is a person who lives principally upon bilberries, and he is generally on his guard so carefully, that he can only be caught off it by those who know his habits as well as our Nibblers do. Nets and ferrets ! *I* know all about it."

" What is to be done ? How am I to do it ? " earnestly inquired the Prince.

" Well," responded the rabbit, " I should not think it right or fair to tell every chance-comer ; but as you are a friend of our good Murlingford, I have no objection to give you the information you desire. After all, the matter is not very difficult. The Bilberry men are always most off their guard when they have had their dinner, especially if it be a more hearty one than usual. Now do you go a little further on the downs and gather as many bilberries as you can manage in the next hour or so. Do the same thing to-morrow morning, and go on doing it until you have gathered a large quantity. Then come out to-morrow evening before the moon is up, and put your bilberries in heaps a little way off from the big yew-tree where the haggister says she first saw you to-day. Hide behind the yew-trees then, and wait quietly to see what happens. If any creatures come and eat your bilberries, you will see them from your hiding-place. Do not interrupt them; let them eat their fill, and when they have done so, your opportunity will have arrived. Step boldly forward, taking great care to put out your right leg first at every step, drawing the left up to it. Then exclaim in a loud voice as you advance:

> "Robin a bobbin a bilberry ben,
>   Ate so much flesh in his time,
> That every one of the Bilberry men
> Must live upon bilberries only, and then
> Must tell every secret he has in his ken,
>   When fairly demanded in rhyme."

"If you say these lines correctly (and in order that you may do so I will at once repeat them again) you will find the Bilberry men most civil, and ready—as indeed they are bound to be by their laws—to give you every information you desire if you will only ask it in rhyme."

The rabbit then said over the verse to the Prince several times very slowly, until at last he had it quite by heart. Then he warmly thanked the rabbit for what he had told him, and asked whether there was any return he could make for his kindness. The rabbit gravely shook his head.

"I like parsley," he said in a mournful tone, "and scarcely get as much of it as I desire; but I could not receive payment for any service rendered to a friend of Murlingford. Anything you could do to alleviate the sufferings of my persecuted race would be a personal favour to me; but I fear this is beyond your power. If you could abolish weasels, exterminate ferrets, and burst all the guns in the world, I feel sure that other enemies, equally hateful, would speedily spring up to prevent the enormous multiplication of our race, which would otherwise follow. No; the Nibblers must continue to suffer. Something, however, you might do to show your sympathy with us. There are many ways in which we are served up to gratify the palates and satisfy the appetites of mankind. We expect to be roasted: in a pie we are at least respectably placed. We know we are calculated to adorn a pudding, and our limbs in a fricassee do us no discredit. But we feel—I do confess we do feel the indignity of being simply boiled and eaten with onion sauce. Avoid hereafter the infliction of this disgrace upon any members of my race who may be brought within the influence of your kitchen arrangements, and you will have done something to repay the little service which has been rendered you by Bufflekins."

The rabbit ceased, and the Prince, who cared little for the flesh of a rabbit, and happened to detest onions, immediately assured the worthy animal that he would remember his request, and act upon the suggestion therein contained. This appeared entirely to satisfy the rabbit, who, having thanked the Prince for the promptness and courtesy with which he had replied, gravely wished him good-by, and disappeared down the nearest hole.

Prince Maraflete now saw his way clearly before him. Indeed, one great comfort throughout the day had been that there had been no doubt or mystery in any of the directions which had been given him. The first great diffi-culty having once been surmounted by the finding of Murlingford, all the rest had, so far, been plain sailing, and there was now another simple thing to be done, which he determined to do with as little delay as possible. He therefore proceeded at once to the higher part of the downs, on which bilberries grew in profusion amongst the heather, and for the next hour occupied himself in picking them. He would gladly have gone on doing so all the rest of the day, but the rabbit had told him to resume his occupation on the next morning, and therefore he only went on picking for an hour, especially as he had nothing to carry them in except his hat and pocket-handkerchief, as putting them into his pockets would have resulted in spoil-ing both his clothes and the fruit at the same time. He gathered a good many in his hour, and, having carried them down towards the yew-trees, covered them up with grass and heather, and left them for the night. Then Prince Maraflete went home, terribly anxious about the result of next day's adventure. He heartily wished that the delay of twenty-four hours could have been avoided, but was sensible enough to know that it was best to obey implicitly the directions of Bufflckins, and accordingly restrained his impatience as well as he could. He was, however, up betimes in the morning; and, in order to secure enough bilberries, directed the whole of the female part of his establishment to assist in the gathering. They were rather surprised at the order, but by no means averse to a holiday on the downs, whereon some thirty or forty damsels were assembled at an early hour, and before dinner-time had collected in clothes-bags an amount of bilberries such as probably has never been gathered at once either before or since. The Prince accompanied the expedition and worked manfully with them; and when he saw the quantity which had been gathered, he was amply satisfied with the energy and activity which had been displayed. He therefore dismissed the party, telling them to leave their bags of bilberries on the downs, whence he would send to fetch them, and promising to give them a dance very shortly, by way of reward, for having so promptly executed his commands. This sent them away so highly delighted, that they forgot the somewhat extraordinary nature of the task they had been told to perform, to the neglect of their ordinary duties, and could talk of nothing else but the dance for the rest of the week.

Meanwhile Prince Maraflete, having returned to the palace and eaten a hasty luncheon, once more approached the downs full of hopes and fears strangely intermingled in his royal bosom. Fortunately for him, however, he had no time to waste in musing and wondering over what was going to happen. There was the work of several hours before him, to bring down bag after bag of bilberries, empty them out under the yew-trees, arrange them carefully into heaps, and then carry off the bags and hide them at some distance from the place. All this took him until quite late in the afternoon, by which time he had the pleasure of contemplating twelve good-sized heaps of bilberries, arranged beneath the yew-trees in circular form, and bearing good evidence of the fidelity and completeness with which the directions of the venerable Nibbler had been carried out. Then the Prince hid himself behind one of the yew-trees. The sun was setting, but there was still light, and the moon would not be up for several hours. But he was too anxious to go home to dinner, and had, in fact, left word that he should not dine at the palace that night. A chicken sandwich and a flask of old Madeira were all the dinner which Prince Maraflete partook of that evening, and with these he whiled away the time beneath the yew tree until the sun had nearly set; then he waited for some time without seeing anything.

The shades of night fell fast around him; the birds had ceased their songs—not a twitter was heard even from a restless sparrow; the gnats no longer hummed around the branches over his head; silence reigned over the whole face of Creation, and all Nature was seeking quiet and repose. The silver light of the moon, imperfectly seen at first, now began to get stronger and stronger, and gradually lit up the woods and downs with a soft, mellow light, which filled the Prince with sweet and melancholy feelings as he gazed upon the exceeding beauty with which it endued everything which it touched. There *is* something melancholy even in the very loveliness of moonlight, for it is a marked contrast with the bright, cheerful light of the sun, just as the peaceful beauty of an exquisitely chiselled marble statue contrasts with the beauty of a human form still animated by life and soul.

The Prince had now waited several hours, and would doubtless have felt very impatient, but that something seemed to tell him that his watching would soon be rewarded. He had been told by the Nibblers to be at the appointed spot before the moon was up. This, he thought, plainly indicated that anything which was to happen would do so *when* the moon was up. That certainly was the case now. He would still wait patiently, and hope for the best. So he waited and watched a little while longer, and then, all of a sudden, there took place something which filled his heart with joy. Out from a holly-bush there stepped a little man—a very little man—about two feet high. He was dressed in a close-fitting coat of dark green, with shiny black buttons, his trousers and leggings were apparently made of dark-coloured velvet, and he had close-fitting red morocco shoes upon his feet. His head was of a remarkably round shape; his black hair curled round it in a curiously regular manner. He wore no hat or cap, and a red handkerchief completed his attire. The expression upon his face was not unpleasant—on the contrary, there was a gentle but timid look about his eyes, and his small features were regular, and agreeable to look upon. He crept out into the space beneath the yew-trees, and looked round him with a wistful air. He peered up into the branches above his head, then he looked to the right, then to the left, and, all of a sudden, he perceived the heaps of bilberries. He took a step backwards in astonishment, and almost immediately afterwards exclaimed, in a shrill, but musical tone of voice,—

"Eh! Free feastings! Free feastings! Fillbelly Bilberry! Fillbelly Bilberry!"

Scarcely were the words out of his mouth when another little man came hurrying in from the other side, then another and another, until Prince Maraflete counted twelve of the small people assembled together beneath the yew-trees. But the most extraordinary thing was, that they were all so exactly alike that no one could have told one from another of them. They had all precisely the same dress, the same hair, and the same features, and they all behaved exactly in the same manner. They looked at the bilberry heaps, then they shook each other warmly and affectionately by the hand, as if to congratulate themselves upon the discovery, and then, without more ado, each little man sat himself down opposite a heap, and began to eat the bilberries with a palpable sense of enjoyment, which it was really pleasant to witness. For a moment the Prince thought that the Bilberry men—for these were evidently the people whom he sought—were now sufficiently off their guard to be accosted, but he was not forgetful of the old rabbit's instructions, and therefore restrained his impatience, remembering that the proper time of action would not arrive until the strange little men had had their dinner, and that, moreover, it was evidently probable that to interrupt them in the midst of it might put them out of temper, and thus produce results very different from those which he desired.

So he still waited quietly behind the yew tree, whilst the Bilberry men ate as if they had never had such a dinner before. They kept up a running fire of conversation as they did so, but Prince Maraflete could not make out what they said, though he was pretty sure that they expressed satisfaction at having discovered a repast ready to their hand, and some surprise at anyone having been so kind as to prepare it. At last one of them jumped up, ran into the thicket, and returned with water, which he brought in an old tin cover of a box, which seemed to have belonged to a box of biscuits, and had probably been thrown down by some one after a pic-nic on the downs, with very little idea that it would ever be made use of as a drinking vessel for the Bilberry men. They all drank the water with as much relish as if it had been the finest wine, and then they fell to at the bilberries again, until each little man had almost or quite finished his heap. Then they began to stretch themselves out, and pick up scattered bilberries, and put them in their mouths one at a time, and occasionally yawn, and, in short, to give all the usual signs of having finished a very satisfactory dinner.

Prince Maraflete now felt that the critical moment had arrived, and that he must make the attempt upon which so much depended. Accordingly he hesitated no longer, but, bearing in mind the old rabbit's directions, he stepped forth from behind the yew-tree, putting his right leg well forward, and drawing his left leg after it. At the second step he took thus he was clear of the tree, and full in sight of the dinner-party, each of whom began to start to his legs directly, whilst a look of terror came over the faces of all, so ludicrously alike in each case that at another time the Prince would have died of laughing. But he had no thoughts of laughing now. Taking his third step quickly forward as before, he instantly spoke as he had been told:

> " Robin a bobbin a bilberry benn,
>   Ate so much flesh in his time,
> That every one of the Bilberry men
> Must live upon bilberries only, and then
> Must tell every secret he has in his ken,
>   When fairly demanded in rhyme."

As soon as ever he had thus spoken, the look of terror vanished from the faces of the little men, and they all quietly resumed their seats, muttering to themselves words which indicated that they were no longer afraid of the intruder. Encouraged by this reception, Prince Maraflete advanced one step nearer, and thus continued his speech:

> " Tell me, pray tell me, good Bilberry men,
>   Since Fate to your ken all discloses,

How did it happen, and wherefore and when,
    That I was endowed with two noses?
Tell me the fate of my parents so dear,
    My father and mother departed,
Make to me shortly their history clear,
    Since ye are both good and kindhearted.
Since that one nose is enough for a man,
    Why should *my* organ be double?
Help me, dear Bilberry men, if ye can,
    Soon to be quit of my trouble!"

He spoke, and for a moment the little men earnestly whispered together; after which one of them, looking kindly at the Prince, forthwith began to accost him in the most friendly manner, and in the following words:

" Your father was a worthy king,
    Your mother quite a duck,
When her as bride he home did bring,
    He thought him much in luck.
They lived as happy as could be,
    Till near a year was past,
But mortal happiness, you see,
    Is seldom apt to last.
The wicked giant, Blunderfel,
    To works of mischief prone,
Resolved by potent charm and spell
    To make the queen his own.
Rejected by the charming bride,
    At last it came to this—
He caught her on the mountain side,
    And strove to snatch a kiss.
Your father was a valiant man,—
    In mighty wrath he rose!
As only angry husband can,
    He tweak'd the giant's nose.

The coward, howling, fled away,
  But took a solemn oath,
He'd be revenged, on early day,
  Upon your parents both.
He went to witches, bad and black,
  He doubtless paid them dear,
And when again he hurried back,
  His mischief did appear.
The evil he had deeply sworn,
  It was not hard to trace,
For you, poor prince, were shortly born,
  With that unlucky face.
The giant swore that since your sire
  His nose had half undone,
He soon should see (oh, vengeance dire!
  Two noses on his son.
Nor thus the wretch was satisfied!
  By poison rank and keen,
Through his device your parents died,
  The monarch and his queen.
For this, alas! since death is strong,
  No spell can work a cure,
But as regards the other wrong,
  Your remedy is sure.
If you our precepts will obey,
  You'll triumph o'er your foes,
And also find a certain way
  To shunt your extra nose.
The cruel giant, Blunderfel,
  Lives by the ocean shore,
He loves to sniff the briny smell,
  And hear the waters roar.
And to his cave that wondrous knave
  Doth lure both great and small,
Who enters once can no man save,
  For he devours them all.
'Tis left to you, good Prince and true,
  A great revenge to take,
And give the wicked wretch his due,
  For both your parents' sake."

Here the Bilberry man paused, as if to take breath, of which he was probably in want, having uttered the above words with great rapidity. The Prince had listened, as we may well believe, with rapt attention, and as soon as the little man stopped he instantly broke in with the following words:

> " Oh, teach me, kind friends, since the secret ye know,
>   Oh, teach me the way to bamboozle my foe :
>   Oh, let me revenge my dear parents, and, then,
>   For ever I'll favour the Bilberry men ! "

The little man who had first spoken seemed perfectly ready to go on by this time, and as soon as the Prince had said these words, he did so:

> " The way is rather long, you know,
>   But take the early train,
>   By noon you'll reach the cavern so—
>   Next morn come back again.
>   Great caution to you must we teach :
>   Pray wear no creaking boots ;
>   Beware of walking on the beach,
>   Or smoking of cheroots.
>   But walk along the upper road,
>   Above the rocky shores,
>   And when you reach the foe's abode,
>   Just ask if he's indoors.
>   'Mid sundry caves along that coast,
>   His cave you can't mistake,
>   The bones outside, he makes his boast,
>   Would make the bravest quake.
>   And there he lives, this giant great,
>   A monster for to view.
>   If you don't kill him, sure as fate,
>   My boy, he'll settle you ! "

Here the little man paused again, and Prince Maraflete could not help feeling that, although he had doubtless heard the true story of his father and mother's fate, the directions hitherto given him were not sufficiently clear and explicit to enable him to act upon them, since he had neither been told the exact locality in which the giant Blunderfel was to be found, nor how, if at all, his slaughter would affect his own nasal condition. So, determined to be satisfied, he once more tried his hand at a rhyme after the following fashion:

> " Kind Bilberry men, I would dare to inquire
>   The name of the cavern and place,
> Where dwells the foul giant who murdered my sire,
>   And sadly disfigured my face ?
> When found, by what potent enchantment or charm,
>   Can I beard the old wretch in his den,   ›
> Prevent him from slaying or working me harm,
>   And blot out his name among men ?
> And if I'm permitted this foe to destroy,
>   Pray kindly the secret disclose,
> How then may I manage my life to enjoy,
>   By losing this surplusage nose ?"

Having thus addressed the little men, Prince Maraflete anxiously awaited their reply, which very soon proceeded in the following words from the same person who had spoken before, and who certainly appeared to be quite as ready to give as the Prince was to ask information :

> " Take train unto the nearest town,
>   Then walk unto the right,
> A man, whose corduroys are brown,
>   Will shortly come in sight.
> You'll want no magic art or spell,
>   Just ask this worthy man,
> ' Where lives the giant Blunderfel ?'
>   He'll tell you—for he can,

Then walk as I have told you, and
  On entering the cave
Hold branch of yew-tree in your hand,
  To circumvent the knave.
Then tell him who you are, and say,
  In short but pithy rhymes,
That it is your intent to slay
  The monster for his crimes.
And if your threatenings he stops,
  Or mischief tries to do,
Just shout the war-cry, ' Lollipops !'
  And strike him with the yew.
Then take his life, with sharpened knife
  Well whetted on a stone,
Cut off his nose when closed the strife,
  And clap it on your own,
Between your two, if boldly you
  Hold his, and do not fear,
Your surplus nose, I tell you true,
  Will shortly disappear.
And therefore then, like other men,
  In nose and face you'll be,
The dear old yew you'll honour then
  O'er every other tree."

Here the Bilberry man ceased, and the Prince felt that he had now received all the information which was necessary to enable him to proceed upon the expedition which he had already made up his mind to undertake. He therefore thanked the little men in the neatest verse which he could compose on the moment, and assured them that he should never forget the kindness which they had shown him. They were about to reply, doubtless in appropriate terms, when the distant sound of a cock crowing broke upon their ears, and with hasty glances at each other, which seemed to indicate that they had outstayed their appointed time, they smiled pleasantly upon the Prince, and scuttled off into the bushes as fast as they could. Prince Maraflete made no effort to detain any of them for the purpose of further inquiries, but, as soon as they had left the place, immediately followed their example. He hastened back to the palace, threw himself upon his bed without undressing, and for the next three hours lay thinking over the strange things which had happened to him during the last few days. Then he jumped up, undressed, and had a cold bath, which greatly refreshed him; then he dressed himself again in a suit of shooting-clothes, packed a small carpet-bag, and proceeded to select from his armoury—which was very extensive, and contained an enormous variety of weapons of destruction—the sharpest knife he could find, which he put into the sheath which belonged to it, and stuck it in his belt. He then chose a grey wide-awake, which he always wore for grouse-driving, and, thus equipped, set out for the railway-station, carrying in his hand a stout staff of yew, which he made out of one of the branches of the largest yew-tree before he started.

It was rather early, and there were not many people about to recognize him, or annoy him with those manifestations of loyal applause which loving subjects usually bestow upon those who are good enough to reign over them. So Prince Maraflete passed quickly and quietly along, entered the railway-station with his wide-awake slouched forward so as to conceal his face as much as possible, and, carrying his carpet-bag in his hand, took a ticket for the nearest town, which was close to the sea. When he arrived there, he left his carpet-bag at the station, grasped his yew-stick firmly in his hand, tried his boots carefully to be sure they did not creak, and, taking the right-hand road, marched boldly forward, leaving the town behind him. Before he had gone half a mile, there suddenly came out of a cross-road a man with a black velveteen coat, and corduroys which were undeniably brown. By this time the Prince had overcome any little doubt or hesitation he might ever have had as to following the various directions he had received from different sources, since all had hitherto gone on well with him. So, without losing a moment, he hailed the man with a loud—

"Halloa!"

The man turned round directly—

"The same to you, and many of them," said he. "What do you want?"

"Pray," said the Prince, "can you tell me where the giant Blunderfel lives?"

"Take the first turn to the right," promptly replied the man, "and it will bring you to the upper road which runs level with the beach. The giant's cave is about a mile on to the left, between the road and the sea. You can't miss it."

With these words he turned away, scarcely waiting to receive the thanks of the Prince, who immediately followed his directions, and, taking the turning which he had pointed out, speedily discovered the upper road, and began to walk along it. It was a good road enough, and very pleasant for a morning walk under ordinary circumstances. On the left hand of the Prince high cliffs towered up towards the sky, sometimes almost perpendicular, and sometimes sloping gradually back from the road at such an angle that an active traveller might have clambered up them if the chalky surface afforded him sufficient hold for his feet. They were chalk cliffs, and shone out white and glittering in the rays of the sun, very trying to the human eye which sought to gaze upon them, unless a friendly mist hung over them, and softened their, dazzling brightness. Upon the Prince's right hand was a space varying from ten to thirty yards, which was occupied here and there by small patches of vegetation, where from time to time some one had endeavoured to turn the ground to account by way of a garden; here and there by huge boulders of chalk, which seemed to have fallen from above, and to have found a lower resting place. The gardens, however, had evidently been deserted, and there was no dwelling-house near any of them, whilst beyond them and the boulders of chalk there was a rapid descent to the sea, which, according to the levels of the road, lay sometimes thirty, sometimes fifty, and sometimes a hundred feet below it, with an intervening strip of beach, varying in its width, according to the indentations of the shore.

The descent to the sea from the road was for the most part to be only made by clambering over the chalk and the gardens, though here and there was a sort of footpath, and at rare intervals a cart-road seemed to have been cut through, as if for the purpose of fetching shingle from the beach. But there was a wild, deserted look about the place, as if those who had formerly lived there had for some time past ceased to do so, and the Prince had no difficulty in coming to the conclusion that he could not be far off from the abode of the giant. Any doubt, indeed, which he might have entertained upon the subject was speedily removed by the appearance of a gigantic board at the side of the road nearest the sea, upon which were inscribed in deep red letters the following words:

" Any person or persons trespassing upon these premises will be speedily devoured.

" (Signed) Blunderfel.*"*

By this the Prince perceived that he was certainly very near to the enemy whom he had come to seek, and the words on the board, far from discouraging him from his enterprise, stirred up within him the spirit of his ancestors, and fired him with an intense desire to destroy one who had wrought him and his such wrong. Stepping boldly past the board, Prince Maraflete stood at the edge of the descent to the sea, and looked down upon the ocean. It was a lovely scene. The waves were gently murmuring as they broke themselves languidly on the beach, as if it was impossible they could ever roar and bluster. So gently, so softly they kissed the shore, that it was like a tender mother lulling a child to sleep, and indeed there was something soothing and sleep-inspiring in the whisper of each receding wave as it gurgled back through the pebbles of the beach with a sound like a "hush" uttered in a low sweet voice. The light of the sun lit up the surface of the waters, which heaved with an almost imperceptible swell, which alone showed you that it was the real, mighty, living sea, and not an enormous pond upon which you were looking. Far away in the distance the white sails of several fishing-boats sparkled in the sunlight, and still further there rose against the sky the dim, shadowy outline of the cliffs of another country. The Prince stood gazing upon the ocean with those feelings of mingled delight and awe which it often inspires. There it lay at his feet, so quiet and beautiful, so peaceful and pleasant to look upon, and seemed to invite man to venture upon its bosom with confidence in its goodwill. Yet, let the wind rise, or some cause unforeseen by man ruffle its present serenity, and how speedy and vast a change would come upon it. The roaring waves, the dashing spray, the mad foam dancing on the crest of the billows, would transpose the peaceful ocean into a mad, dangerous enemy, just as passion possessing the soul of man converts him from a sane and reasonable being into one to be dreaded and avoided.

So thought the Prince as he looked down upon the waters at his feet, and marvelled at the loveliness upon which he gazed. To the right and left the coast appeared to be much of the same character, save that the white cliffs came nearer to the sea upon his left, whilst away to the right they gradually receded, leaving a plain between themselves and the sea which gradually grew more and more extensive as the hills fell back further from the sea, and assumed the more fertile appearance of an inland range.

As the Prince was doubting what course to follow, the sound of oars suddenly fell upon his ears, and, looking up, he perceived a boat rapidly nearing the shore. It was manned by persons who were evidently of the fishermen class, and apparently they had been plying their trade with some success, since the boat moved slowly, and the Prince could see within it the glittering scales of fish. Closer and closer drew the boat, and in another instant she grated against the beach, and several of the crew leaped out and began to haul her in.

"Yeo-ho!" they cried in a loud voice as they did this, and the Prince stood watching them with interest, and thinking what a happy cheery existence must be that of a fisherman. The next moment, however, his thoughts were turned into another channel. A sudden crunching of the beach was heard, as if some heavy animal was passing rapidly over it; then there came a kind of a sound which was something between a growl and a roar, and the next instant there arose a shriek of terror from the unhappy fishermen, as an enormous figure rushed in upon them from the rocks behind, and seized one, a stripling of some seventeen or eighteen years, catching him up by the waist as if he had been a baby.

"I'll teach you to come trespassing here, and waking me up with your confounded noise!" shouted the giant, for such indeed, beyond all doubt, was the new-comer. "I've caught you, have I, you vile scum of the earth? I'll pay you out! I'll settle you!" And as he gnashed his teeth savagely upon the unhappy wretches, they cowered before him like quails before a hawk, not knowing whether he would not immediately destroy them all, and too completely subdued by fear to attempt to seek safety in flight. The luckless youth whom he had seized, feebly attempted to free himself from the clutches of the monster who held him; but the latter calmly took him by his middle and, laying hold of him with his teeth, shook him just as a dog would a rat, and then dropped him senseless on the beach, whilst he raised a short club which he held in his hand, and shook it at the others in a threatening manner. "I'll eat ye!" he cried. "I'll eat ye all, and this young villain first: see if I don't! I'd eat *him* now at once, to show you I mean it, only I had a late breakfast this morning off an organ-grinder I caught in the road, and I think the beast disagreed with me, for I haven't got half an appetite just now. You are not very tempting morsels either,— you briny, salt, fishy wretches; but I'll eat you all the same, if it is only to put an end to your howling when I'm asleep."

The fishermen were apparently too much overcome with terror to do anything but submit to the will of the terrible giant who stood over them, growling and gnashing his teeth as he uttered these threats, which he appeared both able and willing to put into execution. But the Prince felt that now, if ever, he must act. It was a dreadful moment, and had he been a coward he would even now have shrunk back from the task. To do so, however, never entered his head. The knowledge that the destroyer of his parents was before him, stirred up his courage to fever heat, and the blood of long generations of noble ancestors boiled in his young veins as he leaped down upon the beach, and rushed forward to take his share in the events which were passing below. As he did so, however, he did not forget the directions of the Bilberry men, that he was to address his enemy "in short but pithy rhymes;" and when he was but a few yards off he stopped for an instant in order to do so. The noise made by his footsteps on the beach had already attracted the attention of the giant; and, indeed, I never understood why the Bilberry men had told the Prince not to wear creaking boots; because, whatever boots you wear, you *must* make a crunching kind of a noise when you step upon shingle; and I am inclined to believe that the worthy little man only threw in this bit of advice, as well as that about not smoking cheroots (which the Prince never did), in order to surround the matter with mystery, being perhaps unwilling that the Prince should think the business so very simple, as it really was. Be this as it may, the noise of the new-comer's feet caused the giant to turn his head, and forthwith to become acquainted with his presence, which he made the occasion for another savage growl and several wicked words uttered in a deep and sullen tone. Nothing daunted, the Prince spoke out boldly in the following words :

> " Turn, wretch and tyrant, turn to meet
> The vengeance of Prince Maraflete ! "

" Prince Merryfeet ! " shouted old Blunderfel in accents of scorn. " Who the dickens is he ? You vile jingler of doggrel rhymes, you had better be Prince Very-fleet in taking yourself off, unless you want to go into a pie along with this fisherman chap ! If you're really Prince Very-sweet, I may presently treat you thus ! "

As the giant spoke he grinned a horrid grin, and gnashed his teeth again.

Now the Prince was one of those many people who hate having their names punned upon or made the subject of jest, and therefore the language of the giant was offensive and irritating to his royal ears. Still he preserved his temper, knowing how much might depend upon his doing so, and again accosted his enemy, whom he had been directed to acquaint with his reasons for attacking him, which he did in these words :

> " Think not, base wretch, to hide your shame
> By feeble punning on my name :
> Your end is nigh, and you had best
> Think more of prayer than idle jest.
> I'm Maraflete ! this double nose
> The truth of my averment shows—
> You slew my kin, and, not content
> With this, gave *me* this ornament.
> For this twin nose shall you atone,
> Vile dog, by forfeiting your own ;
> And, for my parents' murder, know
> That with your nose your life shall go."

As the Prince spoke the giant appeared to be wrapt in thought, as if trying to remember which of his many crimes was being thus recalled to his memory. It did not take him long to remember; and no wonder, since it is improbable that he had amused himself more than once with the singular pastime of punishing an enemy by arranging that his son should be born with two noses. So he recollected all about it long before the Prince had done, and burst out into a hoarse laugh as it all came back to him.

"Ho, ho!" he cried. "So you're *that* fellow's son, are you—that poor fool of a King with the baby-faced wife that both lost their lives for offending me! Yes, yes; right enough. I settled them both, and so I will you, though by a different fate, for you are young and tender, my chicken."

With these words the giant turned round from the fishermen, who were still cowering on the beach, and prepared to receive the Prince. The latter hesitated for one moment; he had been told what he was to do on entering the cave, but there was no cave to enter, for the giant had left it, and he was uncertain whether the same directions would hold good in an encounter on the open beach. There was no time, however, for delay, and he thought that as he was evidently "in for it," he had better do as he had been told, and hope for the best. So he advanced boldly down upon the giant without another word, which appeared rather to confuse old Blunderfel, who was accustomed to see people run away from him as fast as they could. In order to make the Prince do so, he now gave vent to a series of most inharmonious roars, which had no effect whatever upon our hero, although they showed him plainly enough the ferocity of his enemy, if any further proof of the same had been wanting. He grasped his brand of yew more firmly than ever in his hand, and came on like a brave prince as he was. When he was scarcely three yards from the giant, the latter sprang forward and aimed a fearful blow at him with his club, which he with difficulty avoided by springing aside; and at the next moment, before his enemy could recover himself, he dealt him a thwack on the side with his yew-staff, being unable to reach his head. The effect, however, was satisfactory, for the giant uttered a yell of pain as soon as the yew touched him.

However, a person of his bulk and strength was not to be disposed of by a single blow, and in an instant he had recovered himself, and his club was upraised for a blow which, if successful, would have finished the Prince Maraflete's life and history together. At the same moment the giant's face, inflamed with rage, assumed an expression so awfully hideous that any ordinary man would have been frightened out of his wits. Not so the gallant Prince, who, though he saw the blow coming, and felt that no strength of his could avail to turn it aside, never lost courage for an instant; but even as the club seemed to be descending upon his head, set his heels firmly in the shingle, and shouted at the top of his voice—

"Lollipops!"

The effect was like magic, which was not surprising, seeing that it undoubtedly *was* magic with which the Prince was fighting his battle. The club dropped heavily from the giant's nerveless hand; and so big and weighty was it that, narrowly missing Prince Maraflete's head, it embedded itself in the beach, and, for aught I know, remains there to this day. At the same moment a ghastly pallor overspread the features of the wretched Blunderfel, who seemed as if

" Lollipops " had undermined his constitution and deprived him of all strength and courage. No less delighted than astonished at the success of his war-cry, Prince Maraflete lost not a moment in profiting by the opportunity which was afforded him by the effect which it had produced upon his enemy. Springing eagerly forward, he struck him again and again with his staff of yew, and leaping up as high as he could, smote him violently even in the face. The monster tottered, stretched out his arms wildly, and after another well directed blow, fell helplessly upon the beach.

The Prince was not naturally a cruel man, but the memory of his parents' wrongs drove pity from his breast; and remembering that he was, after all, only executing a murderer, and fulfilling the directions of the Bilberry men, who had, moreover, told him plainly that if he did not kill the giant, that individual would perform the same operation upon him, he nerved himself bravely to the task. Drawing his knife from his girdle, he leaped upon the monster's body, and drove the weapon home to his wicked heart. The giant gave one groan, which was heard ten miles off, and is to this day spoken of in that part of the country as the loudest clap of thunder ever heard. Then, as was but natural under the circumstances, he immediately expired. The Prince waved his knife triumphantly in the air, and then remembered that, having taken vengeance for his parents' death, he had next to consider his own case.

It was not a pleasant thing to cut the nose from the face of a dead enemy, and still less so to clap it on one's own; but nevertheless it had to be done if he wished to be cured, and he determined to go through with it like a man. So he boldly and firmly seized the nose of the monster in his left hand and prepared to cut it off with his right, when, with a cry of surprise, he suddenly let it go, and started up from the stooping attitude which he had of necessity assumed. The nose was of Indian-rubber! Yes, there was no doubt about it—plain, palpable, elastic Indian-rubber, and yielded to the pressure of his hand just like the faces which are made of the same material, and which you can squeeze into any shape you please. Prince Maraflete hesitated, but only for a moment, for his directions had been precise and positive. The nose must be cut off unless he desired to remain double-nosed all his life. So he boldly plunged his knife into the necessary place, and was delighted to find that the article which he required came quite easily off the face, and was in another moment safe in his hand.

His next proceeding had also been prescribed to him with sufficient exactness to prevent the possibility of mistake. Seizing the Indian-rubber nose in his right hand, he clapped it boldly between his own, and held it firmly there, confidently awaiting the result. It was as immediate as extraordinary. A warm feeling, by no means unpleasant, stole over his whole face; then came a sensation as if a thousand pins and needles were very gently pricking his forehead, cheeks, chin, and noses; then a species of dizziness came over him, and he fell prone upon the beach, but only for an instant, for new life and vigour seemed suddenly to possess him, and, springing to his feet, he instantly raised his hand again to hold on the Indian-rubber nose. There was no occasion to do so; it had disappeared, and so had the two noses which had been his plague through life. Instead of them, in the natural place in which such articles are found, namely between his eyes and his mouth, he felt a regular, an aquiline, a perfect nose, evidently prepared to discharge all the functions which properly belong to such an organ. Prince Maraflete's ecstasy knew no bounds. He shouted aloud for joy. He jumped—as far as the shingle on which he stood would permit him—and threw his arms about in the extravagance of his delight. His courage, his perseverance, his careful obedience to the directions he had received, had thus been fully and satisfactorily rewarded; and he could henceforth show his face among men, relieved from the consciousness of being inferior to others in any personal attraction. This was indeed something for which to be thankful. Thoughts of gratitude mingled with his joy, and he formed upon the instant great plans for doing good to everybody and everything within his kingdom.

He firmly resolved that each and every one of the creatures who had contributed to his happiness should be handsomely rewarded. He would forthwith cause to be erected a most magnificent home for decayed Bilberry men; he would abolish the slaughter of "Nibblers," make it a capital offence to kill one of their race, and exalt them at once to the rank of domestic animals. Haggisters should henceforth be for ever sacred, and he would appoint Murlingford, the cab-driver, to a high position at Court. All these and other plans of a similar nature passed through his brain upon his first awakening to the knowledge of his complete cure, and he was entirely honest and sincere in each and all of his intentions. The first thing to do, however, was to get home again; and yet, before he did so, he thought he was bound to see whether there might not be some other work to do with reference to his fallen enemy. He had forgotten the latter for a moment, whilst occupied with his own nasal affairs, but now looked down upon him with some idea that he ought perhaps to receive some kind of interment. What was his surprise to find that, during the brief interval which had elapsed since the giant's fall, his carcase had entirely changed into seaweed, an enormous heap of which lay in the place lately occupied by the body of Blunderfel.

After staring for a moment in astonishment, the Prince resolved within himself that, under these circumstances, he need trouble himself no further about the matter. He looked for the fishermen, but they had taken advantage of the encounter between the giant and himself to slip away, and were nowhere to be seen. There remained only the inanimate body of the stripling whom the monster had dropped after shaking him in his teeth, and no other creature was in sight. A short distance off the Prince perceived the entrance to the giant's cave, which he deemed it his duty to explore. There was, however, nothing to repay him for his trouble. A few dried bones lay at the entrance, and inside there was nothing but the ordinary furniture of a giant's dwelling, which is too well known to need description. There were no prisoners to release, which rather surprised the Prince, who, knowing the general character of such beings as Blunderfel, had expected to find a larder full of mortals ready to be eaten, numerous captives awaiting their doom, and not improbably a distressed princess or two whose deliverance he might have accomplished. But none of these things were to be seen, and Prince Maraflete retraced his steps to the spot where lay the young fisherman, and stood thinking over the best course to pursue.

Now what that course was cannot but be a matter of great interest to all who have read this veracious history.

But as it led to other adventures of great importance and stirring interest, it cannot be included within the limits of the present story. We must leave Prince Maraflete upon the beach, and everybody may settle for himself what he did next. Perhaps he went back into the road, walked off to the station where he had left his carpet-bag, took the next train, and went home to the palace in time for dinner. Perhaps he did something quite different. At all events, we leave him in a position vastly better than that in which we first found him; having vanquished and slain the destroyer of his parents, and, moreover, succeeded in getting rid of the great blot which had hitherto darkened his existence, so that he could no more be known among men by the undesirable appellation of "The Two-nosed Prince."

PART II.

WE left Prince Maraflete standing upon the shore which had been the scene of his triumph over the giant Blunderfel, and considering what should be his next step. Of course there are many good, simple, matter-of-fact people who will say that any sensible young man would have been satisfied with having duly performed all he had undertaken, and would have happily gone home again by the next train.

But if Princes and heroes generally were in the habit of doing such common-place things as this would have been, they would never meet with adventures worthy of being told, and there would soon be an end of all Fairy stories and similarly interesting chronicles. Besides, in the present instance there was another reason why the Prince should take a different course from that which now seems so simple and natural.

Immediately before him lay the body of the young fisherman with whom the giant had first begun his attack upon those who had landed upon the beach. Unlike the carcase of old Blunderfel, this had by no means turned to seaweed; but lay there, still and inanimate, before Prince Maraflete, who stood for several seconds gazing down upon it with sorrow that a cruel fate should have overtaken one so young. Presently he thought he observed a tremulous motion in the limbs, and stooping over the prostrate form, distinctly saw the chest heave.

The young man, then, was not dead, and the Prince was

far too kind-hearted to leave a fellow-creature in distress. What, then, should he do?

No help was at hand: it would have been impossible for him to have carried the young man back to the station, or to any house, for there was none such near, and if there had been the weight of the burden would have rendered any such course extremely difficult.

Casting his eyes around, whilst he stood considering what had best be done, the Prince suddenly observed the boat in which the fishermen had reached the shore, and which they had abandoned in their flight, only too glad to make their escape from the dangerous neighbourhood in which they had found themselves. Here, then, as it seemed to Prince Maraflete, was a means by which he might be able to save the unfortunate victim of the giant's ferocity, and at the same time find a way of escape for himself from a spot which he was desirous enough to leave behind him. He therefore carefully raised in his arms the senseless though still breathing body, and prepared to place it in the boat. As he did so, however, he made a discovery which filled him with astonishment, and in some degree added to the difficulties of his position.

The supposed stripling was decidedly of the other sex. It was not a boy, but a young woman, who had been thus strangely left in his charge. There was no doubt about it. Clad entirely in that blue serge which constituted the ordinary dress of the fishermen upon that coast, and wearing a man's coat with large buttons upon it, the appearance of the figure had been exactly that of a boy, and all the more so as the hair was not worn long but curiously turned back over the head, and confined by a close-fitting cloth cap. But a closer inspection disclosed his mistake to the

Prince, and showed him that it was indeed a woman, and moreover a woman of much personal beauty, whom he was about to lift into the boat.

Her complexion had certainly somewhat suffered from continual exposure to the sun and wind, but there was a healthy brown upon her cheeks apart from the tanning of the sun. Her features were finely cut, the eyelashes which shrouded her closed eyes were unusually long, and her limbs seemed to have been cast in an exquisite mould.

The Prince did not observe all this at once; but the beauty of the girl gradually dawned upon him during the many opportunities which, as will presently be seen, were afforded to him for gazing upon her as long as he liked. At the particular moment of which we are speaking, he had resolved to place her in the boat, and saw no reason why he should change his mind. Accordingly, he lifted and carried her, as gently and carefully as he was able, over the side of the boat, and laid her down upon some canvas which lay therein. Then he made a species of pillow for her head and shoulders by folding up a rough overcoat which one of the fishermen had left, and carefully covered her feet with another.

Having thus made his companion as comfortable as he could, he looked round the boat in order to see what there was on board which might be of use to him on the voyage he was about to take, and what might be got rid of so as to lighten the boat. On second thoughts, however, remembering that the vessel was not his own, he felt that he had no right to throw anything away unless it should be absolutely necessary in the event of a storm. His intention, moreover, was only to coast along until he should come to some favourable landing-place in his own country; and, as he did not contemplate being afloat for more than a couple of hours at most, there was little need of lightening the boat for so short a period, and he therefore abandoned the idea, although there were a number of fish which somewhat added to her weight, and which he had half a mind to throw overboard. He refrained, however, and having taken hold of a punt-pole which he found, endeavoured to float the vessel therewith. Finding this, however, beyond his strength, he landed once more on the shore and pushed the boat with all his might from the beach. Slowly she gave way, grated over the shingle, and in another moment almost floated on the water. Then Prince Maraflete, imitating the fishermen whom he had often watched on the shore, gave her another great push as hard as he could, and running into the shallow water as he did so, gave a spring into the boat, and the weight of his body thus giving an additional impetus to her, in another instant she floated gaily on the waves.

The Prince now looked round for the oars, and found that they were somewhat heavy, and the boat rather too big to be easily managed by one person, especially if he did not happen to be accustomed to rowing. There was a mast, it is true, but our hero had heard and read a good deal about accidents which had happened to sailing vessels through the ignorance of people who thought that they could arrange sails without previously knowing anything at all about the matter, and as this was precisely his own condition, he very wisely resolved to leave sailing alone.

So he was just about to set steadily to work at the oars, when he was interrupted by an occurrence which, had he given the matter a thought, ought not to have surprised him as much as it undoubtedly did. His companion was sitting up and gazing upon him with mingled astonishment and alarm, disclosing as she did so a pair of the most beautiful brown eyes that he had ever beheld. The motion of the boat, aided by the time which had elapsed since she had been so roughly shaken by the giant, had restored her to consciousness; and, as her senses gradually resumed their former condition, she became aware of the fact that she was lying in the bottom of the boat, which was moving slowly through the water. For a moment she lay perfectly still, as if not yet quite certain where she was and what had happened; and then, as memory regained her power, she began to remember all that had occurred, and to wonder what had become of her companions.

So she sat up, and the first discovery she made was that none of the fishermen with whom she had landed were with her in the boat; but that the latter was being guided by a young and handsome stranger, who did not seem to be particularly handy with the oars at which he was labouring. The exclamation to which she gave vent was that which attracted the attention of the Prince, who instantly stopped rowing and returned the maiden's gaze with interest. Thus they sat looking at each other for several moments without either of them saying a word, and apparently each waiting for the other to speak first.

This state of things, however, could not of course endure long, and after the pause had continued for a few seconds, Prince Maraflete, probably thinking it incumbent upon his royal position to make the first advance, remarked in a courteous tone of voice—

"I hope you feel better."

The beautiful eyes opened wider than ever at these words;

and, rapidly passing her hand over them, the maiden spoke.

The tone of her voice was decidedly musical, and although her words were not such as betokened of themselves culture or refinement, there was something not unpleasing in the manner in which they were uttered.

"Where be I?" she said. "And where be my mates? Where's Lanky Bill, and Cork-eye and Bandylegged Harry?"

"Madam," returned the Prince gravely, "if, as I presume, you refer to the fishermen who lately occupied this boat, they are doubtless safe, but have procured that safety by flight."

The eyes were still fixed in wonder upon the Prince's face during this speech, and upon its conclusion the maiden gave vent to the single exclamation—

"Lawks!"

It was not uttered loudly, it was not uttered uncivilly, and although the word was not one which the ladies about his court were in the habit of using, the Prince perfectly understood it to express the surprise which his companion felt at the situation in which she found herself, and her instant and entire comprehension of the position. Even thus, however, it was not exactly an easy observation to answer, inasmuch as it conveyed no particular expression of like or dislike of the circumstances, and suggested no course to be followed and no opinion to be offered by him to whom it was addressed, if indeed it could justly be said to be addressed to anyone. So the Prince was rather doubtful as to what he had better say next, being anxious to remove from the breast of the maiden any fear which she might possibly entertain at finding herself separated from her friends and alone in the boat with a stranger; and at the same time wishing, with a delicacy which was natural to him, to avoid thrusting his conversation upon one who might not desire it. Upon the whole, however, he deemed it more polite to say something; and, therefore, leaning forward upon his seat he observed—

"You have had a severe shock, but you are quite safe now, madam, and there is nothing more to fear. You shall shortly rejoin your friends."

As the girl still stared at him with open eyes, without speaking a word, he continued—

"I am very thankful to have been of service to you. I am afraid you must be hurt as it is. It was very fortunate I happened to come up just at the right moment."

As he spoke the girl's face lighted up with a brighter look than it had yet worn, and she exclaimed with sudden interest and earnestness—

"Did you wallop the old 'un ?"

"If you mean the giant," replied the Prince, "I have rid you of him for ever. He will trouble the world no more."

The girl uttered a shout of joy at this news, and immediately cried out in a tone and manner which at once removed from the Prince's mind any apprehension of her being troubled by fear or timidity at his presence.

"Well done you, mate ! Tip us your fist !" As she spoke she made an effort to rise as if to come forward and shake hands with her preserver, but sank back again with another exclamation of "Lawks ! how stiff I be, to be sure ; I can't move no faster than an old crab !"

Although unused to such language as this, the Prince found something in the tone and manner of the damsel which was pleasing as well as novel. Besides, he was in the humour for an adventure, and his present position appeared to promise him one. So he civilly replied to his companion that he sympathised greatly with her, and trusted she would lie still and rest, there being no occasion whatever why she should exert herself at that moment.

He spoke in courtly phrase, and when he had made quite a pretty little speech of this kind, his companion answered him by bursting out into a hearty fit of laughter.

"Bless you!" she said, "How fine you do talk, surely! Don't you go for to mind I. I be only a bit stiff, I say, *that* ain't no account. I'll be all right in a jiffy." Although unacquainted with the precise nature of a jiffy, the Prince felt that the girl intended to convey an assurance that no long period of time would elapse before she should have recovered from the effects of her accident, if such be the correct term to apply to a severe shaking in the mouth of a giant. He therefore expressed his satisfaction at her statement; and then, taking up the oars, which, during their conversation, he had neglected, he began to row. He had not done so very long, and was taking particular pains about it, and thinking how well he was getting on, when the girl suddenly remarked "Why, what a muff you are with them oars, to be sure! Let *me* bear a hand and help." This rather annoyed the Prince, but he felt he must make excuses for the rudeness of one who had evidently never enjoyed the advantages or received the polish of a court education. So he merely remarked that he was sorry he did not row well enough to satisfy her, but feared that her stiffness would not be improved by her taking part in the work. She would take no denial, however, and having risen to her feet, came and sat down on one of the rowing seats, and insisted upon taking an oar and instructing her companion in the mysteries of the art. Prince Maraflete was by no means an unwilling pupil. In fact, the romance of the situation, the beauty of the girl, her simplicity, and the innocent freedom of her manners, nay, her very voice and accent, and the novelty of some of her expressions to his royal ears, all had for him a species of fascination which rendered the whole affair one of agreeable interest to the young man. Her observations were amusing as well as unusual.

"What baby hands you've got, to be sure!" she cried. "Why, one of Lanky Bill's would make three of yours, I declare! *You* ain't done much rowing, I reckon."

The Prince at once owned the correctness of her guess, and she proceeded to make other observations of a like character, until at last she remarked without any preface or preparation—

"What's your name, young man?"

It was long since the Prince had been so plainly addressed, but he had ceased to be surprised at anything which his fair companion said, so he calmly replied—

"Maraflete, madam, at your service."

"Now don't madam me, Mr. Maraflete," promptly responded the maiden. "I'm no madam at all, but just plain Polly Perkins; so now you know."

This piece of information could not but be interesting to the Prince, who now began to inquire more particularly as to the residence, occupation, and friends of the girl into whose company he had been so strangely thrown. There was no mystery about any of these. She was apparently one of his own subjects, living in a straggling village upon the coast, not far from the scene of the adventure with the giant, which had ended so disastrously for the latter. She remembered no father or mother, but had lived from early childhood in the hut of one " Old Ben the fisherman " and his wife, so she said ; and had been reared among fish, nets, and boats, until she understood all that concerned a fisherman's existence.

It was therefore not wonderful that she should be able, as she certainly was, to instruct Prince Maraflete in many matters concerning the management and navigation of a boat; but as I was unfortunately not there myself to hear what she said and the lessons she gave him, it would be trifling with my readers if I were to endeavour to repeat them, or to use nautical terms which I have occasionally met with in books, but of the nature and meaning of which I am somewhat ignorant. I only know that the maiden laughed a good deal at some of the Prince's notions about a boat, and told him plainly that he was a " regular land-lubber " as far as rowing was concerned; but somehow or other he did not seem to mind anything she said, and they got on very comfortably together all this time. The two good people were so occupied in giving and receiving lessons that they did not perceive that, instead of coasting along the shore as the Prince had intended to do, they had gone some way out to sea. This, however, made no difference in their enjoyment. The Prince did not mind the motion of the boat upon the waves, especially when he was so pleasantly occupied in acquiring knowledge which might hereafter prove useful to him; and, as for his companion, she was perfectly at home upon the ocean, and seemed as happy as her best friends could have wished.

After a time she proposed a sail, observing that there was just enough wind to make it pleasant. So, with the aid of the Prince, who exactly obeyed every direction she gave him, the girl set the sail of the boat, which began to move rapidly through the water. For a time this was very delightful, and the Prince thought he had never found the hours pass so quickly. Presently both he and his companion discovered that the morning's exertion had given them an appetite.

"If we don't have some breakfast," exclaimed the girl emphatically, "my name ain't Polly Perkins!"

The force and beauty of this expression had due weight with Prince Maraflete, who, under the direction of Miss Perkins, chose some of the fish which lay in the boat, and assisted her to broil them, the means of doing which were all on board. Some coarse bread was also at hand, and with this and some salt, the two companions sat down to as good a breakfast as ever man or woman need desire. It was rather a late breakfast, to be sure.

The Prince had started from home early that morning, but it will be recollected that he had made a railway journey, after which he had to walk to the place whereat he encountered and slew the giant, and all the transactions which followed had of course occupied a certain amount of time. It was therefore in fact well on to mid-day when he and his new friend had their breakfast, to which they both did ample justice. So intent upon it, indeed, were they that it was some time before they noticed what was going on around them. Slowly, but surely, a kind of mist stole gradually up, more and more obscuring the light of the sun, which had shone so brightly when they commenced their voyage. At the same time the wind, of which there had been hitherto no more than enough to fill their sails and gently carry them forward, began to increase, and with it came a low moaning sound across the water, as if wind and wave knew that they were going to have a tussle together, and neither of them much liked the thoughts of it. Still Prince Maraflete and Polly Perkins continued their repast until the swell of the sea increased so much that the boat began to rock and roll in a manner of which the Prince became unpleasantly aware, and forthwith he called his partner's attention to the fact.

"I do declare it's getting rough," she replied, "and lawks! see how dark 'tis growing. Young man! shiver my timbers if we ain't in for a storm!"

Although this was another expression which was new to Prince Maraflete, it perfectly conveyed to him the meaning of the person who uttered it, and indeed, on looking around him, it was impossible to doubt the truth of her statement. The wind was rising rapidly, the moaning sound was being magnified into a threatening roar, the waves grew larger and the white foam rode upon their crests as if betokening strife and agitation in the depths below.

Polly bid the Prince hasten to help her furl the sail and take down the mast, which he immediately did, and not before it was time to do so, for the boat was rapidly becoming unmanageable, and the main object the two had in view was to give as little as possible for the wind to take hold of.

And now the sky was almost as black as night; they could see but a few yards about them either before or behind (fore or aft I believe to be the technical terms), and knew not the direction in which they might be going.

Presently a vivid flash of lightning lit up the whole face of the ocean, and then the heavy artillery of heaven opened, and the thunder rolled deeply and loudly above their heads. Insensibly they drew near to each other, and sat down in the bottom of the boat, knowing that they could do nothing, for the excellent reason that there was nothing to be done.

Their best and safest plan, said Polly—to whom the Prince at once deferred as an authority—was to let the boat drift before the wind, and wait for better weather.

This did not seem probable at present. Large drops of rain began to fall ; few and far between at first, then faster and more frequently, until at last the waters above seemed to have entered into a compact with those below, and the clouds sent down powerful and constant reinforcements to the seething ocean.

Fortunately for our two friends, there was a sufficient quantity of tarpaulin on board to aid them in keeping out the wet, besides the two fisherman's coats already mentioned, in one of which the Prince carefully wrapt his companion ; and, drawing her close to himself in the bottom of the boat, which appeared but natural and reasonable under the circumstances, pulled the loose tarpaulin round and over them both in such a manner as to make as good as possible a protection from the fury of the tempest which raged above, below, and around them.

It was altogether a strange situation for a Prince, and one in which he had little expected to find himself when he left his Royal Palace that morning. There, indeed, he had every luxury at his command, and (save for the deformity with which he had been afflicted and which had now happily disappeared) nothing to prevent his passing a life of ease and seeking for happiness where he could most readily find it. But instead of enjoying in tranquillity those blessings which Providence had placed within his reach, here he was in an open boat, lying under a tarpaulin-covering with a companion far below him in social position, and tossed to and fro upon the waves of a tempestuous ocean.

It was certainly a very curious position, and he could not help laughing inwardly as he thought of the expression which the faces of all the great lords and ladies at his court would assume if they could see him at that moment. As they could not do so, however, it did not much matter; and so he lay listening to the winds and waves without much fear that his courtiers would ever know of it, or that the newspapers of his country would be able to fill their columns with an account of his proceedings.

The position was not so very uncomfortable after all. His companion was so pleasant that he by no means objected to their close quarters. She was not in the least frightened; but, on the contrary, showed an absence of fear which greatly pleased the Prince, who contrasted her behaviour with that which he felt very sure would have been the conduct of many of his court ladies, to the manifest advantage of the former. She talked with him cheerfully, and told him that the storm seemed to remind her of something which happened many years ago (as it seemed to her) when she was quite a little child; she could not tell him precisely what it was; but she remembered quite well being in a ship or boat, and hearing the same sounds which she then heard.

The Prince questioned her a good deal about her life with the fishermen, and she answered him with a good-humoured and frank simplicity which highly delighted him. He had already left off addressing her by the formal title of " Madam," against which she had from the first protested; and as they began to make friends more and more, he insensibly slipped into calling her "Polly," which she seemed to think quite natural, and they were ere long talking as if they had known each other all their lives.

The fact is, that when human beings are thrown together in hours of difficulty and danger, not only are the broad but artificial distinctions of rank and position speedily forgotten, but the restraints and barriers of everyday social life are broken down, and people get to know much more of each other in an hour than they might do in half a lifetime of ordinary existence.

So Prince Maraflete and Polly Perkins became better acquainted in the open boat and under their tarpaulin than might otherwise have been the case though they had lived in the same country for an hundred years under the ordinary conditions of life.

I do not know precisely how long they remained where they were, but they did not feel disposed to move, because they knew that there was nothing to be gained by doing so; whereas by staying as they were they kept each other dry and warm, and cared less for the fury of the elements which raged above them. The storm indeed rather increased than abated: the winds roared tremendously over their heads, the waves ran mountains high and every moment threatened to engulf the fragile bark in which the two companions lay. But it was not so ordered. The little boat mounted up high on the top of one wave, and the next moment shot down into the trough of the sea as if she was going straight to the bottom there and then. Yet she rose again and danced like a fairy on the crest of the next wave, repeating the same experiment the moment after; but continually rising again, as if she was only playing with the waves, and knew they were friends who did not really mean to hurt her.

All this time it had never occurred to the Prince or to his companion that there was anything in the least degree unnatural in the suddenness and violence of the storm, which they regarded as one of those freaks of nature to which mankind is subject, and of which people must make the best when they occur. The two young creatures little knew the reason and meaning and origin of that storm; nor could they have done so unless they had been gifted with more than the common knowledge of mortals. The truth is, however, that it was entirely caused by the previous events of the morning. Nowadays you cannot kill a giant, or perform any of those creditable feats of daring which were so common in the days of the Seven Champions of Christendom and at other periods of history, without producing results far more general and serious than was formerly the case.

Steam and electricity have so altered the whole face of the world that everything of this kind becomes quickly known; and, instead of passing quietly on from one country to another, killing evil dragons, knocking troublesome ogres on the head, disappointing cruel and crafty magicians, and delivering various lands from torments of this kind until you have finished as much of this sort of work as it suits you to do—instead of this, I say, you cannot keep your doings quiet for a moment, or perform one of these brave and useful acts without finding it a topic of discourse all over the civilized world, and yourself an object of conversation for all the gossips of society.

Moreover, giants are not persons to be slain and put out of the way without any fuss or bother. They have generally established themselves pretty firmly, and have made friends or contracted alliances by means of which they can withstand that force of public indignation which might otherwise pursue and punish them for their wicked deeds. In this respect old Blunderfel differed in no respect from other giants of the like nature. He had many friends in the monster world, who regarded his wickedness with approbation, and viewed his cruelties as the pardonable eccentricities of a lively disposition. He was, moreover, as is well known to the careful student of history, first-cousin once removed to the King of the country of the Hump-backed Ogres, a nation who have always been notorious for their bad character and evil doings.

No sooner had the giant fallen before the bravery of Prince Maraflete, than some kind friend or officious personage, whichever way you please to take it, communicated the fact—probably by wire, but this we have no certain means of knowing—to his relations, and the whole community of wicked giants and other creatures of that description, knew what had befallen their friend within an hour of his death.

Now you will wonder how it is that I know the thing which I am going to tell you ; and, therefore, in order to put the truth of my story beyond a doubt at once, I state openly that I had it from the sea-gulls.

I am fond of walking by the sea when the weather is a bit rough, and these birds are always more communicative at such seasons than at any other. They wheel and whirl about, skim the crest of the wave after a foam bath (a favourite remedy for invalid sea-gulls, and much recommended by the cormorants, who are the great sea-bird doctors, and of high medical reputation upon the coast), and if you happen to catch them at the right moment, that is, just after a bath, and are fortunate enough to understand their language, you may learn a great many wonderful things about the sea and its business.

Most luckily for me, I had, in very early youth, lessons in the sea-gull language from a bird who was a temporary resident in our garden at home. I do not know how he was caught at first; but they clipped his wings and put him in the garden, saying he was a good hand at catching slugs and other enemies of the vegetable world. Anyhow, he spoke the sea-gull language like a native, and was good enough to teach me all he could. I should have learned much more, only his wings grew, and, when he found this was the case, he flew away one fine morning without saying a word to anybody, and never came back to his slug-hunting, probably preferring the wild waves and the foam-baths, in which I think he showed excellent taste.

I never forgot his lessons, and was thereby enabled to gather from the conversation of these birds how it was that Prince Maraflete and Polly encountered this terrific storm, and were brought into such peril of their lives.

It seems that the race of giants have always tried to keep on good terms with the weather authorities, and especially with those who have to do with the wind department. Of course, as a matter of theory and principle, these things are governed by strict rules and regulations, and all the officials connected with the wind and weather offices are persons of the highest integrity and most strict probity, utterly incapable of being bribed or persuaded in any way or in the slightest degree to swerve from the plain path of duty before them. But somehow or other the fatal word "influence" has a place in this as in every other department;

and the kings of the giants know how to exercise their influence in a manner so skilful and judicious that they could generally arrange a small storm on very short notice, and even, when the occasion seemed to require it, could cause mankind to be troubled by a great tempest. Very awkward customers they must be to have for enemies, thought I, when the sea-gulls first told me this; and I forthwith resolved to keep on good terms with all giants, especially about hopping-time, for an honest man of Kent, with a good hop-garden and the hops just ready to pick, would have a bad time of it if the king of the giants got up a tempest at that particular moment. It is hopping-time whilst I am writing this, and my hops are about half picked, and here I sit listening to the wind getting up much faster and higher than I like to hear it on the sixteenth of September, and I only hope those wretched giants are not at the bottom of it !

Well, as I was saying, the giants heard the news of old Blunderfel's death, and it put them in a terrible rage. Especially annoyed was the deceased giant's first cousin once removed, the King of the Hump-backed Giants, who rejoiced in the sweet-sounding name of Puffblock, the origin of which I have never been able to discover, as when I asked the sea-gulls they only screamed, and either did not or would not understand.

King Puffblock had not cared for his relation when alive; in fact, he had rather hated and constantly abused him for a lout and a fool, both of which he was himself in an eminent degree. But somehow or other, by some strange law of nature, as soon as ever a fellow is dead, one often discovers that one was really very fond of him and will miss him a great deal.

So as soon as the news of old Blunderfel's decease had reached King Puffblock, he first flew into the violent passion which giants always think it right to assume when they hear any news which is not decidedly good, and then he began to declare that he had lost one of the best and dearest friends he had ever possessed. Next he ordered general court-mourning of the deepest character, which, in the giant country and according to old ogre custom, consists in cutting off the left leg of the trouser below the knee and painting the leg either vermilion or sky-blue according to taste. It may be observed that it was probably the existence of this custom which eventually led to the almost total abolition of trousers and the adoption of knickerbockers by those of the giant race who wear anything at all. The expense of continually cutting off one of your trouser-legs was not unnaturally found to be considerable, and although the change was violently resisted by the tailor interest, who had derived great profit therefrom, it was at length carried out to its fullest extent, so that at the present day one scarcely ever sees a giant in trousers anywhere.

When Puffblock had given this order, which he did immediately on recovering from his first fit of passion, he turned his thoughts to vengeance, and took instant steps to communicate, through the stormy petrels, with those agents who were the most likely to be able to procure a tempest with the least possible delay. When this had been done, he further arranged with various fishes of the worst class, and especially with all the devil-fish he could get at in the time, to swim around and direct the boat, in which he heard that the Prince had embarked, so that it might be drifted on to the shores of his country, and its occupants be delivered up into his power.

Thus, whilst Prince Maraflete and Polly Perkins lay comfortably under the tarpaulin, sheltered as much as could be from the wind and weather, and becoming better acquainted every minute, they were gradually being carried into the presence of enemies more terrible and a danger more grievous than the winds and waves. They kept well under the tarpaulin meanwhile, and did not look out, knowing well enough that they could do nothing whilst the storm continued to rage so furiously. They talked together, however, and the Prince found that although Polly's language was not precisely that to which he had been accustomed, her ideas were all nice and good, her intelligence was considerable, and she was certainly a most pleasant companion. He could not comprehend how a mere fisherman's daughter could be so refined in her thoughts and so agreeable in her conversation; and little by little he began to enjoy her society and really to rejoice over the accident which had thus thrown them together.

Still the wind howled and the waves roared, and the boat tossed to and fro, and it seemed not improbable that this their first meeting would also be their last in this world of woe. But, as it is "a long lane which has no turning," so also it is a long storm which has no end, and, in sober truth, such a storm never existed. So the wind, being tired of making such a fuss about nothing, dropped down, first to a mere common gale, next to a slight breeze, and then almost to its ordinary state of composure.

The sea, having been considerably excited and thoroughly stirred up in its deepest feelings, took longer in composing itself, and its bosom heaved with an uneasy motion for some time longer.

But the boat no longer pitched up and down as before;

it rode more gently upon the billows, and the companions became sensible that the danger of shipwreck—and consequent drowning—was over for the present, and that they might rouse themselves to some effort of their own to direct their vessel where they thought best.

As the lady was conscious of her own superiority in the art of navigation, she suggested to Prince Maraflete that she should take the oars as soon as the sea was calm enough for them to row again.

The Prince, however, being far too polite to allow a lady to work whilst he remained idle, entirely objected to this arrangement.

"Well," said the girl, "you had better let me do as I say. You're a precious muff with the oars, you know. You never could have been brought up a fisherman, *that's* plain enough. What *are* you when you are at home?"

A little nettled by the contempt which she showed for his rowing capacity, he replied, with some dignity—

"I am the Prince of the country—Prince Maraflete."

"Are you?" she exclaimed in surprise. "A Prince! well, I never!" She looked at him with her large eyes wide open for a second or two, and then continued—"You are very like other men, too. Are all princes like other men, I wonder? And, I say, why should one fellow be a prince more than another?"

"Because he is born so," replied the Prince, with prompt decision.

"Yes, I know *that*," returned the damsel; "but why *should* he be born so? Is one man better and wiser than another because he is born in a palace and the other in a cottage? and if he is *not* better and wiser, why should he be a prince and the other not be one? I cannot understand it."

"A prince," answered Maraflete, gravely, "who rightly understands his position and properly uses his opportunities, ought to be wiser, better, and braver than other people. His power is great—so are his responsibilities. He should set an example of high, honourable, and moral conduct to his subjects; he should choose good and noble-minded companions, and, with them, set his people an example of the manner in which duty may be done and good work performed in every station in life; he should be first in every good work — brave in battle — wise in council — and the encourager of all that is virtuous and upright in his country."

" Dear me ! " said the girl, " that all sounds very grand, but he can't be best at everything after all. You see you don't row any better for being a prince. Bandylegged Harry could beat you at that, and so could all of them on the beach."

The Prince was about to reply to this observation by some profoundly wise remark, when an event occurred which put an end at once to their conversation, which had been carried on whilst they were about to quit the tarpaulin but were waiting a few minutes, as the sea was becoming calmer and calmer.

The event was indeed one which could not fail of attracting their attention—the motion of their boat suddenly and completely changed ; and, instead of tossing about to and fro upon the ocean at the will and caprice of the dancing waves, she began to move straight and steadily through the water, just for all the world as if somebody was pulling her along by a rope.

Somebody *was* pulling her along by a rope, which quite accounted for the sensation which the Prince and his companion experienced. Whilst they had been snugly lying under the tarpaulin, and delaying to rise and keep a lookout, as they ought of course to have done, the rascally fishes and other allies of their cruel enemies had done their work so well, that the boat had drifted nearer and nearer to the country of the Hump-backed Giants, urged by hidden currents continually in the same direction.

When it came within a short distance of the shore, a couple of giants were directed by King Puffblock to wade out and tow the vessel in ; and this they proceeded to do without delay.

So when the two travellers, suddenly aroused to action and energy by the change in the movement of their boat, sprang up and rushed eagerly forward to ascertain what it meant, they found themselves only a few yards off from a strange country, their boat being hauled in through the surf by two huge and misshapen monsters, and a number of the same sort of creatures standing on the shore, evidently awaiting their arrival.

The sight was not one which was calculated to inspire feelings of hope or pleasure. Immediately before them were a number of small rocks stretching away into the sea, and preventing any vessel from being safely landed. These rocks were covered with green, slippery seaweed, and between them were many small pools in which crabs, shrimps, and other marine beings, which are more agreeable boiled than in their native element, had their abode. Beyond these rocks was the beach, upon which stood the natives, who were watching the boat ; and beyond the beach again the country seemed rocky and barren, so that there was nothing particularly likely to tempt a sailor to land at that spot.

Our poor friends, however, had no choice in the matter. The two giants pulled away with such a will that the boat was shortly upon the low rocks, over which they scrambled, still pulling, until they had hauled her into a small creek, and wedged her so tight in the rocks that she could move neither one way nor the other. This happened almost at the same moment as Prince Maraflete and Polly Perkins rushed forward; and as they did so, they were at once visible to the giants on shore, who immediately set up a yell, or rather a roar of triumph.

The two monsters who had hauled the boat now came staggering back over the rocks, on which they could scarcely keep their footing; and having finally secured the vessel, made signals to the companions that they must disembark. This they would gladly have declined, but there was no help for it.

Each of the monsters was at least twice the size of an ordinary man, whilst the hump upon the back of each threw his head and shoulders forward in a slouching manner, and gave to a brutal and villainous countenance even a more repulsive appearance than it might have had if set upright upon an ordinary body. Their hair was matted on their heads, and there, as well as on their beards, was of a grizzly red colour, whilst their beards were short and shaggy, their eyes grey and stony, their hands huge and coarse, their skin rough and knotty, and their whole appearance disagreeable in the extreme. In voices which sounded like the hoarse bellow of an infuriated bull, and in words too unpolite to be here written, they again ordered the Prince and Polly to come out of the boat, at the same time

PRINCE MARAFLETE.—p. 86

gnashing their teeth and shaking their fists in a threatening manner.

The two unfortunate mortals saw but too clearly that they had fallen into a fresh misfortune, from which escape seemed impossible.

For an instant they stood irresolute, as the thought perhaps crossed the mind of each that it would be better to trust themselves to the sea than to the tender mercies of the repulsive beings whom they saw before them. But it was useless to hesitate, and the danger could not be avoided. So the Prince, clasping Polly's hand tightly, bade her be of good heart, and all might yet turn out well.

She, for her part, although she had trembled violently at the first sight of the hideous monsters, plucked up courage at her companion's word, and promised to do as he told her.

In that dread moment each felt drawn closer to the other, and the hearts of the Prince and fisher-girl were at the same time touched with a warm and tender feeling such as sometimes originates, and is always strengthened, in the hour of common danger or affliction.

Together they descended from the boat on to the rocks, and were immediately roughly seized by the two giants, who with many violent words (some of which they understood, whilst some, being spoken in the giant language, and the Hump-backed dialect, were perfectly unintelligible) dragged them across the rocks to the mainland.

It was a slippery, ankle-spraining passage, but they reached the shore safely, and were immediately surrounded by some forty or fifty ferocious giants, all hump-backed, nearly all carroty-haired, and every one of them so frightful a specimen of humanity that in a civilised country he would have made the fortune of any good Christian who would have shown him about in a cage. They flourished clubs, they howled, they yelled, and threatened the prisoners in such a manner that they quite expected that their last hour was come; especially as, amid the volley of abuse which was being hurled upon them, they distinctly heard the word " Blunderfel " repeated several times, and at once understood that they had fallen into the hands of friends of that departed monster, and friends, too, who had, somehow or other, become acquainted with his recent fate.

Some of the giants went so far as to lay hands on the Prince and Polly and drag them off in different directions; but others who were in authority interposed, and without further injury they were hauled along by the rabble up the beach, and presently ushered into the presence of the dreaded Puffblock, the King of the Hump-backed Giants.

The crowd now fell back to a short distance, leaving the prisoners standing immediately in front of this proud and powerful monarch. Now it is well-known that the ordinary custom of giants is to choose for their king or leader the person among themselves who has attained the largest size and the greatest strength.

In the country of the Hump-backed Giants, however, this custom was so far varied that they always selected the ugliest giant for their chief. The ugliness of Puffblock's family had been for ages so proverbial, that in his case the monarchy had practically become hereditary; but even had it been otherwise, it is more than doubtful whether any other individual in the whole community of giants could have disputed his pretensions to the crown upon his own merits, or demerits as some might call them.

In addition to his being the possessor of a hump larger and more misshapen than that of his brethren, his hair was of a coarser and at the same time more vivid red, and bristled up around his head in a manner which at a little distance off gave the appearance of a stubble-field on fire.

Moreover, he looked distinctly one way with one eye and the other way with the other; his nose was twisted round upon his face in a manner which would have been ludicrous if it had not been also horrible to behold; and his ears were of such enormous size that, solely on their account, he had been nicknamed "the donkey" in his youth, and had only crushed out the nickname by the execution with awful cruelties of any one who ever dared to utter it. His mouth, stretched from one side of his face to the other, twisted down at each corner in a peculiar and unpleasant manner; his chin had always upon it a beard to match the hair of his head, save that it hung down (as is not unusual with beards) instead of bristling up, and always presented a remarkably scrubby and not over-clean appearance. Add to this that he had lost two of his front teeth from an accidental blow from the tail of a tame alligator, that he never washed his face for fear of catching cold, and that the habitual expression upon his countenance was one of combined cunning, malice, ill-temper, cruelty, and sottish vice, and you have before you the pleasing picture which presented itself to the eyes of the luckless Prince Maraflete and Polly Perkins, when the withdrawal from around them of the turbulent and noisy crowd, awed by the presence of their mighty and savage sovereign, left them standing face to face with that terrible personage.

A growl of savage satisfaction broke involuntarily from the latter as he regarded his captives with a smile of bitter malevolence.

For one instant he gazed upon them, and then he broke

forth in a voice which sounded to the Prince more than anything else like an enormous hurdy-gurdy fearfully out of tune.

"What ho!" he cried, in scornful accents. "Have we here the giant-slayer — the murderer of honest men by magic arts—the deceiver—the traitor—the cut-throat villain —the runaway would-be sailor?"

At these words Prince Maraflete drew himself up to his full height, inspired with all the courage of his race, and undauntedly replied to his foul accuser—

"Sir," he said, "whoever or whatever you be I know not, but none of the names you have just spoken apply to me or to this lady, and I beg you to be more polite."

The blood rushed to the giant's face as he heard these bold words, and for a moment he made as if he would have rushed upon the speaker and trodden him down under foot then and there. But, remembering that both the captives were wholly and completely in his power, and not desiring to cut short the pleasure which he anticipated in tormenting them, he curbed his rising passion, and thus replied to the Prince's speech—

"What! young malapert, dost thou deny the charge? We will soon see about that, and as for this wretched wench whom thou calledst a lady, she shall soon rue the day when she consorted with such knaves as thee."

The Prince again hastily interposed—

"Do with me," he cried, "what may be your will; but this damsel can have done no wrong: she is guiltless, or, if she has erred in any respect, it has been my fault, and mine alone. Let her go free, then, and deal with me as you list."

At this moment Polly found her voice, and the true heart

and brave spirit of the girl showed itself at once. She seemed for the moment to forget her own danger and the fearful presence in which she stood.

"Oh, Prince!" she said; "now I know you *are* a Prince, and I see what you meant by saying that a prince should be better and braver than any one else—for so you are." And then turning and facing the giant boldly—"Mr. Monster," she said, "if so you be rightly called, and you look it all over, don't pay no heed to what *he* says. I'm as bad as what he is, and a deal worse, so polish me off if you please, and let this young chap off, there's a good monster!"

The giant King smiled grimly upon the pair.

"Is it so?" he remarked as if to himself. "'Tis the common way of those human fools."

Then, addressing the two captives, who had warmly clasped each other's hands after Polly's bold speech, and now looked at him with brave hearts reflected in their countenances, he exclaimed in a loud voice—

"Let him off? Let her go free?" he asked ironically. "Why, I should be a fool as well as a monster if I did it. No, no, my young friends. I am sure you are too fond of each other to wish to be separated. We will see what we can make of you both together—so we will; and you deserve it, too, for I believe both of ye were guilty in the affair of our cousin Blunderfel. Ye shall be together. Fear ye not—It will please the dainty wench to see the monsters eat her sweet Prince alive, or boil him with sea-weed sauce, or, since we give ladies the preference (*she* a lady, forsooth!) in the giant's country, perhaps she shall be skinned by crabs first—we shall see—we shall see—"

Then King Puffblock set up a hideous laugh, and all the

surrounding giants chimed in, making a frightful bellowing, by no means agreeable to the ears of the unhappy prisoners. Then the King continued to address them—

"Prince," he said, "since Prince thou claimest to be, what hast thou to say why thou shouldst not be scrummaged up, spiflicated, and totally extinguished for thy foul crime in the murder of our cousin Blunderfel?"

"I have committed no crime," boldly replied the Prince, upon which there instantly arose among the giants a low, hoarse murmur of—"A trial, a trial; he denies it!"

A sarcastic smile sat upon the face of King Puffblock.

"Reptile, scum of the earth, vagabond," he said, addressing Prince Maraflete with these uncomplimentary epithets; "since thou dost deny thy crime, know that it is the ancient law and custom of the Hump-backed Giants that any prisoner who does so, shall have a fair trial, and this thou shalt have forthwith."

The Prince, having no objection to make to this proposal, and knowing that it would be useless to make it if he had, calmly bowed his head in silence, while the giants received the words of their King with a low growl of satisfaction.

"Now," said the latter, "I will be judge as usual—swear me a jury."

Immediately twelve giants came forward and went through the ceremony of being sworn as jurors, which simply consisted in having a cord of seaweed hung round their necks, after which each in succession made a declaration that the prisoner should not get off, if he could help it. This did not seem to Prince Maraflete much like a fair trial; but he thought he had better let things take their course, and during this process employed himself in comforting Polly, who was now weeping bitterly, and accusing herself of having been the cause of his misfortune, as, but for her condition, he would have gone quietly home and never embarked in that fatal boat.

When he pointed out to her, however, that all was doubtless ordered for the best, and, moreover, bade her remark how rejoiced the giants were to see her cry, she immediately ceased doing so, and determined to give way to grief no longer.

As soon as the jury had been sworn, King Puffblock called for the witnesses, and Prince Maraflete's heart sank within him when the first who presented himself, a dirty-looking miscreant of a giant, upon whom he had never set eyes before, duly took the oath to tell a lie, a thundering lie, and nothing but a lie, which appeared to be the usual giant oath upon the trial of prisoners.

The King then commenced the trial by asking the witness giant if he had known Blunderfel, to which, breaking his oath at once by telling the truth, he replied that he did. He was next asked if he knew that Blunderfel was dead, to which he replied yes. How did he know it? He had seen it in the register of deaths in Blunderfel's district.

Knowing that this must be a wicked untruth, the Prince interposed and demanded that the register should be produced, since of course it must be possible to do so, and if his accusers could have produced the register itself, or at least a copy of it, and did not do either, he submitted that the evidence of a witness who merely said he had seen *it*, could not be received.

King Puffblock, however, cut the matter short after his own fashion.

" That may be *your* law, poor fool," he remarked; " but

it is not giant law, which is the law we go by, as being much the best by which to make sure the punishment of a prisoner. *I* take it that the witness has sufficiently proved that my poor cousin is dead. Now then, witness, who killed him?"

The witness slowly lifted a very dirty forefinger and pointed at the Prince, upon whom he scowled fearfully at the same time.

"How do you know?" asked the King.

"Saw him do it," calmly replied the giant, to the great indignation of Polly, who wished to break in with an expression of opinion by no means flattering to the giant, but was, though with difficulty, restrained by the Prince.

"How did he do it?" asked the King.

"Came behind him when he was at dinner and stabbed him in the back," replied the witness.

"That will do," said the King. "Call another witness."

"But," hastily interrupted the Prince, who was not disposed to see his life deliberately sworn away without an effort to preserve it. "I want to ask this witness some questions—may I not do so?"

"Certainly not," replied the King. "And besides it would not be the least use, for he wouldn't be such a fool as to answer you."

"Surely," exclaimed poor Maraflete, "you do not call this a fair trial, if you will not let me cross-examine the witnesses."

"You may call it just whatever you please, you confounded rapscallion," answered Puffblock. "It *is* a trial, and so you'll find it, and as to your asking questions of the witnesses, that would be contrary to the law of the Hump-backed Giants, and you sha'n't do it."

Having thus silenced the luckless Prince, he proceeded to call another giant, who gravely deposed to having also seen the death of Blunderfel by the hand of the prisoner.

" How did he do it ? " asked the King.

" He shot him through the heart with a pocket pistol," said the giant.

" How can that be ? " asked the poor Prince, but was again ordered to hold his tongue under pain of having it plucked out by the roots, whereupon he desisted from any further attempts to arrest the course of injustice.

Another witness was produced, who replied to the question as to how the prisoner had slain Blunderfel in a different manner.

" He put poison in his broth," said he, and forthwith another was directly called and asked the same thing.

" He killed him with a magic word," was the answer, and this reminded the Prince of the war-cry which he had, in truth, so effectually used.

Remembering, however, that he had now his companion to think of as well as himself, and being most desirous to escape quietly, if he could, from his unpleasant and dangerous position, he thought it best to make one more attempt to do so.

" Sir," he said to King Puffblock, " I pray you listen to me for a moment.   There are four witnesses who have declared that the deceased giant was killed in four different ways.   Three, therefore, *must* be wrong.   Why not all ? And if wrong as to the manner of the death, why not equally so as to the person who caused it ? "

" Never thou mind, poor knave," responded the giant,

with a terrible grimace. "It is quite right—it is the true, good old-fashioned giant way of giving evidence. Don't you see that the more kinds of death they swear to, the better chance there is that one of them may be right, and that is all we want."

The Prince vainly attempted to protest against this extraordinary doctrine as to evidence, but the King, with fearful gnashing of teeth and words too dreadful to be written, quickly silenced him, and then called another witness, who, being strongly marked with the small-pox, and squinting frightfully, was considered by his countrymen one of the handsomest monsters in Ogredom.

"Now, Lumpster," said the King; "do you know the prisoner?"

"I know him well," calmly replied the person addressed, who was an entire stranger to the Prince.

"Do you believe him to be well affected to giants generally?"

"Sir, Sir," interposed the Prince; "how can his mere belief be legal evidence?"

"*Will* you hold your jaw?" roared the King-Judge, whilst the witness responded without hesitation—

"I have frequently heard him speak against all giants, and Blunderfel in particular, whom he vowed he would kill upon the first opportunity. Moreover, I have heard him say that although a steak from a buffalo-hump was good, one from that of a Hump-backed Giant was far better, and he wished for no better dinner."

At these words, a suppressed growl went round the circle of monsters, expressive at once of their admiration of such cleverly-invented evidence, and their joy at the certainty that it would tell against the luckless prisoner.

" King ! " cried the latter, beside himself with rage and indignation, " Is *this* a trial ? Why, I never saw that fellow before in the whole course of my life ! "

" That has nothing to do with it," coolly replied King Puffblock, " but your outbreak may be pardoned in consideration of your palpable ignorance of the great laws of evidence."

Then, turning to the jury, he addressed them in these few but emphatic words—

" Gentlemen, you have heard the evidence : it is proved that our poor Blunderfel is dead : it is sworn that this knave of a prisoner did it; and if so, it does not much matter how. As to the girl, being taken prisoner with him, according to our law she follows his fate. Is he guilty or not ? "

The jury hardly waited for the King to finish before they all bellowed forth the word " Guilty," with great apparent delight, and the Prince saw at once that nothing he could have said in his defence, if indeed he had been allowed to say anything, would have made any difference.

King Puffblock now turned upon him savagely.

" Well, you cantankerous young cormorant," said he, " you pestiferous, palavering, problematical, peripatetic, perambulating perjurer, what have you to say why you and the girl should not be immediately killed and eaten with oil and onions ? "

The Prince, knowing that some kinds of giants delight in using the longest words they can think of, without being always particular as to their real meaning or application, was not astonished at this address; his chief concern at this moment being how to proceed with regard to Polly. Had he been alone he would have uttered his war-cry and charged upon his foes; but if he did so, he feared lest she might be injured in the tumult and struggle which would doubtless follow. He therefore made a reply to the monster before resorting to any other expedient.

"Sir," he said, "I cannot believe that you would inflict wanton and reckless cruelty upon two innocent persons. Do not so disgrace yourself and your people. If I fall I shall not die unavenged, for I have powerful allies, as you will learn to your cost. But I pray you do not take any rash and violent measures, but treat us as strangers and travellers should be treated, and let us go."

"Let you go!" roared the ogre, as his eyes flashed fire and his face grew red with rage. "You indefensible, irreparable, incomprehensible, illuminated idiot, do not dream of such a thing for a moment. You will never go home, my boy, so don't think it," and so saying, he took a step in advance towards the captives.

The Prince now thought that the moment for action had arrived, and that there was nothing for it but to fight. Having no weapon in his hand, but only in his belt the knife with which he had slain Blunderfel, and which, had they but known it, would have been the most conclusive evidence that the giants could have brought against him, he boldly drew it forth as the giant moved towards him, and at the top of his voice shouted the magic war-cry—

"Lollipops!"

Fancy his horror and surprise when he found that it produced no effect whatever.

"Lollipops be sucked!" cried the giant, with a ferocious chuckle, which, under the circumstances, was awful to hear. "What's the use of the word without the branch, you lollipopuous lout?"

In an instant the Prince remembered that the instructions of the Bilberry man had bade him wave in his hand a branch of yew-tree when he attacked his enemies, and it flashed across his mind that the power of the word had been somehow or other bound up with that of the tree, and that it had lost its magic force without the latter. He hastily turned to his companion.

"Oh, Polly!" he cried, "I fear we are lost. I can do nothing without yew."

"Nor I without *you*, my darling Prince," replied the girl, evidently mistaking his meaning, and receiving his words as a declaration of attachment which, although made at an unfortunate moment, was welcome to her soul as strawberries to a parched throat in hot weather.

With these words she threw her arms fondly around him, and proposed that they should die together, which, in fact, appeared to be the most likely thing to happen to them, whether they liked it or not.

The Prince, who had not meant his words to be thus interpreted, was somewhat embarrassed; but his heart had already inclined so much towards the companion of his misfortunes, that her response was by no means disagreeable to his feelings. He clasped her, therefore, tenderly to his heart, and declared his readiness to die, if die they must, in that pleasant position. The giant, however, had only taken one step forward, and now stood regarding the pair with an amused expression of face.

"Smash my grandmother's kaleidoscope," said he, using a favourite expression of his family, "if you die together, or live together either, you cooing, coddling cucumbers. Here, Biffkins, Furze-bush, Muddleman, tear them asunder, and put them in separate caves until we settle how to dress them. See if they are fit for frizzling, and let old Boilemup the cook make her report at once."

At these words three of the monsters approached the two unhappy mortals and forcibly tore them from each other's arms. It was in vain that the Prince struggled to the utmost of his strength, and shouted his war-cry more than once. The word had lost its magic power, and only produced derision on the part of his foes. Polly could of course do nothing, and the two were parted, their arms securely bound behind their backs with seaweed, after which they were roughly dragged towards the rocky heights which towered up at a short distance from the sea.

As they approached they saw several doors cut in the face of the rock, which they rightly conjectured to be the means of entrance to the caves of which the giant King had spoken. There were regular wooden doors, with huge bars of iron across them, which rendered them doubly strong, and it took a giant's strength to swing them back. This, however, was effected by those who had the prisoners in charge, and in a few minutes Prince Maraflete and Polly Perkins were each thrust through one of these doors, and found themselves within the caves in which King Puffblock had commanded them to be placed.

These were not particularly pleasant places. They appeared to be quite dark, save a glimmering of light beneath and at the sides of the doors, which did not fit very closely, as giants are careless workmen, and rarely turn out their work in a well-finished style. With this exception, however, there was no light in the caves, and no furniture of any kind. The Prince was at first quite overcome by the misfortune which had befallen him, and sat down, about to give himself up to despair. He started to his legs, however, immediately, principally on account of the pavement of the cave being composed of loose flint stones, many of which had the sharp side uppermost. It is not so easy to stand up or sit down just when you wish to do either, if your arms happen to be tied behind you, as was the case with Prince Maraflete. He managed to rise, however, and stood in a most uncomfortable manner, with the most uncomfortable thoughts crowding upon him. The principal one, however, was that which concerned his fair companion.

He, indeed, had to some extent deserved his fate, for he had undoubtedly slain the relative of those who now had him in their power, although he believed that in so doing he had only been carrying out a sentence most fully deserved, and executing an act of righteous vengeance. But poor Polly had done nothing, and now she was about to suffer, probably to be devoured, entirely through him and because of his doings. The thought was maddening, and the sense of his own helplessness still more so. What could he do? No hope seemed to remain. Oh, if he had but brought the branch of yew-tree with him! How differently everything would have turned out!

It was, however, useless to lament, for crying over spilt milk never as yet did anybody the least bit of good, and all he could see for it was to bear his misfortunes like a man and a prince, and devoutly to hope that he might disagree with the giants who should eat him.

Apparently this event was not likely to be delayed, for whilst Prince Maraflete was still occupied by these thoughts, the door of his cave was flung violently open, and a flood of light streamed in, disclosing the figure of a square-built, enormously fat old woman, with gray, grizzly locks, confined under a paper cap closely fitting to the head, and with a very red face, puffed-out cheeks, which almost concealed her nose, and eyes starting from her head as if she lived in a perpetual state of amazement. This old woman had a soup-ladle in her hand, and was evidently the cook of the giant King's establishment, whose report upon the condition of the prisoners he had directed to be made.

She came staggering into the cave, and without any ceremony hit the Prince a whack over the shoulders with her ladle, exclaiming at the same time in a deep but not un-pleasant voice—

"Well, my joker, let me see what you are made of."

The unhappy prisoner was of course full of indignation at this discourteous method of salutation, but as he could do nothing, thought it better to say nothing either, and so remained perfectly silent. Waddling up to him, the old woman began to feel him all over in a quiet and business-like sort of manner, pinching the fleshy parts of his body between her finger and thumb, after a fashion decidedly uncomfortable, poking him in the ribs with her fat forefinger, and squeezing his legs and arms with her hands, as if to ascertain his fatting capabilities. This went on for the best part of a minute, and then she left off, set her arms akimbo, and after looking at him for a second or two with the utmost gravity, remarked aloud to herself—

"He'd fill out, he would indeed, fill out to be a real fat 'un, if they'd only give him time. But that's just what they never do! Drat 'em, say I, dressing their game when it's little better than skin and bone! It don't give a cook a chance, it don't; and then they go and grumble because there ain't enough fat and gravy!"

Prince Maraflete felt a shudder pass through him as he stened to this unfeeling soliloquy; but although it foreshadowed but too plainly his approaching fate, at the same time it gave him a faint ray of hope, that the evident desire of the cook that he should not be eaten until he was somewhat fatter, might delay that fate, and thus give an opportunity for something in his favour to turn up. The old woman gave him a parting poke with her soup ladle, and then went off to inspect Polly, with whom her interview was doubtless of the same sort; but the sea-gull who told me this part of the story did not know exactly what passed, or what was the precise report which old Mother Boilemup made to King Puffblock. Whatever it was, however, it, or something else, delayed the execution of the prisoners for that night, and a great mess of fried fish and seaweed sauce having been furnished to each of them from the kitchen of the great monarch, they were left to get such sleep as they could under the trying circumstances in which they found themselves placed.

In order to allow him to eat, the giant who had brought the Prince his food had set his arms free, and indeed there seemed no reason why they should not remain so, since it was evidently impossible for him to escape through these doors, which no single mortal man could have moved if unlocked, and which, as a matter of fact, were securely fastened, each with a mighty padlock of vast strength.

So Prince Maraflete, finding his arms free, in the first place rubbed and stretched them until they had quite regained their circulation, and then, being a sensible fellow, and finding the food good, fell to and made a remarkably hearty meal. This concluded, he found a fairly comfortable spot upon the pavement, and having sat down, more carefully than before, began to think over all that had happened.

His past adventures rose before him like a picture. The affliction of his youth—his dream—the fulfilment of it, step by step, up to the conclusion of his interview with the Bilberry men—he recalled every incident, and it seemed to him that his path had been marked out for him, and his course made easy in a manner wonderful to think of, up to the moment of his victory over the giant Blunderfel.

Since then, indeed, things had certainly gone wrong. He asked himself why? Had he been too arrogant in the moment of his triumph? Had he trusted too much to his own wits, ascribed too much to his own valour, acted too much upon his own judgment? Perhaps this was so: but then he had no Bilberry man near him to warn him against entering the boat, and they had certainly never so much as hinted that such a temptation would be offered to him.

He was sorry enough, and humble enough, too, now. Oh, what a fool he was to have left behind him that branch of the sacred yew-tree which had helped him so much ! What, by-the-by, had become of it ? He thought carefully over every event of the morning, and at length came to the conclusion that he must have dropped it from his hand when he drew his knife to cut off the giant's nose, thinking that he would have no more occasion for it, or, more probably, not thinking at all. He would give half his kingdom to have it now, he thought, but no such good luck was possible.

Then his thoughts turned to the Bilberry men once more. Had they no power to help him now ? Perhaps they had, if he only knew how to get at them. But they—the Nibblers—the Haggister—and even old Murlingford the cabdriver, seemed to belong to another part of his life now, and he saw nothing before him but the grim reality of a cave turned into a dungeon; a cook ready to make him into a tender dish; and giants waiting to satisfy their appetites therewith.

Overcome as he was with grief—more indeed for his poor Polly's fate than for his own—he felt a strange drowsiness steal over him as he sat; and presently he sank into a deep sleep. He dreamed: and in his dream once more the noble pair who had visited him in the summer-house of the royal gardens appeared to stand before him.

"See our poor darling," said his mother; "how sad that he should be in this dungeon, and in the power of the blood-thirsty ogres! Can nothing be done for him?"

"Truly there can," replied the figure, whom he had known at once to be his father. "The girl has the power in her own hands, if she only knew how to use it."

"Oh!" said the queen in a plaintive tone, "will nobody tell her?"

"Of course they will," returned the other, "the mermaids desire nothing better, for they hate the giants, and would gladly cheat them of their prey."

"Let us ask the mermaids to tell her, then," eagerly rejoined the female form.

"You forget," said the other sadly, "We MAY not. But if our boy was to ask them in rhyme, they would come and help him, and would tell the sweet one what to do."

"Oh, then, why does he not ask the mermaids in rhyme? Ask the mermaids in rhyme—ask the mermaids in rhyme—"

And with these words ringing in his ears as if just uttered, the Prince awoke.

Nothing could be more clear or distinct than the directions which he had just received, and he had too much to be thankful for in the results of his last dream to feel any hesitation about obeying those who had again instructed him in the same manner. The only difficulty was, that he saw no mermaids to ask, either in rhyme or prose, and had not indeed any very distinct notion of what sort of a being a mermaid might turn out to be. However, one thing was perfectly certain, namely, that he could hardly be in a worse position than that in which he then was.

So he determined to make the experiment at once, and after thinking over the proper way in which to address a mermaid for a few moments, he cleared his throat and gave utterance to the following words:

> " Little mermaids, little mermaids,
>   Down beneath the deep-blue sea,
> Come and bring your welcome succour
>   To my Polly and to me.
> Little mermaids, little mermaids,
>   We are in an awful scrape;
> Come to me and come to Polly,
>   Teach us quickly to escape ! "

Scarcely had the Prince finished speaking, when he heard a low dripping sound close to the outside of his cave door, just as if water was running off something on to the rocks, and presently a voice of great sweetness uttered the following words:

> " We hear you, dear Prince, and we come to you, since
>   To rhymes we are always compliant,
> No matters we mince, and we'll none of us wince
>   At the rage or the threats of the giant.

Your Polly, we know (she has not told *you* so,
  And never would show it with *you* by)
On her bosom wears low a gem, than which no
  Rich queen has more splendid a ruby.
To you we confess she *is* a princess
  (Don't tell, or do aught that's unwary),
Who, truth to express, was brought to distress
  By the wiles of a wicked old fairy.
She put in a boat, and pushed off afloat
  This child of a queen, whom she hated,
Wrapt up in a coat with nought to denote
  To whom the poor dear was related.
The fishermen kind the infant did find
  (By sun and exposure 'twas drowning),
And when the babe whined they never opined
  'Twas a princess they'd rescued from drowning.
The beautiful gem from proud diadem,
  Which hung round the neck of the baby,
Denoting her stem—was nothing to them,
  Who never sought riches to lay by.
They left it to deck her beautiful neck,
  Round which a blue riband did bind it,
And there, for to check her life those who'd wreck,
  If you look you will certainly find it.
Her arm, if she raise, this jewel displays—
  And says, without fearing or blinking,
"On this, giants, gaze!" they'll stare with amaze,
  And yield to her orders like winking.
But how you, forsooth, can tell her this truth
  Alone you could never discover ;
So we, worthy youth, in manner uncouth,
  Have come to assist you, fond lover.
Come near on the floor, knock thrice at the door,
  Say, "I am the man who can do it !"
Then, say nothing more—you'll find that you score,
  And pass very easily through it.
To us leave the rest—it *must* be confest
  We do what is open to no man,
And you, ere we rest, shall surely be blest,
  And triumph o'er every foeman."

The voice stopped, and the Prince felt his heart swell with fresh courage as he listened to the musical sounds which conveyed to him such cheering news. Polly, then, was his equal in rank, and not only so, but was able to accomplish his and her own deliverance from their cruel foes, and to add the claims of gratitude to those which love had already admitted into his grateful breast. Full of delight, he lost no time in obeying the injunctions of the mermaid, first, however, thanking her warmly for the same, in what he conceived to be a neat and appropriate rhyme :

> "Little mermaids, little mermaids,
>   How you make my heart rejoice ;
> Never was there news so pleasant
>   Told by such enchanting voice.
> Be my Polly queen or peasant,
>   She my fondest love may claim,
> Little mermaids, if ye save us,
>   Thank you kindly for the same !"

He then approached the door of the cave, as he had been bidden, and deliberately knocked upon it three times with his knuckles, saying each time as he did so :

"I am the man who can do it."

"So it seems," suddenly said a voice close to his ear as he uttered these words for the third time, and turning round he perceived the fat old cook, who had entered the cave unperceived by a secret passage which led from the kitchen, and now stood beside him, ladle in hand. "So it seems," she said in a sarcastic tone, "and I am the woman who can do *you*, with sea-gull sauce and onions, for them's the king's orders, and they won't wait to fatten you, nohow, so come along with me !"

A cold thrill ran through the Prince as she spoke, for he now perceived that if he escaped it would only be just in time, for the giants had evidently decided to devour him more speedily than the cook's previous words had led him to expect. Even as she spoke, however, the large door of the cave swung slowly back, and the old woman started back in horror and amazement at the sight before her.

Three lovely mermaids were sitting upon a rock close to the entrance of the cave, combing their long hair, and murmuring low but beautifully melodious notes. As the door opened, a kind of stream of water seemed to arise round these charming beings, and upon it they floated quietly into the cave. Wheeling round, and singing as they did so, each in turn brought her tail with a tremendous whack against the old cook's head. At the first blow she gave a kind of gurgling scream, at the second she staggered, and the third stretched her senseless upon the floor, and I never heard what became of her afterwards.

Then the mermaids smiled sweetly upon the Prince, and bade him follow them out of the cave, which he did without the slightest hesitation. They conducted him at once to a similar door at a short distance from that which he had just passed through, and bade him perform the same ceremony to it as he had recently done to his own door with such success. Accordingly he tapped three times at the door, and repeated the somewhat arrogant-sounding declaration that he was the man who could do it. The door never seemed to doubt his statement for a moment, but immediately swung back and disclosed the interior of a cave very similar to that which he had just quitted, save that precisely in the middle of it there was a three-legged stool,

upon which sat the fair Polly Perkins bemoaning her cap-
tivity.

As soon as she understood what had happened, and that
the door had been opened by friends, she sprang up and
rushed at once into the Prince's arms. The mermaids
blushingly turned away their heads until this first embrace
was over, and then addressed the two lovers in the following
manner :

> " You had better refrain from embracing again
>   (Pray, don't at my speaking be nettled),
> At least till 'tis plain that your case, or the main
>   Is surely and certainly settled.
> The giants hard by, are cunning and sly,
>   And if you go billing and cooing,
> Will certainly try (I tell you no lie)
>   To compass your utter undoing.
> Forget for awhile the kiss and the smile
>   (Altho' you may fancy me cruel),
> Till the monsters so vile you've conquered in style
>   By the aid of your wonderful jewel.
> Then, Master and Miss, go hug, love and kiss,
>   As much and as long as you're able ;
> But put off your bliss, or be certain of this,
>   The giants will dress you for table."

Thus reminded of the danger from which they had not
yet wholly escaped, the two lovers disengaged themselves
from each other's arms, and began to consider what they
should do next. Prince Maraflete told Polly the news
which he had learned from the mermaids, which she received with great astonishment, but at once owned that she
certainly had a stone hung round her neck by a blue riband,
which she had always been told was some kind of a
charm which she must take care never to lose.

"It was sewn up in a little canvas bag," she said, "and she had never thought much about it."

But as soon as she had been made acquainted with the fact that she was a princess, her delight knew no bounds, though it is only fair to say, that it principally arose from the feeling that it would now be no degradation for her beloved Prince to marry her. Forgetful of their present position, and that the danger to be apprehended from the giants was not yet over, she turned to the mermaids, and, with imploring accents and gestures, begged them to tell her what was her real name, and the names of her father and mother.

The mermaids, however, whether indignant at being addressed in prose (to which they have always had a decided objection) or at Polly's carelessness in neglecting her present danger in order to make these inquiries, only flapped their tails angrily and made no reply. Polly turned to the Prince, and was about to ask him the meaning of this, when a heavy trampling upon the beach attracted their attention, and the next moment they perceived King Puffblock himself, with several attendant monsters, hastening towards them.

No sooner had he caught sight of his two prisoners standing in freedom before the caves in which he had ordered them to be confined, than he broke out in fury and gnashed his teeth vehemently, as he hurried up. Shaking his fist at Prince Maraflete, he exclaimed in a voice of thunder :

" You irredeemable, indefensible, irretrievable, incurable, ignominious imp ! What is the meaning of this ? I'll crunch you to atoms, you gaol-breaking vagabond ! "

At this moment he caught sight of the three mermaids,

placidly sitting on a rock, and still dripping calmly around them as they combed their hair and sang to themselves in their usual low, sweet tones, just as if no one was by.

"Halloa!" he cried, "mermaids on shore! Seize them, my merry men! Tear off their tails! Skin 'em, roast 'em, boil 'em with mushrooms! The nasty, scaly creatures!"

The attendant giants came bustling up towards the mermaids, who sat perfectly calm and unmoved, and continued to sing to themselves as if nothing unusual had happened. At that moment Polly Perkins took a step forward, and in a loud and authoritative tone uttered the word, "Stop."

Struck with astonishment at this strange and bold proceeding, the giants paused with one accord, whilst King Puffblock turned round and looked upon the girl with wonder, which soon, however, gave way to passion.

"What!" he shouted, "you miserable, metropolitan, miserly minx! How dare you——"

Here he stopped short, as if struck by lightning.

Elevating her arm above her head, Polly displayed in her right hand a little canvas bag, open at the top, in which could be seen, distinctly visible to every eye, an enormous and magnificent ruby. As she did so, she slowly but audibly pronounced the words:

"On this, giants, gaze!"

And they did so. To the surprise of no one more than of Polly herself, the attendant giants at once grovelled in the dust, or rather in the shingle, whilst Puffblock, after uttering one word so wicked that no one but a giant could say or write it, sank groaning upon his knees, and in a piteously mournful voice exclaimed:

" Oh, my lungs and kidneys, here's a go! She's got It!
Oh, my knees and nostrils! What shall I do? I *must* do
what she says now. Oh, my eyes and ears! Oh, dear—oh,
dear!"

Polly was as much perplexed with her victory as you can
well imagine, and turned to her Prince at once for counsel
and advice.

" What shall I do next?" she said, and the Prince knew
no better than to refer the matter to the mermaids.

These ladies, however, apparently considering that they
had now done as much as could be expected of them, were
quietly scuffling off into the sea, and paid no attention to the
two mortals who desired their advice. Under these circumstances, Prince Maraflete told Polly that in his opinion they
had better act for themselves, and that the best thing would
be to desire the giants to fit out their own, or a new boat,
and enable them to sail off as soon as they could. Polly,
however, having, in common with a few others of her sex,
a certain amount of curiosity, was not willing to leave the
place without finding out something about her own birth
and parentage.

Upon this subject, then, she determined to address the
kneeling giant, and accordingly did so, accosting him as
" Slave!" without the slightest hesitation, and desiring him
to tell her who and what she was.

" You are the Princess Elvina," replied the giant, "and
your father and mother are King and Queen of the great
Pineapple country. Pray don't kill me!"

Satisfied as she was with this statement of the giant,
which bore out that of the mermaids, Polly—or Elvina, as
I must now call her—pressed him with further questions,
but could discover little more. Persons of his size and

race are generally ignorant, and he was evidently scarcely himself from fear of the power of the gem which the girl still held in her hand.

Prince Maraflete now so earnestly desired her to put all other thoughts aside save those which concerned their escape, that she consented to do so, and accordingly gave orders to King Puffblock that their boat should be taken from the rocks, instantly repaired, and made fit for sea, and proper provisions placed in her. Not feeling certain that she could trust the hump-backed monarch out of her sight, or whether the power of the ruby would operate under such circumstances, she bade him rise and go before her to the rocks, which he promptly and meekly did. Then, at her command, he summoned some of his giants and gave them orders to do what the Princess had directed, which they did without delay.

Prince Maraflete and his fair companion then stepped on board, but just as he was doing so, the Prince felt sure that he saw a gleam of malignant satisfaction pass over the countenance of the giant-king. Grown wise by experience, the Prince determined to make no mistake now. So he begged Polly (for so I must call her still) to step back for a moment, raise her arm with the jewel in her hand once more, and ask the monster what he meant by it? The villain's face fell visibly as he made the reply to which he was compelled by the power of the gem.

"Had you left our coast," he said, "without inflicting any punishment upon us, or restricting our power, we could have raised another storm, and if we had got you here a second time, as we certainly should, your gem alone could not have saved you. It is only absolutely powerful as long as you do not run into the same danger again."

Prince Maraflete instantly whispered in Polly's ear, after which she turned to King Puffblock, who was still standing on the beach, with his giants scattered around him.

" Before I leave this shore," she remarked, " you will be good enough to be changed into stone, every giant of you, and so remain until I come and change you back again to giants."

One deep, awful groan passed through the ranks of the monsters as she spoke, and the next moment her words had been obeyed. Not a living giant was to be seen, and in the places where they had been standing there were only to be seen a number of huge blocks of stone bedded on the shore, some upright, some leaning on one side or the other, and some flat upon the ground.

To this day they remain in exactly the same position ; and any one who doubts the truth of this story has only to sail or steam off to that coast, and he may see them for himself. It is true enough that people point to these great masses of stone as the remains of some grand temple or other building of the olden times, and every antiquary has his own theory upon the subject. Nevertheless, I will back my sea-gull against the wisest antiquary that ever wore spectacles, and will always maintain that these are the remains of King Puffblock and his hump-backed giants, and have nothing to do with anybody or anything else.

As soon as she had thus comfortably disposed of her enemies, the lovely Polly tenderly embraced her Prince, and they once more re-embarked in their boat, and set sail in good spirits and full of hope, though they had not the least idea where they were going. A light breeze sprang up, which carried their little vessel swiftly through the water, and after a couple of hours they found themselves approaching land again, but of a very different appearance from that which they had just left.

Luxuriant vegetation appeared to prevail on every side, forests of palm trees reached almost to the water's edge, and the two travellers both agreed that the country was one which at first sight gave a traveller the wish to land and stay there for some time. As they drew nearer, they heard the sounds of music, but were struck with the somewhat singular fact that there was nothing light or mirthful about it, but that, though exquisitely sweet, it was all of a solemn and mournful character.

They pulled gently into a little creek, where they moored their vessel, and landing on the shore, almost immediately encountered a great procession of persons clad entirely in white, accompanied by bands of music, which were to be seen at intervals in the long line. Seeing a venerable personage, evidently of respectability, seated upon a milestone, and engaged in watching the proceedings, Prince Maraflete ventured to accost him, in order to ask the meaning of what he saw.

"It is evident," replied the old man, "that you belong to a strange land, or you would not ask such a question. This is the Pineapple country, and upon this particular day in every year the good King and Queen make a public mourning for the loss of their only daughter, who, on this day fourteen years ago, when only three years old, was stolen, as is supposed by the bad Fairy Tormentina, and has never since been heard of."

At these words the Prince started and looked at Polly, who returned the compliment.

"Lead me to your King," he said, "I would fain speak to him on this matter."

"Peace, forward youth," replied the old man, somewhat severely. "It is not for such as thou and I, being poor, mean creatures, to speak with kings."

"Nevertheless I must do it," quoth the Prince, and was about to step forward towards the procession, when the other laid a restraining hand upon his shoulder; in doing which he overbalanced himself, and fell off his milestone into the road.·

Seeing this, several of the bystanders concluded that the Prince had knocked him off, and ran up to seize him, which attempt the Prince naturally resisted, and a tumult arose. At this moment it happened that the King and Queen were passing in the procession, and, seeing the uproar, the monarch demanded its cause, and desired the strangers, who were accused of having assaulted one of his subjects, to be immediately brought into his presence.

He was a man of noble appearance, but with a deep sadness fixed upon his countenance, and he shook his head in a melancholy manner as he reproached Prince Maraflete with creating a disturbance upon a day which was held as a solemn and sacred time of mourning in that country.

The Prince, holding Polly by the hand, said that he craved pardon most humbly, but that he had hopes that his business might be such as would interest the King and the Queen also.

The latter sighed deeply as she heard these words, and said that she should never be interested in anything again, for her heart was buried with her daughter.

"But," rejoined the Prince, "suppose your daughter was never buried at all?"

At these words the Queen clutched the King's left ear with her right hand, and shrieked violently.

"Was not your daughter's name Elvina?" asked the Prince.

"It was—it was!" shouted both the parents.

"Was she not last seen in a boat?"

"Yes, oh, yes! The nurse left her asleep in the boat for only three minutes whilst she went to gather wild strawberries, and when she returned, both boat and child were gone."

"And had not the child a beautiful ruby tied round her neck by a blue riband?"

"She had, she had!" they shrieked.

"Then," said Prince Maraflete, drawing himself up to his full height, and gracefully handing Polly to the King and Queen, "happy parents! behold your child!"

The effect of this proceeding was marvellous: the father and mother looked for one instant at Polly, for another at the ruby, and then seized upon the girl and embraced her with such vehemence that it seemed as if they meant to eat her.

They never doubted for a moment that it was their own Elvina; and, indeed, you had only to look at the three together, to feel certain upon the point. The girl had her mother's eyes and forehead, and her father's nose and mouth, and was as surely the daughter of the two as anybody ever was anybody else's child.

Intoxicated with joy, the King ordered the bands to change their music immediately, and play nothing but merry airs for the rest of the day. The courtiers came forward with congratulations, the people huzza'd, and everybody appeared to be enraptured with delight.

Prince Maraflete, meanwhile, stood silently watching the effect of his presentation of Polly to her parents, and for some time nobody took any notice of him, for the poor girl herself could not get in a word. At last her father asked her, pointing to the Prince:

" And pray, who is this good friend of yours?"

" Oh, sir," replied the Princess, blushing, " please, that's my young man."

The King bit his lips at this announcement, and began to anticipate all kinds of difficulties in connection with this stranger. The Prince, however, saved him any further trouble, by stepping forward at once, and announcing his real rank and condition, which very much delighted everybody.

Great rejoicings were ordered upon the happy occasion of the Princess Elvina's return, and some wise fellow suggested that they had better have the marriage rejoicings at the same time. It was an excellent match for both parties, so they all agreed that the sooner it came off the better.

The Prince sent word home that he was about to be married; and the news caused much pleasure in his kingdom, where they had long thought that a court without a queen was a dull affair. So the two were happily wedded in the Pineapple country, and shortly afterwards returned to Prince Maraflete's land.

I do not know at this moment whether he ever saw the Bilberry men again; but I do know that at certain times he had bilberries gathered and placed in heaps under the yew-trees, and that they always disappeared. I also know that he never allowed boiled rabbits and onions to appear at his table, and that he always took off his hat when he saw a magpie, and constantly paid cab-drivers double fares, in the hope of rewarding Murlingford by chance. He lived long and happily with his queen. Every one in the country loved and admired her, she was the most popular queen that ever was known in those regions, and everybody but Prince Maraflete saw that "Elvina" was the prettiest name in the world. The Prince preferred " Polly."

LEGEND OF ST. DDERFEL.

THERE are few moments of life which I more thoroughly enjoy than those which I am fortunate enough to pass by the side of a river. I do not speak now of great rivers : I am not thinking of the Thames, the Rhine, or the Danube; these have their beauties, wondrous in themselves, and mightily enhanced by the associations by which they are accompanied, and with which they are interwoven. But I have in my thoughts the rivers of Scotland and Wales, winding along the valleys between mountains of wood and heather, the rivers of the kingfisher and water-ousel, the trout and grayling, and, last not least, the salmon, king of river fish; the rivers, moreover, of the fairies and water-kelpies, hallowed by local tradition, and in the love and veneration borne towards them by those who live near their banks, each a very Thames, or Rhine, or Danube to the locality through which it winds its pleasant way. I love to stand upon the pebbly bed of one of these rivers which has been left dry enough in the summer months to allow you to walk close down to the water, flowing on in its narrowed channel, still broad enough to be a respectable river, and too deep to be waded across by any one who does not want to be wet through at least as high as his knees—close down to the water, I say, I love to stand, to watch the eddying current, and to listen to the pleasant, babbling sound. It always seems as if the Spirit of the River was speaking to me, and telling me how, in its rapid, continuous course, it is setting an example to man how he can most wisely and happily regulate his life. The water is so wise; when it comes to little banks and uneven places in its bed, it gently flows over them without making any bother about it, and this, says the river, is the way in which men should treat the little unpleasantnesses and smaller misfortunes of life, instead of allowing such things to distract and worry them, and perhaps even to alter their whole course of existence. Then, when huge boulders of rock stand out into the stream, the river glides quietly round them, accepting them as necessary evils which must be endured, since they cannot be cured, which is the way in which men should treat their greater difficulties and the hardships of their lives, instead of fuming and fretting, or sitting down in despair. These are things that rivers never do, says the Spirit, and moreover, as they move constantly forward, they explore with their water every hole and corner within their reach, neglecting nothing, giving a kindly wash to everything that comes in their way, and holding a pleasant conversation with all objects, living or inanimate, with which they come in contact. So a wise man, and one who desires to make his life useful and pleasant to himself and others, will always seek for information as he goes along through the world, will ever have a cheery word for his fellow-travellers, and be ready to do a kind and friendly action to any that require it. And, if he does so, just as the river grows broader and wider as it nears the ocean, in which it finally loses itself, and merges its waters in the infinite space of the sea, so the man's life will become grander and more noble as it approaches its close, and he will have gained the affection and respect of all those whose respect and affection are worth gaining, before the stream of his life, too, floats out upon the ocean of eternity.

These are some of the thoughts that come into my mind as I stand listening, as I imagine, to the voice of the River-Spirit. And he tells me of other things. Wild legends of ancient times; strange tales of love and war, of happiness and woe, of courage and of treachery—tales brought down from the distant mountains, where his stream takes its rise; from the romantic sides of the heathery heights which tower above him; from the deep, dark woods with which his banks are fringed, and from the gloomy valleys cut far into the mountain-sides—tales and legends so interwoven with the supernatural and so fascinating to the imaginative mind, that I can hardly find language to express the ideas which, in wordless sound, the River-Spirit seems ever to convey to me as I commune with him, silently but earnestly, in his very own domain.

One of these—the tale of the River-Sprite—a harmless, pleasant tale enough, I will try to tell, and if it be not all I could wish it to be to those who read, let them blame the mortal who repeats it, and not the Spirit who has perchance whispered it to unworthy ears.

Everybody has heard of St. Dderfel, the famous and blessed saint of North Wales. At least, anybody who has *not* heard of him can never have visited that beautiful country, and cannot have the face to pretend to have a drop of Welch blood in his veins. St. Dderfel was—and perhaps is, if we only knew—a very powerful and withal a most worthy saint. His wooden statue, seated upon a wooden horse, stood in the church of Llanderfel, and to this day the portion of the horse which time and the spoilers have left undestroyed, may be seen in the porch of that venerable edifice.

St. Dderfel's powers were thankfully recognized by the people who dwelt in the district round Llanderfel, and more especially so since they were mainly exercised in curing the diseases of animals, which the Saint did in the most wonderful manner. Whether, during his life, he had been a veterinary surgeon I cannot say, but the healing powers of his statue were miraculous and undeniable, and for miles round there was scarcely a Jones, a Roberts, or a Davies who had not had a horse, cow, or pig, cured by application at the shrine of St. Dderfel. For years—perhaps for centuries—the worthy Saint had gone on, quietly and comfortably, curing people's animals, and the fame of his shrine spread wider and wider, and its riches likewise accumulated by the offerings of the thankful recipients of the favours to be obtained thereat.

At length, London itself heard the tidings of the famous Welch saint, whose reputation had become too great to be confined to his own country. But as many things which are good and estimable in the country, become contaminated when brought into contact with London fog, London smoke, and London wickedness, I grieve to say that the reputation of the Saint fared no better. Mutterings against his sanctity were heard, doubts of his power openly expressed, and even whispers let fall that priestly deceit and trickery were at the bottom of it all. For those were days when priests were out of favour, unless indeed they were prepared to change their old creed, to declare that the Pope was possessed of no authority in the country, and that Henry the Eighth was the only and rightful head of the Church within these realms. Some of them did so, and were rewarded for their compliance with the wishes of the King; others refused, and were speedily thrust out, whipped, and sometimes burned, to the great delight of all good Protestants, who little foresaw that they themselves would have to undergo the same pleasures when the bigot Queen Mary had in due time succeeded to her tyrant father's throne.

In those days there was a regular crusade against religious houses, images, and the shrines of saints, and not a few relics, which had been the objects of reverence or of superstition to many thousands of people, were burned at Smithfield and elsewhere, whilst the offerings which pious people had for ages past presented at the shrines, were gathered together to fill the coffers of the King, who thus found that his alteration in the religious establishment of the country was not unattended with pecuniary advantages to himself, which were exceedingly satisfactory.

So when the fame of St. Dderfel reached London, accompanied by reports that his shrine was not without some rich offerings, it was determined by the ruling powers that a commission of inquiry should be sent down to look after the matter, and, if needs be, destroy the abomination. The persons selected for this business were worthy and discreet men, who had no prejudice for or against anything, so that matters might be directed according to the wishes of the King and his trusty servant Master Cromwell, whose face was steadily set towards the abolition of monasteries and the spoliation of religious houses throughout the land.

The worshipful Justice Allen was one of these Commissioners; Serjeant Davis, learned in the law, was the second; and the third was a respectable person of the name of Philipson, who loved the King and hated the Pope with sufficient ardour to qualify him for the office.

The news of the coming of these Commissioners filled the inhabitants of North Wales with mingled disgust and consternation. They, poor, simple people, were unable to discover what harm their favourite saint had ever done; they firmly believed that through his power their cows, pigs, and sheep, had frequently been cured of diseases which threatened to destroy them; and when they were told that this was either a delusion, or that if it had really occurred, was the work of the priests or the devil, or both; the only conclusion to which they could come was, that neither the priests nor the devil deserved all that was said against them, or were quite so bad as they were represented to be by the public opinion of the day.

For some time they could hardly make up their minds to believe that this needless commission (as they thought it) was really about to visit Llanderfel, and when the matter was placed beyond all doubt, their anger and indignation knew no bounds. It is at this precise period that our story begins.

It was upon a beautiful August afternoon that a pedestrian was making his way over the hills behind Bala. He was a stalwart, well-built man, with an oaken staff in his hand, and a small wallet strapped upon his shoulders. He stepped boldly forward through the heather, gaily whistling a tune as he proceeded to make his way towards Llanderfel, bearing downwards from the mountain to the pleasant valley through which the Dee winds its cheerful course.

When he reached the edge of the hill, he paused before commencing the descent, and looked down upon the lovely view beneath. It was wild—wilder than would be seen at the present day, for the population was more thin there than now, and far more of the land, even in the valley, was innocent of plough and harrow, and knew not the lowing of the oxen or the bleating of the herds which seek their pasture there to-day. Yet was the view lovely indeed, and the traveller might well be excused his pause to gaze down upon it with gratified eyes.

Immediately beneath him the steep side of the mountain gradually fell away into an easy decline, down which a pedestrian might descend without difficulty, provided he were sufficiently sound in wind and limb, and not overladen with baggage or other encumbrance.

At a short distance down the hill the steepness altogether disappeared, and a wide ledge of table-land afforded room for an old-fashioned stone house, apparently too small for a farm-house, and yet too large for the dwelling of a shepherd. At a few paces from this building was a low stone wall, from which the ground again became steeper, and far below in the bottom the traveller could see the river, gurgling and brawling along as if the whole place belonged to it, and nobody and nothing else had a right to be there. For a full minute the man looked down upon the scene at his feet, and then he exclaimed in a cheery tone of voice :

"Oh, the Dee, the jolly old Dee! how like it is to home, and kin, and country, to me and mine. Was there ever such a river to wind itself round a man's heart till he loved it as if it was a human being? Oh, the dear old Dee! How I love to see you again, old river! 'Tis years since I have done so, and the sight of you makes me a boy again."

With these words, the traveller rapidly began his descent, forsaking the path which he had hitherto followed, and proceeding in a straight line down the mountain side. As he went, he hummed a merry tune, and was evidently in exceeding good humour with himself in particular and the world in general. Down, down he went, until he had passed the dwelling already mentioned, crossed the wall, descended the steeper incline beyond, and found himself at a distance of some hundred feet or more below, in a rough country road which led, though by a somewhat zig-zag and roundabout path, from Bala to Llanderfel.

Scarcely had he pulled up to recover his breath, which had somewhat suffered from the rapidity of his descent, before he descried two horsemen approaching him at a short distance. They came from the direction of Bala, and by their manner of looking around and occasionally halting, appeared to be somewhat uncertain of their road. They were both clad in long dark cloaks, and appeared to be persons of great respectability, as far as our friend the traveller could venture to form an opinion upon such a subject. I do not know indeed that he would have troubled himself to form any opinion at all about it, had not the horsemen, as soon as they caught sight of him, shouted aloud in order to attract his attention, and having succeeded in doing so, ridden up and accosted him at once.

"Friend," said the elder of the two, a grave and sedate looking person, who evidently had a dignity of his own, and knew it. "Friend, how far are we from Llanderfel, and is this the right road to conduct us thereto?"

"Now, by St. David," replied the traveller, "it is strange that thou shouldst ask me such a question, when thou and thy mate are but a short two miles from the church and shrine of the blessed St. Dderfel."

The first speaker gravely shook his head as he made reply.

"Speak not to me of shrines and saints," he said, "for sadly does such talk savour of that popery which has so long brooded like a foul cloud upon our dear country, but which is now on its last legs, thanks be to the All-Wise. It is to aid in cleansing the land from such abominations that I and my companion do ride here to-day, and we would fain be guided to the best hostelry which may be near this Llanderfel."

As the worthy man spoke, he to whom his words were addressed regarded him with glances which plainly told that he scarcely appreciated the subject of his discourse, and somewhat chafed at being detained upon his journey. He listened to the end, however, and then returned answer.

"'Tis long since I was here, sirs, and things may well have changed since then. But the 'Horse-shoe' was the sign of the inn at which man and beast were wont to find bed and stall, meat and fodder, in old days, and belike it's so still."

"And where is this 'Horse-shoe,' friend?" asked the younger of the two horsemen, a somewhat shorter man than his companion, and not without a pleasant expression upon his countenance, which betokened a cheerful soul within.

"'Tis in the main and only street of Llanderfel," responded the traveller, "and you have but to follow your nose in order to reach it."

"Art thou journeying the same way?" demanded the

elder of the two riders; "haply thou mightest conduct us to this same hostelry; and, moreover, tell us thy name and station. We are men, I may say, under authority, and may be of service hereafter to those who aid us in our present endeavour."

"I know not thy authority," returned the other, "and what thy endeavour may be I cannot tell. As for me, my name is John Griffith, and from these parts I set forth years back, to go upon the salt seas. I have but lately come home, and I go now to see what old friends may be left alive, and to visit the shrine of St. Dderfel before I go on to Llangollen, which is my native place. An ye will come with me I have nought to say against it, though a seafaring man on foot is but poor company for two mounted gentlemen."

"Friend," observed the elder man, in reply, "thy name and thine errand may be well enough, so far as it is right and proper that John Griffith should revisit the home he left as a boy. Not so, however, thy purpose of visiting this idle shrine. It is time to tell thee, young man, that thou hast fallen into worshipful company. I am Mr. Justice Allen, and here is the learned Serjeant Davies, and we journey to Llanderfel to make speedy end of that abomination which thou callest the shrine of St. Dderfel, who is no more a saint than is this good horse of mine a cow——"

Scarcely were the words out of the speaker's mouth when, to the terror and astonishment of all these men, a loud, sonorous, and unmistakable "moo" proceeded from the mouth of the animal which the worthy justice bestrode, whilst at the same moment its ears seemed suddenly to change their character, and from behind each of them arose a veritable horn, the head of the animal being at the same instant converted into that of the animal which had just been mentioned. For an instant the whole party remained silent with surprise, and before any of them found his tongue the phenomenon had passed away as suddenly as it had appeared. The horns vanished from the place in which they had just been visible, the head resumed its former appearance, and the horse, quietly shaking its mane as if nothing had happened, ceased to utter any other sounds than those which are natural to its species.

Each man looked at the other two for another instant, and then honest John Griffith burst forth with a nautical exclamation of surprise, which I think it better to omit.

"So much for you, Mr. Justice," he continued. "No saint, ain't he? And your horse ain't no cow neither? Well, I never! If you haven't learnt a lesson now, I don't believe as ever you will."

"What mean you, man?" somewhat haughtily replied the person addressed. "Some momentary confusion has clouded your understanding. There is no cow here and no saint yonder, whatever you may think."

"No saint and no cow!" shouted Griffith. "Why this other gentleman must have seen it as well as I! Come now, master; tell us like a man; wasn't your mate's horse a cow just now if ever there was a cow upon earth?"

Too discreet to commit himself by any answer to such a question, the wary lawyer smiled, as he remarked:

"I am no judge of animals, Master Griffith, since that is thy name; but neither the Justice nor I are to be *cowed* by magic art when we are on the King's business."

"On the King's business!" cried Griffith. "What!

does his royal Majesty's Grace's mightiness go for to concern himself with our little doings down here?"

"My man," gravely responded the elder rider, "the King's Majesty is concerned for all the matters which belong to the welfare of his subjects, however remote be their dwellings from his city of London, however humble their position in life. He is supreme over their spiritual matters as well as over their temporal possessions, and he is grieved to see darkness, ignorance, and superstition still among them. It is in his name and by his command that we are here to-day, of which thou wilt hear more anon. But say, is this the Dee we are approaching, and how far are we from Llanderfel?"

As he spoke, the road along which they had been slowly descending, brought the party close to a bend in the river, which commanded a view right and left as they stood upon a bridge which spanned a small tributary rivulet which at that point joined the main stream. To the right, scarce a mile from where they had halted, rose the village of Llanderfel, towards which the wood-fringed river varied considerably in its breadth and depth, but never varied in the dark colour of its water, the sweet tone of its murmuring over its pebbly bed, and the surpassing beauty of its wooded banks. To the left the stream stretched away towards Bala, behind which the eye rested upon the heather-clad hills in the far distance; whilst, on the other side of the river-bed, immediately opposite the travellers, rose a large wood, which screened the mountain-side as with a huge green curtain, all the way up to Llanderfel.

" 'Tis a fair scene," remarked Mr. Justice Allen to his companion, "and not only pleasant to the eye, but wholesome for the soul to contemplate."

"True," returned his companion; "but man has other component parts beside soul and eye, and for my part I feel an internal sensation which reminds me that the body requires occasional nourishment. Push we on, say I, to this same hostelry of the 'Horse-shoe.'"

Whilst this short conversation passed, John Griffith had remained quiet, leaning upon his staff, and apparently thinking earnestly over the last words which had been addressed to him by Justice Allen, to which he had as yet made no reply. Now, however, he again joined in the conversation.

"Yes," said he, "this is the Dee, and yonder is Landerfel; but an ye go to say or do aught against our old saint, I like not to be the man to guide ye thither."

"Friend Griffith," calmly rejoined the lawyer, "saint or no saint, I must have my dinner, after which such a matter can be better discussed."

"Maybe so," returned Griffith; "but I marvel much why ye should come hither with words against a saint whose power is as little doubted in Wales as is his goodness. Why my own grandmother's red cow was down, time back, with a complaint of which she seemed likely to die, and the cow-doctor said that so 'twould be. What does the old lady do but trot off with a basket of eggs and honey to the shrine at Llanderfel. Many a time, as a boy, have I heard her tell the tale, and how she fancied the horse on which the figure of the saint sits, bowed his head to her as she knelt there. And who can say he did not? Anyhow, when she got home again, there was the red cow on her legs again, and never had another day's illness till her time came. And then to say St. Dderfel is no saint! Marry, come up!" say I.

What reply his companions might have made to the last exclamation (which I frankly own to be one which I never understood myself), or to the statement by which John Griffith sought to establish the reputation of his favourite saint, can never be accurately ascertained, for at this precise moment began a chain of curious events, which have principally induced me to tell this story.

The road ran for a very short distance parallel with the river; but a bridle-path apparently led from the road along the river bank in the precise direction of Llanderfel. This appeared not only to be a short cut to the village, but to afford the advantage of turf for the horses' feet, and to command even a better view of the river scenery than could be obtained from the high road. The travellers therefore were tempted to deviate from the main road, and to follow the aforesaid path. They had not gone twenty yards thereupon, before a strange, wild, unearthly yell arose from the river. It was not a yell which it is easy to describe; it was not such a scream as a nervous young lady may be supposed to give when a mouse unexpectedly runs over her face just as she is going to sleep; it was not such a howl as a boy of tender years may raise if a sharp and sudden pang lets him know that a wasp has crawled up the leg of his trowsers; nor was it such an enraged bellow as proceeds from an elderly and corpulent gentleman when you inadvertently set your foot heavily upon his gouty toe. But it was a compound of all three; and, moreover, it was so loud, that it seemed to occupy the whole space and engross the full powers of hearing possessed by the three travellers, so that, in fact, they could hear nothing else whilst it continued.

At one and the same moment, by a natural impulse,

they all clapped their hands over their ears, and as this, in the case of the two riders, made it necessary that they should drop their reins, there was nothing to prevent their horses from running away. Fortunately, however, or unfortunately, as you may happen to think, the animals showed no such inclination, but held down their heads and trembled violently, as if under the influence of great alarm. The sound rang in the ears of the three men for several seconds, and they regarded each other with looks of the greatest astonishment. It seemed to come either from the river itself, or from the woods on the other side, and as none of them had ever heard anything like it, they had not the least idea what it meant, what they had better do, or whether indeed it was necessary for them to do anything at all.

John Griffith, simple and unlettered as he was, first found his tongue, and broke the silence which had followed this dreadful yell.

"This comes of reviling saints!" he exclaimed. "The devils are loosed upon us, and none to help us. Holy St. Dderfel, aid us!"

"Peace, man!" interrupted Justice Allen, who seemed to recover some of his habitual self-possession at the sound of the other's voice. "Peace! and prate not to us further of thy saints. It is, doubtless, because of the sad ignorance and benighted condition of these districts that strange noises are permitted, and, perchance, strange creatures are allowed to appear on earth, whom, let us trust, our coming will henceforth banish for ever. Come, forward and——"

At this instant the speech of the worthy Justice was cut short by two things which happened at one and the same moment.   A huge splash, right in his face, as if a full bucket of water had been dashed into it by a strong arm, with an unerring aim, choked his voice, and drenched his head and shoulders, whilst the same awful yell arose from the river, and rang again through the very heads of the terror-stricken hearers.   The water must have been thrown by some agency very close to the unlucky Justice, for it struck him in such a volume and with so great a force, as very nearly to knock him backwards off his horse, yet nothing was to be seen, and nobody appeared to whom this strange attack could be attributed.   An invisible hand had dealt the blow, and the power which had directed it was as unseen as extraordinary.   But whatever may have been his faults, want of courage was not one of those with which the worshipful Justice was afflicted.   Confident in the righteousness of his cause, and the justice and wisdom of the errand on which he travelled, he was prepared to defy the worst efforts of those who dared to withstand him.   He recovered himself as speedily as could be expected after such a violent and unexpected blow, and, spluttering with rage and indignation, called on his companions to support him.

"What, ho!" he cried.   "Is it thus the King's servants are treated in these outlandish parts?   Come on, Serjeant Davies; come on, trusty friend, and let us remember who and what we are.   And you, man Griffith, an ye be not in league and fellowship with the powers of evil, come to my side, and let us pass boldly on our way."

So saying, he clapt spurs to his horse, and raised his riding-whip with a threatening gesture, as if about to face and overthrow some visible and tangible foe.   At the same time, though he did not much fancy the business, Serjeant

Davies urged his steed forward to his companion's side, and for very shame's sake, John Griffith felt obliged to range himself with the others. But at this moment a wild chorus of mocking laughter arose all around them. From the trees, from the grass, from the hills, from the woods, but principally from the river itself, peals upon peals of laughter came ringing in their ears, as if their appearance or conduct, or both, were furnishing immense amusement to a large concourse of bystanders.

Now it is bad enough to be laughed at by your friends, it is a great deal worse to be derided by your enemies; but to be made the object of jeers and contemptuous merriment by unseen persons is positively unbearable and irritating in the extreme. So did the three men feel it, and more especially those two gentlemen who properly considered that their dignity and position entitled them to be treated with respect.

Drawing himself up to his full height upon his horse, and assuming as martial an appearance as he could summon to his aid, Mr. Justice Allen urged his steed forward, and cried out to his companions to pay no heed to the foolish sounds about them. At these words the laughter was re-doubled; but this was not all. Neither of the two steeds could by any means be persuaded to move an inch; and as honest John Griffith did not feel disposed to march in advance of the two gentlemen, they all three stood there in a row, presenting an appearance sufficiently absurd, and feeling extremely uncomfortable. Their discomfort, how-ever, was presently increased in no small degree, for there suddenly arose out of the river two separate and distinct waterspouts, one of which directed its attention to the worthy Justice, whilst the learned Serjeant experienced the full benefit of the other. Whether in consequence of the respect he had shown for St. Dderfel, or from his being a native of the locality, or from what other cause, I know not; but certain it is, that while this was going on, and his companions were entirely drenched, John Griffith remained as dry as a bone, and stood staring with open eyes at the discomfiture of the others.

Meanwhile the laughter continued, and so did the water-spouts, for at least a couple of minutes; at the conclusion of which time the one ceased and the other died away, until the three men found themselves again left in silence, and the two gentlemen stood, or rather sat, looking at each other with rueful countenances, and looking for all the world as if they had just walked through a pond. Davies was the first to speak, and shivered with wet as he did so. His language was strong, though perhaps not stronger than most men would have used under similar circumstances. He wished the saint and Llanderfel itself with a person whose name bears a strong resemblance to that of the saint, though of a character extremely different. He declared that he should certainly catch his death of cold, besides being half-starved, which was already the case, and expressed a fervent wish that he had never been induced to set out on such a journey, or to visit a country so wild and strange.

On the other hand, Justice Allen took a different view. Not only was his heart more deeply set upon the enterprise in which they were engaged than was the case with his companion; but being impressed with a full sense of the dignity and importance which attached to them both, as bearers of the King's authority, he felt bound to resent and protest against anybody or anything which offered

LEGEND OF DDERFEL.—p. 139

opposition to that authority in any manner whatever. It is but just to say, that this feeling was more powerful in Justice Allen's breast than any consideration of the personal annoyance to himself which was caused by the interruption to his journey, and it stimulated his courage in a remarkable degree. Raising his voice once more, he boldly shouted to his comrades:

"Come on, my friends, come on! In the name of our royal master, King Henry the Eighth, I demand and will make a passage. This is rank Popery, or something worse. Forward!"

As he spoke, he struck his horse sharply with his whip, and using the spur at the same time, prevailed upon the animal to proceed. That on which Davis was mounted followed the example; and as John Griffith now felt bound in honour to stand by his companions, the three men advanced some dozen yards further without interruption. Then, without any warning, there suddenly appeared around them an innumerable quantity of water-birds, emerging from the river, and making right at the travellers. Moorhens, dabchicks, ring-ousels, swifts, and various other winged creatures, came crowding upon them, led by a kingfisher, who darted to and fro with a rapidity which made his bright plumage appear like a flash of lightning passing before their eyes. More formidable still, there appeared several herons bringing up the rear, and apparently prodding several tardy members with their long beaks, as if to urge them forward to the attack. The feathered army hovered round the travellers, flapped their wet wings in their faces, uttered shrill and discordant cries close into their ears, made unpleasant feints, as if about to peck at their eyes, covered their horses' heads and necks with such a feather-bed of wings, breasts, and tails, that they could not see a foot before them, and altogether behaved in a most incomprehensible and audacious manner.

. It was evident that the winged army intended to dispute the passage of the Royal Commissioners, who indeed began to feel that their journey was like to be of a far more disagreeable character than they had at all foreseen. They struck right and left at their assailants, but with little effect, and the more angry they grew the louder grew the chattering and chirping, the more constant the wing-flapping and pecking, until the horses again resolutely refused to proceed, and there seemed no possibility of passing through the opposing force. Not one of the latter, however, touched John Griffith, who hardly knew whether to be pleased or not at being thus spared, as he was well aware that it might not improbably expose him to the charge of being in some way or other connected with those who were thus impiously withstanding the servants of Royalty. So it was, however, and, in order to clear himself from a charge of this nature, Griffith thought it necessary to lend what assistance he could to the two gentlemen, and accordingly raised both voice and arm in their behalf.

For fully five minutes they were kept at bay by these strange opponents, and then in one instant the latter disappeared as suddenly and unexpectedly as they had come. In another instant, not one of them was to be seen, and again the same chorus of wild, mocking laughter rose from the river.

" I like it not, I like it not, Master Allen," said Davies, who now presented a somewhat doleful appearance, his green hat, which had been placed jauntily upon his head, having been utterly torn and disfigured by the beaks and talons of his foes, whilst the blood which flowed from his left cheek bore witness to the sharpness and severity of the attack which had been made upon him by an elderly moor-hen. "I like it not," he repeated for the third time, which was scarcely necessary, for no one doubted his statement for a moment. "Beshrew me, but I wish we had come by the way of Ruabon with our escort, instead of being tempted to come the other road on account of what we heard of the beauty of the Bala country. Confound the country and its beauty too, say I, if these be its inhabitants, and such as this their abominable manner of receiving travellers."

"Brother Davies," returned Allen, as he wiped the blood from his wrist, which was suffering from the peck of a heron, and calmly adjusted his dress, which had been greatly disarranged by a combined assault on the part of a determined body of dabchicks, "Brother Davies, I like it no better than you, but all things come to an end, and if our great and glorious King can master the Pope and oust his power from our land, as he hath done, be you sure it is no river demons that can long withstand him. On, in the King's name!"

With these words the brave Justice urged his steed forward once more, and the party advanced without further interruption until they arrived at a spot where a long and curiously contrived wooden bridge spanned the river, by no means at its narrowest part, from one side to the other. The bridge was ascended by steps on each side, and was not a structure which you would have cared to cross with a heavy weight, or one which had any great architectural beauty to recommend it. There it was, however, to serve its purpose, which it doubtless did to the satisfaction of all concerned, and almost to the foot of this bridge the travellers advanced in security. Then a strange thing occurred. Out of the river there sprang, with one simultaneous spring, a vast quantity of fish—salmon-trout, perch, and I know not what beside—right up into the air. This, however, was not all. Leaving their natural element, the whole body darted through the air full upon the travellers. It was one flash— one glitter of shining scales, dripping with water, and they were at them and on them in every direction.

Davies was nearly smothered by trout, and felt as if perch by dozens were sliding down his back, while Mr. Justice Allen was struck about the middle of the waistcoat by a salmon, which must have weighed thirty pounds at least, and felt at the same time a nip in the calf of his leg, which must have proceeded either from the teeth of a pike or from some other fish endowed with similar weapons of offence.

This was too much for both men and horses. The latter fairly turned tail, and the former being too much surprised and startled to prevent them, set off at full speed in the direction of the road which they had lately quitted. This they very soon reached, their pace on the retreat having been much faster than in the advance, and no obstacle or hind- rance whatever being offered to their progress. They con- tinued up the road in the direction of Bala for twenty yards or more before their riders recovered from their confusion and discomfiture sufficiently to pull them up. This, how- ever, they presently did, and for several seconds the two men sat staring at each other in mute astonishment. In truth, they presented but a sorry spectacle, though, as there were no bystanders to behold them, it mattered but little, since, after all, it is the gaze of our fellow-creatures, and the opinion which we think they will form upon our appearance, which have the greatest share in causing us to care how we look. With clothes wet through and through, and by no means without rent or tear, with hats broken, bent, and out of shape, with blood stains on hands and face, and a general look of having been recently dragged through a pond full of fish whose scales came off easily, our two friends certainly looked less respectable by many degrees than when John Griffith had first encountered them that morning.

So thought that worthy person, who, although his route lay in the opposite direction, and nobody had interfered with his advance, felt bound, by the laws of good fellowship, to retrace his steps and follow his flying companions, whom he joined at their first halt. Neither of them liked to speak first, but the same thoughts were evidently struggling in the breasts of each. Wonder, alarm, and indignation prevailed alternately, until at last the latter passion obtained the mastery in the bosom of Mr. Justice Allen, and he burst forth in terms of reproach, directed alike against the river and the whole neighbourhood. Such treatment had never before been heard of in England, if this north part of Wales might so be called. That two men, bearing the authority of the lawful sovereign of the realm, and sent by him on a special mission for the good of his people, should be interrupted, hindered, nay, absolutely assaulted, on their journey, attacked by birds, drenched with water, pelted with fishes, their lives and limbs endangered, and their enterprise likely to be defeated, and that by powers which did not dare to show themselves boldly and openly like honourable foes! —The thing was too shameful—too monstrous, and would certainly bring down severe and deserved punishment upon the locality.

Whilst the irate Justice expressed his sentiments in these words, and consoled himself with such reflections, the learned Sergeant was occupied with other thoughts, to which he shortly gave utterance.

"My worshipful friend," said he, "in all that you say there is, as usual, much forcible logic and good sense: the King's majesty has been insulted, and vengeance must assuredly follow. But, meanwhile, let me respectfully ask you whether you think it is absolutely necessary that we should attempt to proceed further with our journey this afternoon? We have done our duty so far, and doubtless we will not return until we have accomplished the purpose for which we left London; but the delay of a few hours will not materially interfere with this, and whilst our bodies are refreshed and our strength recruited, it may be that the unseen powers who have opposed us will repent of their folly in setting themselves up against the King's authority, and thus to-morrow we may be allowed to proceed on our way without further molestation."

These words made due impression upon the person to whom they were addressed. Like his companion, he had had nearly enough for one day, and they accordingly agreed to find shelter at the nearest place offered, and there to pass the night.

John Griffith would gladly have left them, in order to proceed upon his own way, but the two gentlemen pressed him so hard that he agreed to stay with them.

The next question was where they should pass the night, and Griffith thought it but right to warn them, that if they found shelter in any farmhouse or cottage in the neighbourhood, it would be well for them to conceal their errand if they valued their safety; for such was the reverence which the people felt for their favourite saint, that the would-be spoilers of his shrine would have fared but badly had the purpose of their coming been disclosed.

I have already mentioned the fact that, in his descent into the valley, John Griffith had passed a house, which was perched, as it were, upon a flat piece of ground which interrupted the continuous steepness of the mountain side. To this building the travellers now directed their attention, for although it was at some height above them, yet there was a sort of path by which it might be reached, and the horses which the two gentlemen bestrode, being used to mountains, were able to make their way upwards without much difficulty. So, leaving the river and the valley, they slowly ascended until they reached the low stone wall to which attention has been made, a breach in which, some yards in length, served for the gate by which might be entered the court, so to call it, of the dwelling.

This court, indeed, was nothing more than a grass plat, and over the grass the travellers proceeded up to the very door of the house itself. It was an old, tumble-down place: the walls, indeed, were substantial enough, being built of large rough-hewn blocks of stone, but its slated roof had evidently not been repaired for some time, for the absence of slates here and there disclosed huge rafters, which had been long exposed to the wind and rain, the chimney in the middle of the roof seemed as if it only wanted a decent excuse to fall down altogether, and the whole place bore about it an air of loneliness and desolation which did not promise much to weary travellers. But a thin wreath of smoke, which curled upward from the chimney, betokened that the house was inhabited, and our friends were too wet and too hungry to stand upon ceremony. So they rode up at once and knocked loudly at the door, shouting at the same time in order to attract the attention of the inmates.

For some moments they appeared to have failed in their endeavours, for no one took the slightest notice of their summons, which they therefore repeated more vehemently than before. Presently a shuffling of feet was heard within, and the door was opened by an old woman.

A very old woman she seemed to be, for she was bent nearly double with age, and her nose reached forward and came down with a hook towards her chin, which curved upwards to meet it with a similar hook, evidently showing that the two had been engaged for a considerable period in the attempt to come together.

She had a queer-fashioned old cap upon her head, in the which were confined the few scanty grey locks of hair which Time had left her; she was clad in a dress of coarse material, and as she leaned upon a crutch and gazed with evident surprise upon her visitors, there was a poverty-stricken look about her which gave but little hopes of the hearty meal of which they were one and all prepared and anxious to partake.

John Griffith was the first to speak.

"Mother," he said, "can you give these gentlemen and me food and shelter for the night? We have come far to-day, and there has been a wetting in the river which causes my friends to be anxious to dry and rest themselves before they go forward on their journey."

The old woman listened to these words, and then replied, in a tremulous voice, and in a language which was entirely new to the Justice and the Lawyer, but which their companion understood, for it was the language of his native land—the Welsh of his childhood.

In the same tongue he addressed the old woman when she had answered his first speech. She immediately brightened up, said a few more words, and by voice and gesture invited the men to enter.

Interpreting her speech to the others, Griffith explained that she had said at first that her man was poor, and they had little in the way of food to offer—it was but a short way to Llanderfel, where good accommodation could be had, and the gentlemen had better proceed there. But on hearing her native tongue spoken by one of the strangers, she had changed her tone, and said that the party was welcome to such poor provision as she could afford in the way both of food and shelter.

Having ascertained this, the travellers' first care was to provide a lodging for their horses, for which they had not far to look, for at one corner of the house, built into the side of the hill, was a stable, quite as good as the house itself as far as warmth and comfort were concerned. Here they placed their steeds in security, and forthwith re-entering the house, were conducted by the old crone to the room which served both as parlour, kitchen, and general living room for her and her husband.

The latter, a weather-beaten old man, with a face which was one mass of wrinkles, so that you could hardly discern one feature from another, was seated in a crazy old chair by the side of the fireplace, and carefully watching a huge pot which was resting upon the fire, and from which fast rising bubbles told of hot food within.

This was a joyful sight to the hungry travellers, and they signified as much forthwith, both by word and gestures. Their delight at first appeared to be hardly shared by the old man, who probably viewed with the reverse of satisfaction the diminution of his own supper by the application thereto of the appetites of these fasting strangers. A few words, however, uttered to him in his own tongue by John Griffith, and doubtless speaking of payment certain to be made, reassured and comforted his venerable soul, nor did he express himself otherwise than cheerfully with regard to their arrival, so far as they could judge from his voice and manner, for his words were not only spoken in the same strange language as that used by his wife, but were mumbled forth from a toothless and antiquated mouth in a manner which, had they been the purest English ever spoken, would have gone far to render them beyond man's understanding.

The old crone, who had disappeared for a few seconds, now re-entered the room with a bundle of sticks, with which she replenished the fire, and made the pot boil the better. She then addressed herself to John Griffith, who forthwith informed the others of the purport of her communication.

There were no such things as beds, it turned out, in the house. She and her man slept on a wretched pallet at one corner of the only other room on the ground floor, but there were two rooms above, and if the gentlemen would be content with bundles of clean straw, they would be very welcome to stay the night.

There being no alternative, so far as they could see, the travellers expressed themselves satisfied, and even grateful for the proposed arrangement, and whilst the old woman continued to busy herself about the preparations for the supper, they ascended the stairs and found the rooms as

represeuted. One, which lookcd out over the valley of the
Dec below, was a large room in tolerable repair, though the
moonlight found its way in at more than one crevice at one
end. However, it was weather-tight for the most part, and
the weather was moreover fine, so the worthy Justice and
his friend resolved that they would appropriate this, whilst
Griffith prepared to occupy the other apartment, which was
smaller, and looked out into the small yard adjoining the
stable. Each of the two gentlemen carried a small closely
packed bag strapped to his saddle, and these they now
opencd, and were able with the contents to make themselves
somewhat more comfortable, and presently to appear in
dry garments, and requiring nothing but food for the inner
man.

This was presently provided, for the old woman had
made such addition as she could to the supper, and a
savoury mess of potatoes and other vegetables, stewed up
together in a manner which rendered the food uncommonly
palatable to the hungry men, served for their repast, and
had ample justice done to it.

After a day which had been rendered fatiguing, as well
by the excitement as the labour which they had undergone,
the travellers were not sorry to retire to rest, and humble
as was the couch upon which they stretched their weary
limbs, it was not long before sleep overpowered them, and
they forgot their annoyances and difficulties in dreams
which we may trust were pleasant.

Davies was the first to wake. He could never exactly
tell what it was that woke him, but something did so, and
that most effectually. He started—sat upright at once
upon his straw bed, and listened attentively. Surely a
voice had been speaking to him—whispering in his very

ear. Impossible! it was an idle dream, he would lie down
again, and compose himself to sleep. But sleep refused to
return at his command. Again he heard whispering—
again he sat upright and listened. The moonlight was
streaming in through the window of the room, and also, if
the truth be told, through the crevices in the roof. The
night was calm and still, so still that, far away down in the
valley, the pleasant murmuring of the Dee came up to the
ears of the listener in the hill-side dwelling. But, as he
listened, other murmurings came up also, more and more
distinct, until at last it shaped itself into words proceeding
from a human mouth.

> " Say, who has dared to make complaint
> Against Holy Dderfel, Cambria's saint,
> And who, more daring, here would bring
> The ban of an apostate king ?
> Saint Dderfel's fame all Wales can tell,
> And all her children love him well,
> For blessings on their flocks and kine
> Oft won by pray'r at holy shrine.
> Back, back, ye men of Saxon breed,
> Let shameless Harry change his creed,
> And let each Southron shift his hope
> From pope to king, or king to pope.
> But if 'gainst Cambrian saint he turn
> His new-born zeal, then let him learn
> That he who questions Dderfel's might,
> Must first o'ercome the River-Sprite ! "

As these words of direful import fell upon his ear, Davies,
remembering the experience of the River-Sprite which he
and his friend had already had, felt the reverse of comfortable, as, according to his view of the case, further proceedings on the part of the individual in question (whoever or

whatever he might be) were undoubtedly threatened. He lost no time, therefore, in endeavouring to arouse his companion, which, however, was at first no easy matter, for, overcome by the exertions of the previous day, Mr. Justice Allen was sleeping the sleep of the just, and snoring the snores of both just and unjust too, if the listener were to judge by the volume of sound which proceeded from his corner of the room.

At last, however, the difficult matter was accomplished, and Serjeant Davies succeeded in making his companion aware that something unusual had occurred. Sitting upright upon his bed, with a last heavy snort, half awake and half asleep, the poor Justice could not at first exactly comprehend the reason of his being disturbed. As quickly as he could, however, Davies explained the reason, and begged him to listen, in case the words which he had just heard should be repeated by their unseen visitor. Accordingly, both men remained perfectly silent, straining every nerve in order to catch the faintest possible sound. This lasted for about a minute, when the same voice which Davies had previously heard again broke upon their astonished ears in the following words:

> " River Dee, River Dee,
> Speak thy mind out, fair and free ! "

The next instant, without the slightest warning of any kind, and whilst the moon was still shining clear in the heavens above, and no sign of rain or wind whatever, a low rushing sound was heard, and in at the window, and at the same time through the crevices of the roof, rapid streams of water came dashing into the room, and flooded the place in a couple of seconds. Before they could leap from their straw beds, the latter were saturated with wet, and the water stood a foot deep on the floor, and was rising rapidly, in such a manner as to threaten to fill the room. The two gentlemen shouted hastily for help, for there seemed no possibility of escape from drowning.

The old people of the house were some time before they could hear; but John Griffith was soon roused by the noise, and came rushing from his room in some anxiety as to the cause of the outcry. Scarcely had he opened the door than a wonderful phenomenon ensued. Not only did the water cease to descend, but not a drop of it attempted to cross the threshold of the open door, but the whole body of water stayed as if pent up in an iron cistern, presenting to Griffith's eyes the extraordinary sight of a pool of at least three feet in depth, in which stood his two companions shivering and wretched, whilst various articles of their clothing floated hither and thither around them. Then, singular to relate, the water began to sink and disappear as fast as it had come, and indeed performed this feat with so much rapidity, that by the time the old woman of the house had got upstairs and reached the room door, it was scarce an inch deep, and in the space of another minute, damp boards, moist straw, and men as moist and damp as either, were the only remaining evidences of the strange and wonderful event which had taken place.

Both Mr. Justice Allen and Serjeant Davies were thoroughly out of temper, which was perhaps not extraordinary under the circumstances. Their language was in accordance with the warmth of their internal, rather than the chilliness of their external, feelings. They denounced the house, the place, the country, and everything connected with it, especially the river and the so-called saint, for whom no epithet was too opprobrious.

The old woman of the house, however, was so evidently terrified at the occurrence which had taken place, that although the two gentlemen were at first inclined to condemn her forthwith as a witch, and one that must have been in league with those who had so injuriously treated them, they speedily retracted their opinion, and became mollified in their views of her behaviour. Anxious to conciliate her guests, she hastened to fetch fresh bundles of straw, which she deposited in the living-room down stairs; and having lighted a fire, hung all the wet articles of raiment before it to dry, all the while bemoaning in her own tongue the misfortune that had happened, and calling Heaven and all the saints to bear witness that she would rather have suffered any hardship in her own person than that guests in her house should have been treated in so scurvy a manner.

Yielding to her persuasions, and having dried themselves as well as they could, and warmed their shivering limbs at the fire, the travellers again sought repose upon the new straw beds which had been provided for them, and suffered no further disturbance during the remainder of the night. When morning came, they took solemn counsel together as to the course which they had best pursue in order to carry out the King's orders, which might on no account be neglected.

Upon the following day they were to meet the third Commissioner, Mr. Philips, who was coming from Ruabon, where a small party of soldiers and certain officials were to assemble, before proceeding to Llanderfel. To reach the latter place, therefore, was still their object, and they desired to do so upon that same day. In fact, as Serjeant Davies wittily observed, although great attempts had been made—and not altogether without success—to throw cold water on their proceedings, the enemy, be he who he might, had not succeeded in damping their ardour, and they were perfectly resolved to do their duty. They, therefore, determined to make one more attempt to follow the path from which they had been driven on the previous day, and accordingly got their horses ready, and, accompanied by honest John Griffith, again set out.

They did not forget to reward the old woman for her hospitality, although both Allen and Davies felt a kind of shudder pass through them when, in mumbling out her thanks, the crone expressed an earnest wish that " St. Dderfel might have them in his care," which, judging by past events, was precisely the thing which they would have most desired to avoid.

They slowly descended the mountain side, and presently found themselves once more in the road which led direct from Bala to Llanderfel. Here John Griffith ventured mildly to suggest that if they followed this road they would probably find no trouble in reaching their destination. Serjeant Davies rather inclined to the same opinion, but the stout-hearted Justice objected to so simple a proceeding. In fact, he was rather ashamed at the cowardice which he somewhat unjustly imputed to himself with reference to the proceedings of the previous day, and felt that his character was more or less at stake. He, therefore, put it very strongly to his companions that they ought not to be driven to alter their course by even so much as one inch in consequence of the events which had taken place. He reminded them that he and the Serjeant were travelling upon the King's busi-

ness, that the King was supreme in England, both as regarded temporal and spiritual matters, and that as to dispute
his power and supremacy was undoubtedly rank high treason,
so to be influenced and swayed by those who evidently did
so must certainly be very nearly the same. Moreover, he
said, that since the King had proved strong enough to shake
off the Pope, who had claimed to be supreme over the
spiritual affairs of the kingdom, it would be an insult alike
to King and Pope if they allowed any one else, saint, sprite
or demon, to oppose and thwart his Majesty's royal will and
pleasure. Therefore upon their allegiance he demanded
that they should resume their yesterday's path, and ride
along the banks of the river to Llanderfel.

Not without some hesitation did they comply, for although
John Griffith had no fears for himself, he did not wish to be
delayed in his journey upon his own private affairs by further misadventures which might befall the two gentlemen,
whilst as for Serjeant Davies, he justly remarked that
although the King's orders enjoined them to proceed to
Llanderfel, they said nothing about getting there by any
particular road, and he did not see the force of braving unseen foes when there was nothing to be got by it.

Mr. Justice Allen, however, being an obstinate man, and
one that loved his own way, had the same good luck which
usually attends those of a similar temperament and disposition. He *had* his own way, and the three men once more
entered upon the path by the river side, and advanced along
the bank.

There was nothing unusual to be seen in river, mountain-
side, or meadow. The water gurgled round the stones,
merrily as usual, the ring-ouzel started from the rushes in
the shallow water, and fluttered across the river, as if

alarmed by the approach of the invaders of his quiet home, the kingfisher went by like a flash of lightning as usual, but apparently quite intent upon his own business, and nothing appeared at all likely to disturb or molest the travellers.

They proceeded for some distance further than they had done on the previous day, and had in fact arrived at a point about half way between the bridge at which they had left the high road and the village for which they were bound, before anything unusual occurred. Then they came to a small strip of green meadow, not twenty yards wide, beyond which was a hedge, and a bridle-gate through which they would be able to pass into a larger meadow beyond. But exactly as they reached this strip of meadow, it suddenly changed altogether its character and appearance.

From a pleasant looking pasture, which seemed to invite a canter, it became a regular quagmire, shaking and shifting as if only anxious to swallow up and engulf anybody or anything which ventured upon it. So actively did its surface heave to and fro, that the horses naturally became alarmed, and refused to move a step further. Nor was it only the land itself which had such a dangerous look about it. From the mud peered up frogs, toads, snakes, and other disagreeable and venomous-looking creatures, and the frogs indeed set up a hoarse croaking, which was of itself enough to frighten any well-disposed horse.

Mr. Justice Allen, however, was determined not to be discomfited, and spurring his steed forward, raised his riding-whip at the same time for the purpose of more effectually enforcing his will. Horror upon horrors! No sooner had he done so, than the hilt silver of the whip turned into a serpent's head, the rest of the weapon became the body, and slipping from the hand of the astonished Justice, wriggled away towards the marsh as if it belonged to the place. Most men would have been utterly frightened and overcome by this strange and alarming occurrence, but the good Justice was not an ordinary man, and had, doubtless, for this reason been selected as one of the Commissioners whose duty it would be to encounter and defeat much local prejudice, and therein to display a firmness and strength of mind without which the victory could not be won. On the previous day Allen had been taken by surprise, and certainly he was not free from wonder at the present moment. But he had made up his mind to carry the business through, and resolved within himself that ten thousand sprites or saints, goblins or devilkins, should not now turn him back. So he shouted aloud to his companions—

"Come on, come on! In the King's name, come on! I warrant me that the King and my Lord Cromwell will prove too strong for these knaves, an' we face them boldly!"

Scarcely had the word Cromwell passed his lips when a tremendous yell broke from the bed of the river; such a yell of mingled surprise, rage, and agony as had never before been heard by any of the party. At the same time, after one mighty heaving, which evidently agitated its whole surface from end to end, the quagmire in front of the travellers ceased to oppose any obstacle to their progress, and returned to its former condition of a peaceful and innocent meadow. Mr. Justice Allen's whip, moreover, calm and quiet as if it had never misconducted itself at all, came actually into his hand as if it had been there all the time—a sedate, respectable, everyday whip—and every ugly and venomous creature utterly disappeared from sight.

All, however, was not over. In the very middle of the river, rearing itself up above the water, appeared the figure of a man, or at least the head and shoulders of a man, which led the casual observer to the conclusion that the rest of the body and the legs were beneath the water; though, as everything connected with magic is wonderful and uncertain, this might not have been the case, and it is quite possible that there were no body and legs belonging to the head and shoulders at all. Be this as it may, so much of a man's form as I have described was certainly visible to all three men, as each of them declared to his dying day. It is true that they all differed somewhat as to its precise appearance, Justice Allen declaring that the head was covered with dark grizzly hair, with a long gray beard, and singularly handsome features, whilst Serjeant Davies maintained that there was a wreath of weeds which almost concealed the hair, and John Griffith stoutly avowed that the head and hair were of a dark red colour. Still they all saw the head, and all agreed that the breast and shoulders were covered with something very like the scales of a fish. It is unimportant, however, to dwell upon these details, since by far the most interesting part of the strange apparition was the voice which issued from its lips.

Of course they all knew perfectly well that it was the River-Sprite. No one else would be likely to be in the middle of the river or to make such an unearthly noise under the circumstances; so they looked and listened, quite prepared for something extraordinary, though not exactly for what followed. Raising above his head a hand which firmly grasped a salmon of considerable size, he hurled the fish

in the direction of the party, as if it was his manner of
giving vent to a curse upon them and their undertaking.
The fish, fortunately for itself, fell short, and disappeared in
a pool between the Sprite and those at whom he seemed to
aim. At the same moment he raised his voice, and in harsh
and discordant tones thus addressed them :

> " Ride on, ride on, since River-Sprite
>   No more may check the royal might,
>   Nor Dderfel's sanctity avail
>   'Gainst those who would his shrine assail.
>   Ride on, ride on, base Harry's slaves,
>   To do the work of robber-knaves ;
>   Yet pause on sacrilegious way,
>   And list to my prophetic lay.
>   By Cromwell's aid and Cromwell's act
>   (Where hath the rogue a counterpart ?)
>   Comes o'er the land an hour of gloom,
>   And meek Religion hears her doom.
>   Through Cromwell works a king this shame—
>   Yet kings shall live to curse the name.
>   In ages yet to come shall spring
>   A Cromwell to confound a king,
>   For Dderfel's wrong shall king atone,
>   And Dderfel's vengeance shake a throne ! "

Having uttered these words, the River-Sprite threw up
both his arms once more, gave vent to another tremendous
yell, and disappeared with a splash which sent the water
flying right and left, and must have considerably disturbed
any fish which chanced to be in the neighbourhood. The
three men looked at each other in amazement, and then
John Griffith shook his head, and said he did not like this
sort of thing at all. The two gentlemen, however, thought
differently, inasmuch as they augured, from the appearance

and disappearance of the individual whom they had just seen, that they would meet with no further interruption on their journey, and they neither understood nor cared for the allusions of something which a Cromwell would, at some future day, do to a king, so long as they were allowed to proceed to the accomplishment of the business of *their* King, which had caused their expedition.

We, of course, looking back upon the whole course of events, understand all about the matter, and see what a wonderful prophecy was that of the River-Sprite; but the persons who heard it were differently circumstanced. Yet I have heard it whispered that some prophecy of this kind, working upon the jealous fears of King Henry the Eighth, was the beginning of the events which caused Lord Cromwell's downfall, which was very hard upon him, since he had nothing to do with the great river, and never killed a king in his life. Indeed, as a matter of fact and history, the King killed *him*, which was a totally different thing; and, considering the whole circumstances of the case, I think it would have been a far more reasonable prophecy of the River-Sprite if he had foretold that Cromwell should before long (as was the case) fall out of favour with his Royal master, and, as happened to a good many other people who displeased King Henry the Eighth, lose his head in consequence. This, I say, the River-Sprite might have foretold, and, in ascribing it to St. Dderfel's vengeance, would have greatly raised both his own reputation and that of the Saint.

Perhaps, however, he didn't know it, or perhaps he was bound not to prophesy about any person then alive, or perhaps he did not choose to give Cromwell the warning. In fact, river-sprites are such very curious people, that one never knows the exact rules by which they go, and therefore it is not of the slightest use to speculate upon the why or wherefore of anything which they may chance to say or leave unsaid. I only know what this particular Sprite *did* say, and, as I had it direct from a water-ousel, who was descended in a direct line from a bird who heard and saw the whole occurrence, and had constantly told the story to his children, to be handed down to the eggs yet unhatched, I do not think that there can be any mistake about it.

At all events, Mr. Justice Allen and Serjeant Davies found that no further obstacle was thrown in the way of their journey to Llanderfel, and in a very short time they arrived at that interesting village, and found comfortable quarters at the "Horse-shoe."

As they reached the place in good time, they were able to make a full inspection of the church and to visit the shrine of the Saint. Several people followed and watched them closely, but no one interfered with them; and, having viewed the figure of the Saint on his wooden horse, and gazed upon the offerings which the piety of the neighbouring villagers and the passing pilgrims had bestowed thereupon, they returned to their inn and made themselves comfortable for the night.

They required the services of John Griffith no longer, and therefore dismissed him, with the offer of a liberal reward. But this honest John refused, saying that since he had been thrown in with them as comrades during a ticklish time, he had stood by them as a Welshman should, but that he had now heard too much of their errand to care to touch their money, and accordingly he took his leave without doing so. This somewhat surprised the two gentlemen, but they did not allow it to distress them, which was a sensible thing on their part, though perhaps not wonderful, since people are seldom averse to saving their money when they can conveniently do so. John Griffith, therefore, went on his way; and, although no longer protected by his presence, neither the Justice nor the Lawyer suffered any further inconvenience at Llanderfel that night.

Upon the next morning their work was to begin, and their brother commissioner, Mr. Philipson, duly arrived from Ruabon with a body of men who had been sent to support the execution of the King's will. The inquiry which they instituted was one of a sufficiently simple character, it was merely to ascertain that miraculous powers were commonly ascribed by the people of the neighbourhood to the wooden figure of St. Dderfel, and this would be held to justify its immediate destruction and the plunder of a shrine which every true Protestant would of course rejoice to see destroyed.

The belief of the people was not difficult to prove, for it was universal throughout all North Wales. When summoned to give evidence upon the subject, the poor creatures thought they were called upon to bear witness to the power, sanctity, and goodness of their beloved Saint, and testified with great alacrity to the many cures which had been effected through his agency. Sufficient evidence was soon collected to have hanged half-a-dozen sinners instead of one saint, who in those days had still less chance of getting off, and it was soon clear enough that St. Dderfel must be doomed. Hanging, however, was not to be his fate.

The people vainly endeavoured to save him by offering to subscribe for his ransom. It might not be. There could be but one place to which the image might be carried, one manner in which it might be destroyed.

At that time Friar Forrest, having first maintained the

supremacy of the Pope and then that of the King, had come back to his first love, and was opposed to the uprooting of the papal power and the destruction of monasteries. It was, therefore, determined that he should be "purified by fire," which was the pleasant way people had of putting it in those days when they burned a man, although I don't suppose it made it any more pleasant for the fellow who had to be burned. Friar Forrest was burned in Smithfield market, and stuck up for the Pope to the last, just as many stout-hearted Protestants held out against him, in Queen Mary's reign afterwards, and were burned in the same fashion. But in order to show that the Saint could not save the Friar, they took his image, chopped it up, and made it into firewood to burn the victim, which it did with great success.

Mr. Justice Allen, Serjeant Davies and Mr. Philipson thought it their duty to be present upon this occasion, being determined to see the last of St. Dderfel, and saw his remains used in this manner with much satisfaction.

Now the fragments into which the Saint had been split were of considerable size, and as they spluttered and cracked and hissed in the fire, the three Commissioners, in common with other people, could plainly distinguish them. Suddenly, from the middle of the crowd which pressed around, eagerly watching the execution of the unhappy victim, a tall man, wrapped in a long, dark cloak, stepped swiftly, as it appeared to those who saw him, into the very .fire, seized one of the largest pieces of St. Dderfel, blazing as it was, quickly placed it under his cloak, whence came a hissing noise as of water thrown on fire, and in an instant the stranger had disappeared again, without any one making an effort to stop him.

All three Commissioners saw the thing plainly, but Philipson was astonished at its effect upon his companions. They turned deadly pale, trembled all over, and looked at each other with terror written in the countenance of each. After a time they recovered themselves sufficiently to explain the cause of their strange emotion, when they both informed their colleague and friend, that in the person who had so boldly stepped into the fire, and performed the feat which has just been told, they distinctly recognized the features of the Sprite of the River Dee.

It was in vain that Mr. Philipson endeavoured to combat so foolish an idea, and to explain away so absurd a delusion. Both the gentlemen stuck steadily to their story, Serjeant Davies endeavouring, though with a melancholy face, to perpetrate a joke after his own peculiar fashion, by declaring that it was no De-lusion but a Dee-Sprite.

This, however, failed to amuse the company when discussing so serious a subject. Serious, indeed, it turned out to be. Mr. Justice Allen was never the same man afterwards; he changed his religion three times, which was not an uncommon occurrence in those days, but was never any the better for it. The memory of his sojourn in Wales seemed ever with him: he continually fancied that he saw the figure of the Spirit of the Dee following him, and at last he took to drinking, and of course made a miserable end of it. It is said, indeed, that when nearly at his last he heard the doctor who was in attendance upon him, declare that it was a clear case of " Delirium tremens."

" Dee, again ? " he exclaimed in frantic horror—" the Dee—the Dee—always the Dee—oh, that dreadful Dderfel ! " and with this name on his lips expired.

Nor did Serjeant Davies ever thrive after the events of

which I have had to tell. He grew stout, and, strange to say, the more corpulent did he become, the worse grew his temper, until at last he was a perfect nuisance to every one. Any allusion to his Welsh adventures at once excited him to fury, and the names of Dderfel and the river Dee were never suffered to be mentioned in his presence. At last, when he had been enjoying a worse attack than usual of the gout, to which he was a martyr, he so annoyed his niece by his irritability and disagreeable remarks, that to one of the latter she thoughtlessly remarked, "Fiddle-de-dee." Scarcely was the word out of her mouth when he flew into a violent passion, accusing the poor girl of having used a forbidden word, and working himself up into such a temper that he tried to rise from his chair to strike her. The exertion and the excitement brought back the gout, which flew to a vital part, and the learned Serjeant went out of the world in this melancholy fashion.

This account of the end of the two Commissioners is that which is commonly held to be correct in Llanderfel, and I have therefore given it, although I believe that the families of Allen and Davies have entirely different versions as to the lives and deaths of their two respected ancestors.

There is, however, a striking corroboration of one part of my story, the most of which, to tell the honest truth, I learned from the water-ousel, whom I have already mentioned and whose acquaintance I recently made when on a visit to North Wales.

Somehow or other, a large fragment of the image of St. Dderfel on his horse did re-appear in the church of Llanderfel, and may be seen in the porch thereof unto this day. Now, how did it come there? Is it likely that the Commissioners, who were so zealous and earnest in their work of destruction, would have left the smallest vestige of the abomination which they had come to destroy? Is it not certain, beyond all reasonable doubt, that every scrap and fragment of the Saint and his horse was sent up to Smithfield to help to burn Friar Forrest? If so, how can we reconcile this with the undoubted fact of the presence in Llanderfel church of a large fragment to-day? There is only one way of doing so, and that is by believing the story of the gallant rescue made by the River-Sprite.

And when I walk along the banks of the old river, and listen to its pleasant murmuring sounds, they seem to tell me over again these old tales, and to impress on me that it is just as well to believe them, for they lead me to feel that there is an unseen and an unknown world, through, and by, and in which we may be daily walking, although we see and know it not, a world of spirits who protect the good and pure, and who can do so better and more effectually than the Spirit of the Dee was able to protect the shrine of St. Dderfel.

KIMMELINA AND THE DWARF.

I DON'T like snow on the 1st of April. About Christmas I hail it as a natural and not unpleasant thing, which rather adds to one's merriment, and makes the fires look brighter and the blackbirds more glossy and jet-like. In January I don't object to it at all, especially if a bit of frost comes after it, and makes the ground crisp and hard enough to walk upon comfortably. Then, as to February and March, no one who lives in England minds *what* kind of weather he has then to encounter, or if he does, he is not fit to live in England at all, and had better be off to southern lands at once. February and March are months during which, whatever weather we have, one is thankful that it is not worse. But when April comes in, I feel that I have a right to expect softer winds, more sun, birds singing and nesting, lambs bleating, and all that tells one that spring is really here. I said all this to myself when I looked out of my window on this very 1st of April last past, and saw a white world which would have been no disgrace to Christmas. I said it much more when I walked out and found what the snow in the night and the frost at early dawn had done. My apricot blossoms were nipped to death, every one of them; all hope of wall-fruit was over for the year; the hares and rabbits, finding their usual food covered with a white sheet, had visited my young plantations, and satisfied their hunger at the expense of my choicest shrubs, and half-a-dozen thrushes' nests wherein, owing to the previous mild weather, the young birds had broken the shells of the eggs and come forth, earlier than usual, into being, were half full of snow, and contained only the lifeless bodies of the little innocents who had been so severely punished for prematurely entering this wicked world. I said several times then—and I deliberately say it again, that I don't like snow in April, and I do not like it for other reasons besides those I have mentioned. I dislike it because it makes me dissatisfied with my native country, its climate, seasons, and temperature: it makes me wish I was a native of some warmer land, or that, if I still belonged to England, I might be as a dormouse, or something of the kind, during this particular part of the year. I have read of swallows clustering together in great bunches to keep warm through the winter, and I feel as if I should like to cluster too, as long as this weather lasts, but instead of clustering, I am obliged to live on, and keep myself warm as well as I can. But, do what I may, and warm myself as I do, I repeat once more that I don't like snow on the 1st of April.

These were the thoughts which passed through my brain as I passed round a new gravel walk which I had lately made at my house in the country, and looked with a sad eye upon the mischief which the hares had done at one place in particular. They are such tiresome creatures, those hares: they do not attack one little tree and eat it up in a respectable manner, but they nip off the heads of half-a-dozen or more, invariably choosing the best and rarest specimens. I have heard farmers say that they do the same in a field of wheat, nipping along so recklessly that they destroy a great deal more than they want to eat.

They had certainly done me a great deal of mischief in one night, and I began to wish that they had all been jugged before they had come into the plantation at all, and then I tried if I could not make a joke about that expression, founded upon the word " Juggernaut," but I failed to settle it to my satisfaction, and so gave it up as a bad job. Then I thought what a fool I had been not to have put down wire netting all round the place, which I should certainly have done only the length was so great that I thought I would rather run the risk and save the expense. I stepped on one side into the plantation to see whether a particular tree which I knew of was safe or not, and as I did so, up jumped a great hare and scampered off at full speed.

If I had had my gun with me I do not think that anything could have saved that hare's life—unless, indeed, I had missed it, which was certainly possible on a cold morning like that, when one's hands could hardly feel the trigger. I mean that the season of the year would not have stopped me, nor the fact that we do not like to shoot the hares so near the house, nor the thought that the coursing people might be coming that way : no consideration of this kind would have stopped me. That which did so effectually was the fact of my not having a gun with me, so that I could do nothing but start (which I did at the sudden bolting of the hare) and then stand gazing after her as she cantered slowly across the meadow beyond the wire fence of the plantation.

As I gazed, it struck me that the animal was not running after the approved and natural manner of hares. Instead of keeping straight on, as a hare pursued by man or dog would have done, or, if unpursued, throwing up her hind quarters in a jaunty manner, like a young deer, this particular hare, immediately after creeping through the fence, and passing some large, thick tufts of grass and rushes, appeared to run after a zig-zag fashion, first on one side and then on the other, as if unable to steer her course straight, and, in fact, not unlike a man considerably under the influence of liquor.

As I knew, from long study of natural history, that this was very unlikely to be the case with so well-conducted an animal as a hare, I was somewhat at a loss to account for the circumstance, until I put up my eyeglass and looked more attentively at my friend. Then at once the wonder was explained. The poor creature carried a burden which steered her course for her. A stoat had been lying in wait for her, crouched beneath one of the tufts of rushes which I have mentioned, and the instant she had crept under the fence, he had sprung upon her back with the usual activity of his race, and, lying at full length upon her, and grasping her fur tightly both with hind and fore legs, was commencing to operate upon her neck in the same manner as that in which a schoolboy deals with an orange, namely, by biting a hole in it, and leisurely sucking the juice.

Of course I knew how this little affair would end. It could, indeed, only end in one way. When sufficiently exhausted by loss of blood, the unhappy hare would fall lifeless upon the ground, and the stoat, when he had satisfied the cravings of his appetite, would leave the rest of the carcase there, and go forth in search of fresh victims. Thus, then, I should very shortly be revenged for the destruction of my shrubs, and the destroyer would have expiated her offence with her life. But at that instant I frankly confess that I thought no longer of my loss. I felt, on the contrary, intense sympathy for the poor hare, and disgust that her pure and innocent life should be sacrificed to such a miserable little wretch as the stoat. I did not hesitate for a moment, but dashing through the fence, rushed in pursuit, shouting loudly as I did so.

The snow, against which I had been protesting all the morning, now served me in good stead. It so much impeded the progress of the hare that, added to the ground she lost in her wild attempts to run first one way and then another, it enabled me to gain rapidly upon the flying animals. I was scarce ten yards from them when the hare, who had begun to squeak pitiably as she felt the sharp teeth of the stoat in the back of her neck, stumbled and fell on the snow, exhausted by pain and loss of blood. I was quickly up with her, and had the satisfaction of catching my friend the stoat a crack over the back with my walking-stick, as he tried to slink away, which effectually spoiled any future effort of his in the direction of amusing himself by riding upon hare's backs.

Then I turned to poor Puss, who lay panting and bleeding upon the ground, looking up at me with her large, sad, frightened eyes, as if feeling sure that she had only changed one destroyer for another. I lifted her gently in my arms, for she was too much terrified and exhausted to struggle or scratch, and I feared she would die before I could get her to the house. Fortunately, however, the stoat had not had sufficient time to work his wicked will effectually upon the poor creature, and her hurts were not mortal. I had the wound in her neck carefully washed, and such remedies applied to it as my experienced house-keeper deemed best.

The latter did mutter, certainly, at first, some foolish

words about " stuffing " and " currant-jelly," with a little roasting, being the best physic for hares, but after I had rebuked her for her inhumanity, she behaved very well about the business. Everything was done for our new guest that was calculated to promote her speedy and complete recovery, and in a very few days she was pronounced to be as well as ever she had been in her life. I had taken the fancy of having a box made for her in my study, and there she lay, in nice clean straw, with only a few bars placed over the box, so that she might not jump out and run away before she was really well enough to go out again into the wide world.

There she lay, and there I sat and wrote—in my study, I mean, not in the box—and if that was all I had to tell you, this story would never have been written. But, on the third day, as I was writing a very particular letter, and, for the moment, was thinking nothing at all about the hare or her box, I was astonished at hearing a voice distinctly coming from the corner of the room in which the latter stood. It was a low voice—rather weak, as it seemed to me—but the words which it pronounced were perfectly clear, and there was no doubt about them.

" I don't like this box—let me out ! " said the voice.

I turned round in my chair with the greatest astonishment.

" Let me out, I say ! " repeated the voice.

I could hardly believe my own ears, but as they were faithful old servants, never in the habit of deceiving me, I gave credit to them as usual, rose from my chair, and walked across the room to my hare's box. When I got there, the animal was sitting in the very middle of the box, looking up at me through the bars. I regarded her for a moment, and then still thinking that I *must* be mistaken, was about to turn away and go back to my chair, when again spoke the voice, and unmistakably it proceeded from the hare.

" Well—are you going to let me out of this box ? "

I never was so staggered in my life.

" Let—you—out—of—that—box ! " I repeated mechanically.

" Yes—that's what I said," returned the hare. " Why don't you do it ? "

I confess that I knew not what reply to make. It was not the question, of course, which puzzled me, so much as the person who asked it. I have often been asked questions by people whom I did not want to answer, and questions, too, which I did not at all desire to have put. But I never had been questioned by a hare before, and the idea seemed to me so ludicrous, that after gazing at her for a moment with a kind of stupefied look, I fairly burst into a fit of laughter. At this Puss seemed somewhat annoyed, and thumped with her forepaw upon the box.

" I don't know what you are laughing at," she said, " or whether you think it becoming in a gentleman to burst out laughing when a lady speaks to him. Why don't you answer my question ? "

These words recalled me to my senses, or rather, if I may say so, to my ordinary politeness.

" Really, madam," said I, bowing civilly over the box, " I was so totally unaware that ladies of your particular species were in the habit of holding conversations with gentlemen, that I hardly know how to answer your very unexpected question. But since you have asked me, I cannot see any reason for refusing to comply with that which appears to be your request. I will certainly release you from the box, and that with much pleasure."

So saying, I took a hammer from a ledge which was near, easily wrenched out the screws which held down the bars on the top of the box, and raising two of them, made room for the hare to escape if she wished. As soon as I had done this, she deliberately raised herself upon her hind legs, placed her forepaws upon one of the remaining bars, drew up her body thereby, and then jumped quietly down upon the floor.

"I am much obliged to you," she then said (and all this in perfectly good English), "for what you have just done, and for the trouble which you have taken about my concerns. Perhaps I ought to inform you (if, indeed, you have not already guessed it) that I am no ordinary hare. Indeed, I should have told you this long before, had I not been bound by a vow not to speak until to-day. The prescribed time of silence having now expired, I am at liberty to disclose to you the truth."

Whilst the hare pronounced these words, in a grave and deliberate tone of voice, I stood with my eyes fixed upon her in the deepest astonishment. I had shot hares often and often, and heard their sad cries of pain and terror when wounded. I had seen them pursued by greyhounds, and heard the shriek uttered immediately before the lanky jaws of the cruel foe were about to seize the hapless victim. I had often seen them stealing from brake to brake in the woods with graceful action, and I had frequently gazed upon their forms after death, browned with roasting, and well-supplied with "stuffing" pleasant to the taste of man. But never before had I seen a hare, alive or dead, calmly facing a human being and speaking to him in his own language, as this animal was now doing. It was a startling mystery —an event so wholly strange and unexpected that I did not know what to think, say, or do at the moment, and consequently remained where I was, standing and staring like a stuck pig, or any other creature whose position at any particular time may be taken to indicate the most extreme surprise. The hare, however, apparently taking no notice of my confusion and embarrassment, thus continued her discourse :

" Since you know that I am not a hare, you are doubtless consumed with an earnest and unconquerable longing to know who and what I am. That longing shall speedily be gratified. I am a fairy, and one of some importance, having authority over a considerable country and many devoted subjects. Unfortunately, though, I am not without my enemies, of whom the chief, the worst, and the most malignant is the vile Dwarf Bamplukes, who reigns over the Fen country, inhabited by little else than snakes and toads, save the miserable ducks, geese, and wildfowl, over whom he exercises a ruthless tyranny. This monster desires anxiously both my kingdom and my life, and would gladly sacrifice the latter in order to obtain the former. He is up to every wile and dodge ever known or practised by the abominable race to which he belongs, and is continually inventing some new trick, or spreading some fresh net in which to entrap me. By the rules of Fairyland, to which all fairies of my class are subject, in a greater or less degree, I am obliged to assume the form of a hare for one month in every year, and during that period my magical powers are suspended, and I am liable to be destroyed like an ordinary hare. Unhappily for me, the wretch Bamplukes is aware of all this as well as I am, and it is during this month that he sets in motion against me every engine which his fiendish cunning can devise. More than once I have been started by the fearful cry of harriers, and had to fly for my life for hours together before those hateful creatures. The terrible greyhound has before this time tried me to the utmost, and I have several times been in danger from the fox and cat. In each case I have known but too well that my enemies were either paid emissaries of the dwarf, or that information of my whereabouts had been given by him to those whose business or pleasure it is to pursue hares. If the villain had power to transform himself into one of these animals, I could never have escaped his craft so long. This, however, he cannot do, and can therefore only assail me by working upon others, of doing which he never misses an opportunity. The stoat who attacked me a few days ago, and who, thanks to your generous and timely assistance, has paid the penalty of his rashness by the forfeiture of his miserable life, was a paid agent of my deadly and untiring enemy. This I know, not only by the unfailing instinct which guides me in such matters, but from the fact that the brute croaked into my ear, just before he made his brutal teeth meet in my throat, ' This is from Bamplukes, with best love and kiss.' Aye, and but for you, a deadly kiss would it have been indeed. You know now the circumstances of the case as well as if I was to go on talking for a week, and I need, therefore, say no more. But as the month is just up, I will, if you please, resume my own shape, and appear to your eyes such as I really am."

The creature ceased speaking, and almost as soon as she had done so, the skin of a hare fell off from her, as if it had been merely a loose cloak thrown over her shoulders, and disappeared altogether, whilst there suddenly appeared upon the floor as comely a little lady as you would see in a long day's journey, be it where it might. I was never much of a hand at describing, but I wish I could make you understand what the fairy was like. Not above six or eight inches high, I think, but with marvellously well-proportioned figure, her head set jauntily upon her shoulders, her limbs beautifully rounded, and—in fact, she looked "a fairy all over," if I may venture to use so familiar an expression in speaking of so mysterious and exalted a personage as a fairy queen. There she stood, in all the glory of her royal beauty, on the floor, and a prettier little creature I thought I had never beheld.

"Now," said she, laughing merrily, as she perceived my evident perplexity, "I must not forget the great kindness which you have done me, and the service you have rendered by saving my life. In old times I could have satisfied you by giving you 'three·wishes,' as all respectable fairies used to do for their friends 'in the good old times.' But alas! those times are changed, and I have not even the power of providing that everything you touch should turn to gold, or of sending a king's daughter, very beautiful and very rich, to fall in love with and marry you without delay. Shorn of our ancient rights and privileges, as we modern fairies are, I confess (though reluctantly) that I can do nothing of this sort. Nor can I, as I would gladly do if possible, relieve you from the liability to those ailments and diseases with which humanity is plagued. You must continue to put up with bad colds if you get your feet wet without changing your socks as soon as possible afterwards; or if you sit in draughts, or go out in the east wind insufficiently provided with wrappers. You must still suffer from internal pains if you persist in eating unwholesome food, and too much of it; nor can I guarantee that you shall be free from gout as long as you drink champagne and port wine, and take so much sugar in your tea. But I will gladly do for you what lies in my power, and I only wish that it were more. You shall henceforth be able to understand the language of all the animals, with and without feathers, that inhabit your native land. Neither bird nor beast shall be able to speak without your comprehending its meaning; and even the hum of the insects shall be intelligible to your ears. It is no little privilege which I thus confer upon you, and it is one from which you will be able to derive both pleasure and advantage. In return, may I ask you to deal tenderly with hares, and not to kill them unless either wanted for home consumption or gifts, or in the case of their being especially troublesome to the new plantations. And if at the recurrence of my month of trial (of which you shall always have due and precise information) you would suspend and stop all killing of hares in your shrubberies and gardens, and keep down all vermin with redoubled care, you would render me a service for which I should never be ungrateful, and far more than repay any little advantage which I am about to confer upon you at the present moment."

So saying, the Fairy tripped lightly from her position to the place where I was standing, which was very near the mantelpiece. Somehow or other—I never knew how—she suddenly stood upon the latter, by which means she brought herself upon a level with my face, upon which she struck me a gentle blow across the mouth with a light wand which she held in her hand, and uttered at the same time some words of which I have not the slightest recollection, and which it is therefore hopeless to attempt to chronicle. Immediately a curious buzzing went through my head and brain, and I knew that I understood the animal language, of which I had been perfectly ignorant before. The Fairy then tripped forward gracefully to the window, and rested there for a moment. Then she turned and looked smilingly at me—

"Farewell," she said. "You are a good fellow, that I *must* say for you, whatever anybody else may say to the contrary, and if ever you are in danger or difficulty, and want the best advice that a true friend can give you, do not forget that such an one you have, and always *will* have, in the Fairy Kimmelina."

Then she waved her hand in the air towards me, with a friendly and pretty gesture, and the next minute had vanished from my sight. I stood there rubbing my eyes, and wondering whether I was asleep or awake, for some minutes after this strange interview. Then I walked out into the garden and looked about, but saw no signs of either hare or fairy. So I took a stroll round the new walk again, partly to collect my confused and scattered ideas, and partly because I had nothing else to do. I pondered gravely over what had just occurred, and wondered whether such a thing had ever happened to anybody else, and whether there were other fairies about, disguised in other animal forms, and playing their part in the drama of fairy life, unknown to and unsuspected by the race of man. I do not know how long I might have gone on pondering and wondering, if I had not been suddenly interrupted by a brace of partridges, which sprang up almost under my feet, and bustled off in a great hurry, as if terribly frightened. To my intense surprise, instead of hearing merely the sharp but cheerful note with which a partridge expresses his feelings when thus roused, I distinctly heard and understood what the birds said, and it was this :

"Confound the fellow, what does he mean by startling a bird like that, coming up so quietly on the grass. Hang him ! the season has been over these two months and more. What right has he to disturb us ? "

And they were still talking in the same strain when the swiftness of their flight carried them out of ear-shot.

I stood for an instant transfixed with astonishment, and then all at once recollected the words and promise of the Fairy Kimmelina. It was evident that she had not deceived me, nor given a promise which she was unable to perform.

If I could thus understand the language of the partridges, doubtless I should be able to understand other birds and animals equally well, and a leaf of Nature's book, hitherto (so far as I knew) closed to mankind, would lie open before me.

In an instant it flashed across my mind that I should now enjoy an advantage and a privilege which might be of great use to me in many ways, and, if properly employed, would sweeten the evening of my days, and enable me to feel more like the companion and friend of what we arrogant members of the human race are pleased to call " the brute creation," but what I consider as a part of creation in very many respects superior to those who thus term them in contempt.

I pictured to myself moments, minutes, nay, hours of pleasure in listening to the conversations of the various creatures which dwelt in and around my house. I fancied myself sitting on the lawn, under the arbutus-tree, on a warm summer's evening, listening to the blackbird's last song before his bedtime, and hearing the praises he doubt-less poured out on such occasions for all the happiness of his pleasant, easy life ; the robin, too, long noted for his piety, would doubtless chant his evening hymn in such a manner as to leave me in a very proper frame of mind after hearing it, and, with equal certainty, I should glean something amusing, or even instructive, from the twittering of the sparrows around the eaves of my house, and in the ivy which crept up and around it in such graceful luxuriance.

Then I would have conversations with the domestic ani-mals, too. My two daughters had at the time two beautiful "collie" puppies, "Meg" and "Mona," which were kept tied up in the stables, but which the girls daily took out for a scamper in the meadows and gardens, scarcely, I fear, with the approval of the head-gardener, who liked things to be tidy, and had a prejudice against rampageous puppies upon his flower-beds. How pleasant it would be to hear the ingenuous remarks of these animals upon things and people ! Their rough, honest judgment would certainly be valuable.

Eva had a cat, too : a famous cat ; a beautiful cat ; a re-markable cat with an enormous brush (it really was rather a brush than a tail), and ways more fascinating than the ordinary ways of a cat. It was devoted to my child, and I smiled to myself as I thought of all the pretty things it doubtless said to and of her, as it purred out its disinterested affection upon her knee, or rubbed its head lovingly against her cheek.

These, and a great many other thoughts of a similar nature passed quickly through my brain as I stood musing over the words which I had just heard fall from the part-ridge's beak, and I promised myself much future pleasure.

both in connection with the tamer animals at home, and the wilder creatures of the woods, whose feelings I thought I should now be able more accurately to ascertain with regard especially to sportsmen in general and gamekeepers in particular.

I had often wondered, whether the tame pheasants which a keeper has reared with tender care from their earliest infancy, regard him as a ruthless and cruel traitor when they see him, at a later period of the year, conducting and directing the forces which are about to be employed to take away their innocent lives, or whether they have any idea that he is only engaged in the performance of a manifest duty, and that, but for the love of killing them cherished by the sporting master, he would have had no employment and they no existence at all. This point should now be cleared up on the earliest possible opportunity, and there seemed to be no limit to the useful information which I might acquire thenceforward, if I only made a proper use of my ears, and threw myself in the way of those animals who possessed it. Full of these thoughts, and with an internal feeling of elation, which can be more easily imagined than described, I proceeded to complete my stroll round the new walk.

Full of love towards all creation, I entertained a great longing to know and be assured of that, which I felt to be the case, namely, that the birds and beasts had the same kind of feeling towards me, and indeed towards the whole race of man, and that all which I should hear, and, henceforth, understand as well as hear, would prove to me more and more the harmony of creation, and the appreciation entertained by the animals of the kindness and wisdom with which man had exercised that power over them which his reason enabled him to possess.

It was true that this appreciation had not been distinctly perceptible in the remarks of the partridge, but there was much to be said in his defence. I could not say that, as a rule, either mankind generally, or I in particular, had dealt with his race in a spirit of excessive kindness or forbearance upon the farm immediately joining the spot from which he and his companion rose: my son and I had shot no less than fifty-four brace of partridges one day in the last September. Probably many of these had been his relations, certainly his friends and acquaintances, and he might perhaps be excused if, looking at it from a partridge point of view, he did not precisely see the kindness or wisdom of that special exercise of human power. Then, I certainly had come suddenly upon him, when he was doubtless making nesting arrangements with his mate, and when my sudden arrival was trying to the temper of a respectable bird. Evidently, it would be unfair to judge by this exceptional case, of the general opinion of mankind cherished by the breed of partridges, and even if further inquiry should lead one, however unwillingly, to conclude that opinion to be unfavourable, one must own that these birds, together with pheasants and some others, must be included in a different category from the general race, as being peculiarly adapted at once for the sport and the food of man.

So I put the partridge's remarks aside as irrelevant and inconclusive, and quietly continued my walk.

Presently I came to the older and higher part of the plantation, where larch and spruce, Scotch and silver firs, copper-beeches, sycamores, coloured thorns, hollies, and a variety of other trees were growing, and where the birds found the most charming positions for their nests, securely sheltered from wind and rain by the dense foliage. Halfway through this, there is an open green space, with a large oak in the midst of it, around which I have had a wide and comfortable seat placed, upon which I love to sit and listen to the songs of the birds, and watch the beauties of the trees as the summer steals gently upon us day by day.

As I sauntered quietly along towards this seat, out dashed two pigeons from the oak. They are never fired at there, and know, I think, that they are quite safe, so I was not surprised to find that they only flew across to a clump of tall trees underneath which our dogs are always buried, and there gave vent to a few quiet " coos." Now there has always been something both soothing and attractive to me in the cooing of a woodpigeon. I suppose this partly arises from its association with my boyish days, when I spent a great portion of my time in wandering amid the woods in my father's park, in which these birds abounded. But even without such associations, I think any one who has anything tender about his heart must be touched by that soft, pleasant sound, and it had always given me simple and real pleasure to hear it. Moreover, considering that we have always held the woodpigeons as sacred birds in our shrubberies and fields near the house, I felt certain that now, when I understood their language, I should hear some special sentiments of gratitude towards myself and my family, in addition to that general friendly feeling towards mankind which these gentle birds would undoubtedly express. Judge, therefore, my surprise and regret—to use no stronger word—when the words of the woodpigeons were thus distinctly wafted to my ears from the branches of the tall elms before mentioned.

" What a tiresome man that is, always walking about our fields, and coming right under our trees ! He behaves just as if the place belonged to him. Men are so trouble-some and inconsiderate."

"Well," thought I, "these pigeons are certainly either the most ungrateful or the most ignorant of birds. Belong to me, forsooth! I wonder to whom they think the place *does* belong : I have built the house, one may say (it was but a cottage when I came here), made the gardens, planted most of the trees, and now to have it hinted that the place belongs to somebody else. The bird must be a fool," and I felt quite indignant at the observations which I had over-heard, and strode forward on my way with a rising doubt in my mind whether woodpigeons had really any claim to be spared as we had spared them hitherto. They did a considerable amount of damage to the corn, and were not bad in a pie, when killed, and if they did not appreciate forbearance, why hold one's hand? when it would be so easy to show them the difference that might, if I pleased, exist in our mutual relations.

I calmed down, however, after a few strides, and began to make excuses for the poor birds. As *we* (with the one exception of my privileged self) could not understand *their* language, so they were doubtless ignorant of ours, and, this being so, they might not be acquainted with the fact that the country belongs to men and not to birds, and might also be ignorant of our kindly feeling towards their own tribe. Besides, it was but a casual observation; it might not have expressed the real, matured opinion of the speakers, and even if it did, these were but one out of many pairs of woodpigeons which frequented the place, and were not to be taken as expressing the opinions and feelings of all the rest. So I comforted myself with these reflections, and continued my walk, hearing no other conversation which bore upon the particular point which I had been considering, although several creatures amused me by the remarks upon other topics which they incidentally let fall.

A sheep was complaining of the number of daisies in the grass, in the same sort of way that you hear people complain that the cook has put too much salt in the soup. A woodpecker groaned out his complaint that the trees were much harder than they used to be, and wished for a return to the "good old times," by which he forcibly reminded me of several of my human acquaintances, who are very much in the habit of making the same remark, with probably not an atom of better reason for it than the woodpecker. I heard a squirrel, too, telling his mate how that he had found a jay's nest in a very comfortable situation, and, fancying it for his dray, had driven the birds out and taken possession. He described with much humour the complaints, the rage, the dismay of the old jays, imitated their harsh screaming, and roared with laughter as he told the story, from which I learned that tyranny and oppression are not confined to the human species or even to ravenous wild beasts, but that in many, even the smaller, animals, the rule obtains that the strong have things their own way, and "the weakest go to the wall."

I finished my walk and came in through the little iron gate from the wood on to the lawn, and then I met my two daughters with the collie puppies, which were gambolling about them with much enthusiasm and delight, much to the detriment of their dresses, to place their dirty paws upon which seemed to be one of the principal amusements of the puppies.

As they jumped about, they gave vent to their pleasure

in several short barks, which I knew well enough, and had always interpreted before as their manner of testifying frantic delight at being let out. Now, however, that I was able to gather their exact meaning, I found that there was something more.

" Here we are," barked Mona, quite distinctly, "and we don't at all object to having a romp with you girls, for you are not a bad sort by any means. But what a thundering shame to keep us tied up three parts of the day in that horrid old stable! Why should not we be free to run about as well as you? We don't like being tied up—I say it's a shame! "

And they barked the same sentiments in chorus.

Then Eva tried to teach Mona to jump over a stick, which she did once or twice, and then stopped and whined, by which, if it had happened only the day before, I should have understood that she meant a meek and gentle protest. No such thing! What she really said was this:

"No, no; I've had enough of this for to-day. You stupid girl! What fun do you think an honest and well-bred dog can find in jumping over a stick? Do it yourself if you want it done—*I* won't."

This palpably disrespectful language, addressed to her own mistress, a young lady who invariably treats her with the greatest kindness, and to whom she owes most of her pleasant walks and runs, struck me as being ungrateful as well as unpolite, and I felt considerably annoyed, and turned away in some disgust.

I did not think it necessary to tell the girls what opinions had been expressed by their favourites, lest it should in any degree spoil the pleasure they found in their company, and I must say that I rather wish I had not myself been undeceived, and my opinion lowered respecting animals of which I had hitherto thought highly.

Worse, however, was in store for me within the house. If there was one animal from whom rather than from another I should have expected affection towards the whole human race, and especially towards the mistress who so fondly loved her, it was Eva's Angola cat. The creature slept in her room, was her constant companion in-doors, and always manifested its regard for her in what we all supposed to be an unmistakable manner. So when I went into the dining-room at luncheon time, and saw Miss Puss stretched upon the hearth-rug, I thought to myself that I should hear from her some pretty and touching sentiments before long.

When luncheon was nearly over, she rose from the rug, walked demurely round the table, and then, receiving a little encouragement to do so, sprang upon Eva's lap, rubbed her head against the young lady's cheek, and began to purr complacently.

Alas, for my new privilege, and alas, for my old theory of the love of animals for man! The cat's purr, hitherto believed by me to be expressive of a personal contentment and a general benevolence towards everybody, said, as plainly as words could say—

"Scratch my head, now, Miss Eva, and tickle me gently behind the ears. That is what I like, and that is about all you are good for. I dare say you think I am very fond of you, but it is only myself for whom I really care. I should be no true cat if it were otherwise. You do very well to live with, because you have a nice room, and give me tit-bits to eat, but, I like the garden cat better than you to play with, and what is more, I don't like your plan of having me shut into the house at night. It is impudence, that's what it is, Miss, and though I let you scratch my head, because it's nice, I do not mean to be treated as if I belonged to you instead of you to me, which is the real state of the case. Bless you, I don't care for you or Kate, or any of them, only I like the place, and get plenty to eat—there! go on scratching!"

I was at once stupefied and disgusted at the selfish and ignoble sentiments thus uttered by the cat, and have seldom felt so inclined to throw any animal out of the window. As, however, we happened to be on the ground floor, the proceeding would have been useless as regarded harm to the cat, and might have occasioned unpleasant scratches to myself. Moreover, I felt bound in honour not to disclose the animal's secret, nor did I desire to embitter my child's existence by destroying her good opinion of her favourite. So I said nothing, but made an excuse to leave the room early, and walked down to my study, much less certain than before that the gift of the Fairy would be so wholly productive of pleasure as I had anticipated.

When a delusion is pleasant, it is not always desirable to have it dispelled; and having held the views which I have expressed with respect to the mutual relations between man and the other animals, I began to doubt whether I was not rather happier before I found that I had been to some extent mistaken. I smoked one cigarette while I thought this, and then I remembered that, after all, I had heard the opinions of very few animals, and that it was very possible that a wider experience and longer trial of my new power might result differently.

So I consoled myself for what had passed, and was not annoyed by the expressions of impatience and anger which now proceeded from a bee who had got shut into the room, and, whilst buzzing against the window-panes in hopeless efforts to get out, vented, in language now perfectly intelligible to me, his wrath against man and his doings, especially as concerned the making of windows and consequent illegal detention of insects who were desirous of going about their daily work. So the afternoon passed, and I occupied myself in reading and writing until I thought I had earned a little fresh air.

Then I walked through the folding-doors of my room on to the gravel-walk in front, and took a turn in the shrubberies, finally sitting down in a shady spot to give myself up to that calm enjoyment which insensibly steals over one at such moments. The weather was much milder now than on that morning when I had had my adventure with the hare. One of those sudden changes had occurred which make the climate of England at once so pleasant and so dangerous to persons of weak constitutions. The snow and frost had disappeared, the wind had got round to the south, the sun was shining brightly, and it was warm enough to sit with comfort upon the garden chair which I had with me. So down I sat, and listened to all the cheery sounds in which I had so often rejoiced before.

Hark to that blackbird. He is singing, doubtless, to his tender mate whilst she sits upon her eggs in the nest below, and listens to his melodious voice with grateful delight. At least, this has always been my idea of a blackbird's song at this time of year. No! What is the rascal saying? Just listen:

"Sit tight, Mrs. Blacky. If you leave those eggs before I give you leave, I'll peck your eyes out! I fancy I've got a good deal the best of it up here, ma'am, but don't *you* complain. Just you do your duty, or you'll hear more of it by-and-by. Don't imagine that I'm singing here for *your* sake. Not a bit of it. I'm singing partly because I like it, and partly because I've got nothing better to do. How I wish the fruit was ripe! Then I could go and enjoy myself, whilst you watched the nest, which is the duty of a hen-bird."

I listened with perfect horror. Was the fidelity of the bird, then, only a romantic invention of some fanciful mortal? Was neglect and ill-treatment of wives as common among birds as among men? Did my ears deceive me? Again, and this time more strongly than ever, did I doubt the value of the Fairy's gift, and felt a sense of sadness spring up within my heart.

At this moment, however, the clear notes of the robin broke upon my ear, and looking in the direction from which they appeared to proceed, I saw the songster sitting upon a thorn-tree near the billiard-room window. I smiled to myself with a comfortable feeling that now at least I was about to enjoy to the utmost the privilege which I had acquired. From this bird, the pious fervour of whose feelings has so long been celebrated, and whose affection towards mankind has been so frequently proved, I should certainly hear something which would elevate my soul from all the littleness of earth, and teach me what beauty was ever to be found in simple purity, such as would doubtless be expressed in the religious melody with which robins habitually begin and close each day.

Alas! this, too, was but one more delusion to be roughly dispelled. The robin, contemplating the ivy which grew thickly against the wall at the back of the kitchen, which from his position he could well see, thus sang his song—for

I really cannot term it an "evening hymn," though that is the designation commonly applied to a robin's effusion at this particular time of day :

"Very thick the ivy looks : yes, but though I have built my nest there for three years running, I have not found it safe. Right enough it was the first year, but the second I was grossly deceived by the weather, and the nest filled with snow and the eggs spoiled just before my mate was going to sit. Then, last year, a confounded boy came and took the nest, eggs and all. I have began to build once again now ; but the weather is horribly uncertain. It really isn't fair upon a bird. I wish it was warm, so that the currants would get ripe. I do love to steal currants. When there is snow on the ground, it is quite true that those fools of people in the house are obliged to throw out crumbs for me, but they are a lazy set, and don't do it often enough. I don't think much of them, and should never trust myself near them, only that many of them have an absurd prejudice against killing a robin, and that is the only reason why I feel safe. They are a horrid set, though, and keep cats who have no more respect for a robin than for a common sparrow—I don't think much of people who do *that*— brutes ! "

"What ! " thought I to myself, as I listened to these words with as much pain as surprise : "Can it then be that I have been deceived in the robin also ? The partridge, the woodpigeon, the dog, the cat, and the blackbird have all belied my expectations, but now that the robin does the same, my cup of sorrow is full indeed."

With these words I turned away heavily to the house, having risen from my chair, utterly bewildered and dis- appointed at the sentiments of the robin. He had shown no gratitude either to Providence or man, abusing the weather in an irreverent manner, and evidently holding the human race in supreme contempt. By this time I had come to the conclusion that the gift which the Fairy had bestowed upon me had by no means added to my happiness. I was contented and satisfied when, judging of the meaning of the voices of the different animals only by the intelligence which nature had given me, I affixed to each a certain reasonable meaning and interpretation. Alas ! the reality had produced upon me two disastrous and humiliating effects. It had lowered my opinion of my own intelligence, since I had been so lamentably mistaken in my previous interpretations, and it had also made me think infinitely worse of the whole animal creation, and created in my mind a feeling that there was a great deal more selfishness, ignorance, and ingratitude in the world than I had previously imagined. So I retired to my study, and kept to it for some time, reading and writing, thinking and idling, according as the fancy seized me. I eschewed the society of animals, turned cats and dogs equally out of the room whenever either one or the other essayed to enter it, and made up my mind to see as little of any animal as I could help until I had the opportunity of getting rid of a power which I had already found monstrously disagreeable, and which I devoutly wished that I had never possessed. I began to wish I had never known that the hare was other than a common hare, and I really fear that a thought once or twice *would* creep into my heart that I should have been better off if I had let the stoat work his wicked will upon her without any interference on my part.

It was whilst I was in this frame of mind that a knock came at my door one evening, and upon my bidding the person knocking to come in, an object which I have never before seen presented itself before me. It was the figure of a little man, whom I should take at a guess to have been about two feet and a half in height. His head was large for his body, and was covered with thick and shaggy hair, surmounted by a black hat, which seemed to have been just taken off some scare-crow in the fields. His beard, dishevelled and innocent of a comb for at least a month, hung down over his breast, whilst his face, besmeared with mud and dirt, had not one redeeming feature, the lips being thick and coarse, the nose red and protruding, and the eyes bloodshot and set far back in the head, under heavy and lowering eyebrows. His dress was that of the most ordinary day-labourer, his hands were large and rough, his boots old and clouted, and his whole appearance disreputable and unprepossessing in the extreme.

As soon as this strange creature had entered my room, he advanced a few paces, and then stopping, pulled one of his shaggy locks much after the fashion of a ploughboy saluting the squire or parson of his parish.

"What do you want?" I asked in surprise, "and who are you?"

The little man made a violent effort to speak, showing me at once that he stammered fearfully. Now there are two things in the world which annoy me more than any other two which I can think of at the moment, the one is a deaf man and the other a man who stammers. Not but what I pity both of them immensely; but the first obliges me to exert my throat, which is my weakest part, and exertion of which is trying and painful, whilst the latter causes me an amount of nervous irritation which makes me ong to run away in the contrary direction as soon and as fast as possible. So when this small man began to stammer, and that, too, when, having intruded upon the privacy of my apartment, he had me at a disadvantage, and running away was out of the question, I was very much annoyed and vexed. I felt myself getting angry; I knew I *should* be angry, and it required the greatest effort to preserve my self-control for the short period during which our conversation lasted. That conversation, however, was so interesting, and had such important results, that I must perforce retail it, although I cannot give any adequate, or nearly adequate, idea of the little man's tone and manner, or of the excessive irritation and annoyance which the two together produced in me. To put the matter briefly, my strange visitor informed me that he was none other than the Dwarf Bamplukes, king of the Fen country, and hereditary enemy of the Fairy Kimmelina. He said that (as I must doubtless be aware) it was a most unusual thing for fairies, or witches, or dwarfs, or any other beings of the same kind, to disclose themselves unnecessarily to mankind, or to seek the assistance and co-operation of the latter in managing their own affairs. As, however, this course had been pursued by his enemy, he felt that in justice to himself, as well as to me, he could not do less than pay me a visit, in order to open my eyes to the real character of the Fairy, and, if possible, to enlist my sympathies on his rather than on her side. So far as *he* was concerned, he declared himself to be a person whose interests could never clash with mine, or indeed with those of any other human being. He was content to live in his own fens, miles away from my place, and to govern his own people after his own fashion. It was hardly necessary to state the grounds of the quarrel between him and the Fairy. It was one of

long standing, and arose entirely from her imperious temper
and habit of constantly interfering with other people's business.   But what he wished particularly to call my attention
to was the entire want of any common interest between the
Fairy and myself.   Her proper shape was that of a hare,
and she ought to be nothing else.   But what was a hare?
One of the most destructive animals to young wheat and
young plantations that we have in this country; a wasteful
animal, too, that spoiled more than it wanted to eat, and
was really a positive enemy to civilization.   Now would it
not be well either to extirpate such animals, or, at least,
greatly to reduce their numbers?   In accordance with this
view, he confessed that he had endeavoured to destroy a
fairy who patronized these noxious animals, and he could
not but think that it was as much or more for my interest
as for his own to accomplish this.

He did not venture to blame me for having saved her life.
I had acted from a generous impulse (the little chap knew
how to flatter), and he might have done the same under
similar circumstances.   But now that I knew all, were not
my sympathies really with him?   What reward had the
Fairy given me in return for the services which I had
rendered her?   He put it to me, whether it had been the
slightest advantage to me to understand the language of
those with whom, in the order of nature, it was never intended that I should converse upon equal terms, or, indeed,
upon any terms at all; and he asked me plainly if I did
not think those must be wrong who attempted to invert
that order, and to effect a complete and radical change in
the relations which had hitherto existed between man and
the inferior animals.

I confess that I was somewhat staggered by the clearness

and cogency of the little man's remarks, albeit that his stammer deprived them of some of their force. I therefore paused a few seconds to consider my reply, and then, without committing myself upon one side or upon the other, calmly asked what it was which he wished me to do.

He replied at once, that he should like me to form an alliance, offensive and defensive, with him, and endeavour to get rid of the Fairy once for all. I expressed some doubt as to the desirability for either of us of such an arrangement ; and further said, that even if we established friendly relations, and took the same view of hares generally as that which he had expressed, I did not see what there was to be done of a practical nature.

As soon as I had said this, my visitor put on a look of inexpressible cunning, and went on to develop his plan. He said that what he desired of me was this—That I should patiently await the next communication from the Fairy, which would, without doubt, be made when the time approached for her temporary resumption of the form of a hare, and her consequent exposure to his attacks. He proposed that I should receive her communication with apparent friendliness, and show every readiness to concert plans with her whereby his machinations might be defeated. Meanwhile, I should in reality have a secret understanding with him, in accordance with which I should inform him of these plans, and, at a time to be agreed upon between us, should deliver her into his hands, so that he might make an end of her for ever.

This proposal the Dwarf made to me with the utmost calmness, as if such vile and odious treachery as it contemplated on my part were an every day occurrence with him, and there was nothing either unusual or abominable about it. His manner, no less than his words, threw me into a tremendous passion.

"Contemptible wretch!" I cried, boiling over with indignation. "How is it that you dare propose to me such a nefarious project? Are you not ashamed even to harbour within your breast, much more to express in words, a scheme so utterly repugnant to any person possessed of the most ordinary feelings of self-respect? What! Win a poor creature's confidence—and that creature a lady, too!—by pretending friendship, when your real object is to destroy her? What is there in my countenance or appearance which could lead you to suppose it possible that I could be guilty of such cruelty and so great a crime? No! Never will I be a party to such wickedness!"

As I spoke, the little man's face fell at first, but before I had concluded, an expression of fiendish malignity stole over it; and I had scarcely finished before he again addressed me—

"There is no need," said he, "of so much violence. I have only proposed to you what one landed proprietor may fairly enough propose to another, namely, to join him in getting rid of vermin which injure the property of both. If you prefer having your shrubs destroyed, and the young shoots of your choicest trees nipped off, it is certainly no affair of mine, though I confess that I think you have a somewhat singular taste. But think once again. Whatever may be the merits of the quarrel between the Fairy and myself, there can be no doubt that it is she, and not I, whose interests are opposed to your own. If you aid me as I propose, not only will your plants and shrubs be secure, but I promise you that all things shall go well with your farm and flock. No mischief that I can prevent shall occur to you ; and you little know how much is done by my little men at night to those who are my enemies. There shall be no stealing of your fruit and garden produce ; your hens shall hatch their chickens safely ; your ducks waddle about in perfect security ; your sheep shall do better than they have ever done before ; and general prosperity shall rest upon all that belongs to you."

I listened to these words with some surprise, as I had no idea that dwarfs were responsible for the sort of damage to property alluded to by the speaker ; but I could not get over the indignation caused by his first suggestion, that I should employ foul treachery against the hare, nor was that sentiment diminished by this barefaced attempt to secure my compliance by bribery. So I scarcely let him finish before I broke forth again—

"You impudent little scoundrel!" I shouted ; "how dare you offer me bribes to induce me to join you in your shameful schemes? This only makes matters worse, and confirms me in the belief that you have been wrong from beginning to end in your quarrel with the Fairy. I will have no more to do with you, and want none of your aid. Hence! Begone! Darken my doors no more with your hateful presence!"

The little wretch scowled frightfully upon me as I pronounced these words.

"What fools men are!" he hissed out between his clenched teeth. "You are like the rest of them, I see, and are not to be convinced by reason. But since you decline my alliance, and elect to take part with my enemies, look out for the consequences. See how your lambing will go on this year. Watch your hens and ducks, your pears and apples, and all the portable property about your place. No one ever yet offended Bamplukes without suffering for it. I can promise you that you shall be no exception to the rule; and the Fairy shall not escape me after all."

So saying, the Dwarf turned on his heel and made for the door, having reached which, he wheeled round, made one of the most frightful grimaces which I have ever seen, spat contemptuously in my direction, and shambled off, leaving me in as great a passion as I had been for several years past.

After a while, however, I cooled down, and, on considering the matter, was satisfied that I had acted rightly in rejecting the advances of the little man, and consoled myself with the reflection that although I had probably made him my mortal enemy for life, his power of injuring me was doubtless limited; and I had only his own word for it that he had any such power at all. I was rather horrified, it is true, at finding my yard-dog dead in his kennel, apparently poisoned, a couple of hours after the Dwarf had left; and, as the latter must have passed close to the kennel on his way out, the thought came across me that he might have had a hand in it. I dismissed the idea, however, after further consideration, set the black deed down as the work of some tramp or travelling tinker, whom the dog might have annoyed, and thought no more about the Dwarf or his threats.

But the next few months gave me serious cause for uneasiness. My lambing had begun well, and I had been in good spirits about my farming prospects generally. Somehow or other, things now began to go wrong. I lost a larger number, both of ewes and lambs, than I had ever done before; I had more barren sheep than common, and the lambs were decidedly less fine and more feeble than usual. Then I lost a valuable cow, one of my carriage-horses fell lame, and the old donkey died, which had been for twenty years about the place, and was consequently valued as an old friend. As for the ducks and chickens, there never was anything like it. So many rotten eggs were never known, I should think, since the days when tithe used to be taken "in kind." Then, indeed, when the parson was unpopular and strict, and the farmers' wives had to lay out their eggs to be "tithed," I have heard that it was perfectly marvellous how often the tenth egg was rotten; but since that time I am sure there had been nothing like it in any farmyard or poultry-house until this time of which I write. When the chickens were hatched, too, they came out such little puny things as you never saw, and the extraordinary number which were carried off by rats was perfectly astounding. We *had* no rats, we thought, and I firmly believe, on looking back, that the work of destruction was not performed by ordinary rats, but by dwarfs. I know that the yard-man, who understood the rearing of poultry thoroughly, could not account for the loss we sustained at this time by any ordinary method of reasoning. The season had been unusually healthy, no rats were ever seen, and although the worthy man knew nothing of the Dwarf's threats, I am sure that he suspected that a witch, or evil creature of some kind, was spiting him or me, or both of us, and that no care or attention on his part could prevent the mischief. The latter was not confined to the poultry-yard, but prevailed also in the garden depart-ment, where things went on in a most uncomfortable manner. The wall-fruit was for the most part nipped by an untimely frost, although indeed this event was, I am sorry to say, of no such rare occurrence as to require that we should attribute it to supernatural agencies. But as the summer advanced other things went wrong.

Never did the currants and raspberries disappear in such quantities, the cherries failed, the pears suffered from hand-blight, as the saying is, in an unexampled degree, and the hand that plucked them could never be detected. Then the potatoes rotted, the cabbages had no heart, the onions lost their flavour, and the very carrots were bad and insipid. I never had such a bad season, before or since, and it was only too evident to me that malicious influences were at work.

So things continued for some time, and meanwhile I received no news of any kind from my friend the Fairy, which I felt the more, inasmuch as I could not help being conscious of the fact that, but for my loyalty to her, I should in all probability have had a much more prosperous year. I must say for myself, however, that I never repented having acted as I did towards the Dwarf, and often thought to myself that I should do just the same if the scene had to be played over again. I only hesitated once in this opinion, and that was when our favourite old collie, Jock, was run over by the express train and killed on the spot. To have saved this old friend, I felt that I could almost have tried to conciliate the Dwarf; but then I had, after all, no evidence to connect the latter with the accident, and if dogs will wander, and get upon railway-lines where they have no business, of course evil consequences are likely to ensue. So, upon the whole, I felt satisfied that I had acted rightly, and bore all my misfortunes with the best grace I could.

Months rolled on; the hot sun of summer had been mellowed by the autumn mildness, and this again had given way to the cold of winter. The shooting-season was in full swing, and ever and anon I was asked to shoot with some one or other of my neighbours. This caused me some difficulty. As far as my own estate was concerned, I was able to avoid the chance of injuring my fairy friend by avoiding the slaughter of hares, which I did under the pretence of leaving them for the harriers. But my neighbours, having no such reason, and wishing to swell their "bag" by the addition thereto of as many hares as could be shot, it would have been impossible for me to refrain from firing upon these animals, if I had joined the various shooting-parties to which I was invited. I therefore made up my mind to decline all such invitations, and thus forego a pastime of which I was exceedingly fond. I kept, however, to my determination, and lost several good days' sport in consequence.

So time passed on; until spring again dawned upon the world, and nature began once more to revive from the deadening influences of the winter frosts.

I have omitted to mention that, during the whole of this time, I had continued in the possession of the privilege bestowed upon me by the Fairy, and, to tell the truth, had become heartily tired of it.

As I sat alone in my study of an evening, the uncomplimentary whisperings of the mice were anything but agreeable. They spoke as if the house had been built for them and for no one else, and made remarks upon the impropriety of my allowing cats to be on the premises, which I thought impertinent in the extreme.

No less so was the twittering of the sparrows on the roof, when rightly understood, and I was excessively annoyed when I discovered that what is called the "homely cawing" of the rooks really consists for the most part in idle vaunts of the superiority of rookdom over the condition of human beings, and fierce denunciations of the rook-shooting habits of some of the latter.

In fact, it was not only the disagreeable sensation of discovering the ill-will towards one's race which was entertained by many creatures from whom one had expected an opposite sentiment, but there was also considerable discomfort in being no longer able to listen to the song of the birds, as music which lulled one's senses and soothed one's feelings, but in being compelled to detect in every note a meaning, and being forced to exercise one's brain in thinking over—often with surprise and regret—the sense and intention conveyed by the singer.

The privilege was one with which I would gladly have parted long before the time came round when I was likely to see the Fairy again, and although I became used to it after a fashion, I own that I never quite got over the unpleasant sensation of being criticised by my domestic animals, and occasionally sneered at by the very mouse which fed upon my crumbs.

At last, one fine morning I went out as usual and took my favourite course round the new gravel walk. I went all round it from the eastern end, along the southern side, through the higher plantation with the oak seat in the middle, and so to the wood at the north-western end, joining the shrubberies at that point.

It was a bright, fresh morning, and I felt remarkably well and cheerful, as one frequently does under the influence of genial weather. At the moment, I think, I had forgotten the misfortunes which had annoyed me throughout the year, and was really oblivious of the existence either of my friendly Fairy or the hideous Dwarf. Suddenly the latter stood before me; he stepped from behind a holly bush as if he had sprung out of the ground, and stood a few yards off, looking quite as ugly as at our previous interview, and wearing no more friendly expression upon his repulsive countenance.

" Well," said he, in the same harsh tone of voice as that in which he had formerly addressed me, " have you repented of your folly yet? How have you prospered since you rejected my proffered alliance? Have your dogs, cows, horses and sheep done as well as usual? Has the crop of fruit been good? Have the hens laid good eggs? Has there been any trouble with the vegetables? You despised my power when we last met, have you learned better now? If so, it is not too late to repent. I will give you another chance. The day after to-morrow it will be useless to ask me. To-morrow the pig of a Fairy takes again the shape of a hare. It will go hard but that I get hold of her before the month is out, but as I do not want to have more trouble about it than I can help, I will still accept your aid, if you will give it, and will pay well for it into the bargain. All your affairs shall assuredly prosper during the coming year as much as they have done the reverse during the past, if you will only consent to let bygones be bygones and agree to my proposal."

As the Dwarf spoke, swift thoughts chased themselves through my brain, one after the other. Although my readers may doubt it, in truth I am not quite a fool, as it struck me very forcibly that in coming to me again this second time, and pressing me so strongly, after the decided refusal I had previously given him, and that in no very civil language, the little man must have some powerful motive of which I knew nothing.

Whether he had done his uttermost against me, and, being unable to do more, thought he would now try another tack, or whether his power of injuring the Fairy was nearly exhausted, I could not tell, but felt certain there was *something* behind. However, I had but one answer to give, and I gave it, more calmly than before, but in a tone equally determined.

"Sir," I said (for I deemed it well to be respectful to a person who had shown his power to injure me, and felt that perhaps I had increased his desire to do so during the past year by the strong language I had applied to him when so enraged by his first advances), "sir, I am not to be tempted from a course which I believe to be right, either by threats or promises. I know nothing of your quarrel with the Fairy Kimmelina, and do not consider it any business of mine to pronounce an opinion upon it. But when you ask me to betray a lady, that is a thing which I never have done and never will do, and although you may be able to injure me for doing my duty, I hope you will be unable to make me swerve from it."

At this speech the Dwarf bit his lips and scowled hideously.

"Do you know," he replied, "that what I have done to injure you hitherto has been nothing to what I can and will do if you persist in being my enemy? I can lay poison for your dogs; I can ruin your sheep; I can give foot-and-mouth disease to your cows; I can make your garden as unproductive as it has heretofore been the reverse, and I can destroy all the hopes of your poultry-yard. Do not be such a besotted idiot as to tempt me to do all this, when, despite the ungracious manner in which you have treated me so far, I am still ready to be your friend, in return for the small service which I ask of you."

The pertinacity of the little man began to annoy me, and I was still more hurt at the low estimate which he had apparently formed, both of my firmness and morality, since he still imagined that he could win me over to his wicked purpose. I regarded him fixedly while he spoke, and, in his fidgety manner and the earnestness with which he pressed his point, I felt more than ever certain that there was something more in it than met the eye.

" It is useless," I replied, "for you to persist in making to me a request with which honour and good feeling alike forbid me to comply. Your continuing to do so, however, convinces me that you must have some other reason than that which you put forward. What is it? I believe that you cannot hurt the Fairy without my aid (which you certainly will not have), or that she is about to have power over *you* unless you obtain some assistance from a human being."

At these words the Dwarf's face became perceptibly agitated, and he stammered more than ever, as he protested that I was entirely mistaken.

"Do you think for a moment," he said, "that such a pig as the Fairy Kimmelina can ever have power over *me*, except under circumstances that are never likely to occur. No, no. Her power expires to-morrow for a month, and until to-morrow is but a short time. She is many leagues away now, for she is not bound to take the hare's shape until after twelve o'clock to-night, and as it is here that she is to take it, you may depend upon it she will not be here until the very last moment."

"Do not be too sure of that!" said a clear little voice like a crystal bell, which just then sounded close by, and, looking round, I perceived a little figure standing by the side of a small yew-tree, in which I instantly recognised my fairy friend.

She looked steadily at Bamplukes as she spoke, and never in all my life did I witness such an effect upon any human being, as that produced upon him by her appearance and look. His face assumed an ashy paleness; his teeth chattered in his head; his arms fell, limp and loose, by his side; his legs appeared to give way under him; and he seemed ready to sink with horror and affright. A low moan broke from his lips, and he made a movement as if to get away, but the Fairy simply waved her hand, and he remained motionless. Then Kimmelina turned to me.

"Kind and trusty friend," she said (and I felt a burst of pleasure mantling on my cheek as I was thus addressed), "I see that I was not wrong in the judgment which I formed of your character when I first saw you, and since you have indeed proved yourself in every way worthy of the confidence which I reposed in you, it is due to you to let you know the exact position of affairs now, and the circumstances under which we meet. This wretch" (and here she cast a look of deadly hate at the shivering Dwarf) "has told you a part of the truth, but such part only as he deemed it desirable that you should know, in order that he might the better tempt you to join in his wicked and detestable schemes. It is quite true that at dawn of day to-morrow, had he come upon me as he hoped, he would have had me in his power. I am thankful to say this danger is now past for ever, and the villain has completely outwitted himself. He knew that your friendship and allaince with me would have been a great hindrance to his wicked designs, because I should have asked you to place me during the next month in a place secured by charms of which I should have told you, against the inroads of witch, dwarf, or demon of any kind. Such charms can be obtained by human beings, but by them alone, and when used as I should have directed you, my safety would have been secured and his vengeance baulked for the coming month. Moreover, after two more months of taking a hare's shape, in the two next years, I should have served my time in that capacity, and should either have been allowed by our laws to retain my own form altogether, or for a few years longer, to assume for a short period the shape of any animal which I might choose. Of course, I should have chosen one with fewer enemies, and less likely to be hurt, than a hare, and thus the wretch Bamplukes would again have been foiled. It was, therefore, an immense object with him to secure your alliance at all hazards, so as to accomplish his wicked purpose before it should be too late. For this purpose he ran a great risk in coming here to-day. He has not only no power in this part of the country, but my power over him is entire and unlimited, save only during the months in which I am a hare. Had he waited till to-morrow, he feared I should be safe with you. Therefore he ventured here to-day, and has, of his own act, delivered himself into my hands—and he knows it ! "

The Fairy turned round in triumph as she uttered these words in an exulting tone, and the unhappy Dwarf sank all in a heap upon the ground.

" Oh, dear Fairy ! " he mumbled out, as he tried to creep towards the spot on which we were standing, " oh, sweet, beautiful, kind, good, charming Fairy, have pity upon a miserable wretch who owns that he is not good enough to kiss the ground you walk upon!"

"He does, does he?" replied the Fairy with bitter irony, "does he think he is good enough to be whipped to death with stinging-nettles by the little elves of the wood?"

"Oh no! oh no! oh, *please* don't say so," roared the terrified Dwarf, half-distracted with fear as the arbitress of his fate hinted at this unpleasant sentence. "Oh, spare me, beautiful queen, no one who is so lovely as you can possibly be so cruel! Let me kiss your feet, and humble myself in whatever way you please. I am your slave. I own it. I repent of all my sins—indeed I do—oh mercy, pray mercy!" and he raised his voice in a kind of half-whine and half-howl, which was inexpressibly ludicrous.

The Fairy, however, maintained the same tone, and seemed in no degree moved by his prayers and entreaties.

"Perhaps," she said, even more bitterly than before, "since you object to the doom which I suggested, you would prefer being boiled to death in vinegar, tied up in a sack full of vipers, or eaten alive by rats. You can have your choice of these three methods of ending your days."

The wretch rolled upon the ground and groaned in abject misery as Kimmelina spoke.

"I wish," she continued, musingly, "that I knew the precise fate which he had intended for me, in order that I might deal out the same to him, which would be in accordance with the ancient laws and traditions of Fairyland. Speak, wretch!" she added, spurning the prostrate Bamplukes with her foot, "say what you had intended to do with me, had Fate placed me in your power."

The poor wretch could make no reply, but moaned out again—

"Oh, lovely Fairy! oh, great Fairy! oh, glorious Kimmelina!"

"Ha!" said the latter, "this is a wonderful alteration from the words I overheard just now—'Pig of a Fairy!' I think it was. 'Pig,' indeed! And now a happy thought strikes me, sir," she continued, turning to me;—"I noticed just now that a look came over your countenance as I was threatening this little monster, which I interpreted to mean that you thought I was too cruel in my intention of putting him to a terrible and painful death. It may be so, although I think he has certainly deserved it. But a happy thought has just entered my head, the following up of which, while it rids me of my enemy, will, at the same time, relieve me from the imputation of having acted with any unnecessary cruelty. Bamplukes, you are, as you are well aware, wholly and absolutely in my power at this moment. I can jump upon you, kick you, beat you, torture you, nay, kill you, without your being able to escape. Well, I will do none of these things. But since you have called me a pig, I will give others a right to call you the same. Not, however, a good, respectable farmyard pig, from which Kentish pork or Hampshire bacon can be made; not an animal whose feet and ears, properly dressed, may delight the epicure; whose liver and crow may make the farmer relish his breakfast, and whose boiled leg may furnish a delightful dinner to the family. No, no; I will not allow you to be anything so often praised by mortals as that worthy animal. A hedgehog shall you be, and as such drag out the remainder of your miserable existence. Pursued by terriers, thrown into water by boys, suspected and persecuted with dire perseverance by gamekeepers, you and your race shall have no rest nor peace from this moment."

As Kimmelina spoke, she waved her wand over the wretched Dwarf, who was vainly endeavouring to interrupt her with renewed praises of her beauty and power intermixed with the most piteous supplications for mercy. As she concluded, he burst into a frantic yell of misery and anguish, which died away in a sound which appeared to me to be something between a squeak and a grunt.

In the very moment that the Fairy waved her wand, a sudden and fearful change came over the features, form, and appearance of the miserable Bamplukes. His hair, clothes, and boots fell off, sharp bristles came out all over him, his nose changed into a regular pig's snout, and in another instant he stood or rather sat before us a veritable hedgehog. Kimmelina contemptuously kicked him aside, and as she did so, pronounced over him some cabalistic words which, as she informed me, would infallibly prevent his ever taking any other shape than that which he now had, unless two Christmas days should happen to come together, or a whole school of boys decline to have any midsummer holidays. As neither of these contingencies, so far as I could judge from my limited knowledge of the world, were at all likely to occur, it seemed to me that the Dwarf had very little chance of being ever again in a condition to do any harm either to the Fairy or to myself.

I confess I felt some pity for the wretch who had had to undergo so terrible a punishment as was involved in this transformation; but an innate feeling of satisfaction arose and prevailed within my heart, as I recollected that now his powers of doing mischief were removed, my poultry-yard might be expected to prosper again, my sheep would be healthy and lambs numerous as before, and my garden would be no more exposed to the blighting influence from which it had suffered so much.

So I turned to the Fairy with the feeling that she had really rendered me a service as well as herself, and congratulated her very sincerely upon the result of the whole affair. She, on her side, thanked me warmly for the part which I had played throughout the business, and offered, by way of an additional recompense for my services, to enable me to understand what the wind said when it whistled through the keyholes, when it softly agitated the leaves with a light gentle breeze, and when it roared through the top of the high elms, and rocked them to and fro with the violence of its blasts.

"My dear Fairy," I said, in a voice of earnest entreaty, "I must beg you on no account to give me any such power as that which you mention. Do not think me ungrateful when I tell you that I very much regret that you ever gave me the power of understanding the language of the animals. I have been cruelly undeceived in my previous notions concerning several of them, and I am sorry for it. I would far rather not know what the winds say. When they blow from the south they are generally so soft and agreeable that no words are required to make their presence welcome; when they come from the west they mean rain, but pleasant and timely rain, and this I know without their telling me so; the north wind is an honest, homely fellow, against whom I button my great coat, and feel that I understand him, as well as if he told me he meant snow and cold; and as for the east wind, the less conversation I ever have with him the better I shall be pleased. I know he means to injure me if he can. He generally gives me a sore-throat, face-ache, rheumatism, or something of the kind; and it would not be the slightest satisfaction for me to know that he rejoiced in doing so, or to understand that he was threatening me when he blew his bitter blast."

The Fairy laughed as I told her this, and at once offered to withdraw from me the power of understanding the animals, to which I readily assented. Nor have I ever repented the step which I then took. Now again I can hear the chirrup of the partridge, the cooing of the pigeon, the cheerful song of the blackbird, and the notes of all the other songsters of the grove, and listen to them with the same delight I had before that fatal power was bestowed upon me. Indeed, I love to make myself believe that I was mistaken in the interpretation which I put upon their words; and that, after all, their feelings towards mankind are really more in accordance with that love and friendliness which I myself cherish for *them*. But the gracious Kimmelina did not leave me without further conversation.

She apologized very much for having left me for so long a time exposed to the petty persecutions of the Dwarf, and explained that nothing but dire necessity had induced her to do so. For the future, however, she promised that she would herself watch over my household, farmyard, and garden, making the well-doing and prosperity of every department her own peculiar and especial charge. We had a long and pleasant talk together, and she told me many things about Fairies and Fairyland which I never knew before and had never even suspected.

Some of these I shall probably tell to my friends before very long, but I cannot say anything more about them just now, partly because they do not properly belong to this story, and partly because the dressing-bell has just rung, and if I am late for dinner, the Fairies that sit around me at that meal will want to know the reason why; and, although they cannot change me into a hedgehog for this or any other shortcoming on my part, yet none the less do I feel a desire to avoid giving them any offence, and therefore I will leave off at once, and postpone until another time the wonderful stories told me by the Fairy Kimmelina.

THE HISTORY OF A CAT.

"DROWN 'em all, say I," were the first words which greeted my infant ears, and I think it will be allowed that they were not calculated to make my first impressions of the new world into which I had entered as agreeable as might have been the case. Fortunately for me, I did not understand them, and they therefore made no difference whatever to my feelings upon the interesting occasion.

I was one of four kittens, the children of an eminently respectable cat of a superior breed, who resided in a large and convenient house in one of the southern counties of England, which was of course claimed as their own by some of that human race who fancy that the whole world is theirs, and was created for their pleasure; but which in reality belonged to my mother, who enjoyed all its advantages, whilst the people who thought it was theirs kept it in repair for her, paid the rates and taxes, and maintained an establishment, apparently to serve *them*, but in reality to provide, from the remnants of their meals, food for the dogs and cats belonging to the place, and principally for my mother, the acknowledged queen of the cats aforesaid.

I was born on a fine spring morning, in an outhouse belonging to the mansion which I have already mentioned; and the ominous words which fell upon my ears must have been spoken before I had been many hours in the world. They proceeded from the lips of Joe Dennis, one of the under-gardeners, who, being but a boy, was naturally fond of sport, and had that mistaken notion about it which leads a certain class of people to think that sport consists in killing inoffensive creatures.

That, at least, is the only excuse I can make for his brutal speech; I do not think he was guided by any desire to reduce the number of cats on the premises; I do not believe that he cherished any animosity towards our race in particular: it was merely the transient idea that it would be sport to see us all drown, and for the momentary gratification of this idle and passing fancy he would readily have put an end to the existence, scarcely yet begun, of four innocent creatures.

Happily for us, however, such wholesale murders were not tolerated in the civilized community into which we had been born. A softer voice replied, in sweet and touching accents—

"Oh, no, Joe! that wouldn't never do, not to drown all the pretty innocents. Whatever would Miss Mary say, I wonder? Such dear little things, too!"

This voice, as I afterwards discovered, proceeded from Ellen, the kitchen-maid; and it was succeeded by one who evidently had more authority than the previous speaker, and who turned out to be Baker, the yard-man, who had the general control of the various out-houses about the premises, and under whose care were the cows, pigs, and other creatures which submit to the authority of man.

"It wouldn't do to drown 'em yet," he said; "not till Miss Mary has seen 'em; and then I think, if we was to get rid of two, and keep two, that would be about the best job."

The start which my mother gave on hearing this proposal with respect to her beloved offspring was attended with certain results which it is well to chronicle, inasmuch as I shall thereby show what great events may be produced by causes apparently small and trivial. In her start of indignant surprise at hearing half her young family doomed to destruction, she caught her fore-paw in the ear of the kitten next her, and tore it so that it hung down on one side: now this kitten, my baby brother, and I, were exactly alike—a kind of beautifully marked tortoise-shell like our mother; another of us was black; and the fourth a peculiarly lovely kitten of an indescribable colour, not unlike my brother and me, but somewhat darker.

So when Miss Mary came to see us next day, she fixed upon this kitten directly as one to be saved, and then said—

"One of the other tortoise-shell kittens, please, Baker; I think they are the prettiest."

And as soon as she had gone away, and Baker, taking the opportunity of my mother's momentary absence, came to carry off two of us to our doom; he took up the black kitten first, and me, luckless me, next. Something, however, prompted him to look again before he made his final choice between the two kittens of similar colour; and on a closer inspection he perceived the wound in my brother's ear.

"This won't turn out so pretty as t'other," he muttered, "along o' that ear—t'other seems all right;" and with these words he replaced me in the straw bed in which we ·

had been lying, and taking up my unhappy brother instead, carried him away to a watery grave.

Young as I was, the incident impressed itself upon my memory; and I think that the narrowness of my escape has had a chastening and sobering effect upon the whole of my future life.

When my mother returned to find that two of her children had been taken from her, I cannot say that she exhibited either as much surprise or regret as I should have expected. Kittens are expensive luxuries to keep, and I suppose she took into account the fact that two would entail upon her less trouble and anxiety than double that number. Besides, it must be borne in mind that this was not her first family; she had more than once gone through the same process, and was not only in some measure used to it, but was a cat of too philosophical a nature to sit down and lament over occurrences which could not be helped, and which no effort of hers could have altered when once they had taken place.

She deemed it right, however, to take measures to prevent, as far as she could, the repetition of kitten-murder in the persons of my remaining sister and myself. That same evening she removed us from the outhouse and the custody of Baker. She was what human beings call "an indoors cat," or, as I should rather say, she favoured the inside of the house with frequent visits, and did not confine herself to those outdoor regions which are inhabited by stable cats, garden cats, and others of a class inferior to that to which she belonged.

The kitchen was one of her favourite haunts, and she was always on the best of terms with the cook, who happened to preside over that department. Now in our kitchen there were a number of large drawers on one side, in one or other of which, according to my judgment, everything one can imagine was kept. At least I have seen the cook take from these drawers such an infinite variety of articles that I find it difficult to believe that there is anything in the world of cookery of which a specimen was *not* there.

But in this great range of drawers there chanced to be a second drawer from the bottom which had at this time only scraps of paper in it, and this my mother selected as our residence for the present. How she persuaded the cook to open it, I do not know, or whether she found it open and took forcible possession. It is, however, a fact that she carried us to this drawer; and that, as it could remain a little bit open without causing any inconvenience to any one, there being plenty of room in that large kitchen, so it was left, and no one ever thought of interrupting us while we remained there. Our mother brought in a soft old slipper, a torn pocket-handkerchief, and two or three other things, which made us a comfortable nest; and there for many days we abode in peace and happiness, passing a pleasant, dozy, dreamy kind of existence, and growing bigger and stronger every day.

As the days swelled into weeks, a change came over us, and we began to find the inside of a drawer too limited an area for our enjoyment. First, we began to stand on our hind legs, and try to peer over the sides at the world beyond: gradually, we got bolder, and attempted to climb up on to the dresser; and after a little while, we managed to descend upon the floor of the kitchen, and soon found ourselves quite at home there.

The kitchen had two doors, one of which led to the interior of the house and the other offices, whilst through the other you passed into the scullery. This was an outside room, although the kitchen wall, the continuance of which formed its back wall, continued still further beyond the house, forming the west side of the kitchen-yard. The north side was occupied by larders; beyond these came a bake-house, and a dairy standing back in a shady angle, beneath some high fir-trees; next came the large gates, through which was the entrance to the yard and back of the house, and from a point just beyond these gates the high kitchen wall ran to the house again, having a large coal-shed built against it, and forming therewith the east side of the yard.

So the pantry door which opened into the yard, faced due east, and thus, whilst completely protected from the wind by the coal-shed and garden wall, had the full benefit of the glorious morning sun, in which we kittens used to revel with delight. Oh, what games of play we have had upon that dear old scullery floor, and upon the stone-paved yard just in front of the door! Our dear mother often joined in those games, although in a somewhat dignified manner, allowing us little ones to run round and round after our tails, to hide in various corners and scramble up into all kinds of queer places, whilst she sat upon the floor watching us with maternal love and interest, and now and then darting at one or the other of us, playfully knocking us over and giving us gentle pats with her soft, velvety paw.

But, oh! to see her if any strange dog wandered into the yard and approached the scullery door during these performances. Her whole demeanour changed, her bristles stood erect, her back went up at once into the form of an arch, and there she remained, her eyeballs glistening like fire and fixed with a threatening gaze on the intruder, whilst a warlike sound of suppressed fury proceeded from her throat, which generally had the desired effect of making the animal against whom her demonstration was made, take himself off in double quick time.

On one occasion I remember a spaniel pup of the most innocent character had followed its master, the eldest boy belonging to the house, from the keeper's lodge; and, entering the yard at his heels in the most unsuspecting manner, approached the scullery door where we kittens chanced to be playing. So engrossed were we in our amusement that we did not perceive the little fellow until he was close upon us. No sooner did my mother catch sight of him than she went through all the form which I have just described, and then, bursting into a fit of spitting in which I had never seen her indulge before, rushed at the puppy with fury, and struck him a sharp blow with her paw. You never saw an animal so taken aback in the whole course of your existence. He positively howled with fright, put his tail between his legs, and fled for dear life. In fact, I do not believe he could ever again be enticed to the scullery door, and I am sure it must have been long before he ventured to look a cat in the face again.

Well, those were childish, happy days which will never return again. This remark, however, is one which applies to every day of a cat's life. No day, childish or not, ever *does* return again; and the wise cat is she who basks in the sunshine whenever there is any to bask in, gets on the hearth-rug when the weather is cold or wet, and strives to make the best of each particular day when it is there to make the best of, instead of waiting till it has passed by for some time, and then regretting it. Regretting the past is very little better than speculating on the future, except it teaches you to avoid mistakes once committed, and to employ present time in a better and more profitable manner than the time which is gone. However, I am not here to moralise, but to relate my history, simple and uneventful as it may be.

The days of scullery play passed away quickly, and the time soon came when our drawer, being required for other purposes, was closed to us. We were driven, I may say, from our early home; which I believe frequently happens to other creatures besides cats, under more or less aggravating circumstances. In our case, we had not much reason to complain. The kitchen was still open to us; we were general favourites, both with the children of the house and also with the servants, upon whose kindness and consideration the happiness of domestic cats and dogs depends not a little; we roamed freely about, and amused ourselves after the ordinary fashion of our race.

I shall never forget my first sparrow. I caught him in front of the house: he was a young bird, lately fledged, or at all events not quick enough in his flight to escape my rapid dart upon him. I have heard people say that we cats are cruel with birds and mice. I don't know how that may be, or what the world calls cruel, but the fun I had with that bird was rare indeed. I knocked him over with my paw so that he should not fly again; then I patted him; then he fluttered and chirped; then I patted him again; and thus I played with him for full five minutes before hunger suggested that I should finish him off, which

I forthwith did, and never was sparrow more tender and delicious.

There were quantities of birds always in our garden: the people of the house did not allow the nests to be taken, in consequence of which the little creatures multiplied considerably, and the place became a first-rate hunting-ground for cats. Starlings built in the chimneys, of which there were a goodly number; for it was a long, low, two-storied, rambling kind of house, only breaking out into a third story here and there, where the necessity for more accommodation for an increasing family, and the greater strength of the walls, tempted its addition.

Not only a rambling, but what I may call a fragmentary house was it, as if several different houses—different in size, shape, and architecture—had been joined together at separate times, so that the effect of the whole was curious, though not otherwise than picturesque. Anyhow, the irregularities of the roof and the number of the chimneys were advantageous in their way; for while the latter tempted starlings and sparrows to build their nests there, the former afforded great facilities for an honest cat desirous of obtaining a meal off the young of the aforesaid birds, and many a fluttering victim have my relations and I secured and enjoyed upon the pleasant gutters and sunny ledges which abounded thereupon.

There was another circumstance connected with this house which rendered it a desirable habitation for cats. It was covered over with ivy to a very considerable extent—so considerable that there was room for a perfect multitude of birds to build and to roost therein; and as there is no better authenticated fact in history than that birds were created purposely, or at least especially, for the benefit of our noble and illustrious race, it is evident that cats were always intended to inhabit this pleasant locality. Established in such quarters as these, I should have been a worthless and ungrateful kitten indeed if I had not been happy. I was so. In fact, I should imagine that a happier kittenhood than mine has seldom been passed by mortal cat.

Under these circumstances it is not by any means a matter of wonder that I grew up sleek and comely, and was a general object of admiration to the human beings who lived in our house, as well as to the other animals who dwelt around; with the exception always of those ill-conditioned and evil-minded dogs, who can never see anything to admire in one of that race which they feel to be so far superior to their own, although a base jealousy forbids them to own it.

The next stage of existence into which my sister and I passed was one of a comparatively trifling importance, had it not accidentally led to a result which certainly could not be so described. We were banished from the house to the yard and outhouses on some foolish pretence or other; and although cats are of course superior to men and women, yet by some means the latter have obtained a temporary ascendancy in this wicked world, and we were unable to resist the decree.

It did not, however, greatly interfere with our enjoyment. The cow-yard was a pleasant and convenient place; there were plenty of birds and mice there, and an occasional rat to afford us diversion by way of variety. Chickens innumerable pervaded the place, but we knew better than to touch them; for they were under the care of our friend Baker, the yard-man, with whom we should have got into terrible disfavour, had we exercised our sporting propensities in this direction. There were large stones, too, with which part of the yard was paved, and which formed splendid basking-places for us, whenever there was sufficient sun to tempt us to engage in this delightful solace of a cat's existence. Moreover, at the end of the cow-lodge, beyond the seven stalls which had been placed there for the accommodation of the cows, there was a large space shut off, in which calves were confined when necessary, and herein was constantly a good supply of straw, in which we could romp to our hearts' content; whilst at the other end there was even a larger space, between the last stall and the door of the lodge nearest the house, in which a variety of articles were stowed, but which still afforded ample space for us to perform all the antics which a kitten could desire. So we were as happy as the day was long, and might so have continued but for the circumstance which I am about to relate.

One fine Sunday afternoon, the Rector of the parish and his wife walked home after church with some of our house people, came in at the back gate, and stood talking near the lodge door. My sister and I had been playing together, and I had left her but for a moment, and was inside the yard watching a young robin who appeared to me too innocent for this world, whilst she remained playing by the door. Now the Rector's wife was a very nice person, so I have heard people say. Of course, *I* don't know, only that she had a pleasant face and voice, and her eyes were as large and beautiful as a cat's. Nice or not, however, there she was on this eventful day, and I heard her say in an admiring tone:

"Oh, what a dear little kitten!"

"Yes," said the voice of the lady who pretends our house is hers. "It is one of Mary's. I told her to give them away, and thought she had done so ; but they do not seem to have got further than the cow-yard."

Then the two ladies laughed, and a little more conversation passed, wherein the Rector's wife said she should like to have a kitten, and the other lady calmly observed that she might have *that* one if she liked. There was no appeal to Mary, and, what was worse, no inquiry as to what might be my sister's own feeling in the matter.

Without more ado, the robber, having coaxed the poor little thing to come to her, seized her in her hand by the scruff of the neck, lifted her from the ground, and, in a word, carried her off before my very eyes, as I sat on the paving-stones of the yard peeping through the open fence which separated it from the lodge. I never was more amazed and more disgusted in my life ! My only playmate, my friend, the companion of my childhood, was thus ruthlessly snatched from me, and I was left to face the world alone. Cats, however, are not sentimental fools, like dogs, nightingales, and human beings. Our lives are regulated by wise maxims and precepts handed down from a long line of illustrious ancestors ; and, among others, there is one which teaches us to submit quietly to that which we cannot avoid. Another wise saying of the ancients enjoins upon each individual cat the propriety of making herself as comfortable as she can under any circumstances in which she may chance to find herself. I found it infinitely more comfortable not to bother myself about my sister's departure, and, therefore, went on just the same ; and though I felt rather lonely for a few hours, the feeling soon passed away, and I did very well without her.

I saw very little of my mother after our banishment from the house, of which she still remained an inmate. She rarely came towards the cow-yard, and seemed to have but little concern for me; whilst, for my part, having seen her with another litter of kittens before I should have thought she could have forgotten her former offspring, I felt my affection for her sensibly diminish, and looked upon her as a being to be rather avoided than sought after. There was no one to dispute my sovereignty over the cow-yard and lodge, although there were others of my race established at no great distance from my domain. Now and then a stable-cat appeared; but the chief resort of our tribe was the garden and the house of the gardener, old Shrimpton, who always had several cats about, and especially one which was popularly reported to have had as many as a hundred and fifty kittens and grand-kittens, and was a personage of almost as much authority and importance in the shrubberies as my mother in the house.

After a very short time I began to get tired of my cow-yard life. Advancing age brought with it new thoughts and associations, and an increasing desire to see the world beyond the gates of our place. I saw the birds fly merrily over the walls and buildings around me, whilst far above my head in the blue sky, I noticed the rooks flying steadily onward, as if for a long journey; and now and then the harsh note of a heron called my attention to the still higher flight of that ungainly bird. All these things showed me that there must be a world outside our domain much larger than I had yet seen, and the desire to make myself acquainted with it became stronger and stronger. I knew there was a large green field just outside the cow-yard, because the great gates of the latter opened into it, and the cows came in and out that way; but hitherto I had never gone further than a yard or two over the threshold of the gates, for there was nothing particular to tempt me, and dogs were very often to be seen in that direction. Also I knew of the high road which ran past the premises at a very short distance from the door at the end of the lodge, but into that I had never yet ventured, remembering how in earlier days my mother used to purr into the ears of us children stories of kittens run over, stolen, worried by dogs, . and meeting with various other melancholy fates, all because they *would* go out into roads without their mothers.

These tales were no doubt told us in order to prevent our straying from the scullery door in our first yard, and they certainly had that good effect. So I knew nothing of the world at all, until the spirit of enterprise became altogether too strong for me, and I felt that I *must* venture forth at any risk. So on one pleasant evening in the summer time I clambered up on to the roof of an unused pig-sty (the pigs having been banished to a locality further off from the house) on to the wall which ran from the cow-lodge to the stables, which formed the south side of my cow-yard, their back being towards it, and their front facing to the south. Along this wall I crept until I came to the gate, which was about midway between cow-lodge and stables, and which had now been closed for the night, so that I had to scramble down it, which I easily did, and found myself in the green meadow outside.

All was still and quiet: a kind of bewitching stillness which was indescribably delightful, and seemed to tempt me on into the night with a magical influence which I had no desire to resist. It was dark, but the moon was beginning to put forth her soft sweet light, which made everything appear more beautiful than in the staring, glaring rays of the sun, which, as I have since learned, are very unfavourable for sporting purposes, although they have their use, no doubt, and make basking delightful. I stole across the meadow until I reached the hedge on the other side, a hedge I had sometimes contemplated with wonder from the cow-yard door; it seemed such a thick, strong hedge, with brambles over it, and lots of blackberries, which tempted children to tear their clothes and scratch their hands in getting them. It was a real, good old-fashioned hedge that, and linnets, chaffinches, hedge-sparrows, and all kinds of birds were to be seen plying their various trades upon it during the day. Now, however, bird-life was hushed, and I heard not so much as the chirp of a solitary sparrow as I crept softly and stealthily along the hedge. Presently, all of a sudden, a swift flapping noise seemed to pass close over my head, and a low but shrill cry smote upon my ear, which, young and inexperienced as I was, filled me with affright, and made me cower down in the grass as if I had seen a dog. But nothing hurt me; and when I ventured to look up, I perceived a large white owl flitting quietly along the meadow on her peaceful journey in search of the mice to whom she looked to furnish her with a supper. I felt quite ashamed of myself for having been so easily alarmed, and determined to be wiser in future.

On I went, and, after a little while, arrived at a hole in the fence, through which some other animal, probably a hare, had evidently been in the habit of creeping. I thought I would do the same; and after performing this feat found myself in another grass field, along which I proceeded, cautiously looking around me, until I arrived at a small hill, upon the face of which I perceived several animals moving, which—from having seen them in the larder at home when the door happened to be open, I knew at once to be rabbits. They were sporting in the moonlight, and among them were some remarkably nice-looking young ones, with whom I longed to make better and closer acquaintance. So I squeezed myself down as close to the ground as I could, and gradually crept nearer and nearer to a corner where some four or five young rabbits were dancing round a hole. They were quite young, and therefore, I suppose, not so cautious as rabbits of a more mature age would have been. At all events I got so near, that I was presently able to spring in suddenly among them.

"Let *me* dance, too!" I cried, and seized the nearest rabbit in my loving paws, whilst the others squeaked and disappeared down the hole. "Now we will dance, my pet," said I, and the rabbit replied; but as he spoke in his own language I am not very sure what he said, and therefore will not hazard a guess. I only know that we *had* a dance certainly, and I hope the young rabbit enjoyed it thoroughly, for I expect it was his last attempt. He *was* a tender young fellow, and I was not a little proud of having done so well on my very first night's hunting.

I did not go home directly after supper, but crept about in the shadow of the hedges, and listened to the noises of the night for some time, until I thought it would be better to return, so that I might be seen in the cow-yard in the morning, and my absence be undiscovered. This I safely accomplished; and you may well believe that the success of this night's adventure encouraged me to try another and another, until it became my usual habit to have an evening ramble by myself. I had very good luck in my hunting, and life in the cow-yard soon began to appear tame and insipid; so that I wondered how so many cats could endure to be confined to houses, stables, and barns, and occupied in the low pursuit of catching the domestic mouse or the casual rat, when such superior amusement was possible, and such far nobler game was within their reach. A warning, however, was ere long given me of the danger which attended my new pleasure.

One evening I had gone out as usual, and had crept along several hedges in the direction of a neighbouring plantation, about which I knew that young rabbits and hares were in the habit of playing in fancied security. It was rather earlier than usual, for I happened to be hungry, and thought I should like a slight repast about sunset, if I could manage to obtain it.

I was not far from the plantation, and already had my eye upon some tender young animals who appeared to be likely to suit my purpose, and towards whom I was about to creep with my usual cunning, little doubting of success. All of a sudden a bright flash shone for an instant between the branches at one particular spot; then came a loud roaring noise, which I have since learned to have been the report of a gun, but which was at that time as strange as it was alarming to me, and the next moment one of the young rabbits rolled over in the agonies of death. The gamekeeper had been hiding to get a shot, and had just secured his victim. Most fortunate was it for me that he had done so, for otherwise, as I was quite unaware of his presence, I should certainly have come within his sight and ken within a very few seconds, when nothing could have saved me from destruction. As it was, I was most terribly frightened indeed : for a moment all the blood seemed to rush from my heart, and I felt as if something horrible must have happened to me. The next instant the sight of the man scrambling over the fence to seize his prey, recalled me to myself, and, without further hesitation, I turned and fled swiftly along the hedge, never stopping until I was far out of gunshot. I then slackened my pace, but continued my course in a homeward direction, and did not breathe freely until I found myself once more safe within my own cow-yard. That night I contented myself with supping off a couple of miserable mice, and so impressed was I with the scene which I had witnessed, and the danger to which I had been exposed, that I vowed within myself that I would henceforth become a reformed character, attend to my home duties like a respectable cat, and leave hedge-prowling and rabbit-hunting to the wilder and less polished of my race.

Good resolutions, however, are but too frequently made only to be broken. Warnings are soon forgotten ; dangers seem less terrible when not actually in sight or near to one ; and the cat who has tasted the flesh of rabbits and sipped the blood of game, can scarcely find herself able to return to the coarser viands afforded by the house and cow-yard preserves. So, before long, I found the temptation too strong for me, and again I sallied forth upon my evening rambles.

The very first night was one of great good fortune, for I stumbled across a fine hare, which had been fool enough to be caught in a wire which some poaching rascals had set in a hedge. Somehow or other the poor wretch had only been caught by the leg instead of the neck ; how she had managed to be so clumsy I cannot tell; but there she was fast enough, with a wire tightly clasped round her leg, in a state of terrible perturbation.

"Dear me, Madam Hare," said I, close in her ear all of a sudden, "you seem very much out of sorts this evening."

She gave a little start and squeak of affright at my address, and made a great spring forward, but was pulled backwards at once by the wire.

"What a hurry you're in," I remarked quietly. "This is hardly neighbourly."

Then she turned her large eyes upon me, liquid with the tears which had been wrung from her by mental and bodily anguish, and implored me by our common catdom to save her. We were of the same race, she alleged, alike called "Puss" by mankind, and having many points of similarity in our bodies, habits, and dispositions. If I would but help her to get herself free from that horrible wire, there would be no end of her gratitude, and she would do anything she could to please me at any time.

Whilst she spoke in these pathetic tones I kept licking my lips in anticipation of my coming feast, and purring meanwhile comfortably to myself, for I had fully made up my mind that she should please me very shortly, although not exactly in the manner which she might herself have preferred. When she had finished I accosted her in a gentle tone, as follows:

"Dear, pretty, *tender* Puss" (and I laid especial emphasis on the word *tender*), "you are mistaken in supposing that I am able, however willing I might be, to set you free. The wire which holds you tight can only be loosened by the hand of man, and that will probably not be until the time

when, after you have been in a state of suffering for many
hours, the person who set it up comes to see what success
he has had. If you wait for that, you will be savagely
knocked on the head, or have your graceful neck ignomini-
ously wrung. How much better then, since, as you say,
we are kith and kin, to gratify one of your relations, as you
are now able to do, and escape from him who has ensnared
you."

The poor creature knew but too well what I meant, and
as I crept closer to her, set up one of those sad cries to
which hares give vent when in pain or distress. This did
not suit me at all, for the sound would soon have brought
either some man or boy, or an animal who might have disputed with me over the prey. Without more ado, therefore, I seized my would-be relative by the throat with
so much affectionate goodwill, that she soon found it
unnecessary to make any more noise, and I kissed her to
death, as I may say, in a very few moments, and purred
a requiem in her ear as she yielded up her last breath in
my loving embrace. I forbear to say more upon this topic,
as the secrets of relations should never be disclosed to
strangers, but I am very much mistaken if the poacher
got much out of that hare when he came to look at his
wires, whilst, for my own part, I felt extremely comfortable and well satisfied, and when I got home, which I
did very soon after supper, I fell asleep, and had a long
nap in the corner of the cow-lodge, awaking in the morning
with only half my usual appetite for breakfast, so good had
been my meal overnight.

The success of my marauding expeditions by night encouraged me to become more and more venturesome.
Very soon I was no longer contented with the hedges

and rabbits' earths, but began to make my way to the
more distant and (though I knew it not) more dangerous
woods.   Up to this time, I had never known the taste
of pheasant or partridge, save, indeed, when any of the
cooked bones of one of these birds had found its way
to me from the kitchen or scullery, and that was very
seldom.

But in one of my rambles I had met a very pleasant
Tom-cat from a neighbouring farm, who had paid me
some attention, and with whom I had exchanged the
experiences of our past lives.   From him I learned that,
although partridge nests were not easy to find, on account of the bird having no scent by which she
might be discovered when sitting upon her eggs, yet the
thing was not impossible, and that by carefully creeping
along the hedges and banks from end to end, in ·places
where the birds were plentiful, there was sometimes sport
to be had.   In the woods, he told me, the fun was even
better, for there were many pheasants' nests where those
gaudy-coloured creatures were preserved, and it was rare
fun to leap in upon one of them when you were lucky
enough to find it.   He said, however, that there was
certainly more danger there than in the open fields, as
keepers were a class of men who would not be prevented
from setting traps, and took altogether a wrong view of
the proper position and privileges of a cat.   Still, a
cautious and clever Puss (such as he kindly insinuated
that I was) would not easily be caught in a trap, and,
after all, the excitement of a little danger increased and
intensified one's pleasure in any hunting excursion.   So
Master Tom offered to show me the way to the woods, and
I readily promised to go with him.

Something or other, however, delayed our visit for some little time. During the early spring it was too early to find a bird in her nest, and there was not much food to be got anywhere away from home. Then, as the summer advanced, I must needs go and have kittens—tiresome little wretches who were speedily drowned, but who prevented my excursion for some weeks later than I had intended and desired. By this time the nesting season was far advanced, and one fine evening, when I had met my friend Tom behind the hay-rick, he proposed that we should go for a real partridge hunt, to which I readily agreed.

Oh, that was indeed a merry ramble which we had together! We crossed one or two fields, keeping in the shadows of the trees and hedges as much as we could, until we arrived at a field which upon one side was fenced in by a real good, old-fashioned, rough hedge, with a good thick bottom of long grass, and thick with brambles and bushes above. Each of us took one side, and we crawled along gently and quietly, carefully looking into each corner and scrutinising every tuft of grass as we passed along. For some time we found nothing to reward our labour, and I got a great shock at one moment when, softly placing my paw upon a lump of leaves before me, I found that I had unwittingly disturbed a large hedgehog, whose bristles were too sharp to be pleasant, and who need not having given the start and grunt which he did, in order to ensure my leaving him to his quiet nook as soon as I could. We had crept on in this manner for some time, when all of a sudden I heard a rush and a flutter on the other side of the hedge, and peering cautiously, but quickly, through, perceived my mate triumphantly stretched upon a partridge whom he had surprised and seized on her nest. She, poor bird, trusting to her scentless condition, and little knowing the sure and systematic manner in which we did our work, had sat perfectly still upon her eggs, no doubt cherishing many hopes as to the young brood which would shortly be hatched, and picturing to herself much future pleasure in their nurture and education. The poor wretch, however, was literally "counting her chickens before they were hatched," for her hopes were never to be realized. In vain she fluttered, gave vent to a cry of misery, and sought to escape from the forepaws of my crafty companion. In vain she begged for mercy, and urged her present condition as one which should secure her from harm, since she would soon give to the world—and to cats among its other inhabitants—a number of birds who, in the lowest point of view, would be useful to us and to other animals, as wholesome and nutritious food. By killing her, indeed, we should be cutting off our own supplies.

Such considerations, however, had no weight with us, and our present need of supper was our first thought. So, in spite of her protestations, we first silenced her with playful pats which effectually prevented her escape, and having comfortably seated ourselves by the side of her nest, proceeded to dispose of her in the manner most congenial to our tastes. We left little of her but the feathers, and however she may have suffered at the moment in the loss of hopes and life together, she may at least have experienced the satisfaction of knowing that she was about to make two honest cats happy.

We enjoyed her thoroughly, and feeling indisposed for further exertion after so hearty a supper, returned to our several homes after an affectionate " good-night." This success so encouraged us both, that it was not long before we made another appointment of the same sort, and sallied forth for a supper-seeking expedition which we hoped would be attended with as pleasant results. As we crossed the first meadow, my companion observed to me that although a partridge was, as we had recently proved, a tender and delicious bird, he had twice tasted the flesh of one which he preferred. "The hen pheasant," he remarked, "is a bird which tastes even better than a partridge in my opinion, and possesses this great advantage, that there is more of her. To tell you the honest truth, I felt the other night that I could have managed another leg and wing, although politeness forbade my saying so. Now a pheasant forms an ample repast for two cats, and is in every respect as nutritious as a partridge."

He then proceeded to inform me that there were many of these birds in the wood which lay nearest to our house, that is to say, within little more than half-a-mile, and suggested that, as we had plenty of time before us, we should go there at once. I readily consented, and we crept as usual along the hedges until we arrived at the wood. Quietly we stole along the dry ditch which encircled it, and presently crawling up the bank, entered the wood underneath the huge root of a tree which stood in the hedge on the top of the bank, and soon found ourselves in a small track, which had been well brushed-out, and which ran near the hedge the whole way with the same, enabling the keeper to pass along on his rounds. We knew well enough that this was no safe place for us to stop in, since keepers are so sly and wicked that one never knows where they may be, and they carry constantly with them their dreadful guns, and think no more of the life of a cat than of that of a common rabbit. So we speedily crossed the track, and buried ourselves in the wood beyond. It was a glorious place. The underwood grew scantily at the particular spot at which we had entered, and thick flags abounded, forming the most suitable places for the nests of the pheasants, and consequently a splendid hunting-ground for us. We stole along very cautiously, peering into the flags and rushes right and left with great care, and feeling confident that the prey we sought could not be far off. Nor were we disappointed in our expectations, for after a few minutes' search, Tom laid his paw on my shoulder, and bade me look into a thicket of brambles and flags intermixed in a strangely wild manner, and asked me in a low whisper whether I saw anything.

I looked as hard as I could, and for an instant failed to discover what it was that he meant. Then, all in a moment, I caught the eye of a hen pheasant, sitting fast on her nest, and apparently looking straight at us. Tom smiled a grim smile at me, and we both withdrew to concert measures. Just beyond the thicket in which the bird sat, was a small ditch, which in wet weather no doubt served to help the drainage of the wood, but which at this season of the year was entirely dry. My companion proposed that he should go round, creep up this ditch, and so get well behind the pheasant, whilst I kept watch in front. Then, whilst the eyes of the bird were steadily fixed upon me, he would suddenly spring upon her, and if by any accident he missed his stroke and she fluttered forward to escape, I should be there, ready to receive her in a close and loving embrace.

The plan appeared to be excellent, and accordingly I took up my position at once, and waited, with a heart beating fast with anxiety, and a mouth already watering at the thought of our coming feast. But all mortal calculations are empty and vain, and whilst I was full of hope and joyful expectation, I was, without in the least suspecting it, upon the eve of a sad misfortune. My dear friend stole round the thicket with his accustomed skill, entered the ditch several yards beyond the thicket, and disappeared from my sight. I knew he was creeping up the ditch, and expected every moment to see him re-appear in the thicket behind the bird. Suddenly there was a kind of sharp click, a rush, and a wild cry of agony from my poor friend, which woke the stillness of the night in a manner awful to the nerves of a female cat. On the impulse of the moment I rushed in the direction of the ditch, and beheld a sight such as I had never seen before, and hope never to see again. In the bottom of that ditch, where the pheasants were never likely to walk, as they would naturally hop over it, but where a fox, cat, stoat, or any other woodland animal would be most likely to creep along if on a hunting excursion, the cruel keepers had with fiendish art concealed a huge steel trap. Full of thoughts of the pheasant whom he hoped to surprise, my poor mate had forgotten the probability of such a wicked act, and whilst stealing along the bottom of the ditch had set his fore paw exactly upon the trap, which had instantly sprung, and enclosed his poor leg in the deadly and cruel grasp of its sharp teeth, crushing the limb sadly, and holding it like a vice. No wonder that the sudden and terrible pain drew forth a yell of anguish, although his sense of the danger he ran was so acute that he gave no second cry, but writhed on the ground in silent agony. Oh, it was a grievous sight to see! But half a minute ago, a young, agile, strong, active fellow he was, as spruce and handsome a Tom-cat as ever mewed upon the leads of a brick house—and now—wounded—bleeding—maimed—he lay in the ditch, a mere wreck of what he had so lately been, and but too evidently destined to a cruel death. I rushed to the edge of the ditch and regarded him with horror and dismay.

"Tom," I said, "my dear Tom, speak to me—come to me—oh dear! what has happened?" He could only moan in reply, and I was about to give way to a transport of grief, when I perceived a fox standing on the other side of the ditch and regarding the scene with a calm look which, I remember thinking at the moment, did not express as much sorrow as I should have expected, seeing that the fate of my companion was one which might with equal probability have been his own.

"Miss Puss," said he, addressing me as coolly as if he had known me all his life—although perhaps this was excusable under the peculiar circumstances of the case—"Miss Puss, if I was in your place I should be off; you can do your friend no good. He has met with a fate which cats must expect if they come into woods, which properly belong to foxes, and to them alone. He has been caught in the keeper's trap, and will be held where he is until the early daylight brings the keeper upon his rounds, who will speedily knock your friend upon the head, if indeed he does not leave it to his dog to settle him, as is sometimes the case. At all events, *you* can do no good here, and I hope this will be a lesson to you to stay quietly at home."

I heard the heartless words of the fox, but was too much overcome with grief and horror to make any reply. I sat on the edge of the ditch in dumb misery, until my poor

THE HISTORY OF A CAT.—p. 243

mate turned his eyes up towards me, and gave vent to a low moan of agony.

"Fly," he said—" fly whilst you can—I am a lost cat!" These were the last words I ever heard him speak, for I felt that what he had said was true, and that not only was he lost, but that I might not improbably share his fate if I remained where I was. So although I was reluctant to leave a friend in distress, I did what any other cat of sense would have done under the circumstances, and fled from the spot as fast as I could lay legs to the ground.

Poor Tom! I never saw him alive again, and I have no doubt the fox's words were true, and that he met with the sad fate which that animal foretold. Indeed, I may say that I am but too certain that such was the case. Some fortnight after this occurrence, having overcome the fears which possessed me for a time, and having a strong desire to taste what the flesh of a pheasant was really like, I sallied forth again on one fine moonlight night, and made my way to the same wood, which I entered at another point. I had not gone far before I came to an open space, in which, among the scattered trees, stood a large oak. I was about to pass near this tree, when the creaking of a branch attracted my attention, and looking round quickly I perceived that the noise was occasioned by the weight which the branch had to carry beyond its natural burden of twigs and leaves, of which indeed it had few or none. But it bore an awful burden nevertheless. Dead stoats, weasels, and other animals which men hate, because they share their own love for game, were hanging from this melancholy limb of the old oak, and I had not to cast a second glance in order to perceive that among the others were several of my own queenly race, and conspicuous among them hung the body of my murdered mate. Regardless of the possible consequences to myself, I uttered a long wail of misery, which was answered in a meet strain by the doleful hoot of an owl from a neighbouring tree.

It had come to this, then! The true, the noble, the tender-hearted Tom-cat, who had been mine own, was hanging, like a common felon, upon the branch above my head. Our brief intercourse had been sweet; our companionship agreeable; our mutual love delightful: but it had come to this. Alas, for the instability of all feline happiness! Nothing can avert doom. When it must fall, it falls with a certainty which no power of cat can resist, and the best and wisest of us must yield to it, as well as the most foolish and simple of our race. Our great and illustrious ancestress, Puss-Cat Mew, lived and died after her splendid and glorious career. Where is she now? Gone—like my poor Tom! and gone—where? This was a terrible reflection.

There was an old white stable-cat once who had a theory that when an honest and good cat died, who had never willingly spared mouse or bird, but had done his or her duty catfully in the world, it was not an entire annihilation of the animal, but that it passed on to another sphere, where cats—no longer oppressed by cruel enemies—dwelt in unmolested happiness, with never-ending supplies of the best cream, and tender mice and young birds as common as blackberries. She went so far as to surmise that our race would, in that new state of existence, be predominant, and that men, dogs, and other inferior beings, would be in our power, and compelled to serve us. I had never thought much about the matter, not being fond of speculative opinions when so much practical work had to be done in the world, but I thought of it now. If that time ever really arrives to cats, and we are—as we doubtless ought by rights to be—supreme, won't there be vengeance taken for past persecutions? Won't there be scratching? And I know one good hearty scratch which shall be given to a certain keeper with the full force of an honest paw, for the sake of my murdered Tom. Yes, men, and especially keepers, will have a rough time of it if the white cat's theory turn out to be true. All furies (and especially He-cat-e, a most appropriate avenger for a slaughtered Tom-cat) will be let loose upon them, their cat-astrophe will be terrible; they will curse the con-cat-enation of events which has placed them in the power of those to whom they have given such just cause of dire and inexpiable hatred. But I must not forget the thread of my story, even for reflections so consoling as these.

On the night of the murder I reached my cow-yard in safety, and, as I have already hinted, it was a fortnight before I ventured again to the scene of that horrid tragedy. As, however, the affections of a cat are too ardent to be restrained, I did not think it necessary to remain long faithful to the memory of the departed, and before many days were over I discovered that there were other Tom-cats equal in beauty and sagacity to him I had lost. In their society I gradually consoled myself for my loss, and one or other of them constantly accompanied me in my nocturnal rambles; or, if unable to do so, gave me friendly hints as to the best places to find game.

One afternoon, however, I had gone out for a ramble over the fields by myself, not waiting for night, and not indeed intending to hunt, but tempted by the brightness of the sun, and feeling inclined for air and exercise. On the other side of the road which ran near our house, were one or two cottages where the people were not hostile, and the cats agreeable. Immediately behind these was an arable field—there were turnips in it that year, I remember—and on each side of this field was a good thick hedge, a very favourite place for birds, and not unfrequently a safe find for a partridge-nest hunter. Along one of these hedges I crept, now and then stopping to bask for a while in the sun, and then creeping on a little further, listening to the cheerful twitter of the small birds, and wishing they were a little tamer. I was some forty yards from the gate at the other end of the field, when all of a sudden it was swung open, and into the field ran a black retriever, closely followed by two men, one of whom had a gun in his hand. I had scarcely time to notice who they were, but, as subsequent events will show, it was none other than the master of the house which belonged to us, who, with a keeper, was coming home from partridge shooting through this field.

At the first glimpse of the retriever, it is needless to say that I fled at best pace, being moved to do so by my natural instincts. I suppose I had got twenty yards, when there came a sharp whizzing noise all round me, followed by the loud report of a gun. It was fortunate indeed for me that I had taken flight at once; for had it been a matter of forty instead of sixty yards, it might have gone hard with me. However, I must have been quite sixty yards off when the sportsman fired, and the shot had so scattered in that distance, that only a few struck me in the back, and though they smarted somewhat unpleasantly, did me no serious injury. You may well believe that I made the best of my way to the cow-yard, and did not venture out again that day.

A thrill of horror, however, was sent through me next morning when the master of the house came sauntering through our cow-yard at the time of their milking the cows. After remarking that it was a fine morning (which I thought very stupid of him, as everybody could see that for themselves without his telling them), he went on to say:

"I think we have got too many cats about, Baker."

"Perhaps we have, sir," replied that worthy man. "There's a good many about the garden, I know."

"Yes," rejoined the master, "and they do a great deal of mischief with the partridges; before nesting-time comes round again I must have them thinned. By-the-bye, I saw a cat uncommonly like your cow-yard cat at the bottom of the Green Lane yesterday. I hope she isn't a poacher. I shot at her, the one I saw, but she was too far off to kill."

My heart was in my mouth with fear as to the reply, and you may fancy my delight and gratitude when the excellent Baker replied, touching his hat, as was his habit when he spoke.

"No, sir, I don't think our cat never gets out. She's a good cat, she is, and I most times see her about at home here. I don't believe she goes away from home, not at all."

"I hope not," said the other, as he slowly turned on his heel and went away; and so ended the conversation.

I was curled up in some hay at the corner of the lodge, and heard every word, and thus I knew for certain who it was who had fired at me the day before, and how much risk I had run of being detected, and perhaps destroyed.

Influenced by the reflections which naturally followed this knowledge, it was some time after the occurrence which I have just mentioned before I moved from off the premises where I knew that I was secure from such dangers as I had lately encountered. I devoted myself to mouse and bird-catching; slew one rat of an enormous size, whose destruction gained me much credit with Baker, and became, to all intents and purposes, a regular quiet, domestic cat. But the old spirit still lurked within me, prompting me to deeds of daring, and suggesting to me that my present life was tame and spiritless. Now and then, as I crept along the slip of shrubbery up the back of the cow-yard, I saw the master of the house, or some of his friends, returning from some shooting expedition. The keepers who followed them had generally game-sticks over their shoulders, in which, secured by the neck, hung pheasants of gorgeous plumage, horse-shoe breasted partridges, and sometimes other birds, whilst the soft sleek form of a dead hare was often apparent also, grasped by its hind legs in the hand of its arch-enemy, man. As I watched the procession, my mouth used to water at the sight of the game, and my heart to swell with a sense of the burning injustice which permitted the inferior animal, man, to follow these creatures for his pleasure, and exult in their destruction as " sport," whilst any similar attempt on the part of one of my own noble race was met with an outbreak of indignation which vented itself in the abominable devices of steel traps, guns, dogs, and other engines of vile and intolerable oppression. It was shameful, I thought, that this should be the law of the universe, and I cherished much animosity against those who obeyed it.

These thoughts recurred to me again and again, and they

naturally led to my forming a resolution to act upon what I believed to be the right and true principle for a cat, to deceive man and share in the plunder which he selfishly wished to keep for himself. So I gradually lapsed from the path of virtue, and began to slide back into my old practices of expeditions by night. I managed these so well that I was never detected, and kept my good character with Baker throughout the whole time. I must not forget, however, to chronicle an event which occurred at this period of my existence, and which might have been attended with very serious and even fatal consequences.

There were, as I think I have already mentioned, many dogs about the place of various sorts, sizes, and ages.

I have never been able to understand the reason why men—aye, and ladies, too—have such a partiality for dogs, and so frequently make pets of them, when there are cats to be obtained who would serve the same purpose infinitely better. Take him at his best, a dog is generally a snarling, noisy, bone-crunching, rackety animal, seldom, if ever, worth his keep, and of no use in catching mice, whom he commonly affects to despise. In my opinion he is an over-rated animal altogether, and occupies a position in the world to which he is by no means entitled on his merits.

Look on the other side at the cat. Soft, smooth, gentle in manner and appearance, clean in her habits, graceful in her movements, stealing with velvety tread over the ground, and giving vent to her feelings in a voice which neither alarms you by its sharp and sudden utterance, or deafens you with its clamour. Here, indeed, is an animal worthy of all consideration ; and if the superiority of man over the rest of the creation were anything else than an idle and wicked fable invented by himself, it would certainly be shown by his honouring and preferring cats above all other animals in the world. Unfortunately, however, this, together with woman's rights, the abolition of drinking ale and spirits, and the making of all men equal in every respect, is among the blessings reserved for future generations; and we can only deplore, without seeking to alter, the existing folly of the world in not seeing things with *our* eyes as they ought to do.

Dogs, I say, were allowed about our premises, and were sometimes very tiresome and inconvenient, coming suddenly into the cow-yard when least expected, rushing at one with hostile demonstrations, which might or might not be serious, and altogether behaving in a manner truly canine; disturbing the peaceful serenity of existence, and constantly making one wish most devoutly that they had never been invented. One fine day, about the time in my life of which I am now telling, a little white terrier was given to the eldest son of the house, which I once heard him say was of a very pure breed, and which apparently thought it necessary to vindicate the purity of its descent by the most obnoxious behaviour towards cats. I knew by instinct that it was an enemy, and avoided it whenever I could, especially since upon one morning I saw it, from my seat on the top of the cow-yard wall, chase, overtake, and miserably destroy a kitten belonging to the gardener, and I felt sure that it was quite capable of dealing in a similar manner with a full-grown cat.

I was very near having the experiment proved upon myself. On one of my quiet, good, well-behaved days, when I had remained at home without once leaving the premises, and had discharged my household duties with satisfaction to all concerned, I was sitting in front of the cow-lodge, lazily devouring the carcase of a robin whom I had surprised and slain during the afternoon. Baker was milking the cows, and when I heard the door at the end of the lodge open, I thought it was either opened by him in order that he might take the milk up to the house, or by some other of the men about the place.

Not a thought of evil had I, when sitting peacefully and quietly in my own domain, and it was a burning shame that any evil should have been allowed to approach me. Nevertheless, so it was. The aforesaid vile little white terrier, "Venus" by name, but brute by nature, sidled into the lodge at his master's heels, saw me through the fence of the cow-lodge, and, without a word of "with your leave" or "by your leave," sprang through the little gate of the fence, which happened to be ajar, and was upon me before I knew where I was. Oftentimes, when thus attacked by a cur, I have set up my back in a stiff arch, glared with the eyes of a demon at my opponent, and by these demonstrations, supplemented, if necessary, by a little spitting, have easily repulsed the attack.

But none of this would have been of the least avail with my present foe, even if I had had time to prepare myself, which indeed I had not. She was upon me in a moment, made nothing of my feeble attempt at resistance, and before I had time to put myself in an attitude of defence, rolled me over and over, and would have had me in the death grip in another moment. Most fortunately, her very impetuosity defeated its own object: she stumbled over her own fore-paws in her rush, and consequently went clean over me as I rolled in the dust; instantly recovering herself, she seized me as I rolled, but failed in gripping a mortal part. One furious blow I struck her in the face with my full force, and then darted up the side of the pig-sty; the murderous wretch sprang after me, but fortunately jumped short by a couple of inches, so that I had time to make for the roof, where I thought she could not follow me. So impetuous was the creature, however, that at the second spring she got her fore-paws over the side of the sty, pulled herself up, and scrambled on to the sloping roof in frantic pursuit of me. But by this time I had been able to reach the top of the wall, and thence the roof of the cow-lodge, which, being higher and of a steeper incline, could not be climbed by a clumsy dog, and therefore afforded a secure refuge to one, like myself, of a nobler race. Upon the roof I sat in security, scowling down upon my vile foe, until her master called her off, and I was relieved from her persecution.

My escape had indeed been miraculous, and to this hour I cannot imagine how I managed to escape at all. Had that beast of a terrier been a little more cool and collected in her first assault, nothing could have saved me, and although I might have had the melancholy satisfaction of scratching one of her eyes out, that would have been no consolation for my own loss of life.

I was very shy for some time after this adventure, for I never saw a man or boy without fancying that he had a dog at his heels, and I started with a nervous shudder at the sound of every distant bark. My nervous system had indeed received a severe shock, from which I did not recover for some time, and my doctors—the stable and garden cats, for I consulted them both—strongly advised change of air and exercise. This I could obtain in no way so well as by resuming my nocturnal rambles, and I found the fields and woods so pleasant that I not unfrequently stayed away for a whole day, and only crept back to the cow-yard when I was afraid that an absence too much prolonged might lead to injurious suspicions on the part of Baker, which, if they once took possession of that good man's mind, might lead to serious consequences.

On one of these expeditions I was the witness of a deed of blood which impressed itself upon my memory in vivid colours, showing, as it did, at once the cruelty of man and the levity with which he inflicts suffering upon less powerful animals.

At the distance of little more than half-a-mile from our house was a large plantation, or rather a group of several plantations which joined each other, surrounded by pasture fields. There must have been fifteen or twenty acres of this planted wood, and it lay in a hollow for the most part, and on the side of the hill or sloping ground on each side of it, the pasture was covered with thick fern, so that in summer it appeared almost as if it was part and parcel of the wood below. One of these plantations was of chesnut, another of ash, and a third of willow, and on the side banks were larch fir in great abundance, so that there was plenty of variety, and, as if there was not enough of this, at the end was a rough piece of gorze, part of which had been grubbed, and a few Scotch and silver firs planted, which towered above the other trees in all the grandeur and self-consciousness of superior beings.

It may easily be supposed that in such a place as this

there was an abundant supply of game. The rabbits had, I regret to say, been killed down somewhat closely for the sake of the growing wood, and the hares usually preferred higher and drier ground, but the partridges nested there in quantities, and there were always a great number of pheasants. In fact, the gamekeeper's house was within a short distance of the spot, though upon the other side of the hill, and he always turned out a number of young pheasants in the plantations. These were, of course, delicious food for a hungry cat, and, near as they were to the abode of a deadly enemy, there was an element of danger in their pursuit which rendered it still more enticing to an animal of an enterprising disposition.

To this retreat, then, I used to betake myself in the late spring and summer months, and although great care was necessary as regarded traps, the place was not without its advantages, especially as at this time of the year it was extremely thick, and afforded admirable hiding-places in the brambles, rushes, and long grass, with which it was abundantly supplied by nature.

Now it chanced that some one had given a doe to one of the young ladies of our house, at some time or other. I do not know the ins and outs of the story, but this doe had a fawn, and as the creatures did mischief when loose, they were shut up in a lodge in our cow-yard, with bars in front through which they could peer at the outer world, but through which they could not pass.

Naturally impatient of such unnatural restraint, I imagine that the poor animals were glad enough when they were now and then let out into the yard, and sometimes into the adjoining field ; and I only wonder that they did not take right off into the open country at once. They did not, however, for some time; and the young buck was two years old before he became so tired of this miserable kind of life, that he fairly bolted. He lay about in the shrubberies for some time, annoying the owners of adjacent gardens by nightly inroads of a character destructive to their vegetables. At last he thought he might as well go further a-field, and accordingly betook himself to the plantations of which I speak, and took up his abode there as soon as the foliage was sufficiently thick to afford him concealment.

I saw him there several times; and a handsome, graceful creature he was. He came out in the very early mornings, before the world of man was awake, and fed with the sheep on the neighbouring pastures; then, during the heat of the day, he couched in the long grass and the plantations, or made himself a comfortable lair in the thick fern. When night came on he sallied forth again; and when the year was sufficiently advanced for the keeper to put a stack of corn for the pheasants into the wood, our gay young friend took advantage thereof, and had many a pleasant meal there.

By this means, indeed, his place of retreat was discovered; for Croughty, the keeper, found his corn-stack knocked about night after night, and told the shepherd that his sheep had been getting into the plantations. This accusation having been denied, the two men kept watch, and soon found out who was the real culprit. News having been taken to our house, those in authority there determined that the buck could not be allowed thus to trespass with impunity upon a domain sacred to the all-important pheasants, nor to devour the corn appropriated to those noble birds. So more than once the master of the house, in his shooting excursions, visited the plantations, and strove to get a shot at the daring intruder.

It was in vain that he did so, however; for the buck was as wary as his pursuers, and either remained hid in some thick lair, into which they did not happen to enter, or ran back between the men who walked down the wood to drive him out, as if he knew quite as well as they did that the enemy with a gun was standing in front, expecting him to go forward.

At last, one day when I happened to have stayed out all night, the hour arrived when the gay young buck was no longer able to elude the savage arts of those who had vowed his destruction. It happened that I had captured a young pheasant that morning, and had so much enjoyed my repast, that I felt disinclined to leave the place. Upon a bank, where formerly there had been a hedge (but this had long since been grubbed when the fields were thrown together and planted), several huge old pollards reared their mighty frames, throwing out large branches, which formed excellent roosting places for the pheasants, although they rather hindered the growth of the underwood below.

Now there is no more comfortable hiding-place than a good hole in the crown of an oak pollard; and into such an one I crept this day, curled myself round as snugly as possible, and went off into a sweet sleep. I was roused by the sound of voices near me, and, peeping out from my nest, looked down upon the plantations below, and saw the whole of what occurred upon that eventful day. The master of the house was there, but he was not the only person who carried a gun. A young fellow, of some one or two-and-twenty years of age—he cannot have been more—was similarly armed; and I think I never saw a youth whom I would less desire to meet under such circumstances. He was not ill-looking; but there was a cat-killing look about his short, black moustache, which I misliked from the first; and I was very sure that any animal which moved past him slowly enough to allow of his taking a deliberate aim, would run a great danger of being destroyed.

I saw him, indeed, miss several partridges that morning, but I do not for a moment believe that he did so designedly, as the sequel will but too clearly prove, that he was a blood-thirsty monster. Well, this boy, whom I heard the other call "Charlie," was placed on the bank, not far from my tree, where there had formerly been a gateway, so that the bank was cut down, and it was the passage by which an unsuspecting animal would be likely to pass from one plantation to another. Here he was to await the possible coming of the buck, whilst the master of our house went elsewhere, and three or four men proceeded to drive the plantation down.

Presently there was a shout: the animal of whom they were in pursuit darted from some low planted wood, crossed an open space in the angle of two of the plantations, lightly bounded over the wire fence, which stood in his way, and buried himself in the thickest part of the wood before him. The position of his pursuers was at once changed, and the beaters shifted their plans, in order to drive him from his new refuge.

I sat and watched with breathless interest. Presently a partridge rose and flew within gunshot of the elder sportsman, for whom the temptation proved too strong, and he fired upon it, with fatal result to the helpless bird. I suppose that the buck, hearing the report of the gun on one side, thought himself safe on the other, for he now crept quietly down the plantation, and came straight down towards the spot at which Master " Charlie " had taken his stand. Slowly he moved along through the young trees, and could scarcely be said to be moving at all, when at a distance of barely fifteen or sixteen yards, the youth poured upon him a murderous volley. The poor animal plunged and staggered forward, when the second barrel was instantly discharged also, and he fell forward in his tracks.

Still the youth, for some mysterious reason, or from habitual taciturnity, preserved an unbroken silence, and the men were about to beat steadily through the wood, when a small boy, the son of the keeper, who had witnessed the foul deed, raised his shrill voice in notice to his father, and screamed aloud, " He's dead ! "

In another moment the men came rushing to the spot, crying, " Where is he ? " And I heard the keeper eagerly asking for a knife with which to cut the throat of the wounded animal. Two men were upon the buck in another moment; and, in spite of the energy of his dying struggles, the cruel deed was speedily effected, as I learned from the keeper's reply to the inquiry of the master, if it was " All right ? "

" Yes, sir," said the man; " we've unbuttoned his shirt-collar for him."

And this was the requiem of the slaughtered deer ! Poor little creature ! No more would he sport with graceful action among the sheep; no more bound lightly over the fence, and couch himself in the brakes and grass; no more take his humble share of the food provided by the superior animal, man, for his petted birds: he lay there, with his life's blood bedewing the ground; his innocent existence cut short by the cruel hand of the tyrants of creation. My heart died within me at the sight; and I shuddered as I beheld the monsters standing in exultation around their murdered victim. Oh, that I could have scratched their eyes out, beginning with that blood-thirsty "Charlie," and going the whole round of them before I had done!

However, as they were the stronger party, such thoughts were useless, and I had to think of my own safety, which was not beyond doubt, whilst the murderers remained so near my place of concealment. Happily, they were too much occupied with the removal of the body of the slaughtered deer to look out for fresh objects on which to vent their murderous spleen, and ere long they had all left the place. I remained in my tree for some time longer, until everything was quiet, and the shades of evening had begun to fall, then I cautiously descended, made my way through the plantations, in the direction of our house, and returned to the cow-yard a melancholy and an altered cat.

The sight which I had that day witnessed had filled me with many strange, and some desperate thoughts. I thought of the masterful nature of man; of his tyranny, his cruelty over the other animals, and the impossibility of always escaping him if his hand was turned against me. From such ferocity, mingled with such intense cunning, not even a cat's life could be safe, as indeed had been proved by the experiences of my own existence. Was there no method by which one could escape from his power?

No; I knew of none; could imagine none. Would it not then be better to submit, to acknowledge his sway, to give up seeking for my food the animals which he desires for his own, and content myself with acting as his dependent and slave, keeping his house and lodges free from rats and mice, and cking out my miserable existence upon such food as is afforded by these wretched creatures, varied only by a small bird or two, too insignificant for his wants, and therefore to be destroyed without his interference?

These thoughts often crossed my mind whilst meditating in the sun, and musing over the events of the past. But the spirit of a cat rose against the baseness of such submission; and the blood of my noble race boiled and fumed in my veins, as I thought of the noble deeds which had been performed by the cats of old, reckless of man's authority. Who had not heard of "Puss-cat Mew," whose exploits in daring the heat of the burning coal, even though her best garment suffered in the performance; whose self-denial in abstaining from the delightful juice of the cow, until that garment had been restored to its former state; whose fame, in short, throughout her whole existence has been sung by nursery bards continuously, and chronicled in the legends by which kittens and children are ever taught to respect the memory of the great? Who, again, has not read of "Puss in Boots," and the benefits which she bestowed upon the human being who was wise enough to trust her? Beyond all, who has not dwelt again and again upon the doings of the celebrated cat of Whittington? And who that has read of these noble, these glorious animals, but must feel that they belonged to a race which was born to rule rather than to obey?

Fired by such thoughts as these, no base considerations of possible danger, no craven fears for my safety, could longer deter me from roaming forth once more as a free cat. For a day or two I hesitated, but only because I doubted whether to bid the cow-yard an eternal farewell, or to reserve it as a place to fall back upon, and only absent myself during such short intervals of time as might allow the belief that I was never far away.

On the whole, I thought the latter the better plan, but I gave the question several days' consideration ; and during this time I avoided all association with the men and women about the place : even set up my back at Baker when he wanted to stroke me, and spit at the gardener, who attempted to take the same liberty.

At the end of the third day my common sense had prevailed, and I determined to keep up the appearance of being what human creatures call a " domestic cat," although there reigned within my breast the spirit of the wildest of my race. So I purred complacently about the place all the morning ; rubbed myself against Baker's leg as he sat milking the cow, and stretched myself in the sun, opposite the cow-lodge, as if I desired nothing better, and was at the very height of feline enjoyment. But when the shades of evening once more fell, I stole quietly out of the gates, over the field, and down the hedge, away to the big wood as fast as my legs would carry me. I had no settled plan of action ; but I thought I should do well to seek an alliance with some other animals, so that we might assist each other in our attacks upon the creatures which Heaven has given to cats for food, and at the same time guard ourselves against the tyrant man who seeks to claim these animals for his own exclusive use.

Had there been a colony of polecats in those woods, I should have expected to find in those creatures my natural allies, but they were rarely to be seen, and indeed I only knew of them by report. Stoats and weasels were too small and insignificant, badgers too slow and heavy, and in fact the fox was the only animal whose skill might be of much service to me in the life which I desired to follow. But the remarks of the fox who had witnessed the melancholy fate of my poor mate had not afforded me much hope that my advances would be received with favour by others of his kind, and I had really begun to doubt whether it would be desirable to make an attempt which might be repulsed with rudeness, when accident led me to encounter one of the very animals upon whom my mind was running. He was a fine fox—a very fine fox—and had the manners of a gentleman too, for he bowed with the greatest civility as I met him in the run of a hare in the thick brakes which occupied a large space in the wood.

" Good morrow, madam," said he.

" Good morrow to you, sir," replied I, not to be behind in manners.

" There will be a good moon to-night, and we shall be able to see the pretty birds roosting on the trees," said he, in a sweet but somewhat sad tone.

" Yes," replied I, trying to imitate his voice and manner, " and how sad that the plump little beauties of pheasants should sit so high above the ground."

" Sad indeed," responded he. " It shows a sad want of trust in woodland society."

" Alas! it does," said I; " and I have observed the same feeling in hares and rabbits, as well as in the partridge, and other kinds of game."

"Madam," observed the fox, with another polite bow, " it is easy to see that you have studied nature. These beasts and birds are, as you say, shy and timid, but we must cure them of such absurd feelings by treating them tenderly whenever we have the chance."

" It is they who should be *tender* to us," replied I, with a smile, to which the fox responded by another, and in this way we soon struck up a friendship which we hoped might be mutually beneficial. We agreed to go a-hunting together, and to share whatever plunder we might be fortunate enough to get, dividing it equally between us as honest partners.

My new friend's name, which I discovered by the not unusual method of asking him, was Peter, and at first I was much pleased with him, as his conversation was amusing and his manners polite. His address in hunting was also considerable, and I thought that I had done a very wise thing in forming the alliance which I have mentioned. All went on smoothly and well for several weeks; we hunted together when we could, meeting by moonlight and assisting each other in the capture of such unhappy creatures as chanced to come in our way. My skill in tree climbing here proved useful, and the pheasants had to choose their roosting places with caution, as Peter was a capital hand at discovering and pointing out to me any straggling bird who had foolishly gone to sleep upon a bough which would bear my weight. In that case, if I could not actually seize him alone, a blow from my paw, well directed at the wing, more than once knocked the wretched bird off his perch in a state which enabled my companion to seize him before he could recover, and so we obtained suppers which we enjoyed with a rare good appetite.

When the shooting season came on, our success was still more delightful and encouraging. We more than once managed to discover, generally by the sound of the guns, which one or other of us had been fortunate enough to hear, when the sportsmen had been shooting in one of the neigh-bouring preserves. On these occasions, the evening of the sport was pretty sure to find us in the wood, looking after the wounded game, off which we made many a pleasant supper.

"Oh, spare me, spare me," cried an unhappy hare, which we one night caught with a broken fore leg after one of those days in which men had enjoyed themselves by murdering a number of defenceless creatures which their keepers had reared for the purpose of furnishing victims to their bloodthirsty masters. "Spare me, kind creatures! what harm have I ever done to you? I will be your slave for ever, if you will only give me my life."

"My dear madam," replied my friend the fox, in his politest tones, "we would gladly comply with your request, did the laws of the country permit it. Slavery, however, is, as you will doubtless remember on further reflection, illegal in England, and we must therefore endeavour to make you of use to us in another way. What consoles us under this painful necessity is the thought that, with your fractured limb, you could scarcely enjoy life as you have hitherto done, and would probably ere long become a burden to your relations."

The wretch, on hearing these words, cast a piteous look upon me, appealed (as those foolish hares always do on such occasions) to our common descent and blood-relation-ship, and in earnest and piteous tones begged for her life.

My answer, however, was to the same effect as that of the fox, and I told her that she was evidently in so much pain, that I felt we should be doing her a real kindness by putting her out of her misery at once.

On finding that her fate was thus made certain, she hastened it by raising cries of distress which it was necessary, for our own safety's sake, to stop without delay. Clasping her therefore by the throat in a manner which impeded her utterance, we at once dealt with her as we had from the first intended, and made a hearty meal off her then and there. This night, however, as on one or two previous occasions, I noticed a tendency in Peter to devour more than his share, and to treat me with something less of deference than, as a cat and a lady, I was entitled to expect. For instance, he appropriated the hare's head without so much as offering me an ear.

Now I happen to be particularly fond of hares' heads, and did not like to be so treated. I was rather cross in consequence, and my temper was not improved by my companion's tone and manner. Instead of ignoring it, or pretending to be unaware of having given me any cause of offence, he laughed at me, openly and insultingly, for not having been sharp enough to secure the head, told me how good it was, and said I was but a slow little Puss after all, and not half " up to " business.

I did not like this at all, for I felt that while it was untrue as a general remark, in this particular instance no skill or cunning of mine could have prevented him, as a larger and stronger animal, from taking the head, if he was so little of a gentleman as to do so. I said nothing, however, though I thought a great deal, and we separated somewhat coldly that morning. Still, our alliance had proved so mutually beneficial, that neither of us cared to dissolve it, and we had several more excursions together which had similarly fortunate results. Nothing, however, in this world lasts for ever, especially, I think, if it is agreeable and pleasant.

The friendship between the fox and me proved no exception to this general rule. One night we had been out together after one of the shooting parties which I have mentioned. We had partaken of a rabbit which we caught on first entering the wood, and not being satisfied therewith, had glutted our appetites on a hen pheasant which, being wounded, could not escape us. Then we found such an inviting patch of fern hard by, that we made ourselves comfortable beds in it, and lay down to rest after our supper. Whether the latter had been too heavy, or whether the damp weather (for it was moist and inclined to rain) had an effect upon us, I cannot say, but certain it is that we slept far into the morning, and much beyond the hour at which I usually stole back to my cow-yard after one of my nocturnal excursions. It was in fact broad daylight when I opened my eyes, and perceived that I had committed the error, dangerous alike to cat and man, of stopping out all night when I might have been at home.

The morning was somewhat raw and unpleasant, and finding this to be the case, I was not long in coming to the resolution that, as I had missed the hours during which I might have stolen quietly home without being observed, I had better remain in the comfortable nest which I had made for myself in the fern, and doze away a little while longer before I thought of turning out. So I curled myself up again and went comfortably to sleep. I was aroused by a noise which startled me from my slumbers and filled me with alarm. The loud shouting of men was in my ears, and it was evident that something unusual had occurred. In another instant I understood it all. The hounds were out! I distinctly heard the huntsmen encouraging them to enter the wood in search of their accustomed prey, and I started up at once to listen.

My companion was equally on the alert. He shook himself, arose from his lair, and stood silently before me.

"By Jove!" he said, "those brutes are here again; it is really shameful. I have had two narrow escapes from them already in my life. Confound it, what shall I do! That heavy supper of mine has made me feel anything but inclined to run this morning. I wish there was an earth somewhere handy! There is not one within three miles, and it is ten to one that *those* will have been stopped."

As he spoke, I heard through the still air a voice still shouting, "Hie in there—Hie in there," and presently came a whimper from a hound, and then another, and then a loud cracking of whips and a cry of "'Ware hare!" told of the probable fate of some luckless animal of that species which had suddenly found herself surrounded by the pack, and probably been sacrificed in an instant. The matter was now becoming serious for my companion.

"Look out for yourself, Puss," he cried—"I'm off;" and shaking himself once more, he crept quietly away in the contrary direction to that from which came the sounds I have described.

I felt that it was high time for me also to take similar steps, for a cat in the middle of a pack of ferocious foxhounds would fare little better than a hare. I, therefore, also left my lair, and seeing an old oak at a little distance, covered with ivy and easy of ascent, I made my way up to it at once, crawled up the trunk, and ensconced myself safely in a place where I could see for some way around me, whilst the ivy-leaves completely secured me from observation. I had not taken my precaution too soon, for but a few minutes had elapsed before the hounds came crashing through the wood, a fierce-looking, savage crew, only eager to destroy, and thirsting for the blood of any innocent animal which might come in their way. They had scarcely approached the spot from which Peter had so lately risen than the foremost of them gave vent to a sound which betokened that he had discovered by the scent which my poor friend had left behind him that a fox had been lately there. His cry was immediately taken up by another and then another of the savage pack, and loud cries of encouragement from the huntsman, who was riding down a track at a little distance, cheered the hounds on as they dashed forward in pursuit. I kept perfectly still, and listened with breathless attention.

By this time my companion must have reached the outside of the wood, and I expected every minute to hear the cry of "Gone away!" which would betoken the fact that he had left the covert, and had a fair start for his life. No such cry, however, reached my ears, but presently came a wild chorus of shouts and yells which betokened that he had been seen, and a short time afterwards I heard voices of men abusing others in no measured terms of reproach for having "headed" the fox.

The morning was so still that I could hear the voices quite plainly; and I need scarcely say that my ears were strained to the utmost in order to hear every sound. Presently, somewhat to my surprise, on looking downwards I perceived Peter himself creeping through the wood and about to pass under my tree. As he did so I bade him cheer up and be of good heart. Wistfully did the poor fellow cast his eyes upwards to my place of safety.

"Oh, Puss," he said, "this is a bad job. There are a crowd of foot-people outside, who headed me back when I had got a fair start, and I don't know which way to turn in order to escape those howling demons behind. I'm off to the lower corner of the wood. Good-bye."

"Good-bye, Peter," said I, "and good-luck to you;" and off he went.

He had not been gone two minutes before the whole pack of bloodthirsty hounds came yelling in hideous chorus upon his track, frantic with joyous excitement, and revelling in the anticipation of murderous slaughter. Half a minute more and I heard another sound of confused cries from the direction which my poor friend had taken. Presently I saw him pass again at a short distance : he had been headed a second time, and was at his wit's end what to do.

I never felt so indignant in my life! What cowardly brutes men must be! Is it not enough to bring out forty or fifty howling fiends, each larger and stronger than the poor animal they wish to destroy, and strive to run him down and take his life, but they must also permit the baser and more contemptible of their own species to crowd round the wood and prevent his having a fair chance of escape? The men that head foxes in this manner should, in my opinion, be soundly whipped at the cart's-tail as persons altogether devoid of taste, good feeling, and human sympathy.

But I hasten to the end. The Babel of noise in the wood continued for some little time, men shouting, the hounds joining in a chorus which would not have been unmelodious to my ears if my heart had not known its fearful meaning, and the whole face of peaceful nature marred by the horrible clamour.

Again I saw poor Peter pass at a short distance from my hiding-place, but oh! how changed from the bright, brave fox I had so lately seen! His coat was dirty and torn, he dragged his brush along as if its weight was too much for him, despair was pictured upon his face, and he looked like a worn-out, broken-down animal whose condition would have touched the heart of any one who had a heart that was capable of pity for undeserved suffering. Once more yet I saw him. The crash of the hounds' chorus seemed greater than ever, and was coming audibly nearer to my tree, so that, although I knew my place of refuge was safe, I insensibly trembled for myself. The noise came nearer and nearer, and presently Peter came forth into the open space of fern where he had passed the night.

He was evidently dead beat; more puzzled, worried, and bewildered than actually exhausted by physical fatigue; and crept along as if almost incapable of moving. Not two seconds after I had seen him, the foremost hound of the pack sprang out of the wood, close on his traces, rage and excitement gleaming from his eyes, and his whole appearance full of fury and determined murder. Another followed him, and then another, and another, in quick succession.

Poor Peter was within their sight, and almost within their grasp, for they gained on him at every stride.

Escape was impossible. The foremost brute was upon him. He turned with an expression of combined helplessness and rage which I shall never forget, and bit savagely at the hound who rushed in upon him with open jaws. I think he must have hurt him, for I fancied I detected a yell of pain mingled with the howl of gratified malice with which the wretch seized my unhappy friend. But what could one brave fox do against a host of furious and ravening foes? It was all over in less time than it takes me to write it. Torn limb from limb by his ferocious murderers, the unhappy Peter yielded up his miserable life, and his spirit went forth—one more witness against the tyranny and cruelty of man towards that creation which in the plenitude of his infallible wisdom he calls "brute," and which he appears to consider as only existing for his own amusement and pleasure, and for the unscrupulous exercise of his own sovereign will!

The hounds had not well finished their horrible meal, and were still growling over the bones of my murdered comrade, when some of the horsemen, who had guessed what had happened from the alteration of the notes of the pack from eager pursuit to greedy exultation, came bursting through the wood to claim the brush of the poor fox as the trophy of their inglorious victory. As they secured this precious relic, I heard them abusing my poor friend for having been "chopped" instead of affording them a fair run in the open, and, with marvellous inconsistency, at the same time swearing at the men who, by continually heading him, had prevented his doing as they wished, and had driven him back to his melancholy fate. Whilst they sat on their horses and watched the ministers of their savage pleasure finishing their repast upon poor Peter's remains, I trembled in my tree lest any of them should catch sight of me therein, and felt by no means secure that this would not be the case. Happily, however, no one saw me, and after a little longer delay, they turned back into the wood, and men, hounds, and horses were soon out of sight and hearing.

I stayed where I was, however, until the shades of evening began to fall : horror at the sight which I had seen prevented my feeling the pangs of hunger, and I dreaded to meet some enemy if I ventured to quit my safe retreat. At last I could stay there no longer: with a fear which I had never known since kittenhood, I crept tremblingly to the ground, and stole away through the bushes with silent and timorous steps until I reached the outside of the wood. Then I set my head straight for home, and arrived at the cow-yard safe and sound, indeed, but having received a fright which I felt I should never get over till my dying day. It had, indeed, been a sad experience to me, and a proof that no cunning, however great, in fox or other animal, can avert the inexorable decrees of Fate.

There were other thoughts, too, which were brought into my mind and took possession of it after the melancholy catastrophe which I had witnessed and have described. I bethought myself that the life which I had been recently following was one which involved greater risks than a respectable cat of a certain age ought to permit herself to encounter.

I had, indeed, been fortunate hitherto, and had escaped the misfortunes which had befallen more than one of the companions with whom my lot had been cast. I could not, however, expect that I should always be equally lucky, and I felt that the awful scene which had lately passed before my eyes was a warning to me to consider whether I had not better alter my course of life, and return to the steady habits and far safer existence of a domestic animal. Perhaps, however, I should scarcely have been able to do so, had I not had yet one more warning, and that the most serious of my life. So inveterate had my hunting habits become, so intense my love of midnight marauding, so deeply imbued my taste for the game which I thereby obtained, that it required even a stronger influence than that which had been exercised over me by the sufferings of others, to drive me to a change which, though it would doubtless prolong my life, would at the same time render it somewhat tame and inglorious.

I thought I would, at least, finish the season as I had begun it, and in carrying out this resolution I nearly managed to finish myself into the bargain. I stole out one moonlight evening, and took my way to a wood from whence I had previously often gleaned a supper. I crept quietly along the hedge until I came to a likely place through which to enter the preserves, and then proceeded to do so through a hole which had evidently been made by hares in their passage to and fro the wood.

I got through the hedge safely enough, and was about to descend into the ditch upon the other side, when all of a sudden I heard a kind of sharp "snick" behind me, and in another instant was in the fangs of a horrible iron trap. An involuntary yell of agony burst from my throat, and then, sensible of the magnitude of my danger, I kept silent, bearing my pain as best I might, and trying to realize to myself what had really happened.

There was unfortunately very little doubt upon the subject. In the "run" from the hedge down into the ditch, through which any animal was certain to pass who was about to enter the wood at that particular place, the crafty and cruel keeper had set a trap, well covered over and concealed from sight by dead leaves, which his detestable ingenuity had employed for this purpose.

I suppose that in my stealthy progress I had stepped over this with my forelegs, but had unfortunately set down one of my hind legs in such a position as to spring the trap, and it had seized me, not very far above the foot, as it happened, but far enough to hold me tight without the possibility of extricating myself from my awful position. Had I been less quick in lifting my leg from the ground, (which I had done as soon as ever I found the earth, as it seemed, yield beneath the pressure of my foot), nothing could have saved my life, as my thigh would certainly have been broken, and I should never have survived such an injury. As it was, indeed, the misfortune was bad enough; the saw-like teeth of the cruel trap bit deeply into my leg, causing intense pain; and I soon found that this was only increased by every effort I made to free myself from the horrible incumbrance.

So I lay perfectly still, suffering tortures, and expecting nothing but a long night of misery, and destruction at the hands of the keeper as soon as daylight should bring him round to see how his fiendish devices against us poor animals had prospered.

Now it was that all the events of my past life seemed to rise and flit before my eyes as vividly as if they were all actually occurring over again. I remembered every kittenish act of disobedience to my mother, unkindness to my sister, waywardness and selfishness with respect to other cats, and all those faults to which kittenhood is prone.

There rose before me, moreover, all the acts of cruelty I had committed in trifling with unhappy birds and mice whom I had from time to time caught alive, and with whose agony I had amused myself before I finally put them out of their misery.

Any little acts of feline treachery which I had committed came back to me in this my hour of woe, appearing in the retrospect ten times as wicked as I had ever before deemed them to be. And then, above all, I brought to mind my sin — my folly — my ingratitude — nay, my madness in deserting the happy home and quiet safe life which had been apportioned to me, and venturing forth upon that perilous path of amusement and plunder which had led me to my present position. Oh, fool that I was! deluded wretch, not to have realized that a mouse eaten in safety in my own cow-yard was much better than a hare or pheasant devoured under the terrible risks which had to be encountered in their acquisition.

But regret was all too late now! Fate had woven out the web of my destiny: retribution had at last overtaken me, and the blood of slaughtered game which cried out for vengeance upon my devoted head, would be avenged by the dreadful death to which I was certainly doomed. These agonizing thoughts did not diminish my bodily pain, but after a while this became somewhat less intense, and a numbness came over the lower part of my left hind leg, which was the one by which I had been caught. I lay still for at least an hour, when an incident occurred to me which I own I should not have believed if I had been told it by another cat as having happened to herself.

I heard a step: it was the step of a man; could it be the keeper already coming his rounds? It was impossible,

for the night was not yet far advanced, and the guardian of
the game would certainly not appear before early morning.
Yet a man it was, sure enough; but who?   A few
moments decided the question.   Creeping quietly along
the ditch, came a man dressed in the costume of an
ordinary farm labourer, with an instrument in his hand
which I suppose was some kind of a gun, though it did
not look like one of the sort usually carried by sportsmen.
From a conversation which I once overheard in the stables,
I think this was perhaps an air-gun, with which a pheasant
might be shot on his perch with very little noise, and the
shooter remain undiscovered.

I saw at once what the new-comer was.   He was a
poacher—very likely some neighbouring cottager upon
whose garden the hares and rabbits from the wood had
worked their wicked will, and who thought he might as
well repay himself by a midnight foray upon their domain.
However this might be, or whatever his motive for being
there, on he came down the ditch, and rapidly approached
the spot where I lay, helpless and desponding, in the
trap.

I had no thought but that any man who found me there
would either kill me at once, or leave me where I was as
not worth the trouble of knocking on the head.   For once,
however, I was mistaken, and that in a manner most
satisfactory to myself, and I hope also to my readers, since,
had it been otherwise, I should never have lived to publish
to the world this history of my eventful life.   The poacher
came quite close up to me, creeping along very quietly,
and stopped within a couple of yards from where I lay.
He half-started when he saw me, and then muttered to
himself:

"Dash my buttons, here's another pussy-cat they've been and catched! Cleared out *my* house, they have, and most others too, I reckon. Dang it! they sha'n't have this one, neither! I wish I could fill their woods with cats for 'em, I do."

He said no more, but approaching the trap which held me, set his foot firmly upon it, so as to make it fly open. Suffering and half mad with pain as I had been, my natural instinct would have been to have flown at him, or at any other human being who had come within my reach at that moment. Fortunately, however, I understood his words, and knew that his intentions were kind, so that I had the calmness and good sense to restrain myself from any demonstrations which might prevent him from carrying them out. I have often pondered the matter over since that night, and wondered whether the man acted from any innate tenderness of heart, or from a feeling that I, like himself, was a poacher, and had therefore some claim upon his assistance. I am inclined to think, however, that spite against the keepers was the principal motive which induced him to interfere on my behalf, and that, having lost cats from his own hearth through the nefarious action of these wicked men, he thought to balk their cruelty and prevent some other poor person from being visited with a similar loss.

Be this as it may, the pressure of his sturdy foot upon the trap left me free, and although I could scarcely draw my maimed limb from its place of torture, I did so, as you may well believe, with the least possible delay, and scuttled off down the ditch as fast as possible. I had no more appetite for supper that night. Indeed, I think the very sight of a pheasant would have made me sick, and the bitter agony of that night cured me for ever of the dangerous taste for game which I had so unwisely acquired.

All my thoughts were now concentrated upon ·a supreme effort to reach my cow-yard. I dragged myself with difficulty through the hedge, left the wood behind me for ever, and crept slowly homewards over the field, suffering more and more at every step I took. Never shall I forget the intense feeling of delight with which I saw the gate of the home which, but a few hours before, I had quitted with a free and reckless step, but over the threshold of which I now crawled in a feeble and helpless state. I crept into the straw which was piled at one end of the lodge in which the cows stood to be milked, and made myself as comfortable as was possible under the circumstances. Pain, however, prevented me from obtaining the sleep which I so much required, and as the sun's returning rays brightened and warmed the world once more, I raised my head and looked out with a saddened heart upon the scenes in which I had formerly been a blithesome actor, but which I much feared that I should henceforth regard only as a maimed and crippled spectator.

The fowls were gathered in front of the lodge in which I lay, slowly picking up their morning meal, and cackling cheerfully to each other as they confessed their mutual enjoyment of the genial weather. Ever and anon the cock raised his voice of exultation, and crowed defiance to the chicken world, whilst the contented grunt of the pig from the sty near at hand, the friendly moo of the cows hard by, and even the harsh cry of the peacock upon the top of the lodge, spoke of universal peace and happiness.

I alone lay there, a miserable sufferer, enduring, with but little patience, a misery which I had brought upon myself. I raised my voice in a melancholy tone, and in my own native tongue, pleaded earnestly for some mitigation of my pain, though I knew not who could afford it. Scarcely, however, had I given vent to a second and still more piteous mew, when I heard a well-known step passing along the front of the lodge, and presently the friendly voice of Baker sounded in my ear:

"Pussy, pussy, poor old pussy, where are you then?"

I replied by another cry of woe, and pushed up my head from my couch of straw. The good man came to me at once, lifted me up, and saw at a glance what was the matter.

"Why, Puss," he said, "I didn't know as how you was given to straying, but anyhow you've got a lesson this time, which may keep you at home for the time to come. Poor thing, poor thing!"

The answering mew which I gave to this remark probably conveyed no distinct idea to Baker's mind, but it was intended by me as a complete acquiescence in the justice and wisdom of his observation, and an expression of my firm determination to follow the course which he suggested as having been taught me by my misfortune.

He did not confine himself, however, to a word or two of pity, which people are generally ready enough to give to the misery of others, but which does not do much to relieve it. Baker got some warm water, bathed my wounded limb, and bandaged it as carefully as if I had been one of his children. Then he made a nice bed for me in one of the spare stalls, fetched a little saucer of milk, and placing it by my side, tempted me to drink. The only thing I disliked was his fastening me by a cord to a ring in the stall, which was not only disagreeable, but totally unnecessary, as I had no desire to leave the place, and should have had great difficulty in doing so had I wished to ever so much. So it was, however, and I remained a prisoner for some days, during which my leg gradually mended, although it has never again been as strong as the other.

And now I have but little more to add. True to the resolution I had formed in the first hour of my agony, I never more attempted to enter the woods in pursuit of the forbidden game. In the ordinary warfare against rats and mice, and in the capture of small birds who were foolish enough to come in my way, I passed a tranquil and happy existence. I reared several litters of kittens with the usual results of such family occurrences. Some of my family met with an early and watery grave; some were with me for a short time, and were then given away to slavery by the mortals who claim dominion over us weaker animals; some grew up to cathood, and then left me of their own accord; and at this present moment, although I have two sweet little creatures who sport and play about in the most engaging manner, I dare not indulge myself in the outpourings of maternal love, lest my heart should be broken by that separation which, sooner or later, is certain to occur.

I live, therefore, a good deal for and by myself: I pass a quiet, demure, respectable, uneventful existence, warn young cats against a habit of stopping out at night or too great fondness for rambles in the moonlight, and am considered by all the neighbours as a pattern of domestic propriety, and an example to be respected and followed by every well-regulated cat.

I had a little more to say, but I see a sparrow who has evidently hurt himself, and is unable to fly. An obvious duty is before me, and I must hasten to attend to the little flutterer before I am anticipated by another. Suffice it to say, that I have told you the principal events of the first of my nine lives, and if anything should occur in the other eight which is worth telling, I shall be very ready to make it known.

THE GRANNIES OF GIDDYHORN.

AFTER the final discomfiture of Dame Stickels, the noted witch of Brooke Hollow, and the adoption by her and her confederates of a quiet, respectable, and religious life, a great change came over the face of the country which they had so long kept in a state of alarm by their extraordinary pranks. Those who have read of her doings, duly chronicled in the volume bearing the title of "Crackers for Christmas," will be well aware that, as there were few witches in England more powerful and more notorious, so the sudden cessation of her evil influence must of necessity have produced a total revolution in the neighbourhood over which she had tyrannized for so long a period.

People could now walk along the lanes at eventide, even in a high wind, without being scared by the sight of an old woman riding on a broomstick, or a gigantic cat with eyes larger and brighter than those of an ordinary animal. Farmers did not find reason to complain of being spited; labourers went safely from their work without being tempted to join in a witches' carouse; the clergy resumed their wonted sway over minds which had begun to believe that a supernatural power was abroad too strong for even their power to control, and everything seemed to have returned to the natural order by which the affairs of the world are regulated. Even the famous, or infamous, Brooke

Hollow ceased to be regarded by the rustics as a place to be avoided; a cottage or two sprang up near it, inroads were made upon the wilderness of briars and brambles in which the witch's abode had been situated, and the traveller whistled carelessly as he passed along the bye-road, as if no evil thing had ever existed in that part of the world.

But although the generality of mankind regarded this change with satisfaction and pleasure, it must be owned that there were those to whom it brought neither one nor the other. From Wye—and possibly far beyond Wye, if we cared to inquire—but certainly from Wye right away to Lyminge, and perhaps further still—the great range of chalk hills had, from time immemorial, been the cradle of witchcraft, the habitual home and resort of warlocks and other uncanny creatures. The Witches of Wye, the Warlock of Coombe, even the great Wizard of Bockhanger, had all frequented some part or other of this locality, and it was not to be expected that the conversion of the Witch of Brooke Hollow to better things would at once and for ever drive out the whole race of evil creatures. Those who still remained were doubtless much annoyed, and their power greatly shaken by what had occurred; they kept quiet for a time, couching in their fastnesses and secret lurking-places upon the hills, avoiding all contact with humanity, and only venturing out on dark and windy nights, when they would be visible to no mortal eye. There were others, however, besides these of the worst kind, who little relished the altered state of things. It is well known that witchcraft, like consumption or insanity, runs in families, often descending from mother to daughter, or from any near female relative to another. So it turned out that the old rule was unchanged in the case of Goody Stickels. She had a niece who lived in the little village of Brooke, at that time even a smaller place than at present, situate, as we all know, between Wye at the west and north-west, Hastingleigh at the north-east, Brabourne at the east and south-east, and Hinxhill at the south.

: Betsy Stickels—for she bore the same surname as her terrible aunt—had been a mere child at the time of the break-up of the witches' party, and the break-down of their power. She grew up a tall, ungainly, rough kind of girl, and for some time no one remarked anything particular about her. She was, however, perpetually asking questions about her father's family, and especially about her aunt, whom she vastly despised since she had become an inmate of the Scott's-Hall Almshouses, and settled down to a good and tranquil life. Betsy's father was an old man, who had worked on the same farm for forty years; her mother was dead, and she had several brothers and sisters, of whom she was the third, her eldest sister Jane managing the house for their father. It was not with her family, though, that Betsy sought for company or loved to associate. She was for ever seeking for some of the old village crones who knew all the history of past events, and who loved nothing better than to gossip about them.

From this kind of person she learned all the stories of the power which her aunt had wielded, the mischief she had done, and how she had been dreaded by the country people round. After hearing these tales, the chief feeling in Betsy's mind was by no means one of regret for the many misdeeds of her aged relative. On the contrary, she seemed to think that the glory of the house of Stickels had fallen when these evil practices were abandoned, and that her aunt's departure from her former course was deeply to be lamented. This unhappy frame of mind was not checked by those with whom she was wont to talk. They always spoke of Dame Stickels and her associates as persons of great power and authority, and related many instances of their wonderful doings, and the vengeance they had frequently inflicted upon their enemies, without being able at the same time to tell of the pangs of remorse they must often have experienced, and the slavery to evil ones to which they were doubtless victims.

This kind of conversation was little calculated to do any good to Betsy Stickels, and gradually she became more and more silent and reserved at home, and took to roaming about alone at times when she had better have been in bed, and in places which she would have done well to have avoided. At home, indeed, she had no opportunity of conversing upon the subject she loved so well. Her worthy old father, who was a sober, honest, and industrious man, and went regularly to church every Sunday afternoon, never by any chance alluded to the past doings and character of his unhappy sister, and would have been very angry if the word witch had been mentioned in his hearing. He held that the best way to avoid evil relatives and their power was never to mention them, and to this rule he faithfully adhered.

By this means, his children, with the exception of the luckless Betsy, grew up steady, quiet, civil, and well-conducted, and his eldest daughter was considered quite the model young woman of the parish. Indeed, she was pretty as well as good, and went by the name of the " Brooke Rosebud " in the neighbourhood, which was a pleasant thing for her father to know, and to which she was certainly entitled by the freshness of her colour and delicacy of her complexion. The general admiration of her sister unfortunately lessened any good influence which she might have possessed and exercised over Betsy, by exciting in the breast of the latter feelings of jealousy, which not only prevented her from seeking Jane's company or advice, but made her avoid the one and resent the other. Such was the condition of affairs in the household of old Thomas Stickels, and such the feeling between the members of his family at the time of the occurrence of the strange and romantic incidents which it is my duty to narrate.

Some half mile or thereabouts to the east of the gorge which has been so famous for ages under the appellation of "Brooke Hollow," there lies a tract of land almost equally celebrated in the annals of witchcraft, and which was and is known by the name of Giddyhorn. Passing along the road from Brooke to Brabourne, with the chalk hills rising immediately upon your left, this tract consists of some ten or twelve acres, properly bearing the name which I have mentioned, although probably twice as much of the side hill above and adjoining it is of the same rough and ragged character, full of low stunted bushes, rough grass, a few small oak trees, and briars and thorns in abundance, being to this day some of the most barren and unprofitable land in the neighbourhood.

Giddyhorn proper rose and still rises somewhat abruptly from the road. There was a cart road which led into it, which had been formerly made by those who sought to dig chalk from that part of the hill, but they had long ceased to do so at the time of which I write, owing to the bad reputation which the place had acquired from its nearness to the residence of old Goody Stickels. The place was narrow at the entrance, but widened out as you ascended the hill, and for some distance was nothing but a tract of land covered with small beech trees and large tufts of grass, with soil so thin above the chalk that the latter constantly cropped up in sight. The hill was somewhat steep at this point, and when the beech trees ended, a rough mass of tangled wood and brambles succeeded, and then the hill rose abruptly again, rough and barren as I have described it.

To this day there is something quaint and curious about the place, which is still one of the wildest in the neighbourhood. But in the days we write of it was wilder still.

I do not know whether anybody claimed to be its owner, or whether it was common land at that time. No one, however, seemed to exercise any rights of ownership over it, and the foxes and badgers, rabbits and hedgehogs had it as a joint possession, only disputed by the large hawks which constantly hovered over the range of chalk hills, for which they have always had a great liking, and which they still occasionally frequent, and would do so still more but for the deadly warfare which man wages against every creature of prey which does not belong to his own species.

I have said that this Giddyhorn had an evil reputation, but I do not think that any particular charge had been brought against it in the days of the Brabourne witches, further than that it was generally supposed to have been one of their meeting-places, being admirably adapted for such a purpose.

There was a deep chalk-pit in it, with over-hanging banks and thickets of brambles; there were stunted trees here and there, with a decidedly witch-like look about them ; and there was a general want of healthy vegetation, which betokened the influence of evil to those who were always on the look-out for signs of such influence when they saw things different from what they should be.

I suppose it was this reputation of the place which made Betsy Stickels so fond of it. She fixed upon it as her favourite walk, and whenever she got away from home for a solitary ramble, she was sure to make her way to Giddyhorn.

This was observed by her family, and her sister Jane thought it but right to speak to Betsy about it. She disclaimed any wish to interfere with her movements, but warned her that mischief might come of it, reminded her that they lived in a neighbourhood where much scandal had attached to their name, and where people were easily suspected of witchcraft.

A Stickels ran greater danger than anyone of incurring such suspicion, and if it was known that one of the daughters of that ancient family was in the habit of frequenting such a place as Giddyhorn, stories might get afloat which would give her a bad name, and perhaps entail disagreeable consequences upon the whole family.

Betsy received these remarks, kindly intended as they were, with great indignation, telling her sister to mind her own business, and not interfere with her, or she would live to repent it. She added some sneering words about Jane's supposed beauty, and told her that, although she might be as conceited as she liked, and have her own way at home, she had better leave *her* alone, for she should always do what she pleased, and go where she liked, in spite of all the silly pink-and-white minxes that ever were born.

Finding her sister in this unpleasant frame of mind, Jane

said no more to her on that subject, but it was one which somewhat troubled her, and she could not but feel that her sister's conduct was such as might bring them all into trouble. She was too headstrong to be reasoned with by anyone, and her father, being at work all day, and generally pretty sleepy at night, did not know of her frequent wanderings, and never suspected the evil which was gathering round him and his.

As time wore on, Betsy's manner in the family perceptibly changed, and that, I am sorry to say, by no means for the better. She returned short, snappish answers to her father, and as for the rest of the party, her behaviour was simply intolerable. She assumed an air of authority over them, which they thought wholly unwarranted, would listen to no remonstrance, and made herself generally disagreeable to everybody. Still, as she had never made herself very useful in the house, her elder sister did not feel much change in that respect, and her frequent absence from home prevented the nuisance from being so great as might otherwise have been the case.

At last, however, a day came which was certainly an epoch in the history of the house of Thomas Stickels. Two neighbours, Mrs. Cook and Mrs. Cullen, had dropped in for a chat with Jane, and after a bit, strange to say, the conversation turned upon witches. The elder women were sufficiently careful of Jane's feelings not to make any special allusions to her unfortunate aunt, but they let fall several hints about the force of bad example, and how a bad name, once given, always sticks to people, so that at last the girl began to feel that they had something more than a general meaning in their observations.

Little by little it came out that Betsy's frequent visits to

Giddyhorn had been remarked, and that these, coupled with her disagreeable manner and rude bearing towards other people, had given rise to the suspicion that all was not as it should be with her in the matter of witchcraft.

No accusation, indeed, was made against her by the two worthy women who held this conversation with her sister, but they shook their heads gravely, heaved deep sighs occasionally, and "wished it might be all for the best," in the manner which worthy people generally do when they wish to insinuate something against their neighbours.

Their words and gestures greatly disturbed poor Jane, who, fully alive to all the discomfort, not to say danger, which might follow the slightest suspicion that her sister had dealings with the powers of darkness, heard with alarm as well as sorrow the evidence afforded by her visitors that such a suspicion was already afloat.

While she listened in this frame of mind, making but short answers, though at the same time expressing her belief that there was no reason for thinking ill of Betsy, it so fell out that the latter suddenly entered the room. The conversation immediately dropped, as is very frequently the case when people are speaking about a particular person, and are surprised by the entrance of the very individual who has furnished the theme for their discourse. These honest rustics, however, not being so skilled in the art of dissimulation as their betters, were unable to avoid showing that they had been interrupted while talking about something which they did not wish the new-comer to hear. They stopped short—too short in their discourse—hesitated —were silent for a moment—then began to talk about the weather in the most unblushing manner, and in fact behaved in a way which would have shown a far less intelligent person than Betsy Stickels that they were agitated and confused by her entrance.

" What did you stop talking for, when I came in ? " she abruptly asked of all three, addressing her question to no one in particular, and perhaps for that reason no one answered.

Betsy stamped her foot upon the ground at receiving no reply, and then said angrily :

" I *will* know what you were saying : abusing me, I'll be bound, or else you wouldn't have come to a dead stop as soon as I came in."

" Abusing you ! Betsy," answered Dame Cook in a wheedling tone, " Bless the girl, what should you go for to think that for: we was only a-talking about—about—about things in general, was we, neighbour Cullen ? "

" That's all," promptly responded the other—" we wasn't a-saying nothink what you mightn't hear, Betsy, that we sartainly wasn't."

" I don't believe ye, either of ye," sullenly replied the girl. " As for that pink-and-white faced sister of mine, she's always ready to say something against me, and I'll be bound you've been listening to her stories now, that's what ye've been about."

" Oh Betsy ! " interposed her sister : " However can you go for to say so ! I'm sure I never say a word against you, and these good neighbours of ours haven't said aught bad, only that they thought you took so many walks alone, dear, which you know I've told you of more than once, and how folk *would* talk."

" Then you *have* been talking against me, have you ? " angrily rejoined the girl ; " I thought I should find it out.

But I'll let you know I'm not to be insulted for nothing. If my own kith and kin turn against me, I'll find those who will help me. Take care of yourselves, Madam Cook and Madam Cullen, and look after your own affairs before you come abusing your neighbours. I'll be even with you both, I will! And as for you, you meek, poor-spirited, white-faced fool, who can't stand up for your own sister, but join in running her down, I'll pay you out for all your ill-natured interference, and joining with my enemies too. I'll look you down, that's what I'll do!" And as she spoke the girl fixed her eyes steadily upon her sister, and Jane fancied she felt a cold thrill pass down her backbone and right through her breast as she did so. She sank into a chair, whilst the two neighbours, not wishing to be present at a family quarrel, or for some other reason doubtless equally as good, slunk off as fast as they could, leaving the sisters alone.

"Oh Betsy!" said Jane, as soon as the neighbours had gone, and she had in some degree recovered from the strange feeling which had so suddenly come over her; "how can you talk so! You will make us enemies among the neighbours and bring us all into trouble by these ways."

"Hold your tongue," sharply replied the other, "and do not think you are going to bully me any longer. I've had enough of being put upon and kept down, and now I'll have my revenge."

As she spoke, she fixed her eyes again upon her sister, and the poor girl afterwards declared that they seemed to go through and through her. She sank back into her chair again in a half-fainting condition, whilst Betsy, with an expression of triumph in her countenance, muttered something to herself and left the room.

It is worthy of note, for it was remarked by the village people and a good deal talked about at the time, that during the next month nothing went right with either Mrs. Cullen or Mrs. Cook. The former had a fine brood of chickens carried off, to a bird, by the rats, the very night after the above-mentioned conversation at Thomas Stickel's cottage; moreover, her cow suddenly ceased to give milk, her favourite cat was shot or trapped (she never knew which) by the gamekeepers, and the moth got into the wardrobe where she kept her best clothes, and did more mischief than she could have believed possible in the time. As for Mrs. Cook, matters fared even worse with her, for a tramp stole all her linen which was drying on a hedge, the rabbits came in and ate every green thing she had in her garden, and, to crown all, she fell down and sprained her leg so that she couldn't get about for a fortnight. Putting two-and-two together, the good women had little difficulty in attributing these misfortunes to the ill-will and wicked devices of Betsy Stickels; and already an evil reputation began to encircle the girl, and it was freely whispered abroad in the parish that she bid fair to equal if not eventually to surpass in wickedness, her too notorious aunt, the witch of Brooke Hollow.

There were even those who openly spoke of going up to denounce her to Sir Edward Scott of Scott's Hall, or Richard Knatchbull of Mersham Hatch; but this was a serious matter for anyone to undertake, and in case of failure would be pretty sure to bring upon the head of him who had undertaken it the vengeance of the evil creatures whom he had tried to circumvent. So for some time nobody interfered with Betsy Stickels, and indeed there was nothing against her but vague rumour and idle suspicion. But from about the time of the visit of the two neighbours which I have related, poor Jane's health began visibly to decline. She lost her appetite, became unequal to much exertion of any kind, burst into tears upon the slightest pretext, and appeared to have lost all interest in life. Nobody knew what was the matter with her. Sometimes she would rally and seem for a while quite like her old self; then a sudden languor would come over her; unaccountable pains would seize upon her without any warning, and her condition caused much uneasiness to her father and friends.

All this time, Betsy's behaviour was anything but kind or sisterly. She either ridiculed and sneered at Jane's inability to go through her usual work as a pretence to cover her idleness, or else maintained a sullen, stolid indifference to her sufferings which no conduct of her sister's towards herself had at all merited. Now and then, indeed, she was so unkind as to taunt the poor girl with cruel words; and on more than one occasion went so far as to tell her that she had fared no better for interfering with other people's business, and that she hoped she repented having gossiped about her betters and spoken against her own sister to busy-bodies like Mrs. Cook and Mrs. Cullen.

All this pointed so clearly to Betsy being concerned in Jane's illness that the other members of the family openly mentioned it to each other, and one of the brothers of the two girls, James by name and a worthy fellow by nature, actually spoke to Betsy one day upon the subject.

The girl, however, heard him silently and sullenly, and then merely asked him what he meant by talking such nonsense. How could *she* hurt her sister? People might say what they pleased—*she* didn't care—and if they thought that Jane was struck, or charmed, or whatever they chose to call it, *she* couldn't help it. There would always be fools to the end of the world, and nonsense would be talked as long as people had tongues. Jane must take care of herself, and if she *was* bewitched, it just served her right for accusing her own sister of evil, and joining with her enemies.

James was so angry at the girl's way of talking that he took her by the shoulders, and shook her roughly, declaring that he would shake the nonsense out of her there and then. Upon this she got into a furious passion, and told him to look out for himself, and not meddle where he had no business, adding that it should be the worse for him that he had dared to lay hands upon her.

Sure enough, that very same afternoon, as the poor lad was felling a tree, his axe glanced from the wood and inflicted a deep wound on his leg with which he was laid up for weeks; and everyone who knew the circumstances, came, of course, to the only sensible and rational conclusion, namely, that this was witch-work, and that the misfortune had befallen him in consequence of his having been so rash and ill-advised as to fall out with his sister Betsy.

So she was more feared than ever in the family, and no one dared oppose her will or thwart her in any way.

Now, there was a young man who, to use the ordinary language of that part of the country, had "kept company" with Jane Stickels for the last two years, or, in other words, was her accepted lover. His name was Jack Cubison, and he lived just over the hill, in the parish of Hastingleigh, which lies to the north of Brooke and Brabourne.

It may well be supposed that young Cubison did not see his promised bride pining and fading away before his eyes without great sorrow, and an earnest desire that the mischief might, if possible, be stopped. He was a worthy young man, and withal as good-looking a specimen of a Kentish peasant as you could wish to behold. It was his habit to walk over to see his sweetheart of a Sunday (and sometimes upon other days when he had finished his work), and his road lay from Hastingleigh to New Barn, upon the crest of the hill, and so straight down the hill by the foot-path through the plantation on the side hill immediately to the west of a large field, which, from its peculiar shape, as seen from the valley below, was then as now, always known by the name of "the Leg of Mutton Field." But if Jack Cubison wanted a short cut from the top of the hill by New Barn across to old Thomas Stickel's house at Brooke, his way was to keep still further on along the hill, and strike down through Giddyhorn, unless indeed he passed beyond Giddyhorn itself and struck down the hill between that place and Brooke Hollow.

He often took one of these latter roads on the Sunday mornings when he went to see Jane; for, if it was fine, bright weather, the view from the top of the hill was very beautiful, and the breeze which blew from the distant sea across the valley was freshening to the body and inspiriting to the soul. Aye, and such a breeze and such a view as are not to be obtained everywhere. Stand on the top of the chalk range to-day, and face the south, and you will be well rewarded if you have toiled up the ascent for no other purpose than to look upon the scene before you.

Immediately in front of you, some ten or twelve miles

off, you see the beautiful blue of the sea bounding the glorious view beneath your feet. Glance at it for a moment, and then draw in your sight and enjoy each object that lies easily within your ken. Far away to the south-west are the hills above Hastings, dim and faint in the distance, and as you look nearer home in the same direction you see the woody country stretching up towards Ashford, and there rises the great church tower of Ashford herself, busy, bustling Ashford, and the clump of trees between Hothfield and Surrenden rises against the horizon beyond the town. Then, on your right, from Ashford, runs the range of chalk hills on the other side of the valley of the Stour, with East-wall park and woods clothing the side of the hill with magnificent foliage, and King's wood behind, and the little town of Wye nestles down out of your sight hidden by the continuation of the hill on which you stand. At your extreme left, miles away, rises the Beachborough mount, with the well-known summer-house upon its extreme point; beyond it, bearing round to the right, the huts at Shornecliffe camp and the ever-increasing town of Folkestone glitter in the distance; the high trees of Sandling intervene between these objects and you, and still further round stands that universal landmark, the old church of Aldington. Nearer to you, some four miles in a straight line, the great house of Mersham Hatch stands boldly upon its hill, a large red-brick mass, with wings right and left, and well surrounded with high trees behind, whilst its singularly picturesque park lies in front. Then, over the whole valley you cast your eye, to behold indeed a smiling country: the old tower rises out of the middle of Naccult wood below you, the pleasant hamlet of Brabourne Leese is but a little to the left, and then Scott's-Hall " wilderness " just beyond.

There is but one thing wanting to complete the landscape, and that is a river to wind through that lovely valley, and relieve the eye as it gazes upon the woods and pastures, the corn-fields and hop-gardens which lie as in a map before it. Still, having no river but the Stour, which in this part of its course is too small for the purpose, we do as well as we can without one, and nobody can deny that the view from the chalk hills is superlatively fine.

So thought Jack Cubison when he walked on Sunday morning to visit Jane Stickels, and frequently kept along the top of the hills for a longer distance than he need have done, in order to enjoy as much of the view as possible. But in the evening it was not so easy to find the way, and he therefore generally turned down the regular footpath to which I have already alluded.

It happened, however, that upon one fine evening when his work was over rather sooner than usual, and he had been feeling very anxious all day about Jane, he determined to go over and see her, and for some reason or other omitted to turn down the footpath, but kept on across the common land on the edge of the hill until he was just above Giddy-horn. Then he turned down, skirting Giddyhorn, which was now immediately on his left, Brooke Hollow being some half-mile or more to the right as he descended the hill. It was between seven and eight o'clock, upon an April day, when the light was beginning to grow fainter, but the sun had not quite done with the world yet. The air was a little cool, but not otherwise than pleasantly so, and the quiet stillness of the evening gave promise of a continuance of the genial spring-weather on the morrow. Jack Cubison descended the hill cautiously, for it was somewhat steep, and had got about halfway down when his course was suddenly and unexpectedly arrested by the sound of a voice from the Giddyhorn side. It was an odd place from which to hear a voice, and under any circumstances Jack would have been surprised at the occurrence. He was doubly so, however, when the voice distinctly pronounced his own name. There was no mistake about it.

"Jack Cubison," it said; and upon his stopping short and looking in the direction from which the sound seemed to come, it repeated the words again.

Now it has been already stated that Giddyhorn, for certain reasons, did not enjoy the very best of reputations, and many men would have been much alarmed at hearing themselves called by a voice from among its beeches whilst passing them alone towards evening.

Cubison was not sufficiently well-educated to be above the prejudices and superstitions of his class, and I do not pretend to say that he heard the unexpected sound unmoved upon the present occasion. But he had a bold heart of his own, and being, moreover, conscious of no evil motive in the expedition upon which he was journeying, did not feel that he had anything to be ashamed or afraid of, or that any act of his had given any evil ones power over him. So when the voice repeated his name a second time, he hemmed and coughed a bit, as one who wished to find his own voice for certain before he replied to the other, and then said aloud:

"Eh? what say? I be Jack Cubison, sure enough: here I be!" and calmly awaited the reply.

It came soon enough, for the same voice presently said—

"Whither be thou a-going, Jack Cubison? on a fool's errand, I wot."

"Not I," said honest Jack, firing up at once at the

implied insult to himself and his sweetheart, "I bea'nt after no fool's errand, nor I bea'nt no fool for to go where I be going, and that's to see the best lass this side o' Lunnon town."

A scornful laugh greeted this reply, and the voice immediately afterwards rejoined:

"Did I not say thou was't going on a fool's errand, to see a poor, puny, drooping, white-faced chit of a girl, with no more pluck than a mouse, and no more brains than an owlet?"

Jack Cubison forgot his temporary disquietude at the strangeness of the address, in anger at hearing this uncalled for attack upon his betrothed.

"Poor! and puny! and drooping!" he exclaimed indignantly: "who art thou that callest thy betters names? If Jane has been drooping lately, that is no reason why I should shun to visit her; and if it be caused by anything evil that has been at work against her, a malison light upon those who have done it."

A sigh as of pain came from the beeches as Jack pronounced these words, and there was a moment's pause, and then the voice went on again:

"Thou art easily vexed, Jack Cubison; easily vexed in truth—yet why should'st thou suspect evil practices against thy favourite wench? Girls do pine and droop without aught being worked or planned against them, and thy Jane has never been strong. It had been better if thou hadst taken up with her sister Betsy, who is a rare fine girl, and would make thee a better wife altogether."

"Eggs and bacon!" cried Cubison, using in his surprise an ejaculation common in his family, "this beats cock-fighting. To think of naming that gawky, ill-favoured wench in the same day with my Jenny! Nay, nay, master or missus, or whatsumdever thou beest that speakest to me, I'll no Betsy while I've Jane to look at, nor nobody would as had got their senses about 'em—Ha! what's that?" Jack broke off suddenly in his speech as something like a bramble came violently against his leg, though he was standing still at the moment, and inflicted upon him a severe scratch. "Drat the brambles," he exclaimed, "I wish they was somewheres else." He paused and stooped down to rub his leg, when the voice again accosted him.

"Thou usest hard words, good Jack, and undeserved withal. Jane may be pretty to the eye, but beauty is skin deep, and a delicate, unhealthy girl would make a poor mistress for a labourer's cottage. Betsy may be less lovely to look upon at first sight, but she grows upon you, she does; and a finer, stronger, and braver girl is not to be found hereabouts. Moreover, she likes you well, Jack, though you mayn't know it."

"Know it?" cried Cubison on hearing this speech, "no, nor don't want to neither. I don't know who you be that stick up for Betsy Stickels after this fashion, but I be'ant that kind o' chap as twists and turns like a whirligig, I be'ant; and I wouldn't give up my young woman not if Betsy was twice the girl I take her to be, let alone all the queer things they say about her."

"Queer things? what queer things, forsooth?" interrupted the voice.

"Never mind," replied honest Jack, "this ain't the place nor the time to talk about queer things, and I must be getting on," and with these words he took a step forward, as if to proceed on his journey. No sooner, however, did he do so, than the voice accosted him in the sweetest and most persuasive tones.

"Dear Jack, kind Jack, don't be hurrying off in this uncivil way. Come into the beeches and join our pleasant party here. Supper will be ready directly, and we shall be so glad of your company."

Now it must be owned—since this is a true story, and no mere invention of an idle brain—that Jack Cubison, with many virtues, had certain faults and failings, and one of these was a partiality for good living when it happened (which was not often) to fall in his way. He had been full of righteous anger when his sweetheart had been sneered at, he had boiled over with virtuous indignation when it was suggested to him that he should exchange one sister for the other; but when the magic word supper was mentioned, he felt neither indignation nor anger. I am sorry to say that he forgot those feelings for the moment; and not only so, but the strangeness of the invitation, the lateness of the hour, and the ill reputation of the place, were all absent from his mind at that instant, when he foolishly stopped short on hearing the word "supper." He stopped short, I say, and more than this, he turned his head in the direction of the place from which the voice had seemed to proceed. As he did so a most savoury odour seemed to rise from the wood and steal upon his senses: it was the odour of roast meat; lamb, as it seemed to him, and there was something remarkably tempting about it. Had Jack been wise, he would have turned up his nose at the odour and at the invitation which had just been given him; he would have answered the latter with a determined negative, and full of good thoughts and good intentions, would have pursued his journey down the hill in spite of any thing which could have been done to prevent him. But the moment he turned his head, and instead of avoiding the pleasant odour, sniffed it up and enjoyed it, I have no doubt that his powers of resistance to evil were sensibly weakened.

No human being can parley or trifle with evil things or evil people without being the worse for it. There is no mistake so fatal as to think that one can play with what is wrong, or associate with people who laugh at and despise what is right, and yet come off unhurt ourselves.

Jack Cubison had certainly no evil intentions in stopping, or in turning his head, or in listening to the invitation given him on Giddyhorn; but it will be seen that this hesitation of his, and his not being resolute in avoiding the temptation altogether, led to mischief which might have been escaped if he had simply turned his back upon the place, and gone straight on without stopping to parley with what he knew could not come of good, and from which therefore no good was likely to come. He turned his head, I say, sniffed the good smell, and hesitated.

Instantly the voice resumed the conversation, in tones more sweetly seductive than before.

"Nice Jack, kind Jack, dear Jack," it said, "do come, like a cheery old boy, and join our merry party. We won't keep you long, Jack, and we shall all be so jolly together."

Jack half turned away, and said, but in a less determined tone than that in which he had hitherto spoken:

"Well—I don't know—'tis getting late—I hadn't ought to stop; I think not, thank ye kindly all the same," and with these words he took a doubtful kind of half step orward.

"Oh don't say no, dear Jack," again said the voice in a most pressing manner; "just stay for one little five minutes, Jack. There's roast lamb for supper, dear old boy, and oh! the ale! such fizzing good ale!"

This was too much for Jack Cubison. He was, to use his own expression, "a little bit peckish," after his walk; the air was fresh and cool, and a slice or two of roast lamb and a glass of ale had a sound about them which were very tempting to the young man. So he turned round again and made a step or two towards the beeches of Giddyhorn.

The voice continued its invitation, couched in the most pleasant words. "This way, dear Jack; there, just step over the ditch and through the gap to your right, and creep up the bank and you will find us."

Jack did as he was told, for all idea and indeed all power of resistance seemed to have left him—as will always be the case with people who give way to temptation; they slip on and on with marvellous ease, and only discover when too late that it was at the first step they should have resisted, and firmly checked the first promptings of evil.

Jack scrambled across the ditch, which was dry enough, and all of chalk, with no grass or moss upon it, which was mostly the same with the bank, up which he crawled as soon as he had got through the gap in the hedge; and there he was, standing amid the stunted beeches of Giddyhorn, with thick tufts of coarse grass growing beneath, and lumps of chalk cropping up on every side; there was a belt of higher trees between this spot and the hedge, and there it was densely dark; but as soon as Jack Cubison had forced his way through these, pushing the branches on one side with his sturdy arms, he came out into the beeches and found himself at once in light and also in company. A kind of chalk-pit had been scooped out in a place where the beeches grew somewhat less thickly, and yet formed a screen round the spot, though not so as to prevent a partial view of the vale being obtained from it.

The pit was not very deep, hardly deep enough, in fact, to be called a pit; but it was pretty wide, and the tufts of grass around had been pulled up and strewn round it, so as to make a sort of carpet upon which one might sit with ease and comfort. Some people, indeed, were already doing so, as Jack immediately perceived. There was a fire smouldering away in the middle of the space, and around this were several figures upon whom the young man at once fixed his eyes.

The first glance showed him that they were all members of the softer sex; the second, that none of them was without considerable personal attractions. One had magnificent raven-black hair which fell in luxuriant tresses over her shoulders; another had features which were simply perfect in every particular; a third had an expression of face to which the word "bewitching" might have been appropriately applied. The eyes of all the party appeared to Jack to sparkle with marvellous brilliancy, but the thing which surprised him most was the sight of Betsy Stickels seated amongst the rest, and seemingly as much at home as any of them.

It must be owned that his first thought on seeing the girl was that he had done her a great injustice when he had recently called her gawky and ill-favoured. She now seemed to him very much the reverse. Her eyes really shone beautifully in the light of the fire; her complexion assumed a delicacy and her face a depth and richness of colouring which he had never before noticed; and as she rose from her seat to welcome the new comer, the proportions and symmetry of her figure seemed really marvellous.

All the party rose at once to their feet and greeted Jack Cubison with boisterous shouts of merry laughter; though to his mind they died away in rather an unpleasant and melancholy cadence, and the echo did not seem to laugh back as it usually did on that side hill. Betsy Stickels came forward to meet the young man, and taking him affectionately by the arm, expressed her delight that he had come to join their party, and proceeded to introduce him to the others.

There was Dame Punyer from Wye, and Mrs. Kennett, Lamming, Fagg, Peck, and Vidgen, all hailing from the same town, and one or two others, whose names Jack either did not catch or could not afterwards recollect. They were all dressed more smartly than he had ever seen ladies dressed before; and as to Betsy herself, he had no idea that the cottage of old Thomas Stickels, or any wardrobe therein, could have contained such fine clothes as those in which that young woman was arrayed. Jack had no time, however, to ask any questions about the manner in which she had become possessed of such gay garments, for as soon as she had introduced him to her friends they all began to talk at once (which, as women in their ordinary condition never do such a thing, at once proves them to have been creatures of no common sort), and drew him along to the fireside, around which they speedily reseated themselves, the guest being placed next to Betsy Stickels, with a damsel on the other side of him whom he had never before seen, but who was presented to him under the name of Madge Hancock.

By this time Jack Cubison had no more scruples about joining the repast, of the savoury nature of which he was more than ever assured by the evidence of his senses. All thoughts of Jane and of the object with which he had started that evening had completely vanished from his mind, and he felt a strange pleasure in the new scene to which he found himself introduced, and the merry acquaintances which he had just made. They were not only merry, but positively uproarious in their mirth, and Jack seemed to catch some of the intoxication of the moment. He ate and drank freely, and found both the roast lamb and the ale undeniably good. Betsy continually pressed upon him the choicest morsels, and her manner towards him was so affectionate that he felt his heart warm towards her, and when at length she put her arm round his neck and her face very near to his, I am sorry to say that he so far forgot his duty to Jane as to bestow upon her sister a very hearty kiss, which she was perfectly ready both to receive and to return.

In short, as the truth had better be stated without any concealment, Jack Cubison completely forgot his duty, and abandoned himself to the ways and doings of the evil society in which he was, as freely as if he had really been one of them. Betsy was still lavishing her caresses upon him, not without sundry jealous glances at his neighbour on the other side, who was likewise disposed to be affectionate, when Dame Punyer, who seemed to be one in authority, as probably the oldest of the party, held up her hand, which literally glittered with the costly rings upon her fingers, and demanded attention.

"Sisters," she said, as soon as silence had been maintained, "we must not quite forget business in pleasure. We have a new recruit to-night in Betsy's young man, and must make him one of us without delay, so that he may be able to join in our nightly frolics, and share the privileges which we possess. We must ask him first, of course; but after the friendly manner in which he has joined us to-night, there can be no doubt of his willingness to be one of us, and as soon as he has given his consent we can go through the usual ceremony at once."

These words were received with much applause and approving laughter, whilst they fell upon Jack's ears without causing him either alarm or suspicion, so engrossed was he with Betsy and the fascinations of the scene. Then Dame Punyer turned to him forthwith and said:

"Jack Cubison, art thou willing to join this society, well-known on the whole hill-side as 'the Giddyhorn Grannies'?"

Jack knew nothing whatever of the society, or of what belonging to it might imply; but as the question was asked him, he felt the soft cheek of Betsy Stickels pressed lovingly against his own, whilst at the same time she whispered in gentle tones:

"Say 'yes,' dearie Jack; say 'yes,' to please his Betsy."

With no further thought save to make himself agreeable, and to afford the girl some return for her kindness towards him, the foolish young man hesitated not for a single moment, but pronounced the word "Yes," upon which Betsy embraced him with greater fervour than before ; his other neighbour held to his lips a brimming glass of ale, and all the party laughed out a wild chorus of satisfaction at his reply, which sound was succeeded by a curious kind of subdued chuckle from the beeches around, which caused Jack to turn his head to see from whom it proceeded, but seeing nothing, he thought it had been only a strange echo.

Then Dame Punyer rose to her feet and stretched both her arms over the fire, which was now smouldering at her feet ; she muttered some words which Jack could not quite make out, but which seemed to partake of the character of a solemn incantation, and then she said, in a voice deeper and more solemn than that in which she had previously spoken :

> " Sisters of the chalky range,
> Sisters weird and wise and strong,
> Mortal nature we may change
> By the dance and by the song :
> Say, shall one or both be tried,
> Here to-night on mountain-side ? "

As soon as she had spoken these words, a loud cry came from all the party of " Both ! Both ! " and, as Jack stared helplessly about him, not very well knowing what it all meant, Betsy whispered low in his ear again :

" Say ' Both,' my pretty boy," and, accordingly, without thought of any kind on the matter, he joined in with the rest and shouted " Both, both," which seemed to amuse the party not a little. Then Dame Punyer bowed her head, as if assenting to the wish of the party, and turning to a tall damsel who sat next her, and addressing her as Sister Vidgen, gave her some muttered directions, upon which she arose, her black hair falling in profusion over her

shoulders, and her eyes sparkling with extraordinary brilliancy as she thus sang:

1.

" When dark is the sky, and the heavy black cloud
Is able the rays of the moon to enshroud,
Then, then, sisters dread, is our hour of delight,
And Giddyhorn Grannies ride forth on the night.

2.

When once safe and sound, on our broom-sticks astride,
Through the darkness of night as we merrily ride,
The owls and the bats start and tremble with fear,
For they know that the Giddyhorn Grannies are near.

3.

By day-time in cottage and cabin we lurk,
Our charms to prepare and our magic to work ;
But night cometh soon, and then, thrice in the week,
The Giddyhorn Grannies their beeches do seek.

4.

Look down from the heights, and gaze far o'er the dell,
What hamlet or house can escape from our spell ?
Strive all that man can, and do all that man may,
The Giddyhorn Grannies must carry the sway.

5.

Who breathes but a word against us and our fame,
Ere long he shall sadly repent of the same ;
His cattle shall pine and his lambs shall die fast,
Till he cringe to the Giddyhorn Grannies at last.

6.

From Giddyhorn beeches we proudly may look
On Brabourne and Bircholt, on Hinxhill and Brooke,
And know that by spell, charm, love-potion, and dream,
The Giddyhorn Grannies are ever supreme.

7.

Our beeches grow thick in our witch-loving Wye,
And you pass them in coming from lone Hastingleigh,
In passing, turn in, and full soon shall ye find
The Giddyhorn Grannies are loving and kind.

8.

From lone Hastingleigh has come Cubison Jack,
And stept on a path whence there's no looking back;
Our beeches when once he has revelled among
To Giddyhorn Grannies he's bound to belong.

9.

The laugh's on his lips and the smile on his face,
As he yields to his Betsy's endearing embrace;
She'll hold him so safe in her loving young arms,
Need Giddyhorn Grannies no magical charms.

10.

Yet charms must be sought for, and spells must we work,
Lest the path freely chosen hereafter he shirk ;
Man's nature is frail—and by spell strong and deep
The Giddyhorn Grannies their partner must keep ! "

Loud shouts of applause followed the recital of these
lines by the handsome Mistress Vidgen; and as soon as they
were concluded, the whole party arose to their feet, and,
linking arm in arm, danced slowly and solemnly round the
fire in perfect silence for some minutes, Jack Cubison's arms
being securely locked in those of his companions on either
side. Then, at a signal from Dame Punyer, the whole
party suddenly stood aside, and crowded together beneath
one of the beech trees, while new actors appeared upon the
scene. From the dark shadows of the beeches came several
cats, one for each of the ladies, and took the places which

the latter had just vacated at the fire.   They were animals, as it appeared to Jack, of a larger size than common, and their eyes sparkled with the same sort of unnatural lustre which he had observed in those of his companions.

The creatures approached the fire, and after giving vent to several remarkably discordant sounds, differing but little from those which usually proceed from ordinary cats at night, linked their fore-legs as the women had done their arms, and, standing upon their hind legs, began a kind of dance round the embers of the fire of such a grotesque character, that it would have struck Jack as indescribably ludicrous, if the circumstances of his peculiar position had not prevented him from seeing it in that light.   The women remained silently watching while the cats danced, but Betsy kept her arm locked all the time in Jack's, as if fearful of losing him.

When the animals had completed their singular performance, they uttered a few more cries not a whit more harmonious than those with which they had previously favoured the audience, and then retreated within the shadow of the trees.   Then old Dame Punyer came slowly forward, and stood in the middle of the smouldering embers of the fast declining fire.   Turning with her face to Jack Cubison, she lifted her arms high above her head, and pronounced, in deep and awe-inspiring tones, the following words:

> " Son of Cubison, although
>   Thou hast sought our life to know,
>   And to see the magic might
>   Gathered on the hill to-night,
>   More thou hast to seek and learn,
>   If thou wouldst from labour turn—

Turn to lead a life of ease
'Neath the sacred beechen trees:—
Wilt thou for this boon forego
Mortal toil and mortal woe,
And the evils of a life
Ever tried by want and strife ;
And the recompense, forsooth,
Be it false or be it truth,
Which by priestcraft is foretold
To a world in woe grown old ?
Wilt thou this vain shadow quit
For a better fortune fit ;
In the present take thy fill
Of the pleasures of the hill ;
Join the Grannies who adorn
The fair side of Giddyhorn ;
Join with them for weal or woe,
And a mortal's fate forego ? "

Now, whilst the Dame was speaking these words, which she did after a most impressive fashion, Jack Cubison was in a perfect maze of bewilderment. The extraordinary sights he had seen, and the still more wonderful things which he had heard, had confused his brain not a little ; and his confusion was hardly rendered less by the conduct of Betsy, who was all the time squeezing his arm in the most affectionate manner, and urging him in a low voice to say "Yes" in a decided tone, and she was sure he would always be glad he had done so. Whether he actually did say the word or not, I am unable to say ; but I suppose, if not, that it was one of those occasions upon which silence is understood to "give consent," for as soon as Dame Punyer had finished her address, she waved in her hand the tail of a black cat, which she drew from beneath her belt, and exclaimed :

" Here we number sisters nine,
Knowing each the mystic sign—

> Son of Cubison, 'tis now
> Thou must take the solemn vow.
> On the tail of brindled cat—
> On the jar of viper's fat—
> On the toe-bone of the dead—
> And by great Medusa's head—
> To be true, and serve alone
> The dread Power we Grannies own."

As she spoke, she took from the same place a small jar, and another dark-coloured object, which she held in her hand, and beckoned to the young man to approach. At the same moment, Betsy murmured to him in soft and enticing tones :

"Now, my pet Jack, go forward and do as she tells you ; and we'll all be so jolly together : there's a duck, go on."

And at the same time she gave him a little push forward. He moved on with a slow and uncertain step, and the eyes of all around him seemed to glitter more brightly and wildly than ever, while from the bushes in which the cats had concealed themselves came mews and miaulings of a perfectly unearthly character. Still it seemed as if the hand of Fate was upon Jack Cubison, and that he had no power of resistance ; so difficult, indeed, is it for those to resist or return who have once ventured upon the path of evil. Slowly and fearfully he approached, dragging one leg after the other, and feeling the reverse of comfortable, until he had drawn near to the expiring fire, and stood within arm's length of Dame Punyer. Then she lifted her voice and spoke again :

> "Now the time, and now the vow—
> What thou see'st me do, do thou."

Then she devoutly kissed the tail which she grasped in

her hand and held it out to Jack, who mechanically did so too : she then performed the same ceremony with the jar of adder's fat, and so did Jack ; and she next pressed to her lips the dark-coloured object above mentioned, which Jack afterwards declared to be a small bone which might be that of a toe, or finger for what he knew ; but at any rate he followed the old woman's example, and she then restored the articles to the place from which she had drawn them. Then she raised her arms aloft once more, and addressed the young man again in the following language :

> " Sworn on the tail, the jar, and bone of dead,
> Now by each hair on fell Medusa's head
> Swear to be vassal to our sov'reign lord,
> And afterwards receive the magic word.
> But, that we all may know thee firm and true,
> Kneel on the ground and we will kneel with you."

So saying the dame knelt down by the fireside, and the rest of the party, having silently approached while she was speaking, knelt also. She made a sign to Jack Cubison to do the same, and Betsy gave a nod and a wink to him which conveyed a similar wish on her part. Had he complied with her request at once I cannot tell what would have been the result. He had given his consent to join that awful band, he had eaten and drank with them, he had listened to their song and taken a part in their magic dance ; nay, he had now actually taken the oath prescribed to him, or at least had gone through the preliminary steps before actually repeating the words.

If then, he had pronounced those words upon his knees, showing by that position his readiness to acknowledge the same Power whom they obeyed, and implying his readiness to kneel and worship with them, in all probability he would have been theirs for ever.

It was at the very instant that he was about to yield to the command of Dame Punyer, and the request of Betsy, scarcely feeling able to resist if he had desired to do so, that the scene was interrupted in a manner totally unexpected by any of the party.

A sound was heard as of branches being pushed aside by the hasty passage of some one forcing his way through them, and a loud voice sounded upon the ears of those who had hitherto had the place to themselves.

"Hallo!" it shouted, which was not of itself an expression calculated to excite uneasiness or alarm, but which came at a moment when any expression at all was both startling and vexatious to most of the party. They began to rise hurriedly to their feet, but before they could do so the figure of the new comer burst into the open space, and stood before them. It was a man, past middle age, but of a vigorous frame withal, and somewhat taller than the ordinary height. He was clad in common fustian garments, and had nothing remarkable in his appearance save an air of courage and determination, which indeed he must have possessed in order to break in upon that dread company upon Giddyhorn hill-side.

This was no other than John Oliver, the parish clerk of Wye, a man noted for his hatred of all appertaining to witches and witchcraft, and his resolute perseverance in putting down the same. Whether because he was protected by his calling, which brought him so constantly in contact with sacred things, or whether he had some special aid unknown to the world at large, certain it is that the enmity of the evil creatures against whom he ever waged war had not been able to injure him, and he was always upon the look-out to discover and defeat their wicked schemes.

Now it had chanced, strangely enough, that upon this particular evening worthy John Oliver had been over to see a crony of his at Hinxhill, and upon his return had called in to see how his old friend Thomas Stickels was getting on. He found that respectable man well enough in body, but sick at heart on account of the condition of his beloved daughter Jane; so he sat down for a while to comfort him with some neighbourly chat.

Presently Jane herself entered the room, looking so pale, wan, and woe-begone, that she merely seemed the ghost of her former self. John Oliver looked at her with a sad but searching eye, and felt convinced in his own mind that hers was no ordinary illness, but that witchcraft was at work.

He said nothing to this effect, however, either to father or daughter, but spoke cheering words of sympathy to both, and they were well pleased with his visit and conversation.

It was not long before Jane became fidgety, and showed evident signs of impatience, getting up and walking to the window, then heaving a heavy sigh as she removed her seat, and appearing disquieted about something to an unusual degree.

Master Oliver, seeing that this was the case, asked whether the girl felt unwell, or whether anything had occurred to annoy her. She denied that such was the case, but old Stickels gave his friend a sly nudge, and observed in a low voice: "She's a-expecting of her young man—he most times comes this night, as 'twere, and she's a-worritting herself because he's behind."

As this explanation seemed natural enough, Oliver made no reply; but at last Jane's uneasiness became too much for her self-control, and she asked her father what he thought would have come to Jack that he was so late? Her father of course could not say more than that he supposed the young man had been delayed, or prevented coming, and observed that it was not so very late, after all, for Betsy was still out.

This led to further conversation on the matter, and John Oliver was filled with suspicion when he heard of the usual behaviour of his friend's second daughter, and her proneness to be abroad late at night.

As Jane, however, seemed still uneasy, and could not but be fearful that some evil had befallen her lover (as, indeed, there had, though not such as she anticipated), the good clerk, who was about starting on his homeward journey, promised to walk a little way towards Hastingleigh, and to inquire whether anything had been seen of the truant, and, if he met him, to hasten him on his road.

Accordingly, John Oliver went round near to Giddyhorn, although by so doing he was going more than a little distance out of his way. Fancying that he saw the faint glimmer of a light in Giddyhorn itself, where he knew that no light should be, he drew nearer to the place instead of hurrying off in the other direction, as most men would undoubtedly have done. Again the light gleamed through the beeches, and stout-hearted John determined that, danger or no danger, he would find out what it meant. So he went boldly in at the bottom of the hill, climbed slowly up the chalk ascent; and, although the glare of the dying embers of the fire was now hid from him by the foliage of the beeches, a murmur of voices reached his ears which guided him to the very place where Dame Punyer had just concluded her incantations, and was about to administer to the luckless Jack Cubison the terrible oath which would bind him for ever to be one with her and the weird sisterhood of which she was so notorious and powerful a member.

The shout which John Oliver gave when he came thus suddenly among the party had a great and wonderful effect upon them, but it was marvellously increased by his next proceeding. An ordinary man might have been induced to think that the presence of the company he saw before him could be explained, and that it was nothing more than an evening picnic among neighbours which was going on. But John Oliver had too much experience in such matters, to be deceived for a moment. Moreover, had his eyesight been baffled and his judgment misled, he had that about him which would speedily have corrected the former and set the latter right.

Years before, by means of a pilgrimage to Canterbury, he had obtained some wooden beads which the Monks of St. Augustine's had informed him were undoubtedly once the property of, and worn by St. Edward the Confessor. These relics he always wore about him, fastened upon a string round his neck; and he knew well that nought of evil could be concealed or could stand before so powerful and holy a charm.

By this means, or by some other, John Oliver knew at once that those upon whose meeting he had broken in were not what they should be; and he hesitated not for a single instant as to the course he should pursue.

Throwing open his vest he displayed the beads to view, and as he did so shouted in a loud voice, " If there be aught of evil here, let it fly at once! Here stands a man who has gotten a charm which makes every witchling to shake with alarm. Away, evil ones! Away!"

Jack Cubison, who had evidently been under some strange spell hitherto, felt his reason and his courage return together as he heard these same words, though he trembled violently as if from nervous exhaustion as he saw what followed. A marvellous change suddenly came over the appearance of those with whom he had been in company. Beauty vanished from their faces, grace and symmetry from their figures, and he saw only several gaunt, grey, haggard old women, with an expression of mingled fear and pain upon their uncomely features. Betsy, indeed, looked no older than she really was, but all softness and every pretence of good looks passed from her countenance, and she appeared the same ungainly and ill-favoured wench which, until that night, he had always supposed her to be. More occurred, however, than a mere change in the form and features of the witches. Each turned in affright from the relic displayed by the new comer. Each rushed to the beeches behind and seized a broom stick, of which articles several had apparently been concealed hard by, though Jack had not seen them before.

In another instant each witch was astride of her broomstick; upon the shoulder of each leapt a cat, these creatures appearing now to be of the ordinary size of such animals; and with a confused, hasty cry of "Mount and scurry! mount and scurry!" the whole party rose up into the air, and flew off as fast as they could, leaving Jack Cubison and his deliverer the only occupants of the place.

Jack rubbed his hand and arm across his eyes; then he looked up, then down, then on one side and then on the

THE GRANNIES OF GIDDYHORN.—p. 320

other, and felt more queerly than he had ever done before in his life. The good parish clerk, however, did not leave him long to himself and his meditations, strange and interesting as they must doubtless have been.

"Is this you, John Cubison?" he asked, in a solemn, not to say severe, tone. "Is this Jane Stickels' sweetheart, out here on the hill side in such awful company? Speak out and let us know what all this means."

The young man rubbed his eyes again, and looked his questioner in the face without an answer. He was still too confused and bewildered to explain matters as he could have wished. But Master Oliver made no long pause before he repeated his question.

"Tell us how you came to be here, John Cubison," he said sternly, "or it may turn out worse for you than I could wish. Such beings as those with whom I found you are not to be suffered in a Christian land, and those who choose them for companions must look to it, lest they share their fate."

Jack drew a long breath at these words, and making a violent effort to speak, brought out the following remarkable words:

"I never seed nothing like it afore, not in all my born days, I didn't."

Judging from these words, and from the manner and appearance of the young man, that he was probably not far gone in the wickedness of witchcraft, and had possibly been only a victim instead of a sharer in the evil practices which had doubtless been going on, Master Oliver now spoke more kindly, and bade the young man speak out boldly and tell the truth, by which means he would be more likely to escape any ill consequences from what had happened.

Y

Thus admonished, and encouraged withal by the evidently friendly intentions of his companion, Jack Cubison opened his heart and his mouth to him, and told him all that had happened; only forbearing to mention the name of Betsy, partly from a feeling of shame at the recollection of the tender passages which had occurred between them, and partly from a desire to shield from possible danger a member of Jane's family.

John Oliver, however, had a keen eye for such matters, and had, moreover, as we know, been looking out for Betsy as well as for Jack himself. He therefore mentioned his suspicion that she had been among the witches, but as he did not ask Jack the question point-blank, the latter merely spoke of his own confusion and helplessness as having so obscured his intellect as to make him uncertain who had been there and what had been done, and led his companion to believe that he had no knowledge of Betsy's presence.

The two men now walked away together down the hill, and when they came to the turning towards Thomas Stickels' cottage, Oliver told the young man that he must now leave him, as he was obliged to get home to Wye, and promised him that if he would be cautious in future, avoid evil company, and never be out on the hills late at night, he would hush the matter up and not bring him into trouble by letting it get abroad.

Jack thanked him warmly, and proceeded to the cottage, where Jane was still anxiously hoping for his appearance, though she had begun to fear that he would not come. Almost the first sight that greeted his eyes was the figure of Betsy, seated demurely in one corner of the room, as if nothing had happened, and playing with a black kitten which was rubbing itself against her, and purring as innocently as you please. The girl gave one quick glance at him as he entered the room, but said nothing of their having met before, and appeared to be very much in her usual condition.

Old Stickels, however, began at once to ask the reason of his being so late, saying that it was already past their usual bedtime, and that they had given up expecting him at all. He added that he had just been blowing up Betsy for stopping out so late, too, and really thought the world was turning topsy-turvy, since people couldn't be content to keep regular hours and be in bed at a proper time. Jack made the best excuses he could, but the reproachful looks of Jane were almost too much for him, and he longed to open his heart to her, and tell her the whole truth.

This, however, he dared not do, for it would have been dangerous to him if it had got noised abroad that he had been supping with witches in Giddyhorn Beeches. Besides this, Betsy's eye was upon him, and he felt an uneasy sensation which made him desirous of shunning the subject in which they were jointly interested. So he invented some story of having been detained at home, and got out of it in the best manner he could. He was not at his ease, however, and had never enjoyed himself so little in the company of his betrothed. It seemed as if a bar had been raised up between them which had never previously existed, and things were much less pleasant than of old.

Jack strove to get over this feeling, and when, after a few minutes, he thought it was time for him to be off, he put his arm gently round her waist, about to show his affection and fidelity by the not unusual demonstration of a kiss. At this instant, however, a sudden scratch on the ankle made him start back; and, looking down, he perceived Betsy's kitten, which had stolen silently across the room and given him this sharp but unexpected hint to be more careful of his behaviour. At the same time, a peculiar look upon Betsy's face told him pretty plainly that this feat of the kitten was performed at her instigation, and that henceforth it would be unsafe to display his affection for her sister in her presence.

It was late when Jack Cubison left the cottage, and I wonder that he was not disturbed by any evil creature during his homeward journey. I suppose, however, that they had been thoroughly frightened and cowed by John Oliver and his relic, and had either no inclination or no power to venture forth again that night. So Jack Cubison got safe home, and resumed his work next day as if nothing had happened. Still, he could not get over that Giddyhorn adventure by any means. It was all so strange, so uncanny, and so unlike anything that had ever happened to him before, that he kept thinking of it again and again, and the memory of that night haunted him at his work, at his dinner-hour, and even in his dreams.

Leaving him in this somewhat uncomfortable condition of mind, we must turn our attention to the other personages of our story.

Jane Stickels got no better: nay, she got worse; decidedly worse. Her appetite still failed, her flesh fell away, and it was evident that if things went on like this, she would not much longer remain in the land of the living. Meantime, there were strange circumstances in connection with her illness. Whenever her sister Betsy fixed her eyes steadily on her, she felt the same strange, chilly sensation which she had experienced upon the first occasion which I have mentioned. Nay, even Betsy's cat seemed to exercise a hurtful influence over her as it sat on the rug and looked at her with its blinking but bright eyes. She had more of the sharp pains about her heart and side to which I have already alluded; but these happened when Betsy was out of the room, and therefore could not be attributed to her. But, from whatever cause it proceeded, Jane's illness had now certainly assumed an aspect which caused the gravest alarm to Thomas Stickels.

Not content with home remedies, he determined to seek for doctor's advice under these distressing symptoms, and went so far as to take the girl into Wye, to see the good Doctor Donamore, whose house was full three miles from the cottage door. But although the doctor paid every attention to the case, he could do little or nothing. He recommended change of air, to the sea, if possible, and plenty of good meat and port wine; but as these things were quite beyond Thomas Stickels' means, he might just as well have recommended boiled ostriches and fricasseed kangaroos, or held his tongue upon the subject altogether.

On quitting Doctor Donamore's house with his daughter, the old man was about to commence his journey homeward with a heavy heart, when, coming round the corner of the street near the "King's Head," who should appear but our old friend John Oliver.

"What! Thomas Stickels!" cried the worthy man, as soon as he set eyes upon him; "Who'd ha' thought o' seeing you here, so far away from home at this time o' day? Turn in along with me, and let's have a snack together before you go home."

Thus invited, Stickels required no further pressure, but led Jane into the little room at the "King's Head," and there proceeded to partake of the refreshment which his friend had offered. The latter, of course, inquired particularly about Jane, and was grieved to hear that her health was the cause of their journey to Wye, though he knew it must be something serious, as people of Thomas Stickels' rank in those days did not travel so far as three miles from home except under the pressure of some extraordinary emergency.

John Oliver now asked more particulars about the maiden's malady than he had done upon his visit to the cottage upon the famous evening of which we know, and listened attentively to all that was told him. He then asked several questions about Betsy, in whom he manifested an unusual interest, and desired to be informed of her habits, manners and disposition in a somewhat particular way. He asked if she had a cat, if she was much away from home, if she and her sister were good friends, and various other curious questions, and listened with grave attention to the replies which he received.

Whilst they were talking, Jane suddenly turned pale as death, and clapping her hand to her side, exclaimed—

"Oh, father—that pain again. Oh dear! oh dear!" and gasped for breath in evident agony.

John Oliver made no more ado, but hastily removing the string of beads from his neck, passed them round that of the fainting maiden. Strange to say, he had scarcely done so when the colour began to come back to her cheeks, her faintness disappeared, and she presently sat up, declaring that the pain seemed to have entirely passed away, and that she really thought she felt better and stronger than she had done for some months.

"Why, Master Oliver," said old Stickels, as Jane thus

expressed herself, "dash my buttons, if you be'ant a better man than t'old doctor yonder, after all. You be a right down good 'un, you be, for to bring my maid round so quick like."

The other shook his head gravely, and, calling Stickels out of the room for the moment, laid his hand upon the old man's shoulder in an impressive manner.

"'Tis as I feared," he said, in a low and solemn tone of voice. "Twenty and seven years have I been parish clerk of Wye, having come young into the office, and being only now in my fifty-five. There was those here then that hadn't ought to have been, and there's those here now. Thomas Stickels! your daughter is be-witched!"

"Dash my buttons!" said the old man on hearing this terrible statement; and having vented his feelings by this exclamation, could get no further, but sat and stared with eyes wide open at his friend and adviser.

"It cannot be otherwise," continued the latter. "There ain't no doubt of it whatsumdever. Your daughter Jane has been 'looked upon'—she is witch-struck, you may de-pend up'ant: and that's why she's been so ampery this spring, and what's more, there ain't no doctor as knows nothing about it, nor can't do her not no good."

"Then what be I to do?" asked the father, in a tone tremulous with fear and grief.

"Do not fear," replied Oliver. "It is by no common chance that you have come here to-day, and it bodes well for you that such has been the case. We've always had a smart parcel of witches and such like in Wye and hereabouts, and maybe that's the reason why we know more about 'em than most folk. Now there ain't no meeting witchcraft by doctor's stuff. If a poor body's witch-struck, there ain't no call to go for the doctor: bless you, *he* can't help you, no form. But there's them that can, aye and will too, for the matter of that."

Stickels eagerly inquired who it was that could and would help his afflicted daughter, and what he should do in order to procure the assistance which was necessary to secure her recovery from the strange and unaccountable ailment with which she had been attacked.

John Oliver then told him that such diseases, being brought about by secret and magic arts, could never be removed by merely human skill. If, he said, he could have afforded to part with his beads, and they had been hung around Jane's neck, he did not doubt but that the evil spells would no longer avail to hurt her; and that with common care, the natural strength of her constitution would ere long restore her to her former self. But, surrounded as he himself was with dangers, and filling the responsible position which he had so long held, he felt that it would be wrong for him to part with the treasure which had frequently been of such service to him in hours of peril. "But," said he, "if I stood in your shoes, Friend Stickels, which, though old and well-nigh worn out, I see, are the shoes of an honest man, I should lose no time over this business, but go and see the Hermit of Foreland Green. He is a sworn enemy, as I am, to all witches, and he knows well how to withstand them. If you was to take *both* your daughters to him, old friend, 'tis my belief you'd find as how he'd settle the matter for you, and no mistake."

Thomas Stickels asked a few more questions of the good clerk, and much wished him to accompany the party if they acted upon his advice and went to consult the Hermit. He could not promise this, however, but remarked that if they went an hour before sunset they would be sure to find the Hermit; and having again urged his old friend not to lose any time in doing so, bade them farewell, and started them on their way home, having previously resumed his beads. This interview had taken place between two and three, and when they reached their cottage it was getting on for half-past three, and they were both somewhat tired with their long walk. At the door they met one of the younger children, little Billy, who was seated on the step, crying bitterly.

"What's the matter, Bill?" asked the old man, while Jane, who was always kind to the little ones, took the child on her knee, and began to soothe him.

"Betsy's been a-spatting of me, she has," sobbed the boy through his tears.

"Been a-spatting of you, Bill! why what had you been a-doing of that Betsy should spat you?" said the father.

"And where is Betsy?" asked Jane at the same time.

"She's away up-street now," answered the little fellow, still sobbing; "and she spatted me because I hid little Jane."

"Hid little Jane?" asked old Stickels, somewhat angry at the child's story. "Who is little Jane, boy, and why did you hide her?"

"I was a-playing underneath the window," replied the child, "and Betsy she was upstairs, a-mumbling and muttering to herself, she was. I heerd her, and all at once she gave a little scream like, and down from her window there dropped a dolly!"

"A dolly!" exclaimed both the listeners in amazement.

."Yes, father, a real waxen dolly; and, oh! it was so like Jane that I thought it was her picture."

"What next?" asked the father anxiously.

"Well," continued the child, "then I heerd Betsy fall down as if she was a-fainting. Then I took the dolly and called it little Jane, and played with it. It was such a pretty dolly, and it had a beauty great pin in it. Then I heerd Betsy a-flumping about her room and a-coming downstairs; and I took and hid little Jane, because I was afeard as how she'd come and take it; and then she came and asted me for the pretty dolly, she did, and I said I hadn't seen no dolly, and then she spatted me, she did, right off."

Old Stickels hardly knew what to make of this story; but Jane, to whom all Master Oliver's words had been communicated, began to suspect, she hardly knew what, and questioned the boy further. He had always been very fond of her, and at her request, took her to the box-tree in which he had hid the dolly. It proved to be a waxen figure so exactly resembling Jane herself that both father and daughter were astonished. There, in its side, precisely on the spot where Jane had felt her acute pain, stuck a long black pin, half in and half out of the figure. Putting two and two together, they made out that the time of Betsy's dropping the figure from the window with a scream, must have been as nearly as possible the very moment at which Master Oliver had placed the relic of St. Edward around Jane's neck. It appeared but too probable, then, that Betsy was not only in league with the evil ones, but that she was conspiring against her sister's life, and had resorted to one of those regular, old fashioned, abominable witch-tricks by which practices are carried on against innocent persons who are designed by these creatures to be their victims. No doubt the pains in her heart and side which had so tried poor Jane had been produced by the cruel management of her younger sister, who must have known at the time she thrust the pins into the waxen doll that she was torturing and gradually destroying the life of her own flesh and blood.

All this was very sad and very terrible, and both Jane and her father were naturally much distressed. They determined, however, after a brief consultation, to say nothing to Betsy on the subject; but to lose no time in consulting the Hermit of Foreland Green, according to good Master Oliver's recommendation. So they comforted little Billy as well as they could, but told him he should always tell the truth, which he certainly had not done in declaring to Betsy that he had not seen the doll, and that therefore his punishment had not been undeserved. They bade him say no more on the matter, and sent him off to play with a neighbour's children, so that he might not be in the way when his sister returned. She presently did so, and seemed more sullen and morose than ever. I could never make out how it was that she did not immediately discover where her lost doll was; because one would have supposed that her evil friends could and would have done as much for her as to disclose the hiding-place in which her young brother had first put it, and also that in which it had now been deposited by her father. But there is no reliance upon the powers of evil, who will always betray and ruin those who trust in them. Perhaps there were reasons of which you and I can know nothing which prevented the first disclosure, whilst in the second instance I have no doubt that the reason was that Thomas Stickels had carefully hidden the little image in the drawer in which he kept his large family Bible, which was probably the last place to which Betsy or her associates would dare to go, and one over and in which they had certainly no power whatever.

Whether from this or from any other cause, Betsy never mentioned the image, or her loss of it, to her father or sister that evening, but behaved in her usual reserved and surly manner, and retired early to bed. The next day dawned bright and fair, and the old man determined that before it closed he would ascertain what the advice of Master Oliver could do for him. The chief difficulty, however, was how to follow that advice as entirely as he could wish, by taking *both* his daughters to the Hermit. Of course there would be no trouble as far as Jane was concerned; but as for Betsy, in the first place, she never by any chance did as she was told; and, in the second place, a holy man was probably about the last being in the world whom she would wish to see.

After pondering over the matter for a long time, the old man came to the conclusion that Betsy's presence could not be necessary, and that the Hermit could probably do just as well without it. So he resolved to say nothing to her on the subject, but to go alone with Jane upon his errand. The latter was unusually free from pain that day, and felt much better and more light-hearted than she had done for some time past. Always disposed to think as well as she could of others, and to put the best face upon everything, she hoped that her sister had either not really been so guilty as she appeared in the matter of the waxen figure; or that she had now repented of her wickedness, and would practise against her no more now that the doll was no longer in her possession.

Poor Jane little knew what a hard task-master is Sin, and how difficult it is to abandon evil ways if once we begin to pursue them. So well-disposed was she towards her younger sister, even after all that had passed, that she spoke kindly and affectionately to her that morning, and told her that their father was going to take her to get the advice of the Holy Hermit of Foreland Green. The girl changed colour at this, and was visibly annoyed; but she made some scoffing reply, and said no more. She was not in the house, however, when the time arrived at which Thomas Stickels had appointed to set out for Foreland; and therefore he had no opportunity, had he so desired it, of asking her to accompany them on their expedition. It was a fine afternoon when the father and his eldest daughter started on their walk.

The road to Foreland from Brooke was neither long nor hard to find, and the distance for foot-passengers could have barely reached two miles. A footpath from Brooke Street led through the Court-lodge Farm to the Hampton Woods, and so by the farm bearing the same name to Beddleston Farm, and then you found yourself at the corner of the plantation bearing the ominous name of "Hangman's Wood." This, as all the world knows, joins Foreland Wood, and beyond Foreland Wood, immediately to the south, lies Foreland Green. But the footpath at the present day skirts Hangman's Wood in its way to West Brabourne, and presently crosses the road which runs from Hastingleigh and the hill, past Bull Town, and so down to Foreland Green, leaving the wood several hundred yards to the right as you journey south. In the old days of which I write this foot-path branched off through the main body of the wood, and brought you out on Foreland Green, without the necessity of going round by the road ; and this was the line which a person might follow in walking from Brooke to Foreland. But sometimes if a walker desired to make a short cut, he would leave Beddleston Farm to the left on quitting Hampton, and keep between Naccult and Foreland Woods until he came quite to the south-western corner of the latter ; through which ran another footpath, taking him out at the western, as the former would to the eastern, corner of Foreland Green.

It was this latter route which Thomas Stickels and his daughter determined to follow, which they could do well enough on foot, though riding or driving through Naccult lanes was a feat impossible of accomplishment in those days, and indeed for long generations after. The very recollection of Naccult lanes recalls the idea of wheels left in deep, unconquerable clay; horses up to the girths in mud that seemed really unfathomable ; and riders reduced against their better inclinations to hard language and despair. Our two friends, however, having neither cart nor horse, not unnaturally walked; and walking had this convenience, that it exposed them to none of those perils of bad roads and sticky mud which would doubtless have assailed them had their method of travelling been different. There are perils and difficulties, however, even for people who walk, and so found Thomas Stickels and his daughter before long. They had scarcely entered Hampton Wood when they lost their way. It seems a ridiculous thing to write, and so it seemed to Stickels when it happened; for, as he afterwards said, he had known that wood, "man and boy, for better than fifty year," and could have sworn he could have found his way through it blindfold. Nevertheless, upon the present occasion, without being blindfolded at all, he certainly lost his way, and after "blundering about all over the place," as he expressed it, found himself coming out of the wood on the Brooke side, exactly at the point where he had entered it. He stood still, scratched his head thoughtfully, and then confessed to Jane that he couldn't make it out at all. She, poor girl, could not help him in the matter; but they determined to try again, and at once re-entered the wood, but with no better success.

It seemed to have grown to double its size since Stickels was last there; and then the path, formerly smooth and tolerably well trodden, was dirty, slippery, and half-choked with brambles and briars, which made it difficult to get along it. Had they been left to themselves I really doubt whether they would ever have got through the wood at all; but it fell out otherwise. As they wandered hither and thither, wondering what had befallen or would befall them, they heard a voice as of one chanting, and of a sudden they perceived a man in a friar's dress approaching them, and soon saw that he was one of those wandering friars who went in those days from place to place over the country, preaching and praying with those who desired their aid, and living for the most part on the charity of the faithful.

This holy man at once accosted them, and hearing of their difficulty, expressed his surprise. The way was easy to find, he said, and they were at that very moment in the footpath. He was himself bound for Brabourne, and they could follow the path together. The father and daughter were only too glad to agree to this proposal, and from that moment the path seemed to have resumed its original character. No difficulty whatever presented itself; and they passed through the woods and went safely as far as Beddleston, where the good friar quitted them, holding on his way to Brabourne, whilst our travellers took what they thought would be the shorter cut, by turning down towards Naccult Lane. On entering Pitt Meadow, however, through which the road runs from Beddleston to Naccult, and on one side of which, ere you reach the head of Naccult Lane, is a part of Hampton Wood, a new danger presented itself in the shape of an enormous black bull which stood on the bank, bellowing at them in an alarming manner, and apparently disposed to dispute their passage.

They were as nearly as possible turning back and giving up the journey; for Thomas Stickels argued with himself, not without reason, that if he was going to visit a wise man for the purpose of saving his daughter's life, the object of his visit would be entirely defeated if she was killed by a bull on the way. So he hesitated at the gate, and was about to propose that they should return, when the bull, overdoing his part, as some people always *will* do, rushed forward towards the gate, as if with the intention of immediately attacking them.

"Holy Saint Agnes!" cried Jane in her fear; for, having been religiously brought up by her departed mother, she generally used such exclamations as preferable to others of a more idle and sometimes much less desirable character.

The words were scarcely out of her mouth when a marvellous effect was produced. The bull disappeared, vanished as if the earth had opened and swallowed him up, and there was nothing left to impede their further advance. The eyes of the father and daughter were at once opened. It was plain enough now: there was witchcraft at work. Their journey was regarded with no favour by the powers of evil; and hence had come, beyond all doubt, their loss of the way in the wood, and the threatening appearance of this shadow of a bull. The old man questioned his daughter as to whether she had told her sister of their intended expedition; and on learning that such was the case, he at once came to the conclusion that it was her doing, and that this was another proof that his unhappy child had indeed sold herself to work evil with the bad ones of the hills. However, since they now knew the worst, they would be better able to guard against it; and accordingly they proceeded on their journey, and reached Naccult Lane in safety.

The road was almost impassable, but they managed to get over it somehow or other, and arrived at the meadow over which the path led to the corner of Foreland Wood, to enter which they had to climb over one of those stiles which are called, from the shape of their top bar, " hog-backed stiles," after passing which, the path led through some forty or fifty yards of the corner of the wood; and after climbing a similar stile at the other end, they would have reached their destination, or at least that end of the large tract of land known as Foreland Green. But here another and wholly unexpected obstacle presented itself in the shape of an enormous black cat, seated upon the top of the stile, whence it glared upon them with ferocious eyes, setting up its back, and growling in a manner par-ticularly uninviting and disagreeable to the approaching travellers. By this time, however, old Thomas Stickels had begun to know better, and to estimate at their proper value the nature of the hindrances which had been thrown in the way of his journey.

So, being fearless of danger, as a man of Kent should be, and relying upon this knowledge and his own courage, he strode manfully forward, with his stout walking-stick uplifted in his hand, and shouted loudly at the same time,—

"Now, you cat, witch, devil, or whatever you be, out of the way with ye!" and struck fiercely at the animal.

Horrible to relate, though his stick appeared to hit the creature full on the back, it passed through it as if it had been air, and produced no effect whatever, whilst the cat glared and growled more fiercely than before; and with a sudden cry of pain, the old man dropped his right arm helplessly by his side, whilst his stick dropped from his palsied hand and fell upon the ground.. Happy for him was it that Jane was with him.

"Father!" she had cried, when he first spoke, but was too late to prevent the words and the action which had resulted so unhappily; "Father! dear father," she now repeated, "mortal strength ain't no good agin them things. Let me try what mother taught me, now I know what 'tis we have to fight."

And, stepping forward with undaunted mien, she repeated.in a calm, firm tone of voice, the verse her mother had taught her when a little child, as a talisman against aught of evil which might be near her.

> "On our knees we lowly bend us,
> Heaven send angels to defend us;
> Guardian spirits, now attend us,
> Sweet Saint Agnes, come, befriend us!"

As Jane pronounced these words, the eyes of the cat

ceased to glare, she growled no longer, her figure became gradually more and more indistinct, and before the words were concluded it had utterly vanished away, and the stile was left unoccupied. At the same moment strength returned to the old man's arm : he picked up his stick, tenderly embraced his daughter, and thanked her, in his own homely language, for having taught him to trust in Heaven, and not upon his own unaided strength.

The two then passed the stile, walked through the corner of the wood without meeting the slightest difficulty, and, after climbing over the stile at the other end, came out upon Foreland Green. The next thing was how to find the Hermit; and in order to accomplish this desirable object, it was necessary to know where to look for him.

Foreland Green at the present day is all inclosed. You may travel along the road south of Naccult Wood in the direction of Bircholt and Brabourne Leese, and for a mile or more after leaving Naccult Wood behind you, the wire fences by the side of the road, and rough grass beyond them, show you that a common or large "Green" existed there at some time or other. But it was very different in the days of which I write. There were no wire fences then. The common commenced very soon after you had passed Naccult Wood, and extended up to Foreland, Chute's and Fuller's Wood, and some way beyond them, on the north, and on the south was bounded by the more cultivated land of Foreland Farm, beyond which came in the Foreland Meadows, extending up to Bircholt Wood.

Foreland Green was thus, it will be seen, of considerable extent, and bore by no means the same civilized appearance which it does at the present day. Huge patches of rough, coarse grass, varied by rougher and coarser masses of brambles, tangled thickets, and wild-growing, stunted bushes, covered nearly the whole surface of the land, save where vast oaks sprang up here and there, spreading their gigantic branches far and wide, beneath which the underwood could not grow, but which afforded shade and shelter to the animals, and formed a striking and beautiful feature in the scenery.

Nowadays, as you stand on the Green, with your face turned towards the south, you see the mass of building, baronial in its appearance from this point, which is now Mersham Hatch, standing out boldly on the crest of its own hill, from whence it commands so beautiful a view of the whole valley of the Chalk Hills, from Beechborough to Eastwell. Then, however, no such sight was to be seen; firstly, because the thick woods intervened, which have since been felled in every direction; and, secondly, because the Mersham Hatch of those days was not the building which now bears the name, but was situate some half-mile to the west of the present site, and nearer to the famous old wood of Bockhanger.

Seeing the nature and extent of Foreland Green, it is not wonderful that Thomas Stickels and his daughter should pause when they found themselves there, and doubt what would be their best course to pursue in order to find the individual of whom they stood in need.

It was fast approaching the hour of sunset, an hour just before which they had been told by Oliver was the best time to discover the holy man. But, in addition to their ignorance of the precise spot upon which he lived, they were in some little difficulty owing to the nature of the ground, which was rough and rugged, and difficult to travel upon if you quitted the footpath on either side. The footpath led by a winding route through the Green away to Bircholt; and as, after all, it seemed the best plan to follow it, seeing that it was the only way by which they could well proceed at all, they determined to do so. The path was one little used, but Stickels and his daughter felt no alarm upon that account.

They feared no robbers, partly because no such people frequented those regions, and partly because, if they had been attacked, they had little or nothing to lose. Witchcraft, indeed, they had reason to know was abroad; but the sanctity of the Hermit's name and reputation would protect them now that they were once fairly upon the Green which he rendered secure by his residence thereon; and they therefore strode boldly forwards, having, in fact, nothing else to do, unless they had turned back.

Their perseverance was rewarded before they had gone very far. Upon the left of the path, and about twenty yards from it, after they had walked along it for a couple of hundred yards, stood a gigantic oak, towards which the ground gently rose, and around which, owing probably to its roots and branches, vegetation was scanty, and there was nothing to prevent a full view of the tree as you passed by.

It was such a magnificent oak that any one who loved the beauties of nature, and especially those trees which are among the greatest beauties that can delight the eye of mortal, could hardly help stopping to gaze on it for a moment. It was precisely this which Thomas Stickels and his daughter did, and as they gazed Jane laid her hand lovingly upon her father's arm, and said:

"Oh, father, what a lovely great oak! 'Tis rather an

" ellinge " * old place this ; but that oak is mortal fine, to be sure.   I should like to go close up to it ! "

The old man was about to comply willingly with this very natural request, when, even as they turned from the path to approach the tree, a voice addressed them which appeared to issue from the tree itself.   It was not a very harsh voice nor a very soft voice, not a very loud voice nor a very low voice ; but it sounded exactly like the tone of an ordinary man speaking in an ordinary manner to ordinary people.   It made no preface at all to what it had to say, but began at once, and seemed to understand a good deal about the business on which they had come.   And this was the fashion of its address :—

> "Old father, young daughter, from village of Brooke,
> You come for the Hermit of Foreland to look,
> Since Oliver told you he's sure to be seen
> If an hour before sunset you come to the Green.
> The Hermit is here, as reported to be—
> And I'll tell you, without any nonsense, I'm He !
> I know what you want ; what you fear ; what you ask ;—
> 'Tis a difficult, not an impossible task ;
> For things that seem out of our reach, hard and high,
> We oft can accomplish, that is, if we *try*.
> But before I advise you in which way to act,
> I am bound to announce an unfortunate fact.
> This Betsy—*your* daughter—and sister to *you*,
> Has scarcely gone straight, in fact, sadly askew,
> Aside, wrong, perverted, obliquely, aslant,
> Neglecting her mother, she's followed her aunt,
> And unless things go right, in the saddest of pickles,
> She shortly will land all the household of Stickels."

---

* Kentish word for "triste," "melancholy.'

Then the voice stopped, as if to take breath, and poor old Stickels and his daughter looked at each other in great astonishment. Grief, indeed, was mixed with that astonishment; for they now heard it stated in plain terms, and upon that which they felt to be undoubted authority, that Betsy was certainly in league with the powers of evil and was following the bad example of her notorious relative. This corroboration of his worst fears so overcame the old man that he was utterly unable to speak a word, if indeed his ignorance and wonder at the strange position in which he found himself would in any case have permitted him to do so. But Jane had more presence of mind, and had also heard sufficient of the nature of the beings who dwell in forests and inhabit oaks to feel certain that, if they spoke in rhyme, they should be answered in a similar manner. She knew but little of the Hermit of Foreland Green, whether he was a wizard or only an ordinary mortal; but as he had adopted this mode of addressing her and her father, she was sure that she could make no mistake in following his example. She, therefore, faced boldly towards the oak, and without any hesitation spoke in the following terms :

> " We make no doubt but what your words are true,
> But please to tell us what we'd ought to do."

She spoke, and waited impatiently for the answer, which was not long in coming. The same voice presently gave back its response in the same tones:

> " Your illness, my girl, does your sister produce,
> For which she can have not the slightest excuse ;
> But yet, if the cause you're desirous to track
> She's jealous—and that on account of your Jack.

> The truth I declare ; but, be this as it may,
> She finds you undoubtedly much in her way,
> And, wishing herself to be Cubison's wife,
> Is trying to finish your innocent life.
> To this, and to other bad deeds she is stirred
> By witches, of whom you have probably heard ;
> The Giddyhorn Grannies, who meet on the hill,
> And plan to make mortals conform to their will.
> They tried it on Jack, and had won in their " try,"
> If worthy John Oliver hadn't come by,
> The stout parish clerk on that terrible night
> Saved Cubison's soul, and put witches to flight.
> But Betsy, far gone in contrivance of ill,
> Has schemed a long time, and goes scheming on still ;
> And to stop her before her full course shall be run,
> There's much to be thought of, and much to be done."

The voice stopped again at this point, and Jane—who not only found her worst fears about her sister confirmed, and more than confirmed, but heard for the first time the reason of her lover's late arrival upon that eventful evening—was so much struck with horror that she could scarcely summon courage or voice to make an appeal for further information upon a matter so vitally important to the welfare of herself and her family. However, she mastered herself by a tremendous effort, and spoke thus :

> " Pray tell us what we'd ought to do, for we
> Quite ignorant on all such matters be.

Then the voice replied as follows, speaking very slowly and clearly :

> " 'Twixt Coombe and Foreland Green (my own abode)
> The river overflows the Bircholt road,
> Were Betsy there, in spite of tear and scream,
> 'Twould be the best to duck her in the stream ;

And e'er she's dry again, 'twould do her good,
To leave her in the shades of Bircholt wood.
Meanwhile, go home : she'll trouble you no more,
If that you nail a horse-shoe o'er your door.
If such you lack, I hardly need explain
You'll find them by the score in Naccult Lane ;
For horses, best or worst in every stud,
Leave shoes as tribute to the Naccult mud ;
Nail one of these o'er every door you've got,
'Twill make it for Miss Betsy rather hot ;
And if she show the smallest spite or spleen,
The force of words I'll tell you shall be seen :
Look in her face, and say out loud and free,
This—" Pickled Pork,"—or afterwards "P. P."
'Twill always check her, and her power restrain,
If once don't do, why, say the words again.
And if you find you've trouble with her cat,
Souse her in soap-suds, she won't relish *that ;*
And mind, in catching her, before you catch
Cry " Pickled Pork,"—she'll neither bite nor scratch.
As for yourselves, you've only to do right,
And ne'er forget your prayers at morn and night ;
The duty straight before you every day,
Do quietly and well, the surest way
This you will find to make you safely stand
Against the witches who infest the land."

Having uttered these rhymes, the voice was again silent, and both father and daughter felt much comforted by the words to which they had listened. It was not a hard thing to find plenty of horse-shoes, and a very easy one to nail them over every door in the cottage. " Pickled Pork " also was an expression very familiar to the ears—and mouth—of a Kentish peasant, and by no means likely to be forgotten ; and if the use of such words could restrain Betsy's power, and enable them to souse her cat in soap-suds without fear of evil consequences, the result would certainly be beneficial to the family of Stickels. The more difficult part of the task would be the cure of the unhappy girl herself, for if it was only to be effected by ducking her in the running water below Bircholt Wood, and leaving her in the wood afterwards, it would require some tact and management to accomplish.

It was very probable that Betsy would suspect some design against her if asked to accompany her father and sister in that direction; and even if she had no such suspicion, her natural disposition would lead her to refuse the invitation. Moreover, if they got her to the place, to duck her seemed such an unusual proceeding for a father and a sister, that they would hardly like to attempt it; and did not feel very certain that the attempt, if made, would be attended with success. They, therefore, thought that they had better ask for more precise information upon this point; and, after whispering together for a moment, Jane spoke once more.

> " About this ducking, sir, in Bircholt brook,
> To us it don't so very easy look :
> *I* can't duck Betsy,—how she'd scratch and slap !
> And 'tis a queerish job for father, hap."

There was silence after this question had been put, and the two waited patiently for a full minute, hoping to receive an answer which would settle the point which puzzled them. Then Stickels whispered to his daughter:

" T' old chap won't say no more. 'Hap he's gone to sleep, or else he don't choose to go on talking to such as we be."

He had scarcely spoken, however, before the voice again came from the tree; but this time its tones were less distinct, and really appeared to resemble those of a person half asleep, or tired of a conversation in which he was not greatly interested. However, this was what the voice said:

> "If any doubts distract your mind,
> Your way you hitherward can find—
> Father and sister, it is clear,
> Can scarce with ducking interfere ;
> But of these things there are 'mong men
> Those who the mysteries do ken,
> And you are scarcely like to err
> If guided by John Oliver."

With these words the voice ceased, nor did Jane and her father deem it right to trouble the Hermit (for they doubted not that he had been the speaker) with any more questions. They, therefore, expressed their thanks for his kindness very warmly (though whether he heard them or not they could not tell, since no further sounds issued from the tree) ; and, having done this, they proceeded to turn round and resume their homeward journey.

As had been foretold, and as, indeed, they could have foretold for themselves without help, they found several horse-shoes in Naccult Lane, which they carefully carried home. Their journey was quiet and uneventful. No cat sat upon any stile, no bull bellowed in any field, everything seemed to be in its natural and ordinary condition ; and the path through the woods of Hampton was as easy to find as indeed it had always been before that eventful day.

It was, of course, somewhat late when they reached the cottage ; but, as it was now the month of July, there was plenty of light, and Thomas Stickels determined to lose no time in commencing the operations which were to set him and his free from the dangers with which he now knew they had been surrounded.

On entering the house, he threw down on the table the horse-shoes, which he had tied up in his large red handkerchief. Betsy was sitting in the corner, and started when she heard the noise.

"Whatever have you got there, father?" she said, rising from her seat, and approaching him, whilst at the same moment a low, whining "miaw" proceeded from the cat at her side.

"Never you mind, wench," replied the old man; "you'll see soon enough, and find 'em useful things, too, please the pigs!"

So saying, he began to undo the knot of the handkerchief, and soon displayed to view four horse-shoes, begrimed a bit with Naccult mud, but plain and palpable horse-shoes notwithstanding. The moment she set eyes upon them, Betsy gave a little scream, as if startled, and immediately cried out:

"Oh, what nasty, dirty things, father! How *could* you bring them in-doors? Here, let me take and chuck 'em out of the window, and then you can see to 'em to-morrow morning, if so be as you really want such rubbish."

"Bide a bit, wench; bide a bit," replied the old man, gently, but firmly interposing between the girl and the handkerchief, at which she made a grab as if to throw it out of the window as she proposed.

"You hav'n't got no call to interfere with these here things. They won't hurt *you*, if so be as all is right, and as it should be; and I ain't a-going to have 'em throwed out of the window, nohow."

An angry colour rose to Betsy's face.

"It is too bad!" she cried, "to bring such a mess in here—I declare it is."

"A man may do what he will in his own house," returned her father; "so shut your potato-trap, my girl, and give your red rag a holiday."

This expressive command to close her mouth and hold her tongue put Betsy into a still greater rage; and, turning angrily to her sister, she exclaimed, in a loud voice:

"This is *your* doing, you minx, I know; you are always setting father agin me, you are. I'll serve you out for it, I will!"

Jane calmly replied, that she had nothing to do with any offence given to her sister, and knew not the cause of her anger; but Betsy was not to be appeased, and seemed quite beside herself with passion.

Turning fiercely upon her sister, she began to use words of dire and fearful import, which I cannot repeat, not being quite certain what they were; but I know that they left no doubt upon the mind of Jane that her sister was working or trying to work some new and terrible spell against her. The same thing occurred to old Stickels himself, and he thought it was high time to stop it; therefore he faced the girl boldly, and said in the sternest voice which he could assume:

"Come, wench; this here won't do: none o' your tantrums here! *Pickled Pork*, if you please; that's it. P.P.—P.P.—P.P.!"

The girl stopped, as if she had been shot: the colour left her face, she turned deadly pale, and, without another word, crept back to her seat, and cowered in the corner.

Upon this, her father, perfectly contented with the

result, made no attempt to interfere with her arrangements, but carried on his own without further delay. A
horse-shoe was nailed over the front door, and another
over the back door; one over Jane's bed, and another over
that in which the younger children slept. They did not
nail one over Betsy's bed, partly because they thought it
might prevent her going there at all, and partly because
they had only got four shoes, and therefore thought it best
to bestow them where they would be most useful, or at all
events best appreciated.

Having done this, Jane and her father retired to rest,
satisfied that a good day's work had been performed, and
that their cottage was in a safer condition than had been
the case for some time past.

I have no means of knowing what were Betsy's
reflections upon the subject, but I imagine that they
cannot have been agreeable; and the introduction first
of the horse-shoes, and then of the words which had
so disconcerted her, must have made her feel the reverse of comfortable as to the prospect before her. She was
quiet enough next morning, however, although she and her
cat both seemed to mope a good deal, as if the place was
no longer as pleasant to either of them as it had hitherto
been.

Thomas Stickels took an early opportunity of consulting
Jane as to what course should be taken about the other
part of the directions which they had received on Foreland
Green; and they both agreed that the best thing would be
to ask Master Oliver's advice as soon as they could find
time for another journey to Wye. This trouble, however,
was spared them by the timely appearance of the very
man of whom they were speaking. Anxious to hear the

result of their visit to Foreland, he walked over about dinner-time, and looked in upon the family, quite ready to give his best advice. The question of the ducking fairly staggered him at first. It was fully discussed between him, old Stickles and Jane, after dinner, in the corner of the churchyard, whither they had strolled, leaving Betsy indoors.

Oliver agreed that the father and sister could hardly be expected to assist in the operation; but unless they were present, he did not see much chance of getting Betsy to the place appointed. When there, he said, his hatred of witchcraft was such that, coupled with his great regard for the family, it would induce him to undertake the matter himself, cost him what it might. Thomas Stickels thanked him heartily; but for some time no way occurred to them of inducing Betsy to accompany them to the place.

At last John Oliver's face lighted up with a ray of intelligence.

"I've got it," he said; and then proceeded to unfold his scheme.

The park and gardens of Sir Edward Scott, of Scott's Hall, were at that day the great attractions of the neighbourhood; and the mansion of that celebrated man was a noble and stately edifice, famous among the houses of the nobility and gentry of the land. Those were accounted fortunate who managed to obtain the privilege of visiting this place—a privilege accorded to few persons of the rank in life of those of whom we now write. It so happened, however, that good Master Oliver had a brother, who occupied a position no less important than that of gardener at Scott's Hall; and through this influential person he had every hope of being able to obtain the desired permission for himself and friends. This done, he proposed that Thomas Stickels and his two daughters should accompany him upon the expedition.

Now the road from Wye and Brooke to Scott's Hall led directly to Bull Town, and thence down by West Brabourne, north of Bircholt Wood, across the running water there, and so away to Brabourne Leese; so that, in taking this journey, the travellers must perforce pass the very spot where the Hermit (or the voice which they supposed to proceed from that saintly personage) had directed that the ducking of Betsy should take place. At Jane's earnest request, Jack Cubison was invited to join the party, to which he readily assented, having lived a remarkably careful and steady life since his adventure in April upon Giddyhorn hill-side, and feeling himself now tolerably secure against the temptation into which he had fallen upon that melancholy occasion. So the day was fixed, the arrangements made, and a heavy country cart hired, which would take the whole number of them.

Contrary to the expectations of her father and sister, Betsy made no objection to the proposal. She had been rather less troublesome since the incident of the horse-shoes; and the very day before that appointed for the Scott's Hall expedition a circumstance occurred which seemed to have so cowed and terrified her that she was quite a different creature.

It was washing-day at the cottage, and Jane was hard at work in the wash-house, with sundry pails and tubs full of soap-and-water around her, and various articles of clothing scattered about. Betsy was, as usual, doing little or nothing to help her sister; but was watching her in sullen silence, with her cat on her knee, and probably wondering how it was that Jane had managed to avoid the spell practised against her, and seemed to be gaining her health and strength every day.

Presently, the elder sister called the younger to help her to move some article of furniture. Instead of complying, Betsy made some rude remark, and sat still. Irritated at this conduct, the usually mild and good-natured Jane crossed to the place where her sister sat, and said to her somewhat sharply :

"You ain't no good at all in a house, Betsy; you never do nothing to help. I wonder what's the use of ye ?"

And as she spoke, she stretched out her hand, as if to lay it on her sister's shoulder, and rouse her to attention. The moment she did so, up started the cat, set up its back, glared at Jane, and made as if it would fly at her face.

Miss Stickels, however, was equal to the occasion. Remembering the advice given on Foreland Green, she promptly seized the animal by the back of the neck, exclaiming as she did so, "Pickled Pork, Pickled Pork, Pickled Pork," three times quickly in succession; and without more ado, plunged it then and there into the nearest tub of soap-suds, sousing it up and down with real good-will.

Betsy sat pale and petrified, offering no attempt whatever to rescue her pet, which struggled in vain in the hands of Jane, and seemed unable either to bite, scratch, or free itself from the grasp in which the brave girl held it. But as soon as ever she loosed her hold, the creature scrambled out of the tub, uttering cries like those of a human being in sore distress, cries so distressing and so curious that those who heard them could not forget them for a long time, and vowed that no common cat could ever have made them, then, making the best of her way to the window, she sprang upon the sill. There she sat for an instant, then turned her head towards the inmates of the cottage, glared fiercely upon them, uttered a cry of rage and despair which sounded like the expression of a furious person baffled and defeated in some favourite design, and presently darted from the window and fled away down the road.

Betsy still sat silent, nor did her sister say anything to her. Still more strange was it that during the whole of that day the younger girl made no remark upon what had happened, but went on in a quieter and more humble way, as if she knew that she had lost some powerful friend and protector under whose care she had hitherto been able to defy all around her.

So the morning rose upon which the journey to Scott's Hall was to take place. A fine morning it was, the month of August having now been reached, and the harvest weather having begun. Thomas Stickels "tidied himself up a bit," as he said, and told his daughters to "go and clean themselves," so as to be in good time for the start which was to be effected about two o'clock. Punctual to the moment came good Master Oliver, and, all preparations having been made, the whole party clambered up into the cart, and away they drove in the direction of Brabourne.

As they passed the road below Giddyhorn, Jack Cubison could not avoid casting a sheepish look towards Betsy; but she sat in her corner with her face steadily bent down as if looking at some remarkable object at the bottom of the cart, and as the eyes of both John Oliver and Jane were upon him, the young man felt the colour rise to his cheeks as he fancied to himself that they must be thinking of his weakness and folly. He wondered whether any trace of witchcraft could be seen in Giddyhorn beeches during the daytime, and almost expected something evil to start up as they passed the place. They went by, however, without a sign that could lead them to suppose that there was, or ever had been, any inhabitant of the hill-side save the innocent animals that everywhere abounded in that locality. Neither witch, cat, nor broomstick appeared to their sight; and they drove on (very slowly, it is true, but that was on account of the age and badness of their horse, and had nothing to do with witches), until they came to the turning from the hill down by Bull Town to West Brabourne. Here Betsy, to the surprise of all, interposed with a remark, which, however, she made in a meek and placid manner, and by no means in a rude or sullen voice. She merely suggested that, as the day was so fine, and the view from the hill road over the vale so beautiful, they should not turn down by Bull Town, but drive straight on, so as to get as much of the view as they could, and take the turning down by Brabourne Street, a mile or more further on, and so by Wall Farm and the eastern side of Brabourne Leese to Scott's Hall.

Now this would have been a very little further, and was a very good road; but there was one thing about it which John Oliver remembered at once. *It would have avoided the running water altogether,* and in fact the party would not have crossed the stream at all, as it took another direction after passing Bircholt, and the hill road was far above it. John Oliver hastily whispered words to this effect in the ear of Thomas Stickels, who at once negatived Betsy's suggestion, and declared that with the old horse they had got they must take the road which was shortest, and in which there was least hill, and that was the road by Bull Town. There they turned, therefore, and drove down until they had passed Cadman Wood and came near the place at which the road to Bircholt, Brabourne, and Smeeth branches to the left, that which runs straight on leading to Foreland Green. Near this spot (where the water flows under the road, about half or three quarters of a mile from the running water), Betsy suddenly called out that she had a bad pain in her side—the motion of the cart hurt her so, she said, that she really could not go on, and begged them to put her down and let her walk home by the foot-path to Beddleston, and go on without her.

This conduct confirmed all the previous suspicions of the party, if indeed recent events had left any further confirmation necessary. No one supposed that the girl had any idea of the command of the Hermit, and their consequent intentions with regard to herself; but the dislike of a witch to cross running water was well known to them all, and there remained not the shadow of a doubt that Betsy Stickels belonged to that unhallowed sisterhood. Of course no one thought of yielding to her desire to be put down from the cart. Her entreaties were all in vain. John Oliver and Jack Cubison had her between them, and in spite of all she could say or do, she was not permitted to move; and I suppose that, together with her cat, a portion of her power had vanished, so that she could not injure or annoy those who offended her. Be this as it may, she made no great efforts to escape, but moaned sadly as the cart turned down the sharp little descent which brought it within a hundred yards of the place where the stream crossed the road. Here she bounded up in the cart, as if struck with mortal pain, and begged in piteous terms to be set down. They restrained her, however, until they were within a few yards of the spot; and then, apparently overcome by her entreaties, stopped the cart, and suffered her to descend, Master Oliver and Jack doing the same.

To duck a woman was not a pleasant nor a very manly task; and at the present day I hope that most men would have great scruples about doing so, in obedience to anybody's commands, be the "anybody" as great and powerful as possible. But we must recollect that things were slightly different in the days of which we write. Oliver had had long experience of the evil wrought by witches and witchcraft. Cubison had lately had practical proof of the danger to which mortal men were exposed by their crafty wiles; and both men firmly believed not only that it was their duty to society and to themselves to do the work before them, but that it was the best possible thing for the girl herself, whom they regarded as the unhappy victim of the Evil One, to be reclaimed by any and every available means, even though such might involve personal pain and suffering to herself. So their minds were fully made up, and as soon as ever they were well out of the cart they turned upon Betsy with a resolute determination to get the job over as speedily as possible. But the instant they did so the girl gave a short, sharp cry, and set off running with incredible swiftness. The road was somewhat wild at that part: to the left, within a few hundred yards, began the scattered trees which formed the outskirts of the great Forest of Coombe, so famous as the scene of many of the actions of that mighty Warlock who bore among men the name of the Forest. To the right a wild, rough grass tract of land stretched away towards Foreland Green, separated by no fence from the road on which our friends were travelling.

It was in this direction that Betsy, half beside herself with fright, ran as fast as she could, and Master Oliver and Jack Cubison followed her at the top of their speed. Meanwhile, old Thomas Stickels and Jane were left in the cart, where they sat staring at one another as if struck dumb by the scene they witnessed. Betsy kept well ahead of her pursuers for upwards of a hundred yards, flying she knew not whither, and only knowing that she was heading in a direction not far wrong for Brooke, though, of course, that village was some three or four miles off.

The intervening trees which were scattered thereabouts soon took both pursued and pursuers out of sight of the road they had left; and, of course, every step they took carried them farther from it. Meanwhile, in her hurried flight, the girl was obliged to keep near the stream, simply because the nature of the ground and the thickness of the trees at that particular spot prevented her from doing otherwise.

I cannot say how the matter might have ended if the parties had been left to themselves; for Betsy was strong as well as swift, and although Jack Cubison was young and active, his companion could scarcely deny that his best running days were over, and he would have found it difficult to come up with the girl. But all of a sudden she stopped short and sank upon the ground, so that in a very few seconds they were close upon her. Then they stopped too. Immediately in front of them stood the form of a venerable man, clad entirely in the brown dress of a monk, holding a tall staff in his hand,

and apparently determined to bar the way against all comers. His long white beard fell majestically over his breast, his features were grave, his face bronzed as if by long exposure to sun and air, his demeanour was strikingly grand; and even if John Oliver had not known him to be so, the others would have had little difficulty in deciding for themselves that this was the ancient Hermit of Foreland Green.

At the sight of this Holy Man the unhappy Betsy had fallen at once to the ground, where she lay grovelling and moaning as if her last hour were come. The two men stood close by her, reverently awaiting the communication which the mighty individual before them might presently be pleased to make. After a very short pause, he waved his hand in the air, and thus addressed them:

> " How is it that a witch is seen
> Upon the confines of the Green ?
> Take her ! regard not scratch or scream,
> But place her in the running stream,
> And if she should resist your work,
> Employ the charm of ' Pickled Pork.' "

Thus adjured, without the smallest hesitation, the two men lifted the unfortunate Betsy from the ground, and proceeded to carry her to the brook, which was only a few yards distant, near the corner of Bircholt Wood, running in a swift stream, but sufficiently shallow to render drowning highly improbable, even if a witch *could* drown, which has always been a matter of doubt among historians learned on these subjects. She made but a feeble resistance, and no charm was necessary to overcome her strength.

Jack Cubison always declared that the water fizzed and steamed as if made hot by her immersion; but this seems to me to savour of exaggeration, which should always be avoided in the narration of actual facts. At all events, in she went, and was thoroughly ducked in that branch of the River Stour which has probably had the honour of being used for the same ceremony as often as most streams in the southern counties. Whilst the splashing, attempts at screaming, the crying and the struggling were going on, the Hermit had slowly advanced, and stood at a little distance from the scene. Presently, he held his staff aloft, and addressing the two performers of the sacred task, thus gave them their directions, with an authoritative air:

> " 'Tis done ! washed out the witch's stain :
> Oh, may it ne'er appear again !
> Back ! Cubison, return you hence,
> And act henceforth with common sense ;
> For if you wander late, and still
> Join supper-parties on the hill,
> You'll meet worse things than yet you've met,
> And evermore your course regret :
> Now join the cart and t'other two,
> And ever to your Jane be true.
> John Oliver, draw out the maid,
> And take her 'neath the leafy shade
> Of Bircholt Wood ; there rest a bit,
> And when for homeward journey fit,
> Conduct her to her father's roof,
> Henceforth from sin to stand aloof.
> And thou, young maid, whose wicked way
> Hath led thee terribly astray,
> Repent ! and so thou still mayst find
> Some comfort for thy troubled mind.
> For thine own sake, and for our Kent,
> I say again, Repent ! Repent !

> To those who do, Heav'n succour sends.
> Henceforth be firm : avoid bad friends,
> Thy kindred love, and day by day,
> Remember both to work and pray."

He ceased, but his words were accepted by his hearers as orders to be obeyed; so that it was hardly necessary for him to say any more, since no one disputed his wishes. Betsy was immediately lifted from the water, and laid upon the bank, after which Jack Cubison walked off at once, repeating over and over again to himself the expressions which the Hermit had used regarding him, and resolving to follow to the letter the instructions which he had received. It may be as well to say at once that to these good intentions he fully adhered. From this time forth he avoided all light and evil company, led an upright and honest life, and acted in every respect as his best friends could have wished. He became, before very long, the husband of Jane Stickels, and she never had any reason to complain of his staying out late at night, or frequenting places of doubtful character. Nay, such was his steadiness and general good behaviour, that, following at a distance the steps of his great benefactor, Master Oliver, he eventually rose to be the parish clerk of Hastingleigh, and ended a useful career in that honourable position.

But I am anticipating matters which of course occurred at a period subsequent to the day upon which took place the meeting with the Hermit of Foreland Green. From the spot upon which this happened Cubison went straight back to the cart, and found Thomas Stickels and his daughter in a state of great excitement. He allayed their fears about Betsy by telling them what had happened, and when they heard that she had been left in charge of John Oliver to bring home, but that he was first to take her into Bircholt Wood, they deemed it useless to tarry longer. The expedition to Scott's Hall had been only a pretext to attract Betsy to the spot, and they had therefore nothing to do but to drive home again, which they did without further adventure, and the wily Jack improved his opportunities with Jane so well during and after the drive that he induced her to name the day upon which she would abandon the name of Stickels for that of Cubison.

Meanwhile, we must return to the spot where we left the other actors in our history. John Oliver listened with attention to the words of the Hermit, and prepared to obey his directions. First, however, he turned to the speaker, and expressed his thanks for the assistance which he had rendered that day, and the kindly advice he had given. To this speech the Hermit responded with a benevolent smile, and then replied:

> " Those who from hill-side down into our dell come
> To Foreland aid 'gainst witches are most welcome;
> And thou, to witchcraft enemy so clever,
> Good Master Oliver, art welcome ever;
> And may thy gratitude be undiminished,
> When this affair shall be entirely finished."

With these words the Hermit turned round, and retreated slowly through the scattered trees in the direction of Foreland Green, leaving Oliver much pleased by his reply.

"No fear of my gratitude being diminished," said the good man; " and much obliged be I by his good opinion. But now to business."

His business, as we know, was to take Betsy Stickels into the "leafy shade" of Bircholt Wood, and afterwards to conduct her to her father's roof. There was plenty of time for this, for it was not yet four o'clock, and the distance to Brooke from Bircholt by the footpath could be barely three miles.

If I merely wished to finish off the story, a very few words would suffice to do so; but I am so anxious to be particular in relating things which actually happened, that I must not sacrifice truth to my desire to avoid being too long. Truth, you know, is often stranger than fiction, and I think it was so in the present case.

John Oliver turned to Betsy, who was gasping upon the bank after her recent immersion in the water. He spoke kindly to her, and asked if she had heard the Holy Hermit's words and advice; to which she nodded assent, being apparently unable to speak as yet. Then worthy Master Oliver helped her to arrange her dress, which, as may be easily supposed, had become somewhat disordered during the operation she had just undergone; and, whilst doing so, he asked her if she would walk into Bircholt Wood and rest awhile, as the Hermit had suggested. The girl made no objection; and the fear which a careful person might have felt of sitting in wet clothes was here unnecessary, owing to the marvellous quickness with which her garments dried, so that she was really scarcely to be called even damp within a very few minutes of being taken out of the water.

They walked into Bircholt wood accordingly, and sat down beneath the shady oaks, on which, as is not uncommon with such trees in that part of the country, acorns grew and wood-pigeons cooed in great numbers. There is no record that I have ever found of the precise nature of their conversation; but there can be little doubt that John Oliver improved the occasion to the best of his ability, and gave the girl much good counsel, pointing out to her the folly and wickedness of sin—especially the sin of witchcraft—and advising her, well and wisely, as to her future conduct. I imagine, too, that Betsy was not indisposed to listen to such things; for it must have seemed to her, apart from any other and better thoughts, that her evil companions had either deserted her during recent transactions, or that the other side was the strongest, and that they had been unable to aid her. In either case, good policy, if no higher motive, dictated her conduct in making friends with those who had prevailed, and she accordingly did so. She certainly showed no signs of resentment against Oliver for the share he had taken in recent events, and the result of their rest in the wood was not unsatisfactory to either of them.

They stayed there nearly an hour, and then proceeded to walk home, and reached the cottage of Stickels without any adventure. Master Oliver here delivered the damsel into her father's care, telling him at the same time that he had held much goodly conversation with her that afternoon, and was sure that her family would find her vastly altered for the better. To all this Betsy made no reply, but meekly and modestly cast down her eyes, as one that acknowledged she had been in error, and wished to act with proper humility. Oliver declared that he felt sure the day would turn out to have been a happy one for the Stickels' family; and shortly after took his departure, promising to look in again very soon to inquire how they were all getting on. He *did* look in again very soon, and took the opportunity of having some further conversation with Betsy, which he told her father gave him still more confidence in the depth and sincerity of her repentance. He took such interest in the case that he came again before two days were over; and, to cut a long story short, Master Oliver one morning informed Thomas Stickels that his daughter Betsy was immediately about to become Mrs. Oliver.

Stickels was greatly surprised, for he had expected nothing of the sort, and had no idea that his friend's visits to the cottage were the result of anything else than a paternal interest in the well-doing of his younger daughter. She was not yet eighteen, and Master Oliver fifty-five; but in his position of life Thomas Stickels was too glad to see his daughter so well settled to make any objection on the score of age. So they were married, and the neighbours all would have it that John Oliver had been bewitched after all. How that was I cannot now say.

It seems to me a very good place at which to bring this story to a close. Those who like to carry it on further for themselves may settle it in whichever way they please. They can fancy John Oliver's disappointment when he found that after all he had been grievously taken in, and had allied himself to one of the regular, or irregular, "Giddyhorn Grannies." They may picture to themselves a trembling, fearful old man—his powerful charm stolen from him during his sleep—left at the mercy of a ruthless witch of a wife, and obliged to entertain her wicked companions in his once quiet house. They may see him seated, an unwilling guest at his own table, with Dame Vidgen on one side and the awful Dame Punyer on the other, the pitiful object of their constant jeers and scoffs; and they may think of him sitting up far into the night, bound to keep the lamp trimmed and the fire burning until his witch-wife returns from one of the terrible gatherings on Giddyhorn hill-side. Or, if they prefer it, they may draw for themselves quite a different picture.

They may sketch the quiet, homely dwelling-place of the parish clerk, neater than even in his neatest bachelor days, and smartened by the good taste and active industry of his affectionate Betsy. They may see her absolute devotion to her husband, her never-ceasing attention to his every want; and may tell how her time, when not employed in rendering him some service, or in attending to her household affairs, is entirely given up to visiting the poor and needy. Further, they may relate how her example and influence has prevailed to reclaim others, and that Dame Punyer, Dame Vidgen, and the rest, clad in the garb of Sisters of Mercy, have likewise devoted the evening of their days to good and charitable works. Either choice, I say, lies before those who wish to continue this story further. As far as *I* am concerned, I have no more to say at present. When people are "married and done for," it is always desirable to leave them alone for a while and hope for the best. "No good ever comes of interfering between man and wife," at least no good ever comes to the person who interferes; and so I shall leave Oliver and his Betsy to themselves. And having done so, there is really very little more to tell.

Some one asks me what became of the little waxen image of Jane. I have not the slightest idea; but if you can find old Thomas Stickels' Family Bible, or the drawer in which it was always kept, the image, for aught I know, may be there still. Certain it is, that Jane became well and strong, and I never heard that any of the little Cubisons were annoyed by witchcraft or witches.

Thomas Stickels himself lived to a good old age and died, like other people, when his time came. All the actors in the scenes of which I have told have long since passed away. But Giddyhorn Beeches are there still, and the actual place is but little changed so far as its appearance is concerned.

I say no more: it would not be safe—at least it would not be wise—to say more upon such a subject, and so I prefer to leave everybody to think what he or she may happen to please, both as regards the after career of Betsy Stickels, and the existence, condition, and general proceedings of the Giddyhorn Grannies.

THE END.

BRADBURY, AGNEW, & CO., PRINTERS, WHITEFRIARS.

Messrs. George Routledge & Sons'
NEW BOOKS.

———◆———

PRICE
s. d.

6 0 GEORGE MOORE, Merchant and Philanthropist. By SAMUEL SMILES, LL.D. With a Portrait. (*Cheap One-Volume Edition.*)

42 0 The Library Edition of SHAKSPEARE. Edited by HOWARD STAUNTON. With 45 Steel Plates, illustrative of Scenes described in the Plays, designed by G. F. SARGENT.

10 6 CHILDREN OF THE VILLAGE. By Miss MITFORD. With 62 Original Illustrations by Mrs. STAPLES, R. BARNES, MIRIAM KERNS, F. BARNARD, C. O. MURRAY, and others, produced under the direction of J. D. COOPER.

10 6 COMMON WAYSIDE FLOWERS. By THOMAS MILLER. With Illustrations by BIRKET FOSTER, printed in Colours by EDMUND EVANS.

10 6 SHAKSPEARE GEMS: A Series of Landscape Illustrations of the most Interesting Localities of Shakspeare's Dramas. With 45 Steel Engravings, after Drawings by G. F. SARGENT.

10 6 THE EMERALD SERIES: Moore's Melodies—Lalla Rookh —Rejected Addresses—Dibdin's Sea Songs—Dibdin's Sea Ballads—Longfellow's Favourite Poems—Evangeline—Shakspeare's Sonnets—Miles Standish. Nine Vols., in a box.

7 6 SUMMER TIME IN THE COUNTRY. Edited by the Rev. R. A. WILLMOTT. With Illustrations by BIRKET FOSTER and other Eminent Artists.

7 6 The Centenary Edition of THOMAS MOORE'S POETICAL WORKS. Edited by CHARLES KENT. With Illustrations and a Portrait.

7 6 NOTABLE VOYAGES. By W. H. G. KINGSTON. An entirely New Work. With many Illustrations.

7 6 UNCLE TOM'S CABIN. A New Edition. With all the Original Illustrations by GEORGE THOMAS. Red Lines.

7 6 THE IMPERIAL NATURAL HISTORY PICTURE BOOK. With 80 full-page Illustrations. Cloth gilt ; and in boards, 5*s.*

7 6 SPINDLE STORIES. By ASCOTT R. HOPE. With Original Illustrations by C. O. MURRAY, and Coloured Pictures.

7 6 THE MILLER'S DAUGHTER. By ALFRED TENNYSON. With steel Plates from Designs by A. L. BOND.

7 6 RIVER LEGENDS ; or, Father Thames and Father Rhine. By the Right Hon. E. H. KNATCHBULL-HUGESSEN, M.P. With 41 Illustrations by GUSTAVE DORÉ.

6 0 ROUTLEDGE'S EVERY BOY'S ANNUAL for 1880. Edited by EDMUND ROUTLEDGE, F.R.G.S. With full-page Illustrations and Coloured Plate.

PRICE
s. d.

JULES VERNE'S FAMOUS BOYS' BOOKS.
New and Cheaper Editions, with all the Original Illustrations.

3 6 1. The English at the North Pole.
2. The Field of Ice.
3. A Voyage Round the World—South America.
4. A Voyage Round the World—Australia.
5. A Voyage Round the World—New Zealand.

3 6 **THE OSCAR PLETSCH PICTURE BOOK.** Containing 150 Pictures, designed by OSCAR PLETSCH.   Cloth gilt; and in boards, *2s 6d.*

3 6 **THE LIFE OF NAPOLEON.** With 50 Illustrations by VERNET, and full-page Plates.

3 6 **TALES OF A GRANDFATHER.** By Sir WALTER SCOTT. With full-page Illustrations.

3 6 **BUNYAN'S PILGRIM'S PROGRESS.** With 50 Illustrations by J. D. WATSON.

3 6 **THE BOYS OF AXLEFORD.** By CHARLES CAMDEN. With full-page Illustrations.   .

3 6 **FEMALE SOVEREIGNS.** By Mrs. JAMESON. New and Cheaper Edition.

3 6 **CHARACTERISTICS OF WOMEN.** By Mrs. JAMESON. New and Cheaper Edition, with Illustrations.

3 6 **WHITE'S NATURAL HISTORY OF SELBORNE.** With Illustrations. (*Standard Library.*)

3s. 6d. JUVENILES.

In crown 8vo, cloth, gilt edges, price 3s. 6d. each.

3 6 **The Flower of Christian Chivalry.** By Mrs. R. W. LLOYD. With 24 Illustrations.

The Wave and the Battle-Field. From "Tales of Perils by Land and Sea." By LOUISA STEWART. With numerous Illustrations.

Friendly Hands and Kindly Words. Stories illustrative of the Law of Kindness. With 21 Illustrations by C. A. DOYLE and others.

The Seaside Naturalist: Out-Door Studies in Marine Zoology and Botany. By the Rev. W. FRASER, M.A. With many Illustrations.

Famous Ships of the British Navy. Stories of Enterprise and Daring. By DAVENPORT ADAMS. With many Illustrations.

The Tiger Prince: or, Adventures in the Wilds of Abyssinia. By WILLIAM DALTON. With Illustrations.

Heroines of the Household. By the Rev. WILLIAM WILSON, M.A. With 22 Illustrations.

PRICE
s. d.

ROUTLEDGE'S RED-LINE POETS.—*New Volumes.*

3 6 Spenser — Choice Poems and Lyrics. — Keats.

In Four Vols., crown 8vo, cloth, with Illustrations, price 3s. 6d. each.

3 6 **THE AUGUST STORIES.** By JACOB ABBOTT.

August and Elvie.	Schooner "Mary Ann."
Hunter and Tom.	Granville Valley.

MARIA HACK'S JUVENILES.

In crown 8vo, cloth, gilt edges, price 3s. 6d. each.

3 6 Winter Evenings: or, Tales for Travellers. By MARIA HACK.
With Illustrations by Sir JOHN GILBERT, R.A., and WILLIAM HARVEY.

3 6 Grecian Stories. By MARIA HACK. With Eight Illustrations.

KINGSTON'S BOYS' BOOKS.

In crown 8vo, cloth, gilt edges, with full-page Illustrations, price 3s. 6d. each.

3 6 Adventures of Harry Skipworth by Sea and Land.
The Pirate's Treasure: A Legend of Panama.
Foxholme Hall: A Legend of Christmas.

3 6 **NOBLE BOYS:** Their Deeds of Love and Duty. By WILLIAM
MARTIN, Editor of "Peter Parley's Annual." With numerous Illustrations.

3 6 **ROMANTIC TALES FROM ENGLISH HISTORY.** By
MAY BEVERLEY. With 22 Illustrations.

ROUTLEDGE'S TWO-AND-SIXPENNY POETS.

Cut edges, cloth gilt, with Illustrations.

2 6

Longfellow.	Bret Harte.
Moore.	Hemans.
Byron.	Coleridge.
Pope.	Dodd's Beauties of Shakspeare.
Campbell.	Hood.
Lover.	Mind of Shakspeare.

2 6 **BUTTERCUPS AND DAISIES.** With 48 pages of Plates by
OSCAR PLETSCH, printed in Colours by LEIGHTON Brothers.

2 6 **BUDS AND FLOWERS.** With 48 pages of Plates by OSCAR
PLETSCH, printed in Colours by LEIGHTON Brothers.

2 6 **THE WARS OF THE ROSES.** By DAVENPORT ADAMS.

2 6 **THE STORY OF THE CIVIL WAR.** BY DAVENPORT
ADAMS.

PRICE
s. d.

2 6 **WELLINGTON'S VICTORIES.** By DAVENPORT ADAMS.

2 6 **LITTLE SILVERLOCKS' STORY BOOK.** By Mrs. SALE
BARKER. With 100 Illustrations; and in boards, 2s.

2 6 **LITTLE RUBY LIPS' STORY BOOK.** By Mrs. SALE
BARKER. With 100 Illustrations; and in boards, 2s.

2 6 **VOYAGES AND ADVENTURES OF VASCO DA GAMA:**
His Adventures and Conquests. By GEORGE M. TOWLE. With Illustrations.

2 6 **WHEN I WAS YOUNG.** By CHARLES CAMDEN. With full-
page Illustrations.

2 6 **BUNYAN'S PILGRIM'S PROGRESS.** With 50 Illustrations
by J. D. WATSON.

2 6 **STORIES AND PICTURES FROM GRECIAN HIS-**
TORY. By MARIA HACK. With 30 Illustrations by Sir JOHN GILBERT, R.A.

2 0 **EYEBRIGHT.** By SUSAN COOLIDGE. With Illustrations.

2 0 **EDWARDS'S HISTORY OF FRANCE.** Revised and brought
down to the Paris Exhibition, 1878.

2 0 **THE GOOD GENIUS THAT TURNED EVERYTHING**
INTO GOLD. By the Brothers MAYHEW. With Illustrations by GEORGE
CRUIKSHANK.

2 0 **TALES OF FAIRY LAND.** By TIECK.

1s. 6d. JUVENILES.—New Volumes.

1 6 Lily's Magic Lantern. By Mrs. SALE BARKER. With 100
Illustrations.

Annals of the Poor. 45 Illustrations.

The Indian Cottage. 45 Illustrations.

Keeper's Travels in Search of his Master. With 45 Illustrations.

The Basket of Flowers. 45 Illustrations.

Uncle Tom's Cabin. With 45 Illustrations.

The Legends of King Arthur and his Knights of the
Round Table.

---

1 0 **ROUTLEDGE'S SINGING QUADRILLE.** An entirely New
Toy Book for Children. With Popular Nursery Rhymes set to Quadrille Music.

1 0 **ROUTLEDGE'S SINGING LANCERS.** A New Toy Book
for Children. With Popular Nursery Rhymes set to Music.

1 0 **ANCIENT AND MODERN MAGIC.** By a Professor.
Fancy boards.

1 0 **MRS. BROWN ON CO-OPERATIVE STORES.** By
ARTHUR SKETCHLEY.